SUMMER OF 38

A NOVEL BY
GALEN WINTER

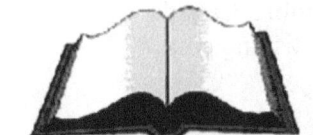

CCB Publishing
British Columbia, Canada

Summer of 38: A Novel

Copyright ©2013 by Paul Winter
ISBN-13   978-1-77143-060-9
Second Edition

Library and Archives Canada Cataloguing in Publication
Winter, Galen, 1926-2012
Summer of 38 : a novel / written by Galen Winter – 2nd ed.
ISBN 978-1-77143-060-9
Also available in electronic format.
Additional cataloguing data available from Library and Archives Canada

Publisher: CCB Publishing
              British Columbia, Canada
              www.ccbpublishing.com

SUMMER
OF 38

Chapter 1

A Peek at the World of 1938

The year 1938 was not what one might describe as an unqualified success. In the United States, the New Deal had been in place for five years, but the 1937 stock market decline continued and unemployment remained high. Many people wondered whether they should have voted for Kansas Governor Alf Landon rather than re-electing Franklin Roosevelt to a second term of office.

In that year, Orson Welles' radio dramatization of H. G. Wells' novel, "The War of The Worlds," scared the hell out of people all over the country. In New Jersey, where the Martians were supposed to have landed, anxiety and terror took control. The frenzied behavior of its citizens clearly proved their misconceived notion that extra-terrestrial aliens were more dangerous than the politicians who ran the state.

Clarence Darrow, the country's most brilliant defense attorney, died that year. So did John Warde. He spent over 16 hours on the ledge of the 17th floor of the Gotham Hotel in New York City. Then he jumped.

In baseball's World Series, the New York Yankees beat the Chicago Cubs. In Madison Square Garden, Joe Louis retained his heavyweight boxing title and got revenge for a previous defeat by knocking out Germany's Max Schmeling after only two minutes and four seconds of the first round of their re-match.

The big band era was underway and the jitterbugs made their appearance. The people of the United States accorded popularity to a song entitled "Flat Foot Floogie with a Floy, Floy." On the positive side of the ledger, "September Song" also made it to the top ten.

A majority of the houses in the country did not have indoor plumbing. In New York City more than 2000 television sets were in experimental operation - an indication of the evil yet to come.

In other parts of the world, more serious problems were faced and dark clouds grew ominously on the horizon. Japanese aggression in China visited a vicious violence on non-combatants. The rape of Nanking gave new definition to the phrase "man's inhumanity to man."

In Europe, the Spanish Civil War proceeded with that special ferocity known only when brother fights brother. Hitler and Mussolini used it to test their military muscle. George Orwell and Ernest Hemingway got raw material for their books: Homage to Catalonia and For Whom the Bell Tolls.

Neville Chamberlain, the British Prime Minister, hadn't yet made his fateful trip to Munich but, in Great Britain, the Foreign Secretary, Anthony Eden, resigned in protest of his government's wimpy policies toward the aggression of Adolf Hitler and the Nazi regime. A month later, with no international opposition, German troops occupied Austria.

The fascist governments of Italy and Germany were in the process of proving the accuracy of Lord Acton's revelation: "Power tends to corrupt, Absolute power corrupts, absolutely." In the USSR, Josef Stalin's widespread purges had already proven the same thesis.

In Latin America, many Republics defaulted in the payment of their bond obligations. In the United States, many cities defaulted in the payment of their bond obligations. The Mexican government was busy nationalizing oil and insurance business interests owned by foreigners. Latent anti-Americanism and a penchant for strong man militaristic leaders caused some Latin American governments to favor the European fascists.

In spite of the popular desire to stay out of foreign wars, the threat of European totalitarianism getting a foothold in the Western Hemisphere was recognized. The United States countered with its Good Neighbor Policy and a headline in the New York Times read: ROOSEVELT TO ARM FOR ALL AMERICAS. 1938 was not a year free from trouble. Still, it could have been worse. It might have been 1937, or 1936, or, for that matter, 1939 or 1940.

Nevertheless, 1938 did have its good moments. Congress established the forty hour work week. Two Pulitzer Prize winning dramas were on Broadway: Abe Lincoln in Illinois and Our Town. In Arizona, near Phoenix, Frank Lloyd Wright built Taliesin West and his architect students planted vegetables in the hope it would help some of the Wright genius to rub off on them.

A Ford automobile cost $666, F.O.B. Detroit. An Oldsmobile went for $777. Evenrude sold the Scout Model of its outboard motor for $44. Butter was 29 cents a pound.

Howard Hughes flew around the world in his new state of the art airship and at an amazing average air speed of 127.43 miles per hour. Douglas "Wrong Way" Corrigan, however, stole the lime-light. He flew from New York to Ireland. He had no official clearance for his flight plan and explained his trip across the Atlantic by saying he must have flown the wrong way. His airplane was a nine year old Curtis Robin. It cost $900 and was referred to in the newspapers as a "crate."

In Hollywood, since Shirley Temple was not available, Merwyn Leroy chose Judy Garland, a little known child actress, for the role of Dorothy in the first Technicolor movie, The Wizard of Oz. The United States no longer stationed its Marines in Nicaragua or Haiti. Lajos Biro of Hungary invented the ballpoint pen.

The pessimists, however, believed "things will get better before they get worse." They were right. War industry promised to provide the economic recovery the New Deal could not deliver. Prosperity was just around the corner. So was the Second World War.

In September of the next year, Germany and the USSR would divide Poland. England and France would declare war and for six years the nations of the world would engage in a struggle that changed the way of human life on the planet. All of the changes may not have been for the better.

1938 was the lull before the storm and during that lull eight people took a banana boat cruise from New Orleans through the Gulf of Mexico and on to the Anchurian coast of the Caribbean Sea.

Chapter 2

An introduction to a young man
suffering from the disease of youth
It is a disease we have all had.
It is cured by the passage of time.

According to Isaac Newton, the apple doesn't fall far from the tree. The two generations of the Eckert family seemed to offer contradicting evidence. Father and son sometimes seemed of a completely different lineage.

David Eckert, to his personal satisfaction called "D. H." by his friends and associates, was the sole owner of a successful manufacturing business in Des Moines, Iowa. His son, Paul Eckert, to his more than mild discomfort called "Pauly" by both father and mother, apparently had little interest in the management of the Eckert Company. D. H. harbored the suspicion his son was preparing for a career as a professional student.

D. H. did not attribute his success in the manufacture and sale of corn oils to intelligence, personality, careful timing, courage or being in the right place at the right time. Though all those elements and his own substantial efforts resulted in a profitable business in spite of a world wide depression, D. H. always claimed his good fortune was due to his established practice of rising with the sun and putting in a full day's work.

Paul Eckert, on the other hand, often went to bed as the sun was making its appearance, but he harbored no deep seated grudge against early rising. He just never felt the need to leave the warm comforts of bed until the sun was well above the horizon. In contrast to his father, Paul attributed his success at the University of Wisconsin to a full social schedule and the practice of sleeping at irregular intervals and places whenever an appropriate opportunity presented itself.

As D. H. aged and his business prospered, he spent more time thinking of the future of his company. The future of his company was his son, Pauly. Of course, D. H. wanted him to enter the business and prepare to manage it for another generation. The possibility that Pauly might not take the reins of the Eckert Company produced in D. H. something akin to a panic terror.

In 1936 Paul got a degree, not in Agricultural Science from the University of Iowa, as D. H. wanted, but in Political Science from the University of Wisconsin. D. H. had been pressured and reluctantly agreed to allow Paul to continue his studies. D. H. lost the war, but he won a battle. He insisted on the condition that his son pursue a study of Business Administration. Paul would have accepted the condition if it required the study of Quantum Physics.

It was not solely a desire for academic knowledge that fueled Paul's interest in returning to the Madison campus. It was also the University of Wisconsin Rathskeller, Lake Mendota's Picnic Point, the Hoofers and, more particularly, Anne Frisch, then in her third year at the University.

Now, two years later, it was June of 1938. Paul was going to receive a Master's Degree in Business Administration. The New Deal's AAA created an atmosphere in which the Eckert Company could continue to prosper and, according to D. H., war industry was beginning to prove Herbert Hoover was right when, seven years earlier, he said: "Prosperity is just around the corner."

It was time, D. H. said to himself, for Pauly to enter the world of business. He made the same statement on a number of previous occasions. In spite of his renewed firm pronouncement, he knew he would do whatever Pauly wanted. He was bluster on top. Under the surface he was a doting father.

* * * * *

On the day of graduation ceremonies, parents descend upon universities to celebrate their pride in their offspring's' scholastic achievement and privately give thanks the financial drain had finally come to an end. On the day before his graduation, Paul Eckert and

Anne Frisch celebrated - first with lunch and then in the privacy of a room in the Park Hotel.

They lay on the bed, side by side. Anne snubbed out a cigarette in the glass ash tray balanced on her naked stomach. They had been silent. "Paul," she asked, "Do you remember when we met?"

"Of course I do," Paul answered. He wasn't entirely sure he did. It was three years ago when he was in his final year as an undergrad and Anne was a sophomore. He was almost certain it was at a drug store called "The Pharm", a place where students often took light breakfasts. He hoped Anne wouldn't ask him to be more specific.

"It was at the Pharm," she continued. "Barbara Wilson asked you to join us and we had our first breakfast together."

Paul was relieved. His memory hadn't failed him. Now he could confirm it out loud. "You had a bagel and I had toast. You traded half your bagel for half my toast. Think of it. A nice eastern Jewish girl eating mid-western toast."

Anne smiled and said: "Think of it. A nice Iowa Protestant boy eating a bagel. If my mother knew I was sleeping with you, she'd faint." She laughed. "You're neither circumcised nor a doctor." She glanced down, then up into his eyes and laughed again.

"Dad would have an apoplectic fit," Paul said. "I'd be disowned. He'd turn my picture to the wall. Sleeping with a liberal! Unforgivable."

They fell silent again.

Paul removed the ashtray and placed it on the night stand. He leaned over Anne and kissed her lightly. Then he drew his head back and said: "Who's going to say it? You? Or me?"

"Oh, Paul," Anne sighed. She hadn't looked forward to this moment.

"We both know it has to come." Paul said and kissed her again. They both smiled. She nodded. It was time. Their relationship ended gracefully. They enjoyed their final intimacies. After dinner they said their good-byes.

* * * * *

At ten in the morning of June 14, Anne Frisch was in New York City and Paul Eckert was in Des Moines. More precisely, Paul was in his bed on the upper floor of the Eckert home. It was Flag Day. In accordance with the agreement forced upon D. H. Eckert by union negotiators, the employees of the Eckert Company got the day off. There was no reason for D. H. to go to his office in the plant.

D. H. was in the living room. As he paced, he chewed on the second cigar of the morning. He was not in a pleasant mood. His factory was idle. Not only did his employees have a day of vacation, but they were getting paid, too. To add to D.H.'s discomfort, Pauly was still in bed.

Upstairs, Paul awakened to the sound of what he thought was ominous, far away thunder. Then he recognized it as the voice of D. H. filtering through the walls and ceiling of the house. Occasionally the higher pitched and calmer voice of his mother was heard.

Paul and D. H. both wrestled with the same problem. He now had a Master's Degree and that was half of the bargain made with his father. His mother already warned him that D. H. was adamant in his decision to no longer pay "another single red cent to keep that kid in school."

Paul, listening to the muted rumblings, was faced with three alternatives. He could try to talk his father into another year at Madison. He could get a teaching job at the University and stay on for another year or so. Or, he could start work at the plant.

He had made a promise to his father and had no good excuse for breaking it. Moreover, during the last two years, maturity began to set in. Life at the University of Wisconsin lost some of its appeal. The more he saw of 18 year old freshmen, the more puerile their life style appeared. With Anne far away in New York, nothing drew him back to Madison.

Paul concluded it was time to join the work force. Yes, he thought, I'm ready. The company is profitable and one day I'll own it. I'd better learn the business and I might as well start now.

His thoughts were interrupted when he heard the not too softly spoken words coming up from the living room. "Wake him up? Wake him up? Hell, he's never been fully conscious before noon since he was four years old."

"Now, David, don't be too hard on him. After all, Pauly is only a boy and he just ..."

"Only a boy? Only a boy? Helen, he's 25 years old."

When engaged in conversation with anyone, more particularly his wife, it was the usual custom of D. H. Eckert to repeat the last few words that had been spoken, but with a rising inflection. This made a question out of every statement. Having, thus, established the issue, he would respond with some non sequitur or exaggeration.

"When I was twenty-five years old, I'd worked in the grain elevator for six years. I had more than two hundred dollars in the bank. I had..."

Helen Eckert dutifully played straight man. She could begin to express any thought, secure in the knowledge she would never be able to finish it. This was acceptable because she was comfortable never having to defend or prove a point. As a result, domestic argument was very rare in the Eckert household.

"Yes, David, I know, but things are different now. Pauly has to find himself."

"Things are different now? Has to find himself? He'll find himself in a by-God hurry or he'll find himself out on his own. He's never going to amount to anything if he doesn't settle down."

Having made his many times expressed position again known, the ceremony was concluded with Helen's ritualistic statement: "I'm sure everything will turn out all right," and she left the room, signaling the end of her participation in the discussion.

Lying in bed, Paul listened to the conversation. He had already made up his mind. He dressed and went downstairs to find D. H. chewing on his cigar and staring out the window. He's probably been pacing, Paul thought. This is as good a time as any. I might as well make my announcement. Then it occurred to him. He might be able to promote a vacation trip at the same time.

"Dad," he said, "I'm glad you didn't go to work today." D. H. thought of the union contract and glowered. "I think we should talk," Paul continued. "Would you be terribly disappointed if I didn't go after a PhD?"

"Disappointed? Disappointed? No, Pauly, no. I wouldn't be

disappointed," stammered a surprised and incredulous D. H.

"The University's all right, I suppose," Paul went on, "but I'd like to start a career in business." D. H.'s jaw dropped. He almost lost his cigar. The shock was too great for complete sentences.

"Career in business? Career in business? Well. Well. Fine. Fine. Yes, very good. I'm sure we can arrange something at the plant."

"I'd like to learn from the bottom up", Paul said. "Do you think I could start in the Accounting Department? You know. Learn where the money comes from - what the expenses are - where the profit margins develop."

D. H. was thunderstruck. What had happened to the boy? It was almost too good to be true. "Profit margins? Profit margins? Accounting Department? Yes. Yes. Very good." His smile was so broad and his joy so great he almost forgave the union for forcing him to give his employees the day's off - and with pay.

"Well, Pauly, if you're going to be part of the company, I guess I can't call you 'Pauly' any more. Wouldn't sound right down at the plant. Do you mind," and then after a short pause, he added "Paul?" Paul didn't mind. Maybe working at the Eckert Company wouldn't be so bad after all.

"I'd like to start sometime this summer, if that's all right with you," he said

"Sometime this summer? Fine. Fine. Sometime this summer. Yes. Fine." It was both surprising and marvelous news. "Helen," D. H. shouted, "I've just had a talk with Pauly. I mean Paul. He's going to come to work at the plant."

"That's nice dear," said Helen from the living room. "When is Pauly going start?"

"Going to start? Going to start? I don't know. Sometime this summer. Pauly, I mean, Paul, when are you going to start?"

"In August or September but, first, I'd like to take a trip," he answered. He paused for only a second while he considered where he wanted to go, and then continued: "I'd like to go to ... ah ... Central America." He selected that destination for no good reason at all. He could just as easily have said Mesopotamia, Mozambique, or the Malay States.

For one agonizing moment, D. H. thought he may have been had. He regained his composure in time to enunciate in loud and clear tones: "CENTRAL AMERICA? GEE SUS AITCH KEE RIST" (with accents on Gee, Aitch and Rist). By this time, Helen entered the dining room, smiling and proud of her boy.

"Oh, David," she said, "isn't that nice. Pauly's coming to work at the company - and taking a trip to Central America. That's marvelous" The words "broadening," "exciting," "educational" and "graduation present" all tumbled out of Helen's mouth during the following thirty seconds. D. H. recognized defeat when he saw it. He didn't even have a chance to object. After a few 'hmmpfs' and snorts, he submitted to the extortion.

"We have a friend who lives down there," Helen said. "You remember him, dear? Rutherford Wilder? From high school"

An expression of distaste quickly covered D. H.'s face. He certainly did remember Rutherford Wilder. He never liked him. Not only had Wilder been his competition for Helen back in the days when she was young and slim and very cute, but Wilder grew up to be a Democrat.

"I think he works for the State Department or something", Helen said. "I'll call Lu Svendson. She'll have his address."

* * * * *

After the phone call, Helen Eckert had the address of Lucy Svendson's brother, Rutherford Birchard Wilder. He was now the United States Consul General in a place called Aguas Buenas in a Republic called Anchuria

Helen wondered if he would remember her. She wrote a lengthy letter and told him of her and D. H.'s lives and of their mutual friends and what had happened to them. Then she told him her son planned a trip to Central America and wondered if he could be helpful to him.

Consul General Rutherford B. Wilder remembered Helen Eckert. He vividly recalled the times the two of them would make an appearance at a Saturday evening Grange Hall dance and then, with the help of horse and buggy, disappear to a more secluded spot. They had grown apart when he went college. He often wondered what she ever saw in Dave Eckert.

Wilder quickly responded to Helen Eckert's letter. He recounted his experiences since leaving Iowa and confirmed that he was now the American Consul General in the city of Aguas Buenas in the Republic of Anchuria. He recommended Paul visit Anchuria and told her he would be pleased to look after him.

He reported the July climate on the coast of Anchuria and made suggestion concerning the clothing Paul should bring with him. He offered to arrange housing in Aguas Buenas. In 1938, the only hotel in the city was the El Palacio. It was an Anchurian National Monument.

Chapter 3

*A Discourse Concerning How the Republic of Anchuria Came into
Being as well as Commentary Concerning the Hotel Palacio*

In 1848, there was only one Republic in Central America. Anchuria was not yet a separate Republic. It was one of the four Provinces which, together, formed the Republic of Sedalia.

In that year, the Republic of Sedalia had been in existence for nineteen years and was trying out its fourteenth President. None of the Sedalia''s first thirteen national executives finished a term in office. Each President had resigned or was overthrown or was assassinated or, in one case, died of natural causes.

Santa Elena was the capital of the Republic of Sedalia. The city was located in the Central Highlands, some twenty miles inland from the Republic's Caribbean port of Ciudad Carillo. Roads between Santa Elena and the capitol cities of each of its other three Provinces were, at best, primitive. Even during the dry season, only the most blatantly chauvinistic Sedalian would claim any of them might become passable.

In those days, anyone who courageously traveled through the Central Highlands ran a substantial risk of being murdered and his horse or mule taken by the Indians or by the Spanish/Indian blooded Mestizos who occupied the largely unexplored mountainous interior. In that part of the Republic of Sedalia, a horse or a mule was infinitely more valuable than the life of a traveler.

Moreover, yellow fever, encephalitis, elephantiasis, cholera, leprosy and various kinds of parasites and amoebae (all hoping to find a home in a human liver) combined to severely limit the number of survivors of those few adventurous souls who elected the overland passage.

If anyone wanted to move an army between Santa Elena and Aguas

Buenas (then the capitol of the Province of Anchuria) he could attempt a march through those Central Highlands, but no one was either brave or insane enough to consider it.

In 1848, the Sedalian navy consisted of a single wooden ship. It was christened "The Patria" and was of questionable seaworthiness. It was commanded by the Admiral of the Sedalian navy. The Admiral was the President's brother-in-law. He had never been to sea. He planned to retire from the service without ever having gone to sea. The navy's anthem, "Rule Sedalia, Sedalia Rules the Waves," was not entirely accurate. Even a madman wouldn't dream of using the sea worm infested, dry rotted Patria to transport an army.

Isolated from one another and to a large extent economically independent, the inhabitants of any one of the four Provinces of the Republic were only casually interested in what went on in any of the other three. Actually governing all of Sedalia from the capitol city of Santa Elena was virtually impossible. To some of the politically ambitious, it seemed unfair that there should be only one "El Presidente" for the entire area.

Cayetano Rodriguez was the Treasurer of the Republic of Sedalia. He coveted the presidency, but could assemble neither the support to overthrow nor the courage to assassinate the current President. Lacking either of the two elements necessary to attain his goal, Cayetano Rodriquez found an acceptable alternative.

Under cover of darkness, he helped himself to as much of the Republic's national treasury as he could carry and fled from Santa Elena to Ciudad Carillo on the Caribbean coast. There he boarded a fishing boat and sailed to Aguas Buenas, the port that served as the capitol of the western Province of Anchuria.

Once in Aguas Buenas, Cayetano Rodriguez called a few planters to the patio of El Palacio. Then, as now, El Palacio was the only hotel in Aguas Buenas. Rodriguez addressed the assemblage, claiming the government of the Republic of Sedalia disregarded the dignity and threatened the authority of the residents of Aguas Buenas.

By the end of the day, Aguas Buenas and the entire Province of Anchuria were proclaimed to be a new nation, free and independent from the Republic of Sedalia. As might easily be foreseen, Cayetano

Rodriquez was named the first President of the new Republic of Anchuria.

With the independence of Anchuria an accomplished fact, the President of the Republic of Sedalia could do nothing about it. He called Rodriguez a traitor, a scoundrel and a common thief. He demanded he be returned to Santa Elena for a fair trial and execution by firing squad.

In Aguas Buenas, a hastily appointed Anchurian Supreme Court rejected the Sedalian demand and established the new Republic's policy of refusal to extradite anyone to any place for any reason. That policy of refusal to extradite remains in effect to this day.

For the nearly thirty years, the El Palacio Hotel was the new Republic's seat of government. Each year, legislators would meet in the shaded interior patio of the hotel and conduct the Republic's official business. A one storied, single bedroom house was built adjacent to the hotel. President Cayetano Rodriguez made it his home.

In 1910, the owner of El Palacio bought the house and added a corridor to physically attach it to the hotel. The official residence of the first President of the Republic of Anchuria now houses the El Palacio's kitchen and laundry facilities.

In the early 1870's, Anchurian government officials formed a company for the purpose of building a railroad from Aguas Buenas to the capitol cities of the other Central American Republics. To attract foreign investors, the company issued bonds promising periodic payments of interest at an elevated rate.

A railroad with a monopoly in Central American land transportation looked like a very profitable investment. In London, Lord Percy Grenville and some of his fellow London entrepreneurs became major investors in the enterprise. Somehow or other, when all the salaries of the Anchurian officials and all of the company's expenses were paid, there was no money left to lay so much as a single meter of railroad track.

When the bonds became worthless, Lord Percy Grenville called on his friends in the English Parliament. Speeches were made claiming the actions of the Anchurian politicians disregarded the dignity and threatened the authority of the British Empire. Compensation from the

Republic of Anchuria was demanded.

No one in Aguas Buenas paid the slightest attention to the demand.

The British sent a gun boat to intimidate the Anchurians and force payments of the bond obligations. The ploy did not work. When news of the approaching gun boat reached Aguas Buenas, the President, the legislators and a most of the citizenry abandoned the city. They found horses and mules and took to the hills, regrouping in the foothills of the Central Highlands at a pueblito consisting of a group of thatched huts. It was (optimistically) called Progreso.

The climate in Progreso was excellent. The city was located fifteen miles from the coast and naval bombardment was not possible. Well above sea level, malaria was not always a serious problem. Progreso was formally designated as the new capitol city of the Republic of Anchuria.

Though Aguas Buenas is no longer the capitol of the Republic, it is the major port and the commercial center of the country. The El Palacio Hotel maintains its reputation as the birthplace of the Republic of Anchuria, the first home of the nation's legislature and the country's first Presidential Mansion. A brass plaque attached to an interior patio wall of the Hotel proclaims those achievements.

The historic character of El Palacio had been carefully preserved. With the exception of electricity and plumbing (which sometimes works quite well) no remodeling of the building had ever been undertaken. If one were to discount the depreciation that might be expected as a result of ninety years of the ravages of tropical time, in 1938 El Palacio was in the same pristine condition it enjoyed in 1848.

The United States Consul General, Rutherford B. Wilder, honored the El Palacio Hotel with yet another claim to fame. He reported it deserved recognition by the scientific community. He believed it should be studied by the world's more eminent entomologists. It contained cockroaches, some of which reportedly grew to over five inches in length. A profusion of spiders and other insects, some as yet unclassified by scientists, all lay claim to the building. In addition, the presence of strange molds and fungi suggest a potential interest on the part of the world's more curious botanists.

And that is why, when asked to recommend living quarters for the son of his long-ago sweetheart, the United States Consul General at Aguas Buenas eschewed the accommodations offered by the El Palacio. Instead, he visited the owner of the Casa Canada and arranged to rent an apartment for the Paul Eckert.

The Casa Canada, Rutherford B. Wilder reported to Helen Eckert, was a small and quiet hostel with a good reputation. It was used by the Central American Fruit Company as a temporary residence for its in-transit employees. It was also used by all visitors to Aguas Buenas who knew the condition of the rooms at El Palacio.

Chapter 4

More about Paul Eckert and his 1938 Preparations for a Cruise to Central America

In Des Moines, Paul Eckert again awoke at daybreak. The Caribbean cruise was on his mind and he couldn't sleep. As he lay on his bed and looked at the ceiling, he wished he had taken a second course in Latin American politics while getting his Political Science degree. He wished he had studied Spanish. He dressed and went downstairs.

D. H. was pleased when Paul joined him for an early morning breakfast. Getting up with the sun was another unmistakable indication that his son was advancing toward that goal of "settling down". Yesterday's announcement of Paul's decision to leave the University and start working in the Accounting Department and today's early rising were good signs.

D. H. was in excellent spirits. Though he had been disappointed in the past, 'with that hope that springs eternal' from within the human heart', he was again convinced Pauly (I mean, Paul) would fulfill all of his expectations. Now if he could only get him to marry a nice Presbyterian girl and start a family.

"Good morning, Paul. Sleep well?" And without waiting for an answer: "It's a beautiful morning, isn't it?" And, again without a pause: "It's great to get up early. Isn't it? Gives a man a chance to think and plan his day in peace. - before the hubbub and distractions begin. Right?" D. H. stopped to take a breath.

Right," said Paul, joining in the conversation.

D. H. watched Paul butter his toast. He was proud of him. "Had a nice talk with Charlie Hanstedt last week. You remember him, Paul?"

"Sure, Dad. He's the banker."

"Right you are. A banker is a good man to have on your side. Can't do much without credit, you know, PaulyPaul."

Paul noticed how quickly D. H. caught his Pauly mistake. He's really trying, he thought, Maybe I should forget about the vacation. That thought evaporated in the aftermath of D.H.'s next words.

"Charlie's daughter is still in town. She's not married, you know."

"Oh, oh," thought Paul, "not Janie Hanstedt." Janie's mother outweighed her husband. Already Janie showed signs of following in her mother's footsteps. Janie, who apparently thought everything was hilarious, had a high pitched and extremely irritating laugh. Living with that laugh would drive a man to commit irrational acts. It was time to change the subject.

"Dad, do you think there'll be another war?"

"I don't know, Paul. The Japs have their hands full in China and they know one of our men can beat ten of theirs. We're too strong for them. They won't let anything happen to give that madman in the White House an excuse to declare war on them. Europe's another matter. I think there'll be war there and Roosevelt might try to get us in it. If he does, the Democrats will lose the next election. That's not our war and we should stay out of it."

"There are people," said Paul, thinking of Anne Frisch, "who believe the Nazis will pose a real problem if they ever control Europe. They claim Hitler's goal isn't limited to just Europe - that he's after world domination. The fascists are not nice people."

"Not nice people? Not nice people? Neither are the Communists. That's Europe's problem, not ours. Twenty years ago we went over there to help them straighten things out. A lot of our boys got killed. Now, they're right back to where they started. There's no point in us trying to do it again. Let them fight it out among themselves."

* * * * *

The purpose of Paul's question was to avoid any talk about Janie Hanstedt. In spite of a University of Wisconsin Political Science undergrad degree, he didn't really care about the probability of war. In the national debate between the interventionists and the isolationists, he had friends on both sides.

Two of Paul's acquaintances dropped out of the University and went to Spain to fight with the anti-Franco Abraham Lincoln Brigade. He never understood whatever possessed them to do it. One of them, he heard, was killed. At the other extreme, some of his Milwaukee friends spent their summers in German-American Bund Youth camps. Paul was never able to determine if they were truly pro-Nazi or merely violently anti-English.

Paul found Fascism to be disgusting. A Europe dominated by Franco, Mussolini and Hitler, if not signaling a return to the Dark Ages as some of his professors believed, meant a monolithic state and the suppression of anyone and everyone who didn't conform. The Communists were equally offensive to him. The bloody purges going on in the USSR wiped out anyone who might become a threat to Stalin. The trees of Fascism and of Communism produced the same fruit.

In Romeo and Juliet, Shakespeare's Prince Escalus looked upon the Capulets and the Montagues and said: "A plague on both your houses." In 1938, Paul and many of his countrymen looked upon the contending countries of Europe and said the same. For them, the most appealing position was that of Colonel Charles Lindberg and the America First people - Stay Out Of It.

Paul agreed. "You may be right", he said to his father, "but I hope they can work out some kind of an agreement to keep peace in Europe. If the Fascists and the Communists can reach an accommodation and avoid a war, maybe the rest of us will be able to get on with our own business."

The Eckerts lived in the center of the United States - politically as well as geographically.

* * * * *

After breakfast, D. H. went to the plant and Paul went to the County Court House. The Register of Deeds charged him twenty-five cents for a certified copy of his birth certificate. The Clerk of Court gave him an Application for a passport. Paul had neglected to bring a pen and the Clerk offered his own Parker, but first the Clerk removed the cap and held it in his hand. The procedure served two purposes. The Clerk

19

would not forget he had loaned out his expensive pen and Paul would not, inadvertently, put an uncovered ink pen into his pocket. The dripping ink would ruin his shirt.

Paul proceeded to fill out the Application. When he came to the space marked "Occupation," he paused. Clearly, he was no longer a student. Both "Corn Oil Manufacturer" and "Executive" were premature and "Office Worker" was demeaning. A pixie inside him suggested the word "Capitalist." Paul took the little fellow's advice.

The next stop was a book store where he bought a Spanish-English dictionary. It was an easily transportable pocket version and contained a few pages of translated useful phrases. Paul picked out the ones he considered to be most important and committed them to memory. They included: "Where is the bathroom?" "Please bring me a beer." "How much?" "I am an American" and, to be on the safe side, he also memorized: "I am not an American."

Ten days later, Paul's passport arrived. He looked at the photograph and winced. The reported occupation of "Capitalist" on the next page brought a counter-balancing smile.

* * * * *

Consul General Wilder recommended Paul get a passage on the S S Arbutus, a Central American Fruit Company steamer sailing between New Orleans and the Anchurian port of Aguas Buenas. The Arbutus, visited the city every month. Paul could board it in Louisiana, sail to Aguas Buenas and disembark. He could spend five days there while the Arbutus sailed on to Villa Smit and re-board the ship when it returned on its voyage back to New Orleans.

The only other way to get to Aguas Buenas was to fly from Mexico City. The airline serving Aguas Buenas was called Transporte Anchuria, C. A. Transporte Anchuria operated two Ford tri-motor aircraft - three on the rare occasions when one of their fleet was not in a shop being repaired. With two flights per week and the necessity of first going out of the way to Mexico City, banana boat transportation by the S S Arbutus was faster and, with all of its shortcomings, more comfortable. It was an easy decision.

A telephone call to the New Orleans office of the Central American Fruit Company secured both the passage and a time-table for port-of-call arrival and departure dates. Paul was advised to buy a hundred dollars worth of Pesos to cover tips, taxis an initial miscellaneous expenses he would incur until he was settled into Casa Canada. As an additional service, the Fruit Company provided him with a list of the inoculations he would need in order to get an Anchurian visa.

Paul learned about the requirement of shots to protect him from smallpox, typhoid, paratyphoid, malaria, cholera, yellow fever and tetanus. He took time to consider the advisability of going to a country where proof of those immunizations was required for the issuance of a visa. With some reluctance, he decided he couldn't cancel the trip and would have to go through with it.

Doc Carmichael, the Eckert family physician, gave Paul the shots. During those procedures, he told Paul how ugly he was at birth. With each inoculation, he described the symptoms of the particular disease it was meant to prevent, together with its terrible consequences. After all shots were administered, the doctor volunteered information about the various venereal diseases found in Central America. He scared the daylights out of Paul. Doc Carmichael casually mentioned that a visitor to Central America can exercise complete control over his exposure to venereal disease. Paul understood what he was trying to tell him.

* * * * *

After the Anchurian Consul General in Chicago issued the Anchurian visa, Paul packed what he considered to be the bare essentials needed for a two week cruise. Since he knew he would be the one who had to carry them, he picked up the suitcases and lugged them around the block. Then he repacked, reducing the number of suitcases from four to two and their weight by 60 percent.

Late in the week, D.H. and Helen drove Paul to the Des Moines railroad station. Three hours later, he changed trains in Chicago, boarding one that carried the proud title: City of New Orleans. He was tired. He hadn't slept during the trip from Des Moines. Paul was over six feet tall and it was going to be a long trip to New Orleans. He needed the extra leg room if he were to comfortably stretch out.

Paul left his luggage on the floor blocking the entrance space to the double seat he occupied. It would discourage others from using it with him. As he watched Chicago pass by the windows of the train, Paul thought of Doc Carmichael's vivid description of venereal diseases. He had no inclination to even consider disregarding the indirect warning.

While Paul Eckert could control his exposure to venereal disease, exposure to murder and revolution were quite different matters. If Des Moines were immune from international intrigue, the Republic of Anchuria was not. Events occurring in Germany and in the Republic of Sedalia, together with events that were happening in Arkansas and in New York City, converged to affect the lives of Paul Eckert and the other seven passengers who would sail together from New Orleans to Aguas Buenas.

Chapter 5

The Saga of Reinhold Reichman
The Presidency of Máximo Peña

In another car of the City of New Orleans, the conductor punched a hole in a ticket and returned it to the passenger who nodded sharply and said "Danke". Reinhold Reichman slid the ticket under the outer band of his hat. "It must be the way the Amerikanishers do it", he mused, having noticed other men's ticketed hat bands. He leaned back and, as he often did, compared the United States with his native homeland. He was critical of nearly everything different from the German life style.

Remembering his bus furtive trip from New York to Chicago, he thought: Their forests are not properly managed. They are full of brush and fallen trees. Now, he studied the back-yards of the structures bordering the railroad tracks. Look at these buildings, he said to himself. They are dirty. Piles of trash are everywhere. They are not neat. Then he recalled another objection to the American way of life. The children do not wear uniforms when they go to school. His mind wandered back to his own youth.

During the summer of 1914, Reinhold Reichman was a school boy in Anklam, Pomerania. It was the time when Germany, Britain, France, Russia, Belgium, Montenegro, Serbia, the Ottoman Empire, Italy, Japan and the Austro-Hungarian Empire, involved themselves in what became known as World War I.

Reinhold Reichman left his school in mid-term to serve his Fatherland. He intended to volunteer for the Air Service and go to the Flugzeugwerft in Lubeck for training as a pilot. It would not come to pass. It was discovered that Reinhold had studied the English language in his Anklam lower school.

Instead of soaring over muddy battlefields with Baron Manfred

Von Richtofen, Herman Goering and other World War I German aces, Reinhold Reichman was given the job of English Interpreter. He spent the war years behind the trenches, questioning British and American prisoners. His major accomplishment was the development of an accented fluency in their language.

Now, over twenty years later, the monotonous nearly hypnotic clacking sounds of the City of New Orleans' wheels as they rolled over the seams in the steel rails carried him back to a different time and to a different railroad trip. It was 1919. It was December. It was cold. Reinhold Reichman was one of many German soldiers crowded inside a box car that slowly made its way from the western front toward Berlin.

Reichman was one of the lucky ones. Other returning soldiers jammed themselves between the cars or, almost frozen, huddled together, clinging to the roofs of the box cars. Now, in the comfort of the American train, he remembered that 1919 trip and the grim and dazed looks of his fellow veterans. Like them, he asked himself the questions: How could the German army have been defeated? What went wrong? Was it the politicians?

The City of New Orleans passenger car jerked forward and Reinhold Reichman came back to 1938. He was on another train. It was summer. It was warm. Germany was again a powerful nation and he was the American representative of the HBG - the Hamburg Bicycle Gesellschäft. He was far away from the 1920s and the devastated and dejected post-WWI Germany. He was on his way to a summer cruise in the Gulf of Mexico and a vacation in the Republic of Anchuria. It would be an important but carefree time in a pleasant land. That is what he thought.

* * * * *

In 1935, Máximo Peña became President of the Republic of Anchuria. He became President through non-electoral means. The Peña revolution was a change of government occasioned by the assassination of President Rivadavia and the leaders of the Anchurian Assembly and Senate. The "popular support" for his coup d'etat consisted of Máximo Peña and less than a half-dozen generals.

Peña established an old fashioned dictatorship. He promoted no economic or social theory. He was there. He held power. He brooked no competition. Whenever resistance to Peña's will appeared, or even appeared to appear, he squashed it – quickly and completely.

One man was murdered by mistake. He was a waiter in a Progreso restaurant. He looked somewhat like Osvaldo Vargas, an official in the old Rivadavia government. By the time the man's true identity was established, he had been beaten to death.

Peña disliked the gringos in general and the Central American Fruit Company in particular. He wanted to nationalize the banana company, but he feared the economic and, perhaps, the military retaliation that could be organized by Llewellyn Black, the President of the Fruit Company. Black was an admirer of Franklin Roosevelt, a heavy contributor to and a powerful voice in the Democrat Party. He could command the attention of the United States Department of State.

Like a dog, warily circling a porcupine as he tried to find the best way to attack, President Máximo Peña studied the Fruit Company. He waited for an opportunity to confiscate its assets and create a state-owned banana monopoly.

By mid-1938, Peña's heavy handed treatment of his opposition made him and his government unpopular. Nevertheless, a few men were willing to run the risks involved in conspiring to overthrow him as long. Others who had done so were in exile (if lucky) or never heard from again (if not).

* * * * *

In the New Orleans headquarters of the Central American Fruit Company, Llewellyn Black was worried. Latin government confiscation of foreign business assets and the recent Mexican nationalizations of insurance and oil companies businesses were disturbing trends. The danger of nationalization of his company's Anchuria banana plantations was a substantial threat. It couldn't be disregarded.

Black had two important allies in Anchuria. Roberto Smit was the

Senator from the Province of Esperanza as well as President of Madera Anchuria, the country's largest tropical lumber company. The other ally, Francisco "Paco" Mendez was the Senator from Aguas Buenas. Don Paco was the President of Mineria Anchuria, a gold and silver mining company. In the National Assembly, the two men formed a solid front, promoting laws favoring their own businesses and destroying any proposal that threatened them.

From behind the scenes, Llewellyn Black joined Smit and Mendez as an equal partner and active participant in their protective programs. Most people suspected Senator Paco Mendez was on the Central American Fruit Company payroll. Most people were right.

Senator Roberto Smit shared the concerns of the Mineria and the Fruit Company. He descried the nationalization of private business and recognized an attack on an enterprise owned by foreigners to be a harbinger of what would surely become an attack on his own lumber empire. He maintained a cynical but accurate opinion of the dangers of governmental interference in the lives of its citizens.

* * * * *

By the summer of 1938, a growing anti-Peña sentiment existed throughout the Republic. With dwindling support from the church and whispers of dissatisfaction in the corps of junior army officers, the overthrow of the Peña regime became more than a remote possibility.

President Máximo Peña knew he had to strengthen his grasp on the country. Peña's admiration of the European fascists was no secret. Centralized authority with ultimate power wielded by one man was a goal he shared with Franco, Mussolini and Hitler. Peña knew Nazi Germany could supply the muscle he needed to stay in control of the Republic of Anchuria.

Anchuria's dictator and his European counterparts had mutual interests. The Third Reich wanted a firm foothold in the Americas - a place from which to expand political influence into Latin America. If the United States entered the coming war, Germany wanted a concealed Caribbean base to supply the submarines that would attack U S ships carrying oil from Venezuela and bauxite from Jamaica.

Senators Smit and Mendez were personal as well as political friends. They both detested Máximo Peña. If he had the support of the Third Reich, he would move against them as well as against the Fruit Company. Any alliance between Anchuria and Germany was a serious danger to them. The liberties and the fortunes of both Smit and Mendez would be imperiled. Cautiously and quietly, the two Senators looked for an acceptable alternative to the Peña regime.

During the summer of 1938, the Republic of Anchuria would celebrate the fiftieth anniversary of their army's glorious victory over the hated Sedalians in the Battle of the Ramasajoti River. Senator Paco Mendez arranged for Senator Roberto Smit to be the keynote speaker at the City of Aguas Buenas' grand celebration of the event. Of course, the two Senators had a hidden agenda. The lives of more than one of the passengers of the S S Arbutus would be affected by the intricate politics of the Republic of Anchuria.

Chapter 6

The Saga of Camilo Rosas

The will of the people is the major force governing the politics of Central America. It is true, national elections are not always held in accordance with the provisions of a country's Constitution. It is also true that the successful candidate for the Presidency of a Latin Republic occasionally receives more votes than there were men women and children in the country. Unsuccessful candidates don't complain. They admired and envied the roguish abilities of the ones who manage the fraudulent count.

Unlike Chicago, managing a fraudulent count is not the only democratic way to win an election in Central American Republics. The Constitution of Anchuria, like those of many of its sister Republics, formally recognizes the citizens' right of revolution. Thus, given enough arms, ammunition and public support, it is legal for those out of office to immediately implement the will of the people. It is not necessary to wait for the next election cycle. Revolution is just another example of democracy in action.

Latin Republics give golden opportunities to those citizens who are willing to work for their own advancement in the world of politics. The life of Camilo Rosas was a rags-to-riches saga equal to that of any fictitious Horatio Alger. Though he was a Sedalian and never set foot in the neighboring Republic of Anchuria, Camilo Rosas set forces in motion that would threaten the revolutionary plans of Anchurian Senators Smit and Mendez..

* * * * *

Camilo Rosas was born in 1906 in Cuidad Carillo on the Caribbean shore of the Republic of Sedalia. He began life enjoying lowly economic status and uncertain masculine parentage. As a boy, he observed a curious fact. Labor seldom produces wealth for the worker. In the world of the laborer, he discovered, the only place where wealth was evident was in the hands of the sindicato - the labor union. Therefore, it was in the sindicato that Camilo Rosas planned his future.

Whenever anyone used the word "sindicato" in Cuidad Carillo, he meant the Sindicato Nacional de Trabajadores de Agricola, commonly known by its acronym, SINDETRAG. The SINDETRAG had exclusive jurisdiction over the Fruit Company plantation workers and the "estibadores" who carried the bananas from the dockside warehouses and loaded them on Central American Fruit Company steamers.

In the port city of Ciudad Carillo, in the Republic of Sedalia, the Fruit Company contributed generously to any charitable promotion undertaken by the SINDETRAG's local boss, who was called "El Jefe". El Jefe's charities were largely undefined and completely unpublicized. The relationship between El Jefe and the Fruit Company was peaceful and downright cordial.

With such an intimate friendship between labor and management, it would be quite ungentlemanly for El Jefe to apply pressure for wage increases. As a result, the wage rate for the Central American Fruit Company workers was low and no strike or other unpleasantness disturbed the dignity and profit of the Fruit Company's Sedalian banana business.

The Fruit Company, to show its own good faith, agreed to hire no one unless he received the stamp of approval of El Jefe. If a Sedalian wanted to work for the Fruit Company, he had to join SINDETRAG and pay its dues. As a second condition to obtaining such employment, El Jefe insisted the worker show his gratitude by making an additional monthly financial contribution, directly to him.

In his early youth, Camilo Rosas attended the school the Fruit Company established for the children of its employees. By the time he was twelve years old, Camilo had mastered the basics of reading, writing and arithmetic. He spent all free time at the SINDETRAG headquarters in Cuidad Carillo where he ran errands for El Jefe.

Sometimes Camilo would earn ten centavos by sitting in the

SINDETRAG anteroom, listening to the giggles and heavy breathing coming from behind the door to El Jefe's office. It was his responsibility to give warning whenever a visitor - El Jefe's wife, for instance - entered the building.

Camilo's diligence was rewarded. When he was fourteen years old, he became a permanent member of the SINDETRAG office staff. Then, in 1925, El Jefe's Assistant vanished from Ciudad Carillo, never to again appear. There were those who believed the Assistant's office affairs were the reason for his disappearance. However, as Camilo Rosas wisely noted, the Assistant's attractive secretary did not disappear with him. There were others who were sure the Assistant had been murdered. This theory was abandoned when the Assistant's wife proved to have an air tight alibi.

The next obvious reason for disappearance was embezzlement. However, the office cash box had not been emptied and the funds the SINDETRAG carried in the local bank were untouched. The Assistant had not absconded with the cash and the third most widely held explanation for his disappearance evaporated..

Everyone concluded the Assistant's death must have been an accident. The SINDETRAG's life insurance carrier paid a double indemnity claim, noting in its records that the insured probably had been "accidentally" caught with someone's wife. This meant he had been killed and either buried somewhere in the jungle or dropped somewhere into the Caribbean. Camilo Rosas was in the right place and the right time. El Jefe appointed him to fill the position of the missing Assistant Jefe of the SINDETRAG's Ciudad Carillo union.

Camilo suspected El Jefe was responsible for the Assistant's disappearance. He knew the Assistant was making demands for increased compensations. He had overheard the Assistant threatening El Jefe with exposing irregularities in the remittances of SINDETRAG's monies sent to don Pablo Ramirez. Don Pablo Ramirez was the President of SINDETRAG. He lived, not in Ciudad Carillo, but in Santa Elena, the Sedalian capitol city.

Camilo never gave voice to his suspicion. If El Jefe committed murder to remove a threat to his leadership of the Ciudad Carillo union, he would certainly kill again if his leadership was again threatened. Camilo Rosas concluded it would be prudent to make no demands of El Jefe. He worked in the SINDETRAG vineyards without great financial reward. His only outside income came from smuggled goods sold through the Central American Fruit Company stores.

For five years, Camilo watched the SINDETRAG's membership grow as the Central American Fruit Company expanded the size of its plantations and learned to combat Panama Disease - Mother Nature's way of destroying banana production. He watched El Jefe grow wealthy, but realized only modest growth in his own financial condition.

Then came the worldwide depression of 1929. In 1930, the Central American Fruit Company cut back its Sedalian operations. Banana workers joined the ranks of the unemployed. The voluntary monthly contributions El Jefe received from each worker's pay checks declined sharply. In the face of such a catastrophe, El Jefe took steps to preserve the level of his income.

The already understated remittances of union dues to don Pablo dropped at a rate substantially larger than the reduction in the number of Fruit Company employees. In addition, El Jefe insisted on an increase in the kickbacks he received from Camilo Rosas a well as from the other laborers who still had jobs.

Within a week, don Pablo Ramirez received distressing news from Ciudad Carillo. He was informed of serious inconsistencies in the accountings prepared by El Jefe. Don Pablo received evidence proving the total amount of dues and contributions collected in Ciudad Carillo, less the amount of authorized expenditures, left balances which, each month, were much larger than the monies actually forwarded to him.

When he became aware of the full extent of El Jefe's bookkeeping errors, don Pablo was livid. He immediately sent a message to the industrious and reliable Camilo Rosas. The message disclosed exactly what don Pablo planned to do to El Jefe when he caught him. Don Pablo's intended acts of revenge came straight from the procedures of the Spanish Inquisition.

Camilo quickly showed don Pablo's letter to El Jefe and recommended he leave the Republic of Sedalia at his earliest possible convenience. After El Jefe read the penalties proposed in don Pablo's letter, he blanched and readily agreed on the advisability of an immediate and permanent vacation. The following day, a Central American Fruit Company steamship weighed anchor at the port of Ciudad Carillo and began one of its return voyages to New Orleans.

El Jefe was an unhappy passenger. Over the years he had amassed a few hundred thousand dollars. The recent stock market crash decimated his equity holdings. Municipalities defaulted on the bonds he held. The product of the years of his imaginative accounting of the union's funds went down the toilet

As he stood at the rail of the Arbutus, watching the Republic of Sedalia slowly disappear on the horizon, the only cash El Jefe carried with him was one-half of the balance in the SINDETRAG's Ciudad Carillo bank account. He tried to keep all of it, but Camilo Rosas insisted they split it evenly. He entered into his self imposed exile a bitter and disillusioned man. "Is there no justice?" he complained.

Camilo Rosas became the new "El Jefe". Honor and wealth awaited him. So did intrigue and conspiracy.

* * * * *

Upon elevation to the post of El Jefe of the SINDETRAG's Ciudad Carillo operation, Camilo Rosas' first act was to assure don Pablo of a proper reporting and a proper remittance of union dues, kick-backs and other contributions received in his office. The welfare of the SINDETRAG (i.e. don Pablo) could support no unreasonable error in the management of such an important activity. Rosas' second act was to assure himself of a fair participation in the same dues and contributions.

Camilo Rosas correctly guessed his newly appointed assistant, an ambitious young man named Jaime Gomez,, had agreed to privately advise don Pablo of the degree of honesty present in the Ciudad Carillo union office's monthly financial reports. Rosas also correctly guessed that Jaime Gomez, would be reluctant to report oversights if he, too, were a beneficiary of them.

If the previous Jefe had been a bit more liberal with Camilo Rosas, perhaps he would still be the Jefe at Ciudad Carillo, but he had been stingy. Camilo's request for a more equitable division of income was not only rejected out-of-hand but an increased payment had been demanded of him. He had no alternative except to send the damning report to don Pablo in Santa Elena and, as a result, the old El Jefe was out and Camilo was in.

Camilo would not make the same mistake. His third act was to assure Jaime Gomez that he, too, would get a piece of the pie. He further promised the young man he would become Jefe of the Ciudad Carillo Sindicato if Rosas ascended to the position of President of the SINDETRAG.

Camilo Rosas' fourth act turned out to be a very important one. He arranged a job for his Uncle Pancho in the Ciudad Carillo Customs House - the Aduana. Uncle Pancho's appointment as night watchman was a happy and popular event. He had to be on the job at 8:00 every evening. Since it was his usual practice to be already heavily in drink by that time, the job didn't really interfere with his social obligations and it certainly had a salutary effect on those around him.

Uncle Pancho no longer left the cantina well after midnight in a completely drunken condition. He no longer staggered home to beat his wife, Maria. When the neighborhood ladies noticed she didn't carry the black and blue emblems of domestic disagreement, they all presumed Uncle Pancho no longer loved her. Nevertheless, Maria was happy.

Uncle Pancho no longer fell asleep in the cantina, taking up valuable bar, table or floor space. He no longer engaged other customers in unwanted conversation or instigated raucous argument and disrupting fist fights. The owner of the cantina and his other customers were happy.

Uncle Pancho could now pay his own cantina bills. That burden was removed from Camilo Rosas and he, too, was happy.

Uncle Pancho was the happiest. He never looked forward to going home to face a shrewish wife. Now he could weave out of the cantina at 8:30 or 9:00 in the evening, enter and lock himself inside the corrugated iron Aduana building, fall into the hammock suspended in the corner of the warehouse and doze off, content in the knowledge that he was one of the very favored and privileged few who got paid for sleeping.

Not a single incident of Aduana robbery had been reported during the entire history of Ciudad Carillo. Uncle Pancho could sleep off his binges in the calm assurance that nothing would occur to disturb his rest or cause anyone to question the caliber of the protection he extended to the properties locked within that building.

Nevertheless, he pried loose one of the corrugated iron wall sheets to provide for his own quick exit in the unlikely event robbers entered the Aduana and endangered his life. Uncle Pancho knew his bright new life was all due to the generosity of his nephew, Camilo Rosas. He was truly indebted to him.

In the four years that followed, Camilo Rosas prospered. His income from the local SINDETRAG dues, the voluntary contributions of the SINDETRAG members, the bonuses from the Central American Fruit Company and the monies received from the furtive sale of smuggled goods made his life comfortable. His assistant, Jaime Gomez was treated fairly and even don Pablo Ramirez was mildly surprised by what almost approached relative honesty in the accounts and remittances from Ciudad Carillo

All parties had a good thing going for them. However, each was afflicted by an innate urge to march forward, to create, to develop, to make their lives better, to get richer. Some call it the American Dream. Some call it greed.

Chapter 7

A (Perhaps Not So) Bloody Insurrection
in the Republic of Sedalia

In 1935, the undisputed president of the SINDETRAG, Don Pablo Ramirez, preferred to live in Santa Elena, the Republic of Sedalia's Capitol city. It was where the country's political activity occurred and don Pablo was politically oriented. He adeptly auctioned the SINDETRAG's votes with the bureaucrats and politicos and, thus, received gifts from all who were indebted to him. Both he and SINDETRAG prospered. Don Pablo was 55 years old and had no intention of retiring from the union presidency - unless his public service was recognized through elevation to high national political office.

Political ferment was in the air in Sedalia in 1935. In the judgment of don Pablo, the President of the Republic and his generals were old and weak and should be deposed in favor of younger, more active and enlightened leaders - enlightened leaders like don Pablo himself. When he very gently approached those politicos who had cooperated with him and received special favors from the SINDETRAG, they very gently informed him they would not stand in the way of a pre-election change of government.

They also very gently informed him that they were reluctant to give support to any proposal for non-electoral change of government until they were convinced there was enough military muscle to insure its success.

Don Pablo faced a difficult problem. The older generals were warmly supportive of the President. The younger army officers would be happy to help dispose of the President - as long as it meant the removal of the old generals and their own advancement in rank. If younger officers were brought into the conspiracy, they might, indeed, produce the muscle necessary to convince the President it was time for him to embark on an extended visit to Miami, Madrid or Mexico City.

However, some of those same younger army officers might determine the Presidency of the Republic was more attractive than mere advance in rank. If they decided to retain political power instead of supporting the ambition of don Pablo, there would be nothing he could do about it. Don Pablo found such a possibility to be completely unacceptable.

There was an alternative. A revolution initiated and manned by the SINDETRAG's banana plantation workers and dockside stevedores might take control of Ciudad Carillo. With the country's major port under the rebel banner, only military intervention could save the President. Don Pablo guessed the generals were not willing to involve themselves in any truly energetic action. They would vacillate.

The younger officers, on the other hand, might come out of the barracks. In some misguided burst of enthusiasm, it was possible they could support President Peña and put down the revolt. To dampen such misguided enthusiasm, don Pablo planned to capture the Ciudad Carillo radio station, announce the revolution and blame the President and the traitorous generals for the country's ills. He would promise to throw them all in prison as soon as they were captured. He would also assure the junior army officers of advancement in rank.

That plan, don Pablo believed, would frighten the President and the generals into fleeing the country. When the radio station made the announcement and called for the army to perform its patriotic duty and support the revolution, it would, don Pablo believed, cause the junior officers to either join the insurrection or, at least, to sit out the mutiny. In either case, the army would be neutralized.

The successful control of Ciudad Carillo was the keystone of the coup. Rebel control of the city would be the necessary credible show of force needed to convince the Senators to openly support him. Don Pablo's most powerful union office was in Ciudad Carillo and its Jefe, Camilo Rosas, had already shown a tendency to be reasonably trustworthy. Don Pablo knew Camilo coveted the Presidency of the SINDETRAG. That, thought don Pablo, would be the bait to insure Camilo's cooperation. Don Pablo went to Ciudad Carillo to confer with Camilo Rosas.

* * * * *

Camilo Rosas was uncomfortable. Something was wrong. Whenever don Pablo wanted to talk to him, Camilo went to Santa Elena. For the first time, don Pablo was coming to Ciudad Carillo. Why? Camilo's accounts and reports to don Pablo may not have been models of accounting accuracy, but they were as fair as any reasonable person should expect. After due consideration, Rosas doubted chastisement was the reason for the visit. Something extraordinary, he felt, was astir. His guess was soon proven to be accurate.

Don Pablo sat in Camilo's office, in Camilo's chair, behind Camilo's desk. Camilo sat before him. After small talk, which Rosas found nearly unbearable, don Pablo approached the reason for his visit with his accustomed caution.

"The government of our country seems to be a good one, no?" he questioned. Camilo watched don Pablo studying him. His answer might be important.

"I do not know if it is good or bad," he temporized. "Unless the government threatens action affecting our SINDETRAG, I take no sides."

Don Pablo did not change expression nor respond. He continued to look into the eyes of the Jefe of the Ciudad Carillo union. Camilo knew his answer was not what don Pablo wanted. He tried again.

"But you live in Santa Elena, don Pablo.," he said. "You are a much better judge. Of course, I trust your judgment."

Then it was Camilo's turn to study don Pablo who looked down at the desk and considered Camilo's answers. Without looking up don Pablo quietly asked, "Do you have political ambition, Camilo?"

Now Camilo understood the reason for don Pablo's trip to Ciudad Carillo. In direct language, those last two questions said: I believe our government is weak and I have political ambition.

As soon as don Pablo raised his eyes from the desk, Rosas looked directly into them and said: "My ambition, don Pablo, is to become President of the SINDETRAG and I will give my full support to any action you may take that will further that ambition."

The conversation became direct. "Camilo," said a faintly smiling don Pablo, "it was the Englishman, Guillermo Shakespeare, who said: 'there is a tide in the affairs of men which, taken at the flood, leads on to fortune'. I believe you will be an excellent President of SINDETRAG." He paused to be sure Rosas had heard the verb 'will be.'

Satisfied when Rosas slightly nodded his head, don Pablo continued. "The President and his generals are old. They no longer have the courage to fight against a real show of force. If they are convinced a substantial effort to dislodge them is in the field, they will quickly leave Santa Elena for retirement in Miami."

"I'm sure you are right, don Pablo," was Rosas' answer. "A substantial effort by a credible force would be successful. What will the army do, don Pablo?"

Camilo shows his intelligence, thought don Pablo. He goes directly to the heart of the matter. "My friends in the Senate will not stand in our way," he said, "but they won't actively support us. Neither will they actively support the government. They will support whoever shows superior force."

"And the army?" Rosas persisted.

"The church should pose no problem," don Pablo continued, again ducking Camilo's question. "Our President has neglected the Bishop and we must remember that the church is sustained by the important families of the Republic. Those "important families" are the Senators and the Provincial Governors. If the Senators support us, so will the Bishop. He is no fool."

"You have planned well, don Pablo," said Camilo Rosas, "and as you have already said, a true show of strength is essential. If the generals are friendly to the President, how can you convince the army to give you the support necessary to remove him?"

Don Pablo Ramirez rose from his chair. He walked to the window and looked out over the City of Ciudad Carillo and beyond, into the blue Caribbean Sea. "Camilo," he said, "You ask an important question. It is the reason I am here today." Then he explained how he planned to arm the SINDETRAG and take control of Ciudad Carillo rather than look for immediate military support.

"I will offer the President safe passage to whatever country he desires. If he doesn't leave, we will commandeer the Fruit Company trucks and go to Santa Elena to force him out."

Camilo analyzed the situation perfectly. If the plot was successful, don Pablo would become President of the Republic and Camilo would become the head of SINDETRAG. If the plot were unsuccessful, don Pablo would be shot and Camilo would become President of SINDETRAG.

However, if Camilo appeared to be involved in the coup, he, too, would face a firing squad. Could he insulate himself from that fate? Yes, he decided, yes, he could. He would keep his plan for self-preservation to himself.

Camilo quickly repeated his promise of active and full support. When don Pablo produced sufficient arms, Camilo would produced a SINDETRAG Worker's Army of Liberation. He would capture Ciudad Carillo and its radio station. Don Pablo agreed to send fifty thousand Pesos in gold coin to cover the expense of creating the army and bribing Ciudad Carillo authorities for their support.

Assurances of fidelity and secrecy were exchanged and don Pablo, satisfied with his work in Ciudad Carillo, returned to the capitol. A week later a messenger from Santa Elena delivered a heavy wooden chest to the Ciudad Carillo SINDETRAG office.

On the following day, Camilo asked Jaime Gomez to come to his office. He opened the SINDETRAG safe, brought out the wooden chest and put it on the desk before him. He watched Jaime's eyes as he opened the chest, put his hand into it and then lifted it out, letting the gold coins trickle back through his fingers.

With Gomez's attention secured, Rosas recalled his promise to make the young man the Jefe of the Ciudad Carillo SINDETRAG when he became the President of the Union. He told him of don Pablo's plan to capture the Presidency of the Republic and emphasized the necessity of organizing a worker's army to take control of the city.

"And that, Jaime," he said, "is why I am talking to you now. If don Pablo is successful, I will be the President of SINDETRAG and you, Jaime, will be the Jefe here in Ciudad Carillo." Camilo paused and looked at Gomez. Then he said, "None of this will happen unless an effective worker's army has been organized."

"Don Camilo," volunteered Jaime Gomez, with remarkable enthusiasm, "it will be an honor for me to personally organize an army and lead it to take the Comandancia, the radio station and the city's generator building."

Rosas looked at the chest. "We have money, Jaime," he said, but we will need guns. They will be delivered to the Aduana soon, so you must be patient. Tell no one until we have the weapons. I, too, will need time. An appropriate payment must be made to the Comandante of the Guardia. The head of the Aduana and the Mayor are important to us. They, too, must receive consideration. I will handle those matters. You will be in charge of the army. Its work should not be dangerous, but it is important that there be a large army, a very large army."

Jaime Gomez was prepared. "When don Pablo is ready to move," he said, "tell me. I will see to the distribution of the rifles."

Jaime paused and looked at the chest before adding: "Of course, I will have to distribute some of the money to the men in order to insure their help." He again glanced at the chest and the golden coins. "Four or Five thousand Pesos should be enough. I will need it on the night before we act. I will call a meeting as the men come from the plantations. I will have an army, ready to move, by seven o'clock in the morning."

Jaime Gomez' willing cooperation was a relief. Camilo did not want to be openly involved in the revolt. He wanted to be able to claim loyalty to the government if the coup failed. Jaime would be his cat's paw. Now Camilo's Presidency of SINDETRAG was assured. It mattered not if the revolution succeeded or failed.

Before the month ended, the head of the Ciudad Carillo Aduana, the Comandante of the Guardia and the Mayor were all richer. The wooden box in the SINDETRAG office was lighter and the Central American Fruit Company's ship, the Arbutus, delivered a shipment of farm equipment destined for the Fruit Company's plantation.

The wooden crates containing the equipment were not inspected. They were stored, unopened, in the Aduana building. The scene was set for the Sedalian Revolution of 1935.

The best laid plans o' mice an' men gang aft a-glee.

Chapter 8

Cherchez la Femme and You Will Find Her

In 1938, Ellie Sue Bradshaw was a twenty-five year old hazel eyed, honey blonde with a soft Arkansas accent. A narrow waist, an infectious smile, and a well-developed native intelligence produced potent female weaponry. Ellie Sue's passage on the S S Arbutus was booked early in the spring of 1938. By July she was anxiously awaiting the signal that would send her on a Caribbean cruise.

Nine years earlier, on October 28th, that Black Friday when United States stocks and bonds lost 26 billion dollars of value, Ellie Sue was a high school freshman in Salem, Arkansas. She didn't pay much attention to Wall Street's cataclysmic event. She was more interested in cheerleading.

Her father, Dr. John Bradshaw, was a physician blessed with both a financially rewarding practice and a very clever stock broker. The doctor followed the broker's advice and withdrew from the stock market in September. He left the stock market a full month before the Crash. As a result, like his daughter, Ellie Sue, he wasn't greatly concerned about the Wall Street disaster, though, occasionally, he wondered about the possible effect the Crash might have on the ability of his patients to pay their bills.

While other people were worried about their finances and went out of their way to be particularly friendly to their bankers, Dr. John Bradshaw was more concerned about the paneling in the den of the new home he was building in the most exclusive neighborhood of Salem.

The contractor claimed the best mahogany in the world was produced in a country called Anchuria. The doctor insisted on the best. He insisted on the best because his socially conscious wife insisted on the best. A special order for the wood were placed with Madera

Anchuria, S.A., a producer of the very best quality mahogany. The lumber mill was located a few thousand miles away in Villa Smit in the back waters of the Republic of Anchuria. The completion of the carpenter's work in the den was delayed for five weeks while the mahogany was sawed and planed and shipped, first to New Orleans and then to Salem.

While her mother paid special attention to the design of her new home, Ellie Sue was paying special attention to Forrest Taylor, the fullback on the freshman football team. Forrest was the son of Jackson Taylor, the most prominent attorney in Salem. Jackson Taylor and John Bradshaw used the same stock broker and Taylor, too, had followed his advice.

The Taylor family's southern blood lines were impeccable. The attorney's grandfather had been a junior officer assigned to General Thomas E. (Stonewall) Jackson's staff during the War between the States. (The Taylors never called it the Civil War). This accounts for the attorney's first name. (If it hadn't been for his mother's rock firm objection, he would have been named "Stonewall".)

Following this same tradition, Attorney Jackson Taylor's first born son was named after the cavalry officer and Confederate General, Nathan Bedford Forrest. The secret of his military success, said the general, was: "Get there first with the most men." History translates that quote as: "Get there fastest with the mostest." General Forrest had a dark side. After the Civil War, he was active in the Ku Klux Klan. His name sake, Forrest Taylor, also had a dark side.

During his time in Salem High School, Forrest Taylor became the high school football and basketball star. He was the idol of his female classmates, including, of course, Ellie Sue. When, during the summer between her junior and senior years, she announced she was going steady with Forrest, her mother was delighted. If Ellie Sue played her cards right, she would become a member of one of the county's oldest, richest and most socially prominent families.

The 'going steady' announcement was occasioned by the promise Forrest felt he had to make to Ellie Sue if he were to be successful in getting into her pants. With the exception of an evening in a hotel in Little Rock after the state basketball tournament, most of the sexual encounters between Ellie Sue and Forrest took place in the back seat of the Taylor family Packard.

Mrs. Bradshaw was not unaware of what was going on. She thought things were moving in the right direction. Dr. John Bradshaw, however, was not thrilled. He had twice treated Forrest for what was commonly called "the crabs". Dr. Bradshaw was often called upon to treat that condition and he knew it was usually contracted in a whore house across the county line. His conversations with the young man did not impress him. He considered Forrest Taylor to be an over-indulged, worthless. pup.

The doctor did his best to break up the romance, finally resorting to sending his daughter to an out-of-state woman's college. Ellie Sue's first year at Missouri's Columbia College was a terrible ordeal. She was lonely. Forrest did not share Ellie Sue's loneliness. He was able to develop a number of pleasant liaisons with coeds who believed screwing a university athlete was a status symbol.

Forrest never developed any interest in visiting Ellie Sue at Columbia. He had no great difficulty in becoming otherwise occupied. He rarely answered her letters and by the end of her first year at college, Ellie Sue accepted the fact that "it was over." Being a healthy girl, she wasn't long out of circulation.

Ellie Sue graduated with a Fine Arts Degree in 1936 and returned to Salem. Forrest Taylor had also returned to Salem, but not as a lawyer. While Ellie Sue was busily pursuing her Fine Arts degree, Forrest was busy flunking out of first the University of Arkansas and then from two other colleges, each with progressively more modest academic admission requirements.

Forrest went to college to play - on the football field, in the campus beer halls and in whatever beds became available. He would have been more successful on the football field if he had been less successful in his other fields of collegiate endeavor.

When the football scholarships stopped and a disappointed Jackson Taylor refused to finance further attempts to turn his son into an attorney, Forrest Taylor reluctantly left academia. Now, back in Salem, he became the local agent for the Philadelphia Fire & Marine Insurance Company.

It may have been an attack of nostalgia. It may have been the simple fact that there were few interesting young men in Salem who attracted Ellie Sue's interest. In any event, with the assistance of bridge partners Dora Bradshaw and Emaline Taylor, Forrest and Ellie Sue began to see each other.

To the joy of her mother and the sadness of her father, Ellie Sue and Forrest married. Ellie Sue learned the fairy tale conclusion: "and they lived happily ever after," accurately describes life only in the moving pictures. She also learned a lazy, egocentric, over-imbibing, spoiled rotten young man becomes a lazy, egocentric, over-imbibing, spoiled rotten husband.

The first time he came home drunk and smelling of another woman, Ellie Sue threw a fit and got a bruised cheek for her pains. After that she didn't question him. One afternoon, while taking a bath, she decided she could no longer endure the marriage. Ellie Sue went to her father's clinic and tearfully explained Forrest's mistreatments and her unhappiness.

Divorce was not that common in the mid-thirties, but Ellie Sue received solid paternal support. Dr. Bradshaw produced an ointment to kill the unwanted visitors Ellie Sue had found in her pubic hair. She made an appointment with a lawyer and a divorce action was commenced.

By mid-June of 1938, Ellie Sue was waiting for her divorce decree. As soon as she received it, she planned to embark on a summer cruise through the Gulf of Mexico and the Caribbean Sea. It would take her away from Salem for a few weeks, let things settle down at home and give her time to think about her future.

Ellie Sue did not discount the possibility of a shipboard romance. It would serve as a catharsis and be a pleasant way to commemorate her renewed single status. She hoped her fellow passengers would include a man who would meet her standards.

In July, the day she anxiously anticipated finally arrived. In deference to the social standing of the parties' parents, the matter of Taylor v Taylor was the first case on the docket. Few people would be in the courthouse that early in the morning. The judge gave Forrest all the debts. There were many of them. He gave Ellie Sue her maiden name and all assets of the marriage. There were very few of them. He provided for alimony in perpetuity. Ellie Sue knew it would be Jackson and not Forrest Taylor who would make the payments. The judge banged down the gavel and Ellie Sue felt like a slave who had been liberated.

Outside the courthouse, Dr. John Bradshaw waited in the family Roadmaster Buick. It was a happy day for him. He was proud of his daughter. In spite of her mother's pressure, she had the gumption to get rid of that bum. Ellie Sue was equally proud of her father. Never once had he said: I told you so. Minutes later a smiling Ellie Sue almost ran down the courthouse steps.

"It's finished, Daddy. It's all over. It's done," she said. She looked in the back seat to again make sure her suitcases were there and, with a cheerful "Let's go", she got into the seat beside her father. They left for Memphis and the train that would carry her to New Orleans and the S S Arbutus.

Ellie Sue's divorce was nearly as much of a relief to John Bradshaw as it was to his daughter. The trip from Salem to Memphis was not one of silence and introspection. The termination of the marriage left no scars on Ellie Sue. She chattered and she bubbled. John Bradshaw was just as happy. Any fears he may have had about Ellie Sue harboring post-divorce feelings of guilt vanished during the ride. Only one serious moment occurred.

"Do you know what you're going to do when you get back home, Ellie Sue?"

"I've been thinking about it, Daddy." She didn't want to tell him she had decided to leave Salem. She knew she would have to tell him, but now was not the time.

"Well, honey, remember," said John Bradshaw, "Salem is not the only place in the world." John and Ellie Sue Bradshaw were certainly father and daughter. They thought alike. Both understood she should start a new life, free from the restraints imposed by either the social pressures of smaller communities or by the familial pressures of parents. Inwardly, Ellie Sue heaved the proverbial sigh of relief. When she returned from the cruise, her father would not stand in her way. The announcement of the plans for her future would not be difficult.

Ten years earlier, in 1928, Dora and John Bradshaw went to Europe on the Holland American luxury liner, Volendam. John didn't play bridge, disliked shuffle-board and took no great delight in looking out at a flat watery horizon. Two books in the ship library, Aldous Huxley's Point Counterpoint and Evelyn Waugh's Decline and Fall, saved him from complete boredom.

At the train station in Memphis, Dr. Bradshaw carried his daughter's luggage to the train named "The City of New Orleans". He kissed her, said "I'm proud of you, kid" and gave her a book. "This will keep you occupied when you things get monotonous." he said. The book was entitled: A History of the Republic of Anchuria.

Ellie Sue said, "Thank you, Daddy," and gave him the paper sack she had elected to leave behind. It containing the orange and two sandwiches her mother had packed for her. She smiled. He smiled. The conductor yelled, "All Aboard" and Ellie Sue waved off the porter who came to put her suitcases on the train. With an exhilarating sense of freedom and relief, she carried them herself.

Chapter 9

The Passing of Camilo Rosas

Ellie Sue began to plan her summer cruise nearly six months before embarking on the S S Arbutus. Paul Eckert had a month to prepare for his visit to Aguas Buenas. In 1935, three years before Ellie Sue and Paul boarded the train that would carry them to New Orleans and to their banana boat cruise to Anchuria's port of Aguas Buenas, another man sailed from Ciudad Carillo in the Republic of Sedalia to Aguas Buenas in the neighboring Republic of Anchuria. He had only a few hours to prepare for his trip.

* * * * *

It was nearly four o'clock in the morning when Camilo Rosas, the soon to become ex-Jefe of the Ciudad Carillo SINDETRAG, heard a tapping at the backdoor of his house. He lit the kerosene lamp, took his revolver from the night stand and went to the door.

"Who is it?"

"It is your Uncle Pancho," said a voice. "Let me in, Camilo. I have important news."

Rosas unlocked the door and an agitated Uncle Pancho, looking over his shoulder to see if he had been followed, entered from the black night. "Put out the lamp," he gasped and, in the same breath, said: "They are going to kill you. You must leave now, Camilo. They are going to kill you."

Rosas put the still lit lamp on the table. "Calm yourself, Uncle Pancho," he said. "Sit down." He poured a glass of aguardiente and pushed it toward Uncle Pancho. "Here. Drink this. Who is going to kill me?"

Uncle Pancho downed the aguardiente with one efficient

48

movement of arm and hand. Not a drop was spilled. "The soldiers," he answered. "I heard them, Camilo. They are going to shoot you."

"Calm yourself, Uncle Pancho. Calm yourself," Rosas said as he poured out more aguardiente. "Now, tell me - slowly. Why are the soldiers going to kill me?"

With the second glass of aguardiente inside him, Uncle Pancho regained some of his composure and told his nephew what had transpired earlier in the evening.

"I leave the cantina, Camilo, and I go to the Aduana. Maybe I doze off," and quickly added: "Usually I do not go to sleep, but tonight I am very, very tired. Then I hear noise and I wake up. I remain very quiet in my hammock. The ones who break into the Aduana, they have the key. They are soldiers, Camilo. They do not see me because I remain very, very quiet.

"The Capitán tells one of the soldiers to open one of the boxes that is marked "farm equipment". Do you know what is in the box, Camilo? Rifles, Camilo. Rifles and bullets. I wonder what kind of farm uses so many rifles and bullets.

"Then the Capitán he tell the soldiers to guard the door and shoot anyone who come in. Then he say he is going to the Telégrafo and wait until it is open in the morning and then he will send the telegrama to the General in Santa Elena.

"Camilo, the telegrama is going to tell the General that what Jaime Gomez say is true and the General should shoot don Pablo Ramirez and he wants the General to say it is all right for him to shoot you, too. To shoot you, too. You got to go now, Camilo, before the Telégrafo is open."

Jaime Gomez! That hijo de puta, Camilo said to himself. He poured more aguardiente, this time into two glasses. After a moment and as Uncle Pancho anxiously watched him, Rosas asked: "Did anyone see you come here?"

"Oh, no, Camilo. I squeeze out between the loose sheets of corrugated iron on the Aduana wall. I fear they will follow me and maybe shoot me so I am very careful. It is dark and no one sees." all will be good

Camilo considered his predicament. His Assistant Jefe, Jaime

Gomez, had exposed the conspiracy. Uncle Pancho was right. He had to leave immediately. "Do n o t alarm yourself, Uncle. All will be good. You will be safe, but you must do exactly what I say. Go to your home. Do not waken Maria. Bring your burro to the back door of the SINDETRAG building and wait for me. Be sure no one sees you."

After Uncle Pancho left, Rosas dressed. He took a metal box from beneath his bed. It contained the money he accumulated during the four years he was Jefe of the SINDETRAG in Ciudad Carillo. He pushed the barrel of the revolver under the belt beneath his coat and hoisted the box up on his shoulder. Then he turned down the lamp and slipped out the back door.

Careful not to be seen, he made his way to the SINDETRAG office. There he opened the safe and removed the chest containing what was left of the gold don Pablo had delivered. He poured the contents of his metal box into the chest and then dragged it to the back door of the building. He closed the door behind him and, under the protection of a moonless night, he hurried to the house of Chico Elizondo.

* * * * *

Chico Elizondo was a fisherman. He was a prosperous fisherman. He owned a fishing boat that was painted. Its sails had few patches. He lived in a house that did not leak during the rainy season. He could afford the roundest girls. Nevertheless, Chico Elizondo was not a good fisherman. He complimented the meager existence he wrested from the sea by income derived from an active import business. Chico was a smuggler.

The antagonism between the Republic of Sedalia and its neighbor, the Republic of Anchuria began with the embezzlement and flight of Cayetano Rodriguez to Aguas Buenas in 1848. The most recent War between the countries was instigated by Lord Percy Grenville and culminated in the Battle of the Rio Ramasajoti. It was ended by the Treaty of Santa Elena that established their mutual border.

Both Republics claimed the Treaty allowed the other country to cheat it. The Treaty only added more fuel to the mutual hatred. The deep seated antagonisms between Sedalia and Anchuria continued unabated. One of the results of those continuing national frictions was the existence of high tariff barriers meant to punish the other country's commerce. Anchuria produced quality rum. Sedalia's high tariff on Anchurian rum created obvious opportunities for a clever entrepreneur. He could buy rum from the Anchurian distillery, smuggle it into Sedalia and sell it at an attractive price. It was tax free.

Chico Elizondo would sail his fishing boat from Ciudad Carillo in the Republic of Sedalia to Aguas Buenas in the Republic of Anchuria. He would buy as many cases of rum as his boat could safely hold and return to Ciudad Carillo. The policy of the Central American Fruit Company created a prime market for his contraband.

The Fruit Company did not want drunken employees. It refused to allow the sale of alcoholic beverage from its company stores. Camilo Rosas bought Chico Elizondo's illegal rum. He sold it to the manager of the Fruit Company store who, in turn, quietly sold it to the banana plantation laborers. It was a profitable business for all three men.

* * * * *

It was dark when Chico Elizondo opened the door to his house and lifted the kerosene lantern to light up the face of the person whose knocking disturbed his sleep.

"Camilo? Is that you? Whatever do you want."

"Let me in, Chico. I have business to discuss."

"Now, Camilo? It's the middle of the night. Tomorrow, Camilo. We'll talk tomorrow," and Chico started to close the door.

Rosas pushed the palm of his hand against the door to hold it open and stepped inside. "No, Chico. We'll talk now. I have important business in Aguas Buenas. It can't wait. I must leave now."

Chico, not yet fully awake, scratched his right cheek. Turning to place the lantern on the table, he looked at his bed and then at Rosas. "Camilo," he objected, "We can leave at ten. It's only a few hours."

"Listen, Chico," Rosas persisted, "I must leave now. Do you understand? Now. It is important. It is very important. I will pay you two hundred - two hundred and fifty Pesos, but we must leave as soon as you can get your boat ready."

Upon hearing the words: "two hundred and fifty Pesos," Chico Elizondo became fully awakened. Fifteen minutes later, as he prepared his fishing boat in the darkness, he wondered why Camilo Rosas was being so generous and what was the important business in Aguas Buenas.

While Chico Elizondo wondered, Camilo Rosas returned to the SINDETRAG office where Uncle Pancho and his burro stood waiting. They loaded the chest onto the animal. Rosas gave Uncle Pancho a bottle of aguardiente together with his final instructions.

"Go to the plaza in the square, Uncle Pancho. Sleep there tonight. Leave the plaza in the morning when there are many people who will see you. Tell them you spent the night there and never mention anything else that happened tonight." Then he added an unnecessary order: "Be sure you drink all of the aguardiente."

When the sun arose the following morning, Uncle Pancho's snoring disturbed the people who came to the plaza. When he regained consciousness, he carefully followed his nephew's instructions and, thereafter, never mentioned a word about what really happened during the previous night. He dismissed those events from his mind. In the course of time, Uncle Pancho came to believe he really had left the cantina, passed out in the plaza and spent the night there.

On the same morning, those who noticed the absence of Chico Elizondo thought he was fishing, and on the same morning, Jaime Gomez went to the SINDETRAG office. He discovered he was too late. The union's safe was open and the chest of gold coins was gone. Though he was disappointed, he consoled himself in the knowledge that he would soon become the President of the SINDETRAG, live in don Pablo's house in Santa Elena and receive just compensation for his services in alerting the President to the planned revolution.

* * * * *

When the sun was over the horizon on that same morning, Camilo Rosas and Chico Elizondo sailed past two shore-line monuments, one on each side of a dry creek bed. The monuments marked the boundary between the Republics of Sedalia and Anchuria. On the maps, the dry creek bed is called the Rio Ramasajoti. Once beyond it, Camilo Rosas left Sedalian jurisdiction and was safely within the Republic Anchuria.

During the hours of darkness, when the two men sailed in a westerly course from Ciudad Carillo toward Aguas Buenas, Chico Elizondo divined the reason for Rosas' generosity. It was obvious he was not taking a vacation. The story of urgent business was probably a lie. If it was a lie, then Rosas was running away. If he was running away, would he not take his money with him? The heavy chest Chico helped him carry from the burro to the boat - was it gold or silver that made it so heavy? Perhaps it contained the same money Rosas would use to pay him the two hundred and fifty Pesos.

Chico Elizondo considered the matter. Rosas came to his house in the middle of the night. He came alone. Perhaps no one knew he went to Chico's house. Perhaps he could kill Rosas, take his money and deny he had ever seen him. Perhaps the guardia would think Rosas stole the money and disappeared. Yes, he would kill Camilo Rosas even though he had only a machete and had seen the revolver hidden in the belt under Rosas' jacket. There was risk, but there was reward, too.

After the sun rose and the boat sailed into Anchurian waters, Camilo Rosas searched the mangrove swamp shore-line or a beach where he could land and disappear with his hoard. Within a few kilometers of the city of Villa Smit, the fishing boat rounded a spit of land and a sandy beach came into view. Rosas told Chico to land.

Chico saw his opportunity. Rosas sat in the middle of the boat, his feet straddling the chest. Chico sharply pushed the tiller away from himself. The wind passed behind the sail and it snapped from one side of the boat to the other. Chico hoped the flying boom would hit Rosas and push him over the side. If it did not, he would have to use the machete.

Rosas sat low in the Chico's boat. He saw the boom coming toward him and had time to dodge its full force. Still, it hit him on the chest and knocked him against the boat's gunnel. As Chico drew his machete, Rosas kept his wits about him. Chico knew what he carried in the chest between his feet. He had helped lift it from the burro and carry it to the fishing boat. Rosas knew with equal clarity that Chico planned to kill him.

Of course, he had planned to kill Chico when the boat was safely ashore in Anchuria. He had already concluded that dead men do not, in fact, tell tales. He would have to kill him now. Camilo quickly reached under his coat and grasped the handle of his hidden revolver. The front sight of the weapon caught in his belt and he struggled to pull it out as Chico raised his machete.

For Chico, the die was cast. There was no retreat. He would kill Camilo Rosas or Camilo Rosas would kill him. He lunged forward with the machete raised above his head. He swung it with full force, aiming at the side of Camilo's neck. Rosas, his revolver still entangled in his belt, dodged to the right and shoved his foot into Chico's abdomen, hoping to kick him in the genitals.

A split second before Chico fell backward against the side his fishing boat. His machete continued its downward movement and the blade struck the top of Rosas' shoulder. It missed the targeted neck, but opened a deep and bleeding gash that immobilized Camilo's left arm.

As he saw the smuggler raise his arm and prepare to strike again, Rosas dislodged the weapon from his belt and shot Chico Elizondo in the forehead. The force of the impact of the .38 caliber bullet knocked Chico over the side of the fishing boat and into the lagoon. Still grasping his machete, Elizondo was dead when he hit the water. His blood drew the sharks.

Rosas dropped the revolver and tried to stem the flow of blood from his shoulder. He pressed his right hand against the wound and struggled to his feet. With its tiller, sheet and sail unattended, the fishing boat nosed into the wind and lost headway. Rosas knew it was imperative that he reach the shore and attend to his wound.

He had no sailing experience, but he knew the tiller steered the boat. With blood still running down his arm, he moved toward the stern of the vessel. He stood upright in the boat and, to maintain his balance, grabbed the boom. With his body, he pushed it to the side. He kicked the tiller with his foot, intending to point the vessel toward the shore line.

A gust of wind came from the Caribbean. It hit the sail and swung it and the boom sharply back against his body. This time the boom pushed Camilo Rosas over the gunnel and into the lagoon. He was alive when the first shark came to him.

The tide slowly carried the unmanned sailing boat to the sandy shore of the lagoon and then ebbed, leaving it on its side, high on the beach.

Chapter 10

The Saga of Carlos Mejia

In the Memphis train station, Paul Eckert leaned his head against the bristly cloth that covered railroad passenger car seats. He looked out the window at nothing in particular and wondered why all trains had the same dusty smell. He'd left Des Moines at midnight, boarded the City of New Orleans in Chicago at five and was now half way to New Orleans.

He looked again at the railroad time table. Four more hours to go. He had to get some sleep. No one was sitting in front of him, so he pushed on the back of that seat. It pivoted forward until it formed a double seat, each side facing the other. He took off his shoes and sprawled his six foot-plus length over the entire double seat. He shut his eyes tightly and was determined he would sleep.

At the Memphis railway depot, John Bradshaw kissed his daughter goodbye and began the trip back to Salem. He kept telling himself she was a grown woman with good sense and he had no cause to worry about her. He worried about her. He knew she should get out of Salem, but he hated to see her move away.

Inside the station, Ellie Sue showed her ticket at the gate and again disregarded a porter who looked like he was willing to take her suitcases aboard the City of New Orleans. She had packed lightly and had no trouble carrying them into the day coach.

She pushed one of her suitcases against the heavy door that opened into the passenger car. She entered and saw what she thought was an unoccupied double seat. No head stuck up over it. When she came closer, she saw a passenger lying stretched out, cater-cornered across the seat. His suitcases further blocked entrance into the seats. His eyes were shut and he appeared to be sleeping.

She thought, he's kind of cute. After a moment's hesitation, she decided not to disturb him and continued on to the next car. There she found a seat and soon the train jolted forward and moved out of the station as it began its run to New Orleans.

The view from the train windows was depressing - railroad yards, gray industrial buildings, the backs of tenements with refuse on the grounds and laundry hanging on ropes stretched across back porches. Ellie Sue turned from the window and opened The History of Anchuria. It was written by Dr. Carlos Mejia.

Ellie Sue forced herself to read two pages. Well, she thought as she set the book down on the seat beside her, if I ever have trouble going to sleep, this book will make me doze off.

* * * * *

Carlos Mejia was a poet, a historian and an economist. He wasn't a doctor. He had only a Bachelor's Degree from the University of Indiana, but it was the custom in his native Anchuria to pay appropriate honor to those who attained such elevated academic status by assigning the title 'Doctor' to any and all of them.

The oldest son of a north coast Anchurian cacao plantation family, Carlos Mejia was sent to the United States to study Economics - a course of action he dutifully followed, although he hated every minute of it. He had no interest in the study or application of the, to him, arcane and particularly opaque world of economic theories and formulae.

Nor had he any interest in the law or in politics. A career in the military or in the church was simply out of the question. Carlos Mejia preferred to live in a private world of thought and contemplation. He loved the classics and read them in both Latin and Greek. He translated Shakespearean sonnets as well as works of Aristophanes into his Spanish language.

Carlos Mejia was uneasy and unhappy in the world of business. Nevertheless, upon his return to Aguas Buenas, he remained on the Mejia finca, ineffectually attempting to learn to manage a cacao farm. In three years he proved beyond all reasonable doubt that he couldn't manage his way out of a wet paper bag. Then his father died and Mejia was relieved when a younger brother took over the operation of the plantation.

Carlos Mejia took advantage of the opportunity to dedicate himself to his real interest - the pursuits of reading and writing. His first attempts at commercial authorship involved romantic poetry. The income produced from two thin books of poems was insignificant or, to better describe it, non-existent. He decided to direct his attention to chronicling the history of his homeland. There were no such books written by Anchurians.

When, during his research, he read a history written by a Sedalian academic, Dr. Mejia was incensed. The outright lies and inaccuracies of the Sedalian book were unforgivable. Its author had the unmitigated gall to tell his readers United States filibusters and Anchurian criminals combined to steal land from the Sedalian Republic in the Treaty of Santa Elena. Any reasonably honest historian knew it was the other way around. Worst of all, the author claimed Sedalia won the Battle of the Rio Ramasajoti. That was absolutely intolerable.

Dr. Carlos Mejia would not allow such patent outrages to go unchallenged. His next two books, "A History of the Republic of Anchuria" and "The Battle of the Ramasajoti" were written to correct the record. The Sedalian infamies in the negotiation of the Treaty of Santa Elena as well as the clever outflanking maneuver of the Anchurian hero, Lieutenant (later President) Espinosa, together with the courageous actions of his brave soldiers at the Rio Ramasajoti battle ground were authoritatively chronicled for the world to see and appreciate.

Now the Doctor's publications were more successful. Both volumes were required reading in all of Anchurian schools. He received a steady income from book sales and was lionized by the Anchurian press. He was praised as the patriot who accurately recorded the history of the native land.

Mejia's fifth opus was an investigation into the economics of the north coast of the Republic of Anchuria and, more particularly, of Aguas Buenas. The book described the raw materials located on the coastal plain, reported the pleasant climate, noted the availability of a cheap labor force and emphasized the favorable tax structure of the

Republic.

Mejia's book described the cacao industry in some (inaccurate) detail and presented statistics showing the growth of the Cerveza Alemana brewery, the newest industry started by emigrants from Germany's post World War I chaos. He also recorded a reasonably accurate history of the development of the Central American Fruit Company.

Inside Anchuria, his book received critical acclaim. The liberals disregarded references to cacao and beer and considered the book to be an exposé of the economic imperialism of the Colossus of the North. No less an expert than Clemente Diaz, the Dean of the University of Anchuria Law School, hailed the book as the nation's first attempt to break the economic chains put in place by the Central American Fruit Company.

The acceptance of the book by the liberals as a revolutionary document was not what Carlos Mejia had in mind. Since his days at the University of Indiana, he admired the Colossus of the North and appreciated the Fruit Company. They were the ones who invested the capital, built the businesses and created the jobs that produced the salaries paid to many of his otherwise disadvantaged north coast countrymen.

The book, published in Spanish with an English version appended to it, was written for the purpose of attracting new investments by United States corporations and developing more jobs for the peons of coastal Anchuria - but speeches were made in the Assembly praising the Mejia efforts to promote "Anchuria for the Anchurians," and he felt it would be ungentlemanly to correct the orators.

Dr. Carlos Mejia's book gave him great national status. His fellow countrymen referred to him deferentially as "don Carlos." The recognition made him happy. The book and its local interpretation, however, did not make the President of the Central American Fruit Company, happy. When Llewellyn Black was not happy, remedial action was soon to follow.

In the Congress of the Republic of Anchuria, Senators Smit and Mendez joined to promote the passage of a bill to provide government funds for the purposes of distributing the Mejia book. The move surprised knowledgeable liberals who were convinced both men were concerned with protecting the banana, the mining and the lumber businesses. Those knowledgeable liberals were quite right.

They did not, however, appreciate the Byzantine scheming of the two men. The legislation easily passed both the Anchurian Senate and Assembly. It became the law of the land. Under the Senators' directions, the Anchurian government bought the remaining undistributed seven hundred and forty-five copies of the eight hundred that were printed.

With the Senators' further guidance, the government hired a New Orleans public relations firm. The firm promised to popularize the book and draw the attention of United States' anti-business liberals to the terrifying extent of the Central American Fruit Company's conspiracy to destroy the liberty of Latin Americans.

The books purchased by the government of Anchuria were all given to the New Orleans firm which received a far from modest fee from the funding established by the Anchurian legislature. The promised public relations campaign never materialized.

The New Orleans firm had somehow forgotten to disclose that its largest client was the Central American Fruit Company. The Mejia books were all "distributed" to Llewellyn Black who kept one copy as a souvenir and burned the rest. No second edition of the book was printed.

Back in Anchuria, Senator Paco Mendez proposed the establishment of a National Library of Anchurian History. The Central American Fruit Company made a big donation to the project and the company was publicly lauded by both Smit and Mendez. The library was built in Aguas Buenas. Dr. Carlos Mejia was appointed as its Director. There he collected books and read and wrote tracts on Anchurian history.

Roberto Smit, Paco Mendez and Llewellyn Black succeeded in deftly removing both Mejia and his book from the political arena. Dr. Carlos Mejia, now securely seated and comfortably shaded in the academic groves, was completely happy.

Well, not completely happy.

* * * * *

In the Spanish language, nouns ending in the letters "ote" usually signal a Nahuac Indian origin. Coyote and guajolote (turkey) are examples. The Nahuac gave the name "zopilote" to the large, black, very ugly birds the Norteamericanos call buzzards.

To some extent, the Aguas Buenas garbage disposal system depended upon the zopilote. It helped clean the refuse from the streets and gutters and remove the dead animals that would otherwise accumulate along the country's roads. For these services, the birds were identified by law as Anchuria's national bird and, as such, a protected species.

In the air they are graceful. On the ground they are ungainly, unsightly, unseemly and hideous, or so say the birds' champions. Dr. Carlos Mejia was not one of their champions. To him the zopilotes were even worse. He could not stand them.

The National Library was located directly across the street from the one storied Aguas Buenas building that housed the Comandante and the Guardia Civil - that is, the Civil Guard that is, the Policemen. Many zopilotes, when not engaged in their street cleaning activities or soaring majestically above the city, perched and rested on the top of the Comandancia Building.

Whenever Dr. Mejia looked out the window of his office on the second floor of the National Library, he would see a line of big, black, hook necked, ugly zopilotes staring directly back at him from the top of the Comandancia building. He stood it as long as he could. Then, one day, he crumbled under the pressure and bought a rifle.

Soon thereafter, as was her usual custom, Dr. Mejia's secretary, Consuelo, left the National Library for lunch and a few hours rest during the midday heat. Instead of closing the Library and leaving with her, Dr. Mejia was ill at ease and stayed behind. It seemed strange to Consuelo, but, after all, don Carlos was an eccentric.

So, she put it from her mind and assigned no special significance to this deviation from his usual pattern. When she returned at three in the afternoon, don Carlos was smiling, relaxed and in one of his more pleasant moods. Only later did she discover the reason for the metamorphosis.

When Consuelo left the building, Dr. Mejia returned to his office. He opened the shuttered window slightly, stepped back, picked up his rifle and took aim. Seconds later, the sound of a shot disturbed the noon day peace of Aguas Buenas. The zopilotes flew from the roof of the Comandancia in confusion, except for one that fell dead in front of the building's entrance. Members of the guardia, with drawn night sticks, charged from the station, ready to put down any insurrection.

The only one in sight was a mestizo peon leading a burro loaded with fire wood. They seized him, pummeled him with their night sticks and hauled him into the Comandancia where he was roughly questioned, then presumed innocent and released. The peon didn't understand what had happened, but never again tried to sell firewood anywhere near the Comandancia.

During the next few months, the scene repeated itself. Some day, between noon and one o'clock, a shot would be heard, a dead zopilote would fall to the street in front of the Comandancia and an innocent bystander would be captured, pummeled, questioned and then returned to freedom.

Ultimately it was determined the shots came from Dr. Mejia's office in the National Library. Now the Comandante of the Guardia had a problem. Don Carlos was a national monument. He could not be arrested, but he could not be permitted to continue to disturb the tranquility of the public in general nor, in particular, that of the Comandante who liked to remove his boots, lean back in his chair and, with his feet on the desk, enjoy a midday snooze.

After two more birds were shot, he screwed up his courage and marched across the street. He confronted Dr. Mejia and confiscated the rifle. Noonday peace and tranquility again visited the streets of Aguas Buenas.

But not quite. After a few weeks, Dr. Mejia could stand it no longer. He got another rifle and history repeated itself. A shot was heard. A buzzard died. A peon was pummeled. A rifle was confiscated from don Carlos. The same scenario re-occurred every few months thereafter.

Chapter 11

The Saga of Clevis Dewlap

Aboard the City of New Orleans, Ellie Sue Bradshaw heard a quiet cough behind her and turned from the window. She showed her ticket to the conductor who was standing in the aisle beside her. He punched a hole in it, making sure no one would be able to use it again. Ellie Sue asked him for a pillow and in due course he re-appeared and gave one to her. She put the pillow against the window and leaned her head on it. Ellie Sue had too much on her mind to allow sleep on the train. The divorce, the cruise and her plans for the future all occupied her thoughts.

Ellie Sue spent little time in the past. The question: "How could I have been so stupid?" occurred to her a few times. She swept it from her mind and, thus unencumbered, planned her march into the future. Salem was no place for her. The last two years in her home town represented nothing more than a backwater in her life. She meant to get into the main current. Hot Springs, or St. Louis, or Memphis, she thought, they were big towns.

It's too bad universities don't teach a girl how to make a living, she said to herself. Well, I'll find something. Ellie Sue again tried to read The History of Anchuria. It was boring. A heroic effort pushed her to the fifth page. I'll save it for the ship, she rationalized, and set it down again.

Then another thought occurred to her. I certainly hope I have something better to do than read a book. She remembered she had been assigned Cabin 12, Deck A, Starboard on the S S Arbutus. There must be at least twenty-four cabins on that boat, she thought. I hope they are all filled. Oh, please, please, put an interesting young man aboard. Ellie Sue's thoughts turned to the prospects of the adventure and romance of an ocean cruise.

* * * * *

Not all people destined for the Arbutus' mid-July passage to Anchuria entertained hopes for such excitements. Clevis Dewlap had no thought of meeting some lovely young thing during his cruise on the banana boat. He seldom gave romance a moment's consideration - unless he was drunk and in a house of ill repute.

Clevis Dewlap was not seeking adventure or escape from an unsatisfactory past. He was returning to a place of security and contentment and he dreaded the trip. It was not his first voyage to Anchuria. In 1932, Clevis Dewlap was a hardwood sawyer in Newhebron, Mississippi. He liked the work and would have been happy to spend his entire life in Jefferson Davis County, but such was not to be.

The Jefferson Davis County Land and Lumber Corporation managed to stay solvent until 1933. By then the depression had so eroded its business that it was unable to arrange credit and was forced to file for bankruptcy. Clevis was unemployed for nearly a year. Then he found work in New Orleans, unloading bananas at the Central American Fruit Company dock side warehouse.

It was there he learned a lumber company known as Madera Anchuria, S.A. wanted to hire a hardwood sawyer. Clevis discovered the Madera Anchuria sawmill was located in a town called Villa Smit. He discovered Villa Smit was located on the Caribbean coast in a foreign country known as Anchuria and he discovered the wages he could earn were more then merely attractive.

With some help from a lady friend named Lulu who could read and write and with whom he enjoyed an occasional professional association, Clevis Dewlap filled out the job application. To his joy, he was hired. He was happy to be guaranteed long-term work during the time when few jobs were available. He was happy to have an opportunity to again be sawing wood, an occupation he truly enjoyed.

The terms of the employment contract were not troublesome to him. He had to work for four years and half of his pay would be withheld. After the four-year term had finished, he would receive the money withheld from his monthly salaries. With that much money, he could afford to hire Lulu for a whole week, take her to Biloxi and still have a pile of cash.

Best of all, when that money was all gone, Madera Anchuria said it would offer him another four-year contract. Clevis Dewlap considered himself to be the luckiest man in the world. In 1934, he boarded the Arbutus for the first time and sailed to Villa Smit.

The 1934 trip to Anchuria was Clevis' first ocean going experience. It was not enjoyable. He was quite uncomfortable when looking at a horizon that seemed to tilt and shift. He was unaccustomed to lifting a foot and putting it down on a deck that had either risen or lowered and was not where it should have been, Clevis Dewlap had no "sea legs". He was a man of the soil. He was a landlubber.

Clevis did not become merely seasick with the slightest pitch or roll of the Arbutus. He was subject to a terrible, great, green, intense and towering seasickness, unrelieved for a single moment from the time the ship left the pier in New Orleans until it docked at its Villa Smit destination. After the first full day of constant and aggravated seasickness, Clevis thought he might die. After the third day, he didn't care.

When he disembarked and again stood on solid and reasonably dry land, Clevis regained his composure. He quickly adjusted to life in Villa Smit and found he had nearly everything he needed for a full and satisfying life. One essential commodity, however, was found to be lacking. The only corn produced in the Republic of Anchuria was grown in the highlands, far from the saw mill. No adequate supply of good corn was available in Villa Smit.

In addition to being a first-class sawyer, Clevis Dewlap was an accomplished amateur distiller. His reputation was well established in the vicinity of Newhebron where his moonshine had been distributed and where quality in homemade drinking whiskey was appreciated. Clevis himself was somewhat addicted to his fine product. Without a reasonable supply of corn, he faced a difficult four years in the Republic of Anchuria.

The problem turned out to be transitory. One of Clevis' mestizo fellow workers taught him the rudiments of making alcohol out of sugar cane. There was lots of sugar cane around Villa Smit

With no Federal Revenue agents to disturb him and - being of a naturally generous nature - Clevis produced and supplied his newly made Anchurian friends and associates with potent libation. Recognized as a distiller of a quality product, albeit cane based, Clevis Dewlap enjoyed a degree of popularity with his Latin neighbors seldom accorded to gringos. His first four years in Villa Smit were not at all painful.

In the spring of 1938, Clevis Dewlap's Madera Anchuria employment contract was completed. He returned to New Orleans. That second sea voyage was as dreadful as the first, but soon he again found himself on solid ground in New Orleans. True to their word, Madera Anchuria paid the $1,800 that had been withheld from his Villa Smit salary. It was the most money any Dewlap ever had at any one time. He could hardly believe his good fortune. Money, however, does not bring happiness.

Lulu was not to be found in the house that had employed her services. She left the trade and married the policeman who collected the monthly installment of protection payments from the madam who owned the place. In his disappointment, Clevis decided to go back to his roots. He bought a suit and a bus ticket to Newhebron, the home town he left by rail five years earlier. (More precisely, the home town he left by freight train gondola and without benefit of ticket.)

In the five years of his absence, Newhebron had changed. The whole United States had changed. He was a stranger in his own land. It wasn't at all like he remembered it. Even the corn likker tasted somehow inferior to his sugar cane alcohol. He kept $150 and divided the rest of the money among his sisters and brothers. He signed another four-year contract with Madera Anchuria and prepared himself for the return voyage to Villa Smit.

Clevis Dewlap did not look forward to the ordeal and agony of the trip. With a history of being involved in the manufacture, distribution and personal usage of intoxicating liquids, Clevis had been sick while on land - many, many times. It occurred to him he much preferred beverage sickness over sea sickness. He carefully calculated the amount of moonshine he would need to stay drunk during the trip between New Orleans and Villa Smit. He produced that amount, carefully packed it in an extra suitcase, and returned to New Orleans.

When Clevis Dewlap arrived at the Central American Fruit Company dock, he watched the men sweating under the hot New Orleans sun as they unloaded the stalks of green bananas from the Arbutus. Five years earlier, as a longshoreman, he had carried bananas from the ship to the warehouse. As a pastime, he reflected, that kind of work was grossly over-rated. Operating a saw in an isolated town in the jungles of Anchuria was an infinitely preferable occupation.

Getting there, however, was not half the fun. This time, Clevis boarded the Arbutus with the hope and expectation of avoiding the dreadful sea sickness. He recognized the Purser and greeted him. "Hallo Looie. Ahm goin back to Veeahsmit again."

"Welcome aboard, Señor Dewlap," the Purser answered. He checked Clevis' name on the ship's Passenger List and sent him to his assigned compartment - Cabin 7, A Deck, Starboard. There Clevis Dewlap unpacked, using most of the drawer space in the room's single dresser.

He opened his extra suitcase and assured himself that none of its precious cargo of Mason jars had been broken. After removing one of them, he carefully slid the suitcase and it under the bunk. Moving to the chair next to the room's small desk, he unscrewed the top of the jar and took a healthy dose of his version of Mother Sill's Sea Sickness Remedy.

Chapter 12

The S S Arbutus

In 1926, the S S Arbutus was named after the fifteen year old daughter of Llewellyn Black, the President of the Central American Fruit Company. The Company owned the ship and Black owned over half of the company's common stock. One would suppose, he had the right to call the ship by any name that struck his fancy.

That supposition, however, would not be correct. He wanted to name it the S S Llewellyn Black. It was his wife, Elizabeth, who insisted it be named after their daughter. It was also Elizabeth who had insisted the poor girl be named Arbutus.

Llewellyn Black inherited a minority interest in an Anchurian silver mining company. As a young man, he went to the Republic to personally determine the value of his holdings. While there, his interest changed from ore to tropical fruit. Llewellyn Black created the third largest banana company in the world.

In 1938, Anchurian politicians (as well as some United States Senators, Representatives and a few Governors) trembled when he frowned. Even more importantly, bankers deferred to him. He was not, however, strong enough to contradict the will of Elizabeth Black.

* * * * *

The S S Arbutus plied its course from New Orleans to the Republics of Anchuria and Sedalia. Its first port of call was Aguas Buenas. After continuing on down the Caribbean coast to Villa Smit and, occasionally on to Ciudad Carillo in the Republic of Sedalia, the Arbutus would reverse its course and sail back to Aguas Buenas and New Orleans.

The ship was a banana boat - a working freighter. Most freighters are black and rust colored. The Arbutus was mostly white. Elizabeth Black insisted on it. Its loading booms, however, were colored a reddish orange by heavily leaded marine paint. Though its primary job was to carry bananas from the Fruit Company plantations to New Orleans, the Arbutus also transported Company supplies, Company personnel, commercial cargoes and, occasionally, passengers. Round trip cruises from New Orleans took fourteen days and cabins on the Arbutus often were occupied by people interested in summer trips through the Gulf of Mexico.

The Arbutus' passenger cabins were designated by number, deck and direction. It was all very logical. Cabin 7, A Deck, Starboard could be easily distinguished from Cabin 12, A Deck, Port. This kind of nomenclature had the advantage of requiring the landlubber tourist to learn the difference between port and starboard and, thus, feel very nautical.

There was only one deck available for passenger accommodations on board the S S Arbutus. It was called A Deck. There was no B Deck. Cabins numbers 7, 8 and 9 were on the Port side of A Deck. Cabins numbers 10, 11 and 12 were on the Starboard side. There were no cabins carrying numbers smaller than 7. There were no cabins carrying numbers larger that 12. The Arbutus had only 6 compartments available for passenger accommodation and, of those, Cabin 12 was usually used to store ship supplies.

The Cabin numbering system had the advantage of allowing the passenger to mislead himself into thinking there had be at least twenty-four passenger compartments on A Deck and, perhaps a similar number on B Deck. As he studied the Arbutus' cruise literature, the summer vacationer might be led to believe there would be a large number of fellow tourists aboard the ship - plenty of people to provide the potential of a ship board romance or otherwise pass the time of day while leisurely floating around on tropical seas.

The term "passenger accommodation" was also somewhat misleading. The passengers' cabins were positive proof the Arbutus was not designed for the purpose of "accommodating" passengers. The portions of each side of the ship that had been rebuilt into compartments were barely large enough to be divided into a passageway and three small rooms.

Each of the cabins contained an upper and a lower bunk. The bunks were not wide, thus making it quite cozy for those who decided to honeymoon on the Arbutus and use only the bottom bunk. However, anyone six feet tall was longer than the mattress. He would hang over at both the head and the foot of the bunks.

A chair, a tiny desk, a dresser and a combination shower, sink and stool area completed the compartment furnishings. Hooks attached to one end of the upper bunk served as the Arbutus version of a closet. A single light bulb hung from the ceiling. The lighting fixture was originally intended to give only enough illumination for a storage space. It was not intended to be used for reading purposes. No one could see such a cabin and justify the use of the word "spacious", which also appeared in the company's advertisements.

The facilities available for the entertainment of passengers were not extensive. A canvas swimming pool, a bit shaky but serviceable, was set up on the fantail. Some deck chairs were scattered about. A bar room and a dining room provided for the passengers' essential necessities. When not used for dining purposes, the dining room doubled as a reading room.

Signs identified each place. The sign above the bar on the Starboard side of the ship said "SALOON". The sign above the bar in the passageway on the other side of the ship said "SALON." Apparently the management felt a little bit of confusion was good for the passengers.

The Salon contained a long buffet table and four smaller square tables. In contrast to usual maritime custom, the Captain of the Arbutus never ate with the passengers. He wanted nothing to do with any of them. Since there were only two bunks in each of the six cabins, a maximum of twelve people could use the dining room at any one time.

One of the Directors of the Central American Fruit Company argued that three tables with four sides would serve a dozen passengers so there was no need to go to the expense of buying an extra table and four more chairs. On a close vote, his motion was defeated.

The "tropical breezes," so often alluded to in the travel publications, were a sometimes thing. Sometimes, in August and September, hurricanes roared through the Caribbean and into the Gulf of Mexico. During those months, the Arbutus would usually be at sea and in position to receive the benefit of the hurricane associated tropical breezes.

At other times there was no air movement. None at all. The cabins became ovens. The management foresaw the possibility of these baking temperatures. Each cabin was provided with a porthole. A perverse fate also foresaw the same possibility. During the twelve years prior to 1938, it arranged for the laying of so many coats of marine paint over the portholes' mechanisms that, atomic energy not yet being available, no known power could open them.

In 1943, the Arbutus was sunk by a Nazi submarine. The German submarine commander was drunk. He mistook the banana boat for an oil tanker. The Arbutus sank to the bottom of the Gulf of Mexico in two large and a multitude of smaller pieces. Such was the force of the single German torpedo. Nevertheless, none of the cabin portholes were jarred open.

It was during the high sea periods that the Arbutus vigorously pitched and rolled. The summer cruise folks who were still able to dine realized why the tables and chairs were chained to the floor. Rather than being able to follow their stormy weather predisposition to violently slide across the entire length of the dining room, the furniture was limited to mere twelve inch lurching. This was enough to catapult the red sauce covered boiled bananas out of the plate and onto the lap, but not quite enough to dislodge the passenger from his chair.

During the storms, the passengers appreciated the Central American Fruit Company management for having the foresight to paint the port holes so tightly shut that they could not open, take on salty water and drown the cabin occupants.

Chapter 13

The Ship's Company
Luis Gogeasgoechea
Osvaldo Vargas

The Ship's Company of the Arbutus was, indeed, a polyglot bag. The Captain spoke English when in a good mood and Greek, his native tongue, when angry or excited. The language used most extensively by the below decks crew was Lebanese Arabic. Spanish came in second and was followed by Swahili. One of the Lebanese crewmen had an acceptable English vocabulary and another could speak Greek. The Mozambique deckhands both spoke Swahili and one of them could handle Spanish. A Honduran was able to communicate in English.

Whenever the potential for a shipboard disaster was evident - like the discovery of a crate about to slip out of the net during the unloading of cargo - the Captain would get excited and scream an order in Greek. The Greek speaking Lebanese crewman would yell out his interpretation of the order in Arabic. Upon hearing it in their shared language, the English speaking Lebanese sailor would shout his English interpretation. The Honduran then translated what he thought he heard into Spanish and, finally, the Spanish speaking Mozambique would repeat a Swahili version for his African counterparts.

After passing through the various interpretations, the order seldom bore any relation to the original Greek words shouted by the Captain. One of the hands might run to the Galley to bring the Captain a cup of coffee while another lowered the ship's flag on the jack staff. The others would scurry about performing functions that had nothing to do with the poorly secured crate. By the time the Captain's order - or some version of it - had passed through the five languages, the once imminent danger would have already occurred.

* * * * *

One member of the ship's compliment was assigned the job of keeping the passengers occupied and happy. That man said his name was Luis Gogeasgoechea. He insisted everyone call him Luis - which wasn't a necessary suggestion since no one could handle "Gogeasgoechea." He claimed to be a Spanish Basque forced to leave his country as a result of being on the wrong side of the Franco revolution. He did not speak the Basque language and he didn't have a Basque accent when he spoke Spanish or English.

A rumor, spread by the crew, identified him as a native of the Central American Republic of Nuevo Leon. The rumor reported he was a felon who managed to get out of that country and into the Republic of Anchuria only shortly before the Nuevo Leon Guardia Civil began looking for him.

Luis Gogeasgoechea told his employers he was Spanish/English bi-lingual and a competent bartender. The former attribute was accurate. The latter suggestion was highly questionable. Nevertheless, it was Gogeasgoechea who tended the six foot long bar in the ship's Saloon. The back bar's inventory of hard liquor consisted mainly of gin, scotch, American whiskey and Cuban and Anchurian rum. It was also held a few liqueurs - an old bottle of dry vermouth, aguardiente, tequila, Ouzo and a sugar cane based alcohol called "Seco". After sampling the Seco, some passengers believed it should be taken from the bar's inventory and used to remove paint from automobiles.

If a passenger asked for a beer or a gin and tonic or a whiskey and water, Luis smiled. If a mixed drink was ordered, he frowned. Luis never mastered the complicated mysteries of mixing a drink. The bottle of vermouth which had long stood on the back bar attested to his inability to mix martinis. It was used only occasionally. A passenger might order a martini, but a second was never requested unless he had suicide in mind.

To give him his due, it must be reported that Luis never admitted defeat. He kept trying to produce palatable mixed drinks even though he had to struggle to maintain his dignity when passengers yelled such things as: "Horse whipping is too good for you" or "My God, man.

What have you done?" or "You should be taken out and hung."

As a part of his bartending duties, Luis made sure platters of the large platano type banana, sliced thinly, deep fried and heavily salted, were always available. Other saloon supplies he oversaw consisted of Cuban and Anchurian cigars, lots of Cerveza Alemana (an Anchurian beer), some Lucky Strike cigarettes (then in their green package) and a dish which once held individual pieces of some kind of rock candy, now indescribable because they had surrendered to tropical heat and melted together into a solid mass. Many passengers thought it was a fine example of native glass blown art and offered to buy it.

Luis was also the Social Director. He interpreted those duties to be limited to finding four passengers who could all play bridge and serving a salty beef broth in the ship's Salon at precisely 11:00 in the morning and 3:00 in the afternoon. On a few occasions, he managed to do so.

Luis' other assignments were: Purser, Steward and Medical Officer. If there had ever been a doctor aboard the Arbutus to protect the passengers from injury and disease, it was not disclosed in the ship's records. On the few occasions when illness developed, it was Luis Gogeasgoechea who responded to requests for medical attention. ("It is not serious. Here. Take the aspirina.")

The Captain of the Arbutus had a high opinion of Luis Gogeasgoechea and regularly praised him. On the frequent occasions when a passenger (more often, passengers) wrote to the Fruit Company complaining of his poisonous martinis or various other derelictions of duty, the Captain always came to Luis' defense. The position of Luis Gogeasgoechea in the Ship's Company was secure.

It would be secure as long as he was the one who determined which alcoholic beverages were to be stocked in the Arbutus.

The Central American Fruit Company auditors noticed large quantities of Ouzo were regularly ordered by Luis Gogeasgoechea. Ouzo is a colorless, anise flavored, unsweetened Greek alcoholic beverage. It is an uncommon drink. The accountants concluded it must have had a special appeal to the passengers of the Arbutus. During every voyage, they put away cases of the stuff.

The Captain of the Arbutus, Stavros Stavropopolous, was the only one who drank Ouzo.

* * * * *

The food served to the passengers of the Arbutus was of good quality and very well prepared. The cook was more than merely competent. He came close to being excellent. He went by the name of Osvaldo Carrera. It was not his real name. Not even the Captain knew the ship's cook once prepared the meals for a President of the Republic of Anchuria and was then known as Osvaldo Vargas. He now performed the lowly occupations of a ship's cook for reasons of health. If President Peña's Secret Police found him, his health would be seriously endangered.

Osvaldo Vargas began his career as a cook in the Villa Fontana Restaurant in Anchuria's capitol city of Progreso. His food preparation was one of the reasons the restaurant was a favorite meeting place of government personalities as well as army officers. Vargas was popular with the young officers and soon was placed in charge of "Security." Translated into English, this meant he would discreetly arrange for the use of the rooms above the restaurant by the younger officers and their female companions.

Lt. Juanito Rivadavia was one of Osvalso's army friends. When he and five others asked him to arrange the confidential use of one of the rooms, Osvaldo was shocked. While homosexuality was not unknown to him, none of the young men had ever indicated sexual ambivalence. Six of the young men using the room, at the same time? Well, it was incredible.

Vargas was relieved to discover the six were not deviates. They needed a place to plan a barracks revolution and overthrow the President of the Republic. Osvaldo Vargas was endowed with a high degree of natural political acumen. From association with politicians who frequented his restaurant, he knew the behind-the-scenes power structure of the Republic. He joined with the conspirators and gave them valuable advice.

When their successful coup occurred in 1932 and Lt. Juanito Rivadavia assumed the Presidency of the Republic, Osvaldo became a part of his government. He did not become the President's cook. He became the President's confidant and his most trusted advisor. Juanito Rivadavia depended on the advice of Osvaldo Vargas not only with regard to relations with the Fruit Company and the United States, but also with regard to the Europeans.

Both Rivadavia and Vargas were nationalists. They were suspicious of Uncle Sam, but the Fascism of a Mussolini, the Communism of a Stalin or the national racism of a Nazi Germany were infinitely less attractive than the alternatives of good relations with the Colossus of the North. Living with a neighbor like the United States was like being inside a lion's cage while a band of hyenas circled around it. If the lion did not eat you, living with it offered unquestionable protection. That "if" was a constant source of worry for many Latin American Presidents.

* * * * *

In 1935, when assassins hired by Máximo Peña, entered the government palace and killed President Rivadavia, Osvaldo Vargas made himself very scarce. He left the palace with only the clothes on his back and the solid gold tea service he felt might be an appropriate reward for his dedicated labors on behalf of the Republic. Since that time, the Peña government had been looking for him. It would be terminally unhealthy for Osvaldo Vargas if he were caught.

When he was one of President Rivadavia's inner circle, Vargas earned extra cash by quietly extending advisory services to the Central American Fruit Company. He gave confidential early warning reports directly to Llewellyn Black's Anchurian Senator, Paco Mendez, whenever any proposed action of the government might affect the Fruit Company's operation.

Of course, Senator Mendez and the Fruit Company supported Vargas and the Rivadavia government. It was not difficult for Osvaldo to ask Llewellyn Black to help him hide from Peña. Osvaldo Vargas became Osvaldo Carrera and easily secured the job of ship's cook on the Arbutus.

A voyage to Aguas Buenas was a culinary education for the

passenger who knew bananas only as a fruit to be peeled and eaten raw. Aboard the Arbutus, the summer cruise tourists ate baked bananas, boiled bananas, fried bananas, bananas twice as large as those found in the grocery store and sweet tiny bananas the size of a man's thumb. Every meal included a new banana experience. Some of the passengers never ate another banana during the remainder of their lives.

Since Osvaldo Carrera was the only Anchurian on board, the discovery of his true identity was a danger only when he walked the streets of Aguas Buenas or Villa Smit. As long as he remained aboard the Arbutus he was assured of continued good health. He was very careful when he left the ship. After all, there was a price on his head and he was no fool.

But Osvaldo Carrera remembered. He remembered when he was Osvaldo Vargas. He remembered the life style and the wealth that came with high position and political power. Now he was reduced to the status of a cook in hiding and at risk of being captured and murdered whenever he was in Anchurian waters.

Osvaldo would work with the devil himself if there were any reasonable prospect of fomenting a revolt that might again elevate him into the councils of power.

* * * * *

The officers and the crew of the Arbutus avoided the passengers as they would avoid the black plague. Association with passengers invariably resulted in questions. Few of the crew spoke English and only occasionally did a passenger speak a strange idiom called "College Spanish." The passengers who had endure such a university study learn everything about the language, except how to read, write or speak it.

Conversations with them were seldom productive and usually disagreeable.

"Tienen ustedes shuffleboard?" Pause. Blank look.

"Do you have a shuffleboard court?" Pause. Blank look.

"Shuffleboard, Shuffleboard." Pause. Blank look.

"GOD DAMN IT, SHUFF FELL BOARD?"

Those last words were delivered with a pause between syllables and in a loud voice. This is the procedure which, it is universally believed, will allow a foreigner to understand what you say and be able to answer in your own tongue. Somehow or other, it did not work aboard the Arbutus.

No, the Arbutus wasn't the Normandie or the Queen Mary, but then, the price of the voyage was very reasonable. Where else could a tourist take a two week cruise in the tropics for $175.00?

Chapter 14

The Saga of John Smit

In 1888, a North American vagabond who called himself John Smith, but otherwise was quite reluctant to discuss anything concerning his background, appeared in London and contacted the Chairman of the Royal Indies Society, Lord Percy R. E. Grenville.

Smith told Lord Percy of his adventures in Central America. He claimed to have been a passenger on a coastal steamer sailing the western Caribbean shoreline. Because of an altercation with the captain (who he described as a black-hearted scoundrel) he was unceremoniously put ashore in the city of Aguas Buenas in the year 1885, penniless and with only the clothing he was wearing.

That's what he told Lord Percy. He did not mention he had been a teller in a New Orleans bank and suffered from a rare form of dyslexia. He could not distinguish between his own money and money belonging to the bank's depositors. He did not mention how he boarded the steamer surreptitiously and with both a new name and substantially more than a few dollars in his carpetbag.

He did not tell Lord Percy he made the decision to visit the Republic of Anchuria because of its lack of an extradition treaty with the United States. He did not tell him about Anchuria's time honored and continuing admirable refusal to send any criminal, political or otherwise, back to whence he came. He did not tell him the "altercation" came about because of the captain's insistence that he pay for his voyage.

John Smith did tell Lord Percy B. E. Grenville and his Board of Director about his wanderings along the Central American coast, about the groves of wild cacao and about the coastal mountain range with its reported rich deposits of silver. More importantly, Smith told them about the large concentrations of mahogany and other tropical hardwood trees located near the Caribbean coastline. It was with the economic potential of a lumber mill that he planned to capture the attention of the English financier.

Lord Percy was still pained by the memory of the losses he suffered in the Anchurian railroad bond investment venture. He meant to recover those losses. This time he would not make the mistake of investing in some untrustworthy foreigner's scheme. This time he would deal with a reliable person - that is: someone who spoke English.

The Royal West Indies Society was ready to support John Smith's plan. With money provided by Lord Percy R. E Grenville and his associates, Smith would construct and manage a saw mill on the Caribbean shoreline close to the tropical forests where the valuable hardwoods grew. When the mill was completed and production began, Smith would sell the lumber to Lord Grenville's Royal West Indies Society and only to the Royal West Indies Society. The price paid to Smith would be established at 25 per cent of the London lumber market quotation.

When the site of the forests was disclosed, Lord Percy asked the pregnant question: "Is it located in Anchuria or is it in Sedalia?"

Smith thought for a moment, looked blank and replied: "I don't know."

Lord Percy paused, looked first at the map and then at Smith and persisted: "Is it to the east or to the west of the Ramasajoti River?"

"The what?"

"The Ramasajoti River. It's the boundary between the two countries, old chap."

"Lord Percy, I've been all over that territory for nearly two years. There ain't any Ramasasa – Ramataka – whatever - River around there. There ain't any river East of Aguas Buenas. There's a bunch of what you might call wet season run-off ditches, but believe me, there ain't no river or stream or creek anywhere nearby. There just ain't any water power in the whole area. I know. I've looked. We've got to bring in a steam engine for power."

Lord Percy sunk back into his chair. The other Directors of the Royal West Indies Society recognized his expression of concern and anxiously watched him. John Smith wondered what it was all about.

Lord Percy was considering the possibility of both Sedalia and Anchurian claiming ownership of forests near a border that neither country could clearly establish. Lord Percy appreciated the economics of working with a group of Latin politicians. Dealing with one government was bad enough. Dealing with two of them doubled the costs of doing business. Mentally, he began to assess the import of John Smith's revelation.

Lord Percy B. E. Grenville considered the magnitude of the problem. There's the President of the Republic, he thought and, he added, his brother-in-law. There is always at least one General, the a Governor of the Province - and his brother-in-law. Every one of them will have their hand out and every one of them must be paid up front.

Profit would be substantially reduced if the budget had to include sponsorship costs payable to both Sedalian officials and Anchurian officials. He thought for a moment, then came forward in his chair and said: "This will delay our venture but I believe the modest difficulty can be overcome."

His Lordship directed John Smith to draft a detailed listing of all machinery, equipment and supplies he would need to build the mill and to prepare a budget for his first two year's cash requirements. He informed his fellow Directors that he would deal with the "jurisdictional problems".

The plain fact of the matter was: no one, Anchurian, Sedalian or otherwise, knew where Sedalia stopped and Anchuria began. Prior to 1888, no one really cared. The land in question was nearly inaccessible mountain, jungle and swamp, mostly swamp. A few primitive aborigines lived there. If they ever learned the whole flat world was not composed of swamp and jungle and if they were smart enough to find their way out, they would have left the place in a heartbeat.

* * * * *

Lord Percy Grenville's plan to stabilize the national boundaries and determine which Republic controlled the tropical wood bonanza was quickly executed. The British Ambassador to the Republic of Anchuria confidentially advised its President of that Republic that his intelligence sources had discovered the Sedalian armed forces were preparing to invade the territory of the Republic of Anchuria.

The British Ambassador to the Republic of Sedalia confidentially advised the President of that Republic that his intelligence sources had learned Anchurian army forces were preparing to invade the territory of the Republic of Sedalia.

Armed conflict between the neighbors was sure to follow. Lord Percy didn't care who won the war. He knew the boundary would be clearly established at its conclusion. The Royal West Indies Society would have to pay only one set of bribes.

Upon receipt of the confidential information from the British Ambassadors, the reactions in the capitol cities of the two Republics were immediate. Speeches were made in the separate Congresses. The imminent invasion of the vile Anchurian (or Sedalian, as the case may be) territorial hungry, oppressive, militaristic, gringo backed monsters from the west (east) was denounced.

Defense of each Republic's borders - "up to and including the death of the last of our patriotic, faithful and brave Sedalian (Anchurian) soldiers" - was promised. Such an announcement caused the officers and enlisted men in both the Sedalian and Anchurian army to seriously reconsider a change of profession.

Banners were carried through the streets. Editorials castigated the old Treaty of Santa Elena that drew a line on a map to separate the two Central America Republics. Under that Treaty's terms, according to the editors, the Anchurians (Sedalians), backed by the all powerful "Colossus of the North", stole the western (eastern) lands historically belonging to them.

Armies were sent forth to do battle and drive the hated invader from their sacred soil. After three months of conflict culminating in the battle at the Ramasajoti River, both countries were relieved when President Grover Cleveland insisted a truce be declared. Representatives of the warring nations met with the United States Secretary of State and a Treaty of Peace was negotiated.

Both countries claimed the United States took advantage of them and sided with their enemy. The war was won by Sedalia - or by

Anchuria - or was a draw - depending upon which historian you prefer. In any case, the finest mahogany forests were found to be located within the borders of the Republic of Anchuria. The Royal West Indies Society made its investment and Lord Percy's Anchurian lumber mill project proceeded at full speed.

* * * * *

Lord Percy had a well deserved reputation for being able to recognize a profit potential at a hundred meters and his abilities as a diplomat and a negotiator were obvious, but he was capable of making terrible mistakes. The purchase of Anchurian railroad bonds was one example. The Anchurian lumber mill was another. John Smith's 1888 proposition for the establishment of a lumber mill on the Caribbean coast did not produce satisfactory economic results for Lord Percy Grenville. To put it bluntly, he and his London associates in the Royal West Indies Society took a bath.

The concept itself was sound. The market for mahogany and other tropical hardwoods was large and growing. Supplies of that kind of lumber were limited. With proper financing and organization, the investment appeared to be a guaranteed money-maker. The organization was excellent and the financing was more than adequate.

Docking facilities and piers were constructed in a mangrove lined lagoon on the eastern Anchurian coast. The saw mill was built and furnished with the most modern equipment. Trees were felled and delivered to the mill where they were cut and planed. The quality of the mill's production was consistently high.

For two years, regular boatloads of tropical woods from the Anchurian coast arrived in London. The Directors were pleased with the progress. Then, suddenly, no further shipments came to London. Like Lord Percy's investment in the Anchurian railroad, the value of The Royal West Indies Society's investment in John Smith's Anchurian tropical lumber venture evaporated.

John Smith, on the other hand, considered the venture to be extremely profitable. His British friends had come forward with the funds required to build the mill and the docks. They also provided the money needed to operate the business for the first two years of the mill's existence.

Unfortunately, just as the business began to attain its profit potential, Smith experienced a re-occurrence of the unfortunate dyslexia that had made it impossible for him to continue his banking career back in the days when he lived in New Orleans.

Smith became unable to recall the terms of his contract with The Royal West Indies Society. In particular, he could not recall the clause which obligated him to sell the wood to the Society at a price equal to 25 percent of the London market quotations. He was, however, able to remember that no extradition of any sort was allowed by the Republic of Anchuria. He also retained the presence of mind to apply for and obtain Anchurian citizenship.

Efforts by Lord Percy and the partners of the Royal West Indies Society to improve Smith's memory failed and a breach of contract proceeding was initiated in London. The Society was satisfied with the English judge's decision which deplored John Smith's faulty memory. It penalized him with a substantial damage judgment and ordered specific performance of the Society's contract. The Anchurian court system, however, paid no attention to the judgment of the British courts and refused to enforce its terms.

When the Society sought redress by prosecuting their claims against Smith in the Anchurian court system, the local judges based their conclusions not on the English contract law, but on the argument that, as a matter of public policy, Anchurian industry should be Anchurian owned. It held in favor of John Smith - or "Juan Smit" - as the name appeared in his naturalization documents.

* * * * *

Only a few years earlier, Juan Smit (as John Smith) had to win a foot race with the police in order to avoid imprisonment in New Orleans. He landed in a foreign country with no prospects and slightly more than five thousand dollars in a carpetbag. Now he was now the sole owner of a very prosperous business.

In accordance with universally adopted custom, as a millionaire

Juan Smit was honored and respected by everyone - with the possible exception of a few soreheads in London. By 1900, a community had built up around his saw mill. It was named Villa Smit and the maps of the Republic of Anchuria so identify it.

By the standards of that time, Juan Smit was a progressive employer. Anyone who completed two years of satisfactory work for the company - now called Madera Anchuria - received lumber for home construction on credit. A company store sold the foodstuff and the dry goods for life's basic necessities and it extended credit. The interest rate was a modest 15 percent (compounded monthly).

Juan Smit married a Spanish/Chuchiba Indian girl and soon the population of Villa Smit increased by the addition of Roberto Smit. In honor of the Englishman who had made Madera Anchuria possible, the child's middle name was Percy. In 1928, in his 70th year, Juan Smit was extradited from Anchuria by a higher court. That is, he went to his reward. That is, he died. His son, Roberto Percy Smit, succeeded him as President and sole owner of Madera Anchuria.

* * * * *

The market for Central American hardwoods continued to be sound even after the beginning of the world wide depression of the late 1920s. Those who sold out their stock before the market crash continued to demand exotic tropical hard-woods in their home constructions. Roberto Smit shared his father's business acumen and Madera Anchuria prospered.

Madera Anchuria experienced very little difficulty with its local labor force. The paternalistic qualities of the company attracted workers. The security of a good house and a wage large enough to provide food for the table and allow cantina entertainment far outweighed the fact of associated credit and interest and debt. True to the Latin character, debt was considered as something that could be paid tomorrow (an attitude universally favored by the current United States Congress).

As Madera Anchuria prospered, its need for technical assistance increased. The local population provided a good supply of manual laborers, but more professional help was hard to find. For one thing, a qualified accountant was needed. The University of Anchuria had no Accounting Department.

Hiring gringos did not produce favorable results. The living conditions in Villa Smit did not appeal to them. The hot and humid atmosphere of the north coast was too uncomfortable for many of them. The Latin/Indian culture of the area was strange. No golf courses, swimming pools, or duplicate bridge leagues existed.

Without special inducement, gringo employees didn't last long. It was Roberto Smit, the son of the company's illustrious founder and now a Senator in the Anchurian legislature, who initiated the practice of offering the four year employment contracts that provided for withholding half of the salary in order to guarantee a full four years of service. It wasn't such a bad arrangement. In Villa Smit there weren't too many places to spend money, anyway.

In 1932, the Madera Anchuria employment contract brought Clevis Dewlap to Villa Smit where he happily operated the huge circular saws that organized the logs of tropical hardwoods into lumber. Some of the mahogany he cut during his first four term found its way to Salem, Arkansas.

Senator Roberto Smit did more than produce the quality paneling used in Dr. Bradshaw's Salem, Arkansas den. He was an important participant in the events that occurred in Aguas Buenas during the summer of 1938, but few of those passengers on the Arbutus would every realize the importance of those events.

Chapter 15

The Saga of Thomas Andersen

Clevis Dewlap was not the only gringo to come to Villa Smit under an employment contract with Madera Anchuria. A few years earlier in 1933, another norteamericano, an accountant, signed an agreement to spend four years at Villa Smit.

Thomas Andersen was born on a farm in North Dakota. He was of Norwegian stock and, supposedly, genetically programmed to enjoy winter sports and, without complaint, survive the cold and snowy months of North Dakota winters. Such was decidedly not the case. Thomas could hardly stand on skis and he was a poor skater. While other school boys were becoming accomplished in those sports, Thomas Andersen was standing on the sidelines, alone, cold, wet and miserable.

He was the youngest in a family of five boys. His clothing was well worn by the time it passed down to him. He knew hunger and he knew hard work. He grew up with a burning desire to accomplish three goals in his life. He would never be a farmer. He would never be cold. He would never be poor.

Thomas attended the University at Bismarck. He found a job in the University library. He stoked the coal burning furnaces at five sorority houses. In the summer months he painted barns and built silos. He saved every penny he earned and was able to work his way through college.

Because he knew accountants worked with figures and figures meant money management, Thomas Andersen decided to major in the study of the Accounting Sciences. Because he knew of no cold country where Spanish was spoken, he selected the study of that language as his minor. Andersen graduated in 1931 when the country was in the throes of deep depression.

As soon as the Prohibition ended, he took the only job he could find and became an accountant for a recently legalized brewery in Chicago. He moved to the windy city, famous for receiving the benefits of the December, January and February breezes coming off frozen Lake Michigan. In spite of all his efforts, Andersen was still cold. He was still poor, but he had severed his ties with farm labor.

In Chicago, Andersen carefully built his savings account and assiduously looked for a job with a southern exposure. When he read the Madera Anchuria advertisement offering employment to a qualified accountant willing to work in the Republic of Anchuria for four years, he saw visions of a hammock swinging between two coconut palms on a quiet beach while fresh breezes came from the deep blue Caribbean Sea.

Sitting in a swim suit on the golden sands of a Central American shoreline in mid-February had an overwhelming appeal to this young man who sometimes thought he spent most of his life standing navel deep in snow as the winds of near gale force whistled around his head and the mercury retreated to the lowest part of the thermometer, there to remain hidden until March - and sometimes April - and sometimes May.

It was an easy election. He signed the contract, packed light clothing and sun glasses and left for New Orleans. As he boarded the banana boat that would carry him to the Republic of Anchuria, he vowed he would see snow again only on Christmas cards and He made a solemn promise: He would never visit a place where snow had fallen. He knew he would be happy in the Tropic of Cancer.

Once in Villa Smit, Andersen learned golden sand beaches are not common in eastern Anchuria. Mangrove swamps lined most of the shores. Commonly, those swamps serve as home for various types of scorpions, poisonous snakes, stinging insects, amoebae and microbes carrying diseases usually fatal to civilized man. The North Dakota accountant also learned, in the wet season, Villa Smit was hot and humid and in the dry season, Villa Smit was also hot and humid.

* * * * *

In 1935, Thomas Andersen awoke in the bedroom of the Villa Smit house Madera Anchuria provided for his use. It was early in the morning and the sun had not yet heated the coastal air. Already humid, the sheet on which he lay was moist. He parted the mosquito netting hanging from the ceiling and surrounding his bed. He arose, showered and brushed his teeth. Then he dressed and, as he prepared his breakfast, he considered his prospects. Spending two and a half more years in Villa Smit did not fill him with undiluted joy.

The social life in Villa Smit was limited. Senator Roberto Smit's circle of friends and associates was particularly exclusive. It did not include company employees. A few other land owners and the local shop keepers formed the caste which might be referred to as Villa Smit's high society. That group, too, was closely knit and did not easily allow foreigners (especially gringos) into their homes. Few of their daughters were handsome, but, when compared to the local Chuchiba Indian girls, they were all Jean Harlows.

The only other North American in the town was a Southerner who spoke with a heavy Mississippi accent. Andersen could scarcely understand him. He was a sawyer and seemed constantly intoxicated. Andersen thought his name was Clay Vastulip. It sounded more Central European than southern. In any event neither of them wanted to spend much time with the other.

It was rumored a cinema would open in Villa Smit. In the meantime, entertainment was limited to three cantinas. Andersen believed it would be unwise to enter any of them unarmed and without a reliable body guard. Each of the cantinas provided the Villa Smit's alcoholic German doctor with a broad base of experience in sewing up knife wounds and mending broken bones. Between midnight on Saturday and noon on Sunday, his practice flourished.

If the social life in Villa Smit was non-existent, well, the accountant thought, he could put up with it for the remaining two and a half years of his contract. Amidst the nearly unrelieved expanse of mangroves crowding the Caribbean coast, Anderson had managed to find a small golden sand beach. It was only a few miles east of Villa Smit and there the Caribbean breezes did, in fact, bring some relief from the hot inland humidity.

Thomas Andersen found a way to fill his Sunday leisure. Spending time on the beach, sunning, fishing and contemplating his future were inexpensive past times and they were immeasurably superior to North Dakota Sundays spent huddling near a wood stove while Saskatchewan Screamers brought Arctic snow and bone-freezing temperatures.

Every Sunday morning after breakfast, Andersen put four bottles of Cerveza Alemana, a half dozen pieces of fresh Anchurian bread, some sausage, a few bananas, a string hammock and a book into a canvass bag. Then he put some fish hooks and line into his pocket, saddled a horse provided by the Madera Anchuria stable and rode to his sandy beach.

Whenever he visited it, he had it all to himself. He couldn't understand why anyone within a ten mile radius wouldn't be on the beach watching the Caribbean and taking the sun at every available minute. Perhaps they took these gifts for granted. Thomas Andersen did not take them for granted. Until the Chuchiba Indian girls became a lot less ugly, he would spend his Sundays in a hammock swinging between two coconut palms on a golden sand beach while fresh breezes occasionally came from the deep blue Caribbean Sea.

* * * * *

On his way to the beach, Andersen stopped and collected some pebbles and the broken half shell of an empty coconut. He would put sand and water into the shell and use it to hold his bait. The bait would be the small crustaceans he would dig from their burrows in the wet shoreline.

Seaside fishing on the Anchurian shore was an uncomplicated matter. Tie the hook to the line. Tie a pebble onto the line close to the hook. Put the bait on the hook. Swing the bait, hook and pebble in an arc above the head and throw the line into the surf. Then tie one end of the line to a stick poked into the sand. Place an empty beer bottle on a piece of drift wood some two or three feet from the stick. Run the line from the stick to the bottle, once around its neck, and then into the water. When the fish takes the bait, the line will pull the bottle from the drift wood and the noise will alert the fisherman. In the meantime, he can lie in his hammock and read or doze in the sun.

As he rode to his beach, Andersen reviewed his status with some satisfaction. He was not cold and he was not farming. The only goal he had not yet achieved was that of wealth. He was careful with his money and his weekend diversions were not expensive. He lived quietly and he put most of his Anchurian salary in the company safe. In just a few years he could return to New Orleans, get the additional five thousand dollars withheld from his four year Villa Smit salary and then begin his search for true wealth.

The trail Anderson followed turned toward the beach. The Caribbean came into view and the accountant saw a fishing boat on its side in the sand. The sail, he noticed, had not been lowered. It flapped in the gentle breeze. It seemed strange and suggested an accident had occurred. His suspicions were confirmed when he approached the vessel. He saw a revolver, a puddle of not yet completely dried blood and a wooden box on the bottom of the boat. Andersen looked up and down the beach. No one was in sight.

He searched the sands surrounding the boat. There were no footprints showing anyone had walked away from it. No body and no foot prints? The boat must have been unoccupied when it arrived on the shore. He picked up the revolver. There were still five rounds in the chamber. One shot had been fired.

Anderson hauled the wooden chest from the boat and was surprised by its weight. He dragged it to the coconut palms that lined the beach. There he opened it. Thomas Andersen received a surprise as great as Ali Baba's when he opened the cave of the forty thieves.

The chest was filled with the money Camilo Rosas earned through smuggling and extortion, together with what was left of don Pablo Ramirez' revolution fund and with the treasury of the Ciudad Carillo SINDETRAG. Andersen sat next to the chest, staring at its contents.

The fired revolver and the blood? It may have been a suicide, but that was highly unlikely. An accidental shooting? Probably. Someone carrying a large amount of money and a weapon for his own protection must have accidentally shot himself while sailing. He must have fallen overboard. The ship must have drifted ashore and when the tide went out, it keeled over and was left high and dry.

So much money, he thought. If he could keep it, he would reach his third goal. He would be a wealthy man. So much money. Certainly someone else had to know about it. If it were learned that Thomas Andersen was suddenly wealthy, that 'someone' would surely appear and claim it or steal it from him.

Anderson took the cap from a bottle of Cerveza Alemana, sat on the chest and thought again. He remembered hunger and the multi-patched clothing he wore as a child. He remembered the basements of the University of North Dakota sorority houses and the soot and the cold of his after-midnight-to-before-sunrise furnace tending. He remembered how he had to guard every penny and spend only when absolutely necessary.

Thomas Andersen made his decision. He buried the chest and burned the boat. He hoped the returning tides would carry all evidence of it back into the Caribbean. The following Saturday he worked late and when everyone else left the Madera Anchuria offices, he took his savings from the company safe. The next morning, as was his usual Sunday custom, he saddled a horse and announced he was going to the beach. This time he would not return to Villa Smit.

When the accountant's absence was noted, due inquiry was made. He was not found. His fellow workers believed some accident had befallen him. The search uncovered only the evidence of a fire and the metal fittings of a fishing boat at the beach where Andersen spend his Sundays. Anderson, it was generally believed, was dead.

Senator Roberto Smit thought otherwise. Andersen had taken his savings with him. Wasn't that a peculiar action for a man intending to spend a few hours at the beach? The company horse, the Senator noted, never returned to the stable. Roberto Smit smelled a planned disappearance.

News of the aborted coup in the neighboring Republic of Sedalia soon reached Villa Smit. When Roberto Smit got word of the disappearance of the Ciudad Carillo SINDETRAG Jefe along with the union's treasury, he guessed the truth. Thomas Andersen had the good fortune to get his hands on the SINDETRAG money. He was probably on his way back to the United States. Smit silently wished him good luck and asked his New Orleans agent to advertise for another accountant.

Chapter 16

The Arrival of the Passengers

During its voyages to Central America, the cabins of the Arbutus were seldom completely vacant. At least a few of them would be occupied by Fruit Company employees, tourists or Anchurian students going to or coming from universities in the States. Occasionally a commercial traveler or a migrant might board the ship, but they rarely formed a part of the ship's passenger list. The eight people who sailed on the mid-July, 1938 passage of the Arbutus were a fair representation of those who took banana boat cruises in the Tropic of Cancer. Two of them, however, didn't quite fit the usual pattern.

As Clevis Dewlap raised the Mason jar to his lips, tasted the moonshine and gave it his professional approval, Dr. Charles and Mary Louise Magnussen boarded the Arbutus.

Dr. Charles Magnussen was a professor of Political Sciences at Bowling Green State University (Ohio). He had a successful history of securing federal grants for study in Latin America. Even during the Hoover Administration, he was able to obtain government funds to enable him and his wife, Mary Louise, to spend the summer months studying the politics and economics of Central and South American Republics.

The Professor's political writings were objective and solidly researched. Though his books never came close to being best sellers, they were used as texts in a number of colleges and the royalties allowed Dr. Magnussen a standard of living higher than that of the average professor.

By the summer of 1938, the Rome-Berlin Axis was established. The Spanish Civil war was raging. Japan continued its aggression in China. Italy had attacked and conquered Abyssinia. Austria was a memory and the coming Munich Pact would seal the fate of

Sudetenland and Czechoslovakia. The hope of avoiding a devastating European war was waning. Whether the Latin American Republics would support the Axis or lend their assistance to what was later to be known as the Allies was a question yet to be decided. It was an interesting time for the political scientist.

Dr. Magnussen's application for a grant to study the politics of Central American Republics was quickly processed. He prepared for a summer visit to Anchuria and Sedalia. There were no rail connection between the capitol of Anchuria and the neighboring Republics. The roads between Progreso and Central America other population centers were unimproved. Overland transportation between the Anchurian capitol and other Central American capitols might have been available, but, unquestionably, it would be quite uncomfortable.

International air travel was still in its infancy and, while it was possible to fly to Anchuria, the Professor and his wife viewed flight in an airplane with a marked lack of enthusiasm. It was one of the few things they agreed upon.

With both land and air transportation unacceptable, the Professor and Mary Louise, arranged a passage on the Arbutus, intending to leave the ship when it docked at Aguas Buenas, spend a some time in Anchuria and, later, sail to Sedalia for further study before returning to Bowling Green.

The Magnussens occupied Cabin 7, A Deck, Port. They did much more than occupy it. They overflowed it. When Mary Louise's steamer trunk, various suit cases, hat boxes and personal paraphernalia (together with the Professor's two suitcases, typewriter and brief case) were delivered to their quarters, there was barely enough room to open the door.

"Spacious accommodations? Spacious accommodations?" Mary Louise questioned, quoting from the Fruit Company's cruise advertising, "There's no place to put anything."

Professor Magnussen took the opportunity to make a helpful comment. "In the event we are asked to spend a year on a safari into darkest Africa, you have packed everything you will need. In exchange for your admirable preparedness, you must put up with a few minor inconveniences, dear" he said. Then he suggested they store the excess luggage in the upper bunk and share the lower one.

Mary Louise gave him a look that would have frightened Attila the Hun. Dr. Magnussen's summer trip to Anchuria and Sedalia would produce up-to-date commentaries in his forthcoming book on the politics of Central America, but Mary Louise made it entirely clear it would not produce any kittenish change in the relationship that existed between them.

For some years that relationship could best be characterized as an armed truce made between long-time and suspicious enemies. While open warfare was a possibility and a constant threat, the parties contented themselves with guerrilla forays into each other's territory.

Dr. Charles Magnussen understood the 'not on your life' look Mary Louise gave him. Over twenty years of skirmishing should teach the combatants something. Two of the things he learned were: (1) At times Mary Louise has only a limited sense of humor and, (2) Discretion is the better part of valor. Such being the case, he immediately withdrew from the cabin telling Mary Louise he would seek out the Purser and ask him to arrange for the safe storage of the steamer trunk and boxes in the ship's hold.

* * * * *

While the Magnussens were engaged in trying to shoe horn themselves and Mary Louise's luggage into Cabin 7, two taxis arrived at shipside. Paul Eckert stepped from the first and paid the driver. He retrieved his suitcases and walked up the gangplank where the ship's Purser, Luis Gogeasgoechea, checked his credentials and confirmed he was not a stowaway. Paul was directed to Cabin 10, Starboard. He would share it with another passenger.

The second taxi carried Ellie Sue Bradshaw. While waiting for the driver to unload her baggage, she watched Paul Eckert as he walked toward the gangplank leading up to the Arbutus weather deck. She admired his build. He appeared to be young. He appeared to be alone. Then she remembered him. He was the man she saw sleeping in the train. Ellie Sue's prospects for a pleasant cruise had just improved. She remembered the book her father had given her. She was pleased at the prospect of not becoming an expert on Anchurian history after all.

When she boarded the ship, the Purser put a check mark next to her name on the Passenger List and, as he did with all travelers, explained the difference between port and starboard. "When you look to the front of the ship, Miss", he said, "the port side is on your left and the starboard side is on your right."

Ellie Sue looked like she was listening, but she had something else on her mind. She said to the Purser: "The passenger who just came aboard - he looks just like my cousin Johnny. I haven't seen him in years." She asked if he happened to be Johnny Schmid and what cabin did he occupy.

Luis Gogeasgoechea reviewed his list and told her: "No, señorita. He is Mister Paul Eckert and he is in the Cabin number 10" Then he added the word "starboard", to display his own command of nautical terminology. To make sure there was no misunderstanding, he pointed to the right side of the ship. Ellie Sue smiled sweetly and said, "My, oh my, he certainly does look like Cousin Johnny". Luis gave Ellie Sue the directions to her pre-assigned compartment – Cabin 9, A Deck, Port.

Though three passengers had not yet boarded the Arbutus, Luis Gogeasgoechea would have happily abandoned his post to carry Ellie Sue's luggage to her cabin. He offered to do so, but Ellie Sue smiled, declined, picked up the suitcases and walked toward the passenger compartments. She is pretty, Luis thought as he watched saw her slim figure disappear down the passageway that led to the starboard cabins.

Slightly disappointed, Luis again reviewed the Passenger List. One of the three yet-to-arrive travelers would be the sole occupant of Cabin 11. His name was Reinhold Reichman. Luis was not surprised to see the Passenger List show he traveled under a German Passport. Many Germans migrated to Central America during the 1920s. Many of their friends and relatives traveled from Germany to visit them. Some of them were jovial and friendly. Some of them were stiff and formal.

The other two missing passengers were assigned to Cabin 8. One was a man named Druckrey and the other was a woman named Nelson. Luis hoped they were lovers masquerading as a married couple. If so, he would not give them away.

* * * * *

Luis expected some of the people already on board would unpack and immediately head for the ship's Saloon. That's what usually happened. He looked at his watch. Then he looked down the empty pier. He could not be two places at once. Should he be Purser and record the passengers as they boarded the Arbutus? Or should he be the bartender and provide the passengers with drink?

Luis decided he would rather be criticized for failing to process the arriving passengers than be criticized for failing to have the Saloon open when arriving travelers sought refreshment. He left his post at the gangplank and hurried to the ship's Saloon. He would enter the three missing tourists in the records when the Arbutus was underway.

Minutes earlier, following the Purser's directions, Paul walked across the weather deck toward the starboard passenger quarters. When he entered compartment 10, he found his cabin mate had already arrived and a battered suitcases lay on the lower bunk. His cabin mate had staked out his claim to it. Paul did not like upper bunks. However, he knew it was first come, first served. He would have to make the best of it.

Paul saw the opened Mason jar on the small desk. It was half filled with a clear liquid. His cabin mate was sitting beside the desk. The man smelled strongly of whiskey. There was no question about it. The Mason jar contained alcohol and the man had been drinking.

"I'm Paul Eckert", Paul said. There was no response to the announcement. Clevis Dewlap simply looked up at him, smiled and showed a mouth, incompletely toothed. After a few seconds, Paul asked, "And who are you?" It seemed like a reasonable question.

"Ahmklay vezdoola playstah mechah" were the sounds which came from his cabin mate. Paul had already noticed a sign on the ladder leading up to the captain's bridge. It was written in four different languages. He was able to identify only two of them - English and Spanish. The sounds coming from his cabin mate must have been one of the other two. Paul gave an immediate response. "I beg your pardon," he said. In Iowa it is a polite way of saying: "I don't understand you.

"Sall rye. Iddoan botha meahtahl. Yallsee ahmabit dranken", was the response.

"I beg your pardon."

A soft voice from the open cabin door behind him confirmed the presence of Ellie Sue Bradshaw. "I believe you are a northern boy. Am I right?" Planning to admit it, Paul turned to see a well appointed and nicely built, hazel eyed, light brown haired young woman standing in the passageway. She spoke with a cute accent. She was pretty. She smiled. He smiled.

"Well. Yes. I'm Paul Eckert. From Iowa. Yes, from Iowa. You are, indeed, right. Iowa. And who are you?"

"I'm Ellie Sue Bradshaw. I'm from Salem, Arkansas and I understand Mississippi talk. This gentleman said his name is Clevis Dewlap. He's pleased to meet you. He says it's all right. It doesn't bother him at all and he says he's a bit drunk.

"I declare", she added as she waived her hand in front of her face as if to dissipate the odor, "I never would have guessed."

She looked down at her suitcases and then looked up at Paul. She smiled again and said: "My, these suitcases are heavy." Paul smiled back at her and, after a second or so, what she said registered with him.

"Oh", he said, "let me help you with them." Without any further acknowledgment of the existence of Clevis Dewlap, seated unsteadily in the cabin chair, Paul picked up Ellie Sue's suitcases and followed as she left the cabin.

"I just can't seem to find Room 9", she said.

"That's because Cabin 9 is on the port side of the ship. This is the starboard side", Paul said, showing off his newly acquired ocean-going vocabulary. They returned to the weather deck, crossed to the port side of the ship and entered the companionway that led past the Magnussen cabin, past the Druckrey/Nelson compartment and on to the door identified by the number 9. Paul set Ellie Sue's suitcases inside her quarters. She smiled at him and said: "I don't know what I would have done without you, Paul. I just don't know how I can thank you," and she kissed him on the cheek.

Paul Eckert's prospects of a pleasant cruise to Aguas Buenas had just improved. "What a nice was to say thanks", he said. He stood in the corridor, not knowing what else to say. Ellie Sue smiled at his embarrassment.

"I believe I'll take a walk around the deck after I've unpacked", she said, knowing Paul would take the hint.

"That's a great idea", Paul answered. "I think I'll do the same. He paused and then added: "Well, good bye (pause) for now".

She shut the compartment door and Paul, still smiling, walked back down the passageway.

* * * * *

As soon as Dr. Charles Magnussen left their compartment to find storage space for her excessive baggage, Mary Louise Magnussen tried to open the porthole. She was unsuccessful so she walked to the weather deck and threw something overboard. That "something" was the ribbon she had taken from her husband's typewriter.

The thought of watching Charles searching and then again searching his writing supplies for the missing typewriter ribbon brought a smile to her face. She was satisfied. She had given him something to worry about during the voyage. Bothering Charles Magnussen was a source of delight for Mary Louise.

At that moment, Dr. Charles Magnussen didn't have anything to worry about. The Professor had no intention of looking for the Purser. He could put up with the cramped cabin space, especially when he knew it would irritate the living hell out of Mary Louise. So, as she casually jettisoned his typewriter ribbon into the Mississippi, the Professor casually jettison any thought of attempting to get storage space for Mary Louise's extremely excess baggage. Instead, he entered the ship's Saloon.

Magnussen recognized the man behind the bar. He was the Purser who welcomed him aboard the Arbutus and directed him to his cabin.

"Excuse me. Is the bar open?"

"Yes it is, sir", answered Luis Gogeasgoechea. "My name is Luis." He seldom told the passengers his last name. They could never remember it, anyway. "I am the ship bartender." He noticed

Magnussen's look of confusion. "Yes", he added, "I am also the ship Purser."

The Professor ordered a martini.

As far as Luis Gogeasgoechea was concerned, Dutch Ginebre was probably the equivalent of English Gin. So he took the Ginebre bottle from beneath the bar, added what he estimated to be the proper amount of the ancient dry vermouth, speared an olive with a flat toothpick, slipped it into the drink and placed it before his customer. He watched the Professor's expression and waited expectantly, hoping this time his martini would draw praise. He was doomed to disappointment.

The Professor's eyes bulged. His right hand shook and, luckily, spilled a substantial portion of the drink. The fingers of his left hand went, involuntarily, to his throat. With nearly paralyzed face muscles and through eyes stretched wide open, he looked menacingly at Luis who backed up and slid out from behind the bar. Keeping his eyes on the Professor and his back to the wall, he slithered out of the Saloon to seek asylum elsewhere.

The martini glass fell to the floor and shattered, solving the problem of what to do with the rest of the drink. The Professor's white knuckled fingers now locked on the edge of the bar. His eyes followed Luis as he retired from the room. The only sound the Professor could make was a periodic rasping caused by the deep intake of air in lungs nearly immobilized by the effect of the drink.

Convinced he had ingested curare if not some even more rare and lethal native poison, Magnussen wondered if Mary Louise or, perhaps, some unknown enemy had successfully planned and executed his demise.

At this moment, Paul, returning from Ellie Sue's cabin, approached the door to the Saloon. Without warning, the door swung open and the Purser backed out of the room. He turned and stepped directly into Paul. The Purser touched the bill of his cap, said: "Perdón Señor", and without another word or even breaking stride, he hurried astern and disappeared down a gangway.

Curious about what might have caused the Purser's sudden departure, Paul opened the door and looked inside the ship's Saloon. He saw another passenger with a broken martini glass on the floor beside him. He was gripping the side of the bar and wordlessly, but angrily, he stared at Paul.

Paul smiled and gave him a cordial "Hello." The stranger continued to grip the bar rail and stare. He made no sound or movement to acknowledge the greeting. Paul nodded at him, closed the door and resumed his stroll on the weather deck. Strange person, he thought. Not at all friendly.

Back in the Saloon, Magnussen's diaphragm relaxed and he was able to draw in a full breath of air and leave the scene of the crime. When he again entered his compartment, he saw Mary Louise had temporarily solved the space problem by squeezing some of her luggage onto his upper bunk. He knew it was a matter of storage convenience and not an invitation.

Faced with the inconvenience of trying to sleep in his now crowded bunk, the Professor reversed his previous decision. He would ask the Purser to put some of Mary Louise's baggage in the hold. He would make sure her cosmetics would be taken to storage. He noticed the ribbon had been removed from his typewriter and guessed what had happened. Revenge was quickly planned. Before dinner, he would bring Mary Louise to the ship's Saloon and give her a martini.

Chapter 17

Reinhard Reichman and the Abwehrabteilung

After the latest disastrous attempt to mix a martini, Luis escaped retribution and hurried to his Purser's station near the Arbutus gangplank. On his way from the Saloon, he caught a glimpse of a man and a woman carrying luggage and correctly guessed they were Druckrey and Nelson. He put a check mark after their names on the Passenger List.

By now, all cargo destined for the Central American Fruit Company plantations had been loaded into the hold and the hatches were securely battened down. Luis wondered if the eighth and last passenger had boarded the ship during his absence from the gangplank. As he wondered, another taxi drove onto the pier and a man in a white linen suit emerged. He retrieved his suitcases and walked toward the ship. That one, Luis thought, would be the German.

As Luis noted the man's arrival in the ship's Passenger List, the German looked at him and announced: "I have worked very hard introducing German bicycles into the United States. Now I will enjoy a pleasant cruise and a vacation in Anchuria."

Luis thought it sounded as if the man was giving himself an order, but it was Reinhold Reichman's way of advising the Purser of his occupation. He hoped the entire crew would soon know he was a German commercial agent. His identity would be established.

As was his usual procedure, Luis began to give Reichman directions to his cabin. Before he could finish his explanation of the difference between port and starboard, the passenger abruptly turned and walked away from him. Well, thought Luis sadly, he must be one of the stiff and formal ones and he walks funny.

Once inside his compartment, the reason for the funny walk became apparent. Reinhold Reichman removed his trousers. A Walther

Heeres pistol with an attached silencer was taped to the inner thigh of his right leg. A box of 9 mm. cartridges was taped to his left. He grimaced as he ripped off the adhesive tape.

Reichman carefully cleaned the remnants of the adhesive from the P-38. Gripping the weapon, he pointed it at a rivet in the bulkhead. He liked the feel of it. Holding it brought back memories of his earlier life.

* * * * *

The end of the First World War brought chaos to Germany. Kaiser Wilhelm II and the order brought by the German military were gone. In their stead was a nation approaching chaos, abused by Clemenceau, humiliated by Orlandini and robbed by Lloyd George. The weak and ineffective Ebert government faced a serious threat of overthrow by the Communists. Confusion and disorder were rampant.

Reinhold Reichman was an unemployed army veteran when he was mobilized into the Freikorps - a kind of private police unit organized to put down the Communist Sparticide revolution of 1919. He fought in the streets. He saw blood. He killed. During the years of uncontrollable inflation that gripped Germany during the following years, he looked to the Worker's Party for salvation.

The German Worker's Party blamed the nation's problems as well as its military defeat on the Jews and the Communists. The exhortation of conspiracy is a convenient and powerful tool for the politically ambitious and the Party's leader, an Austrian veteran of the German army used them effectively.

When that leader, Adolf Hitler, created the Brown Shirts, a paramilitary organization that terrorized Jews and Communists, Reinhold Reichman joined it and became a Sturmabteilung - a Storm Trooper. He remained loyal to the Party even after the notable failure of the Munich Beer Hall Putsch of 1923.

After Hitler and Rudolf Hess were released from prison, the German Worker's Party changed its name to the National Socialists - the Nazis. Its membership grew from 17,000 in 1925 to 800,000 in 1931. That was when the German millionaires Hugenberg, Kirdorf,

Thyssen and Schroder provided the Party with powerful financial support.

The Nazis received 11 million votes in subsequent elections and Adolf Hitler became Chancellor of Germany in 1933. During those years, Reinhold Reichman carried a pistol for the Nazis. On occasion he did more than merely carry it.

In 1935 Admiral Wilhelm Canaris was named head of the Abwehrabteilung, a sub-branch of the German Reichswehr Ministry. The sub-branch was usually referred to as the Abwehr. Admiral Canaris developed it into a sabotage and espionage organization. He recruited agents from the pool of World War I veterans who experienced the turmoil of Germany in the 1920s. He preferred those who had supported the National Socialist Party and looked for those who believed the Communist threat to their country had to be eliminated at all cost. Reinhold Reichman fit the Admiral's profile.

The following year, Reinhold Reichman was a passenger on the North German Lloyd's liner Deutschland, bound from Hamburg to New York City. He was a commercial agent representing the Hamburg Bicycle Gesellschäft. At least, that's what his passport said. It was not the Hamburg Company that sent him to the United States. It was the Abwehr. Reichman's mission was to establish a network of German undercover agents.

The Nazi spy masters in Hamburg had little information about 1930s American intelligence operations. The fact that they had such little information led them to believe the American counter spy unit must be very secretive and well organized. Reinhold Reichman believed it with almost fanatic certainty. In fact, the Intelligence Service in the United States was it was in its infancy.

* * * * *

When the United States formally recognized the Soviet Union, Reichman became convinced America was an active participant in the world-wide Communist conspiracy. He was quick to find conspiracy at every turn and he feared the secretive and shadowy American counter intelligence agencies. When he passed through the U. S. Customs at

New York, he received a terrible scare.

To validate his false identity, one of his suitcases was filled with technical data, photographs and promotional materials for the Hamburg bicycles. The Customs Agent saw them and carefully questioned Reichman about the bicycles. His curiosity was extensive. Where were they sold? What was their price? Reichman was absolutely sure the man was an American secret policeman. The Customs Agent was not a policeman. He was involved in nothing more sinister than planning to give his son a bicycle for Christmas.

Reichman expected to be arrested on the spot. In Germany a Customs Agent would probably be an associate and possibly a member of the Geheime Staats Polizei - the Secret State Police - the ones known by their acronym Ge-Sta-Po. When he was allowed to enter the country, Reichman fully expected to be placed under continual surveillance. He was sure the American secret police were aware of his presence and were waiting for his first mis-step. If they captured him, he decided, he would tell them everything he knew and offer to become a double agent.

Reichman's fear of arrest and the torture that would surely follow kept him in a self-imposed confinement within the decaying New York hotel that catered to longer term residents of modest means. For a week he did not venture from his room. Then paranoia again seized him. What could be more suspicious than a man shunning his own countrymen? If he avoided contact with them, would that not be positive proof that he was a spy, trying to hide his identity?

Reichman left the protection of the hotel and began to visit German restaurants and gymnastic clubs. He met Germans who left 1920s Germany for opportunity in America. Slowly he tested their sentiments and assessed their potentials as undercover agents. Careful to do nothing that might actually amount to spying, each month he sent reports to Hamburg.

The Abwehr received information about the Ku Klux Klan, about Father Coughlin's racist preaching, about the German-American Bund and about he America First organization. Reichman did not mention the sources of his information - gossip from his German friends and articles in the New York Times.

As his fear subsided, Reichman's quasi-covert activities increased and, occasionally, he had good luck. One of his friendly compatriots was a draftsman working for the Sperry Rand Company on Long Island. That plant produced the Norden Bomb Sight. Reichman got copies of the plans and delivered them to an Abwehr courier who posed as a waiter aboard a North German Lloyd's liner.

In Hamburg, the Abwehr was delighted. Reinhold Reichman was regarded as a capable and effective spy. That reputation was accurate. Reichman's fears approached paranoia. His paranoia made him suspicious. His suspicions made him careful. Super caution made him successful. Each of the few agents in his network had been most prudently selected. Each was unquestionably loyal to the fatherland.

Still, Reichman believed he would hear a midnight knock on his door and be confronted by the American secret police. He was happy when the Abwehr gave him an assignment that would take him out of the United States and beyond the reach of the American Gestapo. True to form, Reichman told no one of his new assignment. If any one of his agents was a double agent and knew he was going to leave the country, his enemies would arrest him immediately.

Reichman quietly left his hotel during New York City's noontime rush. He rode the subways until satisfied he was not being followed. Then he took a bus, first to Philadelphia, then to Toledo and, finally, to Chicago. There he boarded a train for the trip to New Orleans and a passage to Aguas Buenas on the S S Arbutus.

* * * * *

Reichman again lifted the Walther and aimed it at the rivet. These Americans are not so clever, he thought. They inspect your luggage when you arrive, but not when you leave. In Germany we are not so careless. Now he worried about the risks he might run upon entering the Republic of Anchuria. Smuggling a pistol through their Customs could endanger his mission.

If they found the pistol, how could he explain it? Why would a bicycle salesman carry a Walther and a box of 9 mm. bullets? His identity would surely come under scrutiny. On the other hand, what if he needed a weapon to protect himself against an enemy that might have followed him aboard ship?

He weighed the fear of being unmasked against the fear of being unarmed and decided to compromise. He would load the pistol and keep it and the silencer. He would throw away the remaining cartridges. There would be less bulk to hide. If all went well, when he arrived at Aguas Buenas he would decide if he should jettison the gun.

Reichman loaded the pistol, attached the silencer and put it in his valise. He locked the valise and put it inside his suitcase. He locked the suitcase and put it under his bunk. After locking the cabin door he walked to the weather deck. No one was in sight. He took the box of 9 mm. bullets from beneath his coat and dropped it into the Mississippi River.

Paul Eckert rounded the corner just as the German turned to go back to his compartment. Reichman panicked. Had the man seen him drop the cartridges? Had he heard the splash?

Paul was otherwise occupied. He was still smiling and thinking of Ellie Sue. "Good afternoon", he said. "Lovely day, isn't it?"

"Yes, it is, as you say, a lovely day", was Reichman's slow and apprehensive response. Then he rather stiffly and formally added: "I am a commercial agent for the Hamburg Bicycle Company. I am taking my vacation. You are taking the cruise?"

"Yes", Paul said. He recognized the German accent and felt the man's sudden conversation was somehow a bit aggressive. "At least I'm going as far as Aguas Buenas. Then I'll leave ship for a few days and re-board on its return trip to New Orleans."

Reichman caught his breath. The stranger seemed naïve, but looks can deceive. Why did he say he would leave the ship at Aguas Buenas? Was it an attempt to remove suspicion? Could he be an American agent sent to follow and spy on him?

"What a nice coincidence," Reichman said. "I will disembark at Aguas Buenas. My name is Reinhold Reichman." He extended his hand. Paul took it and said: "And I am Paul Eckert." The German gave two quick tugs to Paul's hand and released it.

"Eckert? Eckert? You are German?"

"Half" Paul admitted. He was not comfortable and wanted to end the conversation. "My grandfather came over from Stettin many years ago." He took advantage of the short pause that ensued by adding: "I'll look forward to traveling with you. Very nice to meet you". It was the polite way of saying "goodbye" in Iowa. Before Reichman could respond, Paul turned and walked on toward the fantail.

The German watched Paul's retreating figure, nodded his head slightly and then started back to his own compartment. When he entered the companionway leading to his Cabin, he saw a young man and a young woman in the passageway. They stood before the door to his cabin. As soon as they saw him, the man asked: "Can you tell us where is Cabin 8, A Deck, Port?

"It is on the other side of the ship", was Reichman's curt answer. "This is the starboard side."

The man picked up the couple's luggage and both nearly ran back toward the open deck. Reichman watched their retreat and wondered if they had run away in order to avoid being questioned. He wondered if he had caught them in the act of breaking into his compartment. Then a worse alternative occurred to him. Perhaps they were in the act of locking his door after entering it.

Reichman unlocked the door and carefully examined the cabin's interior. There was no indication that anyone had looked through his belongings. However, a professional would leave no tell-tale signs. Suspicion tore at him. Did they enter his cabin? He took the pistol from his suitcase and once more balanced it in his hand. He was glad he had it.

Chapter 18

Getting to Know Ellie Sue

Paul Eckert was in a pleasant frame of mind as he leaned on the ship's rail and gazed out at the docks and the New Orleans skyline. The mild sense of emptiness that remained with him since he and Anne Frisch parted was now replaced by a sense of relief. A simple peck on the cheek had the effect of severing an old emotional tie. No sense of guilt would restrain his pursuit of Ellie Sue.

For the moment at least, not even a thought of the pain and annoyance he would suffer by sharing his cabin space with Clevis Dewlap bothered him. The vague uneasy feeling about beginning a business career was forgotten. There was a spring in his step and a smile on his face when he left the amidships rail and returned to his compartment. A kiss from Ellie Sue Bradshaw was a mood altering experience.

When he entered Cabin 10 and began to unpack his suitcase, he could have used another of Ellie Sue's kisses. Clevis Dewlap was draped over the lower bunk. As Shakespeare would have described it, he was engaged "in swinish slumber". Paul noticed the Mason jar was now only one quarter full. He also saw three pails placed next to Clevis' bunk and wondered if the ship's plumbing leaked.

Paul opened his suitcase and took out the toothbrush, Ipana dental cream and shaving gear. He opened the curtain that separated the cabin from the bathroom/shower area and entered the tiny space. He put the tooth paste and brush into one of the glasses resting on the ledge above the sink and then paused. There was no tooth brush in the other glass.

He looked back into the cabin and at the occupant of the lower bunk. Clevis Dewlap was enjoying his nap. He lay on his back. His mouth was open. The teeth brave enough to show themselves displayed a spectrum of color ranging from yellow to black. A disturbing thought occurred to Paul. Was it possible that his cabin mate might use his tooth brush?

Clevis was a vocal sleeper. It couldn't be described as snoring. It was much worse than mere snoring. He made moist, slurping sounds. Between that wet gurgling, he mumbled. He may have been talking in his sleep, but Paul's ear was not attuned to the Mississippian's accent. To him it was mumbling. Occasionally Clevis let loose a short but loud animal noise. It sounded like a bark but did not come from his mouth.

Paul put his tooth brush and the Ipana back into his suitcase. He would run no risk of cabin mate usage. He took out his pajamas and prepared to put them in the dresser. He discovered Clevis had already stored his clothing and personal effects in the top three drawers leaving the bottom two for Paul.

Great, Paul thought. Just great. I like the top drawers and I can't stand the top bunk. This is just great. Well, in four days I'll be in Aguas Buenas. He repacked his pajamas in his suitcase. I can live out of my luggage for a few days, he told himself.

The smell of the moonshine and the other odors produced by Clevis permeated the cabin. Paul went to the porthole and tried to open it. He couldn't move the clamps that held it shut. The many coats of marine paint covering the hinges showed the porthole hadn't been opened in years.

Paul looked again at the fulsome, but nevertheless sleeping Clevis Dewlap. Then he stepped out into the passageway for less toxic air. A walk around the deck was definitely in order. He hoped Ellie Sue would be taking a similar stroll.

Once on the weather deck and after a few deep breaths, Paul looked for Ellie Sue. He passed the ladder leading to the ship's bridge and again saw the four language sign, nearly three feet square and entitled "WARNING." It was specifically addressed to the passengers and advised them entrance to the ship's bridge was strictly forbidden.

Ellie Sue saw Paul and had enough time to strike an attractive pose at the rail before Paul saw her. "Ellie Sue," he said in a voice that wasn't quite a yell, but was loud enough to show enthusiasm.

"Oh, Paul," she said. "Come here, honey." Paul was accepting the invitation before she made it. He was at her side, watching the gangplank being raised when she said: "Isn't it exciting. We're on our way." She took Paul's arm with both hands, pulling herself close to him. That little movement was a part of Ellie Sue's way of getting a man's attention, but it wasn't at all necessary. She already securely captured Paul's imagination. Now it would be up to him to convince her he was worthy of further attentions.

The engines changed their pitch, the propellers dug into the water and the Arbutus began its journey down the Mississippi River and into the Gulf of Mexico. As the ship sailed away from New Orleans and through the low, flat delta land, Paul and Ellie Sue continued to explore their new surroundings.

They visited the Salon and wondered why the tables and chairs were chained to the floor. They walked to the eyes of the ship. They looked down and watched the prow of the Arbutus slice through the water. Dolphins appeared. Diving and surfacing, they piloted the Arbutus down the river until they tired of the game. They were gone as suddenly as they had appeared.

Paul showed Ellie Sue the notice marking the Captain's bridge as off limits to one and all. They agreed one of the foreign languages was Spanish and after eliminating French, Italian, and German, they speculated about the other two. Parsi and Bulgarian were favored.

They made their way to the fantail and saw a jerry-rigged structure about five feet high, eight feet long and six wide. It was lined with rubberized canvas. A pump lay on the deck alongside the structure. A hose, long enough to reach over the side of the ship and down into the sea was attached at one end of it. Half a dozen folded deck chairs leaned against the side of the makeshift pool.

Paul opened two of them and set them side by side, commenting: "This is the 'luxurious swimming pool' they told us about in the advertisements." Ellie looked inside the pool structure. "There are only six rooms on this boat", she said. "I don't have a roommate so there can only be eleven of us. We can all squeeze into the pool if we're real friendly."

Ellie Sue and Paul sat in the deck chairs and talked and watched egrets and herons flying along the flat watery edges of the river. They were at ease in each other's presence. No strained formality hampered them. After a while, their conversation turned to more personal matters.

"What's a pretty girl like you doing all alone in a place like this?" Paul asked.

Ellie Sue looked down and paused while she confirmed her initial impulse to admit the failure of her marriage. "I just got my divorce", she said. "I was only married for about a year. It was a mistake. I mean the marriage, not the divorce."

To make sure there was no mistake, she said: "Don't get me wrong, Paul, honey. I like the idea of married life. The mistake was my mate selection. I've been a free woman for over a day now." She told of her short marriage and it termination without bitterness. When she finished, she looked up at him and was pleased to see no indication of any change in Paul's demeanor.

Divorce wasn't that common in the mid-1930s. It was the usual custom for women to stay with unsatisfactory husbands. A woman's place was in the home - and too many women were educated only for that career. If they brought a Bill of Divorcement, where could they go and how could they get by on depression style alimony?

Husbands, on the other hand, were under no such constraint. Divorce was, too often, considered as proving the wife was defective, or unloving, or unfaithful.

"A bad experience, Ellie Sue," said Paul. He was quietly pleased to learn Ellie Sue had no attachments. "You're very pretty." He paused and added: "And very smart." He paused again before adding: "And you've got a great sense of humor." He took her hand. "Smile, Ellie Sue. You'll put it behind you and move on to bigger and better things."

"You're very sweet Paul, honey," she said holding on to his hand. "But now it's your turn. What's a nice boy like you doing all alone on a ship like this?" Paul needed no other prompting to volunteer his lack of commitment to anyone. Ellie Sue was happy to receive that information.

The Arbutus continued to move down the Mississippi and toward the Gulf of Mexico. Paul and Ellie Sue continued to watch the delta slide past and they talked. Paul told how he would disembark at Aguas

Buenas, spend a few days and then return to New Orleans. He described his decision to enter into the family business in Iowa and Ellie Sue told of her plan to leave Salem and seek independence in Memphis, or, perhaps Kansas City (which she knew was closer to Des Moines).

They were comfortable with each other.

* * * * *

With all passengers accounted for and the beef broth being prepared in the galley, Luis Gogeasgoechea could relax. He lay in his hammock in the crew's quarters and mentally reviewed the Passenger List. It assigned the title of "Dr." to Charles Magnussen and Luis hoped the man was a physician. That would be good luck. Of all the jobs assigned to him, the duty of being the ship's Medical Officer was the most worrisome.

From time to time, passengers became ill. Luis recognized his complete lack of medical knowledge, but he did his best. The sea sick all received the same advice: Don't eat anything. A cut required a bandage and everything else called for an aspirin. A real live doctor would be a godsend.

Luis's first encounter with Dr. Magnussen and the unfortunate experience with the martini might have injured their relationship. He hoped they could still become friendly. Luis thought of the many passengers who stopped speaking to him after enjoying one of his mixed drinks.

The letters they sent to the President of the Central American Fruit Company were very unkind. Luckily the Arbutus passenger service was a profitable venture for the company. Such being the case, Llewellyn Black gave all such letters to his secretary with the instructions: "Send the Gogeasgoechea letter to them."

The 'Gogeasgoechea letter' was a form that thanked the passenger for bringing the matter to his attention and assured him Mr. Gogeasgoechea would be fired immediately. The secretary had a number of the pre-signed form letters ready for automatic mailing if the Gogeasgoechea complaints came in when Mr. Black happened to

114

be out of town.

Luis thought of the girl in Cabin 9. She was a charmer. A pretty girl with big eyes, Ellie Sue Bradshaw would receive his best service. Luis hoped she would not ask for a martini. He did not want her to hate him.

Luis hadn't met the two people who occupied the compartment between the Magnussens and the girl with the cute accent, but he has already noted their arrival on the Passenger List. Since their passports were issued in different family names, Luis guessed they would probably keep to themselves. If they stayed in love for the entire cruise, they wouldn't cause him any problems. He hoped they would get along.

Luis did not like the German - the one in the compartment next to Señor Dewlap and Señor Eckert. The Latin and the Nordic temperaments are not naturally compatible. The German was too formal, too stiff and too remote to become truly friendly. Luis suspected Herr Reichman would be difficult and demanding. He probably would insist the scheduled shipboard social activities actually take place. He feared the man might even expect them to be held on time. He was sure Herr Reichman would write a letter to the President of the Fruit Company.

Clevis Dewlap was one of the men assigned to the cabin next to the German. Luis knew him. A few months earlier he had watched him regurgitate his way from Villa Smit to New Orleans. In his entire shipboard career, Luis never saw a passenger who ate so little and upchucked so much over such a long period of time.

In his capacity as the ship's Social Director, Luis had already attended to his responsibility to provide for Clevis' comfort during the voyage back to Villa Smit. He had carried three pails into the cabin occupied by the sleeping Sr. Dewlap and placed them on the floor next to the head of his bunk. There was nothing else he could do for him.

The last compartment at the end of the starboard passageway, cabin 12, was unoccupied. It was used to store various supplies - most of which were earmarked for the personal use of Captain Stavros Stavropopolous. The supplies included a dozen cases of Ouzo which, Luis felt, should provide the Captain with a sufficient amount of drink for the time it took to complete the Arbutus' round trip voyage. Cabin 12 was seldom available for passenger occupancy.

The German passenger insisted on sole occupancy of Cabin 11 and the girl in Cabin 9 was also alone. There was no other compartment into which Paul Eckert could be moved. For four days and four nights Sr. Eckert would have to share the cabin with Clevis Dewlap. Luis pitied him. As he thought about Paul Eckert and Clevis Dewlap, Luis concluded that we live in an imperfect world.

Chapter 19

Preludes

It was after four o'clock and time for the three o'clock beef broth. Luis left his hammock in the crew's quarters and walked to the fantail to advise the two passengers already in deck chairs of the availability of the broth in the Salon. As he ascended the ladder to the fantail, he recognized Ellie Sue and Paul. Unseen, he watched for a few moments while, stretched out in the deck chairs, they talked and laughed. He knew they would be uncomplaining passengers and cause no unpleasantness. He went to them and made his presence known.

"Good afternoon, nice young people. I am your Social Director, Luis Gogeasgoechea, at your service," he said with a bow and a wave of his hand. Paul looked up, recognized the Purser and answered: "Good afternoon Mister Go, ah, Gog, ah ..."

"Please call me Luis. Yes, I am also your Purser. I am your Bartender, too. You are Miss Bradshaw?" he asked of Ellie Sue. She admitted it. "And you are Mister Eckert, no?" he continued. "No," said Paul as he nodded his head up and down, "I mean, yes. I am Paul Eckert." Then he added: "And I'm pleased to meet you (pause) Luis."

"It's so nice to meet you, Mister Luis," said Ellie Sue in her soft accent as she extended her hand and stole the heart of the Purser, the Bartender, the Social Director and the Medical Officer. He immediately liked them both. "You need anything, you call Luis, no?" he said. They both agreed and then he looked at Ellie Sue and asked: "You drink the martini?" When she denied it, he smiled and said: "Good. I make bad martini," and he slowly shook his head from side to side.

Then he smiled and announced: "Now we have beef drink in the Salon. If you like, please come." Because he liked them both, he added: "The Salon is on the starboard side. That is this side." He pointed to make sure there could be no mistake and disappeared down the ladder.

Luis went directly to the Dining Salon where Osvaldo Carrera had already delivered paper cups and containers of beef broth. The Magnussens were alone in the Salon when he arrived and Mary Louise had served the broth to her husband. Luis expected trouble from them. The man, Luis noted, seemed a bit cool and it was the wife who did the introductions.

She presented her husband as "Professor" Charles Magnussen and Luis said to himself: Mierde! Un profesor! He would get no help from him if a medical doctor were ever needed. Nevertheless, Luis smiled when he introduced himself, asked them to call him "Luis" and promised to faithfully serve their every need.

A minute later, Paul and Ellie Sue entered the Salon. They took cups of the warm broth. Paul looked at the man and woman seated alone and sipping the warm, salty drink. He elected to ignore them both for two reasons. Paul recognized the man as the one who had so silently glared at him from the ship's Saloon. He wasn't interested in socializing with some miserable old bore. More importantly, Ellie Sue absorbed all of his attention. He preferred her company, exclusively.

"Let's watch the delta," he said, taking Ellie Sue by the elbow to steer her out of the room.

Mary Louise Magnussen wasn't going to miss an opportunity to satisfy her curiosity about a pair of fellow passengers. "Oh, hello, you two," she said, advancing on them and pulling her husband along by the sleeve of his seersucker suit. "We're the Magnussens," she continued without taking a breath: "I'm Mary Louise and this is Charles." Looking at Ellie Sue she said "You are very pretty," and immediately asked: "Are you married?"

Before Ellie Sue could answer, Paul looked at Mary Louise and said, evenly: "Are you?" Professor Magnussen smiled. He was going to like this young man. "Oh, yes," answered Mary Louise, and then she added, "Charles and I have been married for years." After a short pause, "It seems like centuries," and she looked up, sweetly, at her husband.

Mary Louise directed her conversation to Ellie Sue and the two of them sat at a table, leaving Paul and Professor Magnussen standing and somewhat ill at ease. Paul broke the silence.

"I read a book by someone called Charles Magnussen when I was studying Political Science at the University of Wisconsin. Had to do with the politics of the Caribbean. A bit too liberal for my tastes."

"Oh. Are you going to be a Political Scientist?"

"Heavens no. I'm going into business."

"Well, that's probably a good decision. Political Science can be quite dull. I'm Dr. Charles Magnussen and I'll admit I'm the one who wrote the book. Professor Eastman is at Wisconsin. Do you know him?" ("Yes.") "Let me tell a story about him," and Magnussen showed Paul a completely unsuspected human side of the University of Wisconsin mentor.

Magnussen warned Paul against ordering a martini. He recounted his experience of the afternoon and positively confirmed the accuracy of Luis' confession of inability to mix a martini. "With one more bartender like him," he said, "I could destroy the city of Bowling Green in a single afternoon." Now Paul understood the reason for the scowl on Magnussen's face when they first met. He re-assessed his opinion of him.

While Paul and Magnussen discussed mutual University of Wisconsin professor acquaintances, Mary Louise engaged in one of her favorite past times - direct cross examination. Ellie Sue didn't seem to mind. Occasionally, bits of their conversation floated into Paul's earshot.

"Of course, you were wise to dump him, Ellie." "How long have you known him?" "He seems very nice." "Do you play bridge?" "No?" "Good. I don't like women who play bridge." (Professor Magnussen enjoyed the game.) "There are so many other interesting things to do with one's life."

Paul would have preferred to be alone with Ellie Sue, but there was no graceful way he could break away from the Professor. With his alternatives limited, he suggested: "Let's join the women", and they did.

"Paul's going to disembark with us at Aguas Buenas," announced the Professor.

"I know," said Mary Louise, and she smiled.

"He has a Political Science degree from the University of Wisconsin," said the Professor.

"I know", said Mary Louise, and she smiled.

Mildly frustrated, the Professor turned his head, winked at Paul and said: "Paul speaks fluent Mandarin and is a personal friend of Senator Robert LaFollette."

"I didn't know that," Mary Louise said and her face fell.

Professor Magnussen made no other announcements. He quit while he was ahead.

* * * * *

Alone in his compartment, Reinhold Reichman was worried. Were two American counter intelligence agents aboard the Arbutus? Did he surprise them as they were about to break into and search his belongings? Was that why they so quickly hurried away from him? Would they discover his secrets? He doubted it. They were well hidden. But the Walther pistol? They would be suspicious if they found it. It would surely make them suspicious? It could incriminate him? Should he throw it overboard? No, never.

The problem nagged at him. Were they American secret police, posing as summer cruise vacationers? That was the central question. Perhaps he could find out. The Purser. Yes, the Purser. What was his name? Luis something. Reichman would question him. It was past the time for the afternoon beef broth, but, perhaps the Purser would still be in the Salon.

After first entering into the empty Saloon, discovering his error and then walking to the other side of the ship, Reinhold Reichman came into the Salon. Luis was there, but so were another ship employee and four passengers. He would have to wait before questioning the Purser.

Reichman greeted Paul who introduced him to Ellie Sue and the Magnussens. The German clicked his heels and sharply nodded his head in the Prussian manner. Mary Louise stifled a giggle and Ellie Sue turned away so Reichman could not see her expression.

As soon as Reichman learned Charles Magnussen was a professor of the Political Sciences, like a needle seeking the magnetic north, he focused his attention on him. Magnussen? Magnussen, he thought. The name is Danish? Or, Norwegian? It is certainly Nordic. He is a scientist of politics. A professor. For the moment, Reichman forgot about the man and woman he suspected of being American counter intelligence agents. Here was an opportunity to discuss the beauty and glory of the Nazi cause with a political scientist.

* * * * *

When the German began to expound his party line, Paul and Ellie Sue quietly slipped out of the room and escaped to the weather deck. They headed directly to the canvas swimming pool on the fantail. As they sat there, side by side, watching the Louisiana delta, Paul carefully dropped his hand to the arm of Ellie Sue's folding chair. It came to rest on Ellie Sue's hand. It didn't disturb her a bit.

"That funny little German man," she said, accepting the hand holding invitation without objection. "He seems so intense. The way he clicks his heels together. Just like Fritz Feld in the movies."

"Be ferrry careful, Miz Bradshaw," said Paul, feigning seriousness and rolling his rrs in an Iowa attempt at a German accent. "He may be a Nazi zooper shpy on his vay to blow up der Panama Canal."

"Don't be ridiculous," answered Ellie Sue, almost succeeding in keeping a straight face. "It's the Japanese who want to blow up the canal. Besides, I distinctly heard Herr Reichman pronounce the letter "R". Therefore he isn't a Japanese spy. You can't have Eric Von Stroheim playing Mr. Moto. He doesn't even have a scar on his face. You can't be a German spy without having a scar. It would violate all of Hollywood's rules."

"All right, El," answered Paul, "I'll play your silly game." He paused for a moment and then said: "Clevis Dewlap is really an American Army Air Corps pilot. He's been thrown out of the army for..." Paul paused again while he searched for a reason.

"For drinking, honey. For drinking," prompted Ellie Sue. "He got drunk and bombed his own air field by mistake."

"No fair, El. That's typecasting."

"They do it all the time in Hollywood," Ellie Sue pouted. Paul leaned toward her till his forehead touched hers. He said: "OK, OK. I can't stand to see a woman cry. He got drunk and bombed his own airfield. He got drunk because... he fell in love with a girl whose father was filthy rich, but hated him because he was poor. The old man broke it up by sending his daughter to Europe to forget about Clevis."

Without moving her forehead from his, Ellie Sue continued: "He's going to Anchuria to live in the jungles and forget about her."

"Right," Paul agreed. "Being a poor boy, he couldn't afford a passage to North Africa to join the Foreign Legion, so he had to settle for Anchuria." Then he looked at Ellie Sue and said: "It's your turn. Take over."

Ellie Sue's picked up the story. "Professor Magnussen is really a missionary, going into the jungle to save the souls of the benighted heathen. Mary Louise is his secret mistress."

"Mary Louise?" said Paul, moving his forehead from Ellie Sue's in surprise.

"All right. I'll make her Magnussen's cook and housekeeper. Now come back here and finish the story," she said, pulling Paul's head back into contact with hers. Paul finished the fantasy.

"The Magnussens, Dewlap and Reichman end up in the same part of the jungle. Reichman is killed and eaten by the savages Magnussen is trying to convert. Dewlap gets religion and stops drinking. The shock is so great Magnussen goes native and has a long and happy affair with Mary Louise who, it turns out, is a semi-reformed cabaret dancer. Dewlap finds a gold mine, becomes exceedingly wealthy and goes back to the states to find and marry his first love. She is now poor because her father has gone bankrupt. Everyone lives happily ever after."

"Except for the savages," Ellie Sue added. "They all get indigestion."

Still sitting side by side in the deck chairs with foreheads touching, there was a pause in their light conversation. With a more serious tone of voice, Ellie Sue asked: "Who, really, is Paul Eckert?"

Paul looked deeply into her eyes before answering. "Paul Eckert" he said and then slowly added: "is, really, the man who is going to kiss you." There was no objection, so he did.

Chapter 20

Reichman Investigates and Paul Considers

When Reinhold Reichman entered the ship's Salon, intent upon questioning the Purser about the identity of the two people he suspected of attempting to break into his cabin, his introduction to Professor Magnussen set him on an entirely different course. Magnussen's first impression of Reichman was negative. He was more accustomed to the courtesy and polite tact usually found in the Latin American. Reichman's brusque direct questioning almost seemed like an attack on Magnussen's credibility.

"You are a professor," he said in a tone that made the statement sound like a question. "Of Political Science?" Reichman continued without waiting for an answer, "Where is your university?" If Magnussen had hackles on the back of his neck, they would have stood up. "I head the Political Science Department of Bowling Green State University," he answered in faintly measured tones. "Bowling Green in Ohio," he added.

"Ah", said Reichman, moving a step closer to the Professor. "The heartland of the United States. Are you near Detroit? Father Coughlin broadcasts from Detroit. Do you listen to him? What do you think of him? He is very intelligent, No?" There was no pause between the questions.

Magnussen knew he was talking to a zealous Nazi. He stifled his initial impulse to tell the German what he really thought of the Third Reich and Father Coughlin, but he had spent too much time with Latin Americans. Some of their natural civility had rubbed off onto his basic gringo character. He took a half step backwards and limited himself to a bland answer.

"He is a very interesting man. His positions on race are quite controversial."

"I'm glad you agree with him, Herr Professor," said Reichman, taking another step toward him. "His warning to those of us who are Aryan is timely. The greatest danger we all face is Communism. I know. I have seen the Communists in the streets. If the United States is to survive, you must eliminate them. Eliminate them, as we have done in Germany." Reichman's voice had risen.

Oh my, thought Magnussen. He's worse than I thought. You can't have rational discussion when people get emotional and begin to raise their voices.

"They are animals," Reichman continued. "See what they are doing right now. They are killing their own. They purge their leaders. They starve the Ukrainians. They ...".

While he spoke, the Professor thought of the 1934 Nazi assassinations - Rohm, Schleicher and Strasser in Germany - recently, Dollfuss in Austria. After another five minutes of Reichman's lecture, the Professor had enough.

"You must excuse me, Herr Reichman," he said, interrupting the ex-Storm Trooper. "I find your comments on the New Order in Germany to be most enlightening, but I must attend to my wife's medical needs. The poor woman has diabetes and I must give her injections of insulin. Her behavior becomes erratic if I overlook my responsibility. I must go now. I hope you enjoy the voyage," he said, as he moved along the bulkhead and out of the Nazi's range.

* * * * *

Mary Louise sat at the buffet on the far side of the Salon, watching Reinhold Reichman's energetic support of National Socialism and enjoying her husband's obvious discomfort. Once freed from the German's attentions, the Professor came across the room and took Mary Louise firmly by the arm. Without pause or explanation, he led her from the room.

"Charles," she said as he hurried her down the passageway toward their cabin, "I certainly hope you haven't been rude to that nice foreign gentleman. Is he a political scientist," and then, sporting her Cheshire cat smile, she added, "like you?"

Magnussen snorted. "Nothing to joke about, Mary Louise. The man's nothing but a damned Nazi - and no, I didn't insult him though I sincerely wanted to." The professor was irked by his wife's Cheshire cat smile, so he volunteered: "I told him you were subject to epileptic seizures. That when they occurred, you sometimes became violent, cursed and struck out at anything near you. I said I recognized your symptoms and would have to get you to our compartment and tie you down for a while."

The Cheshire cat smile took its leave and was replaced by an I'll-get-you-for-that scowl worthy of Orson Welles.

When the Magnussens left the Arbutus Salon, Reinhold Reichman was left alone with Osvaldo Carrera and Luis Gogeasgoecha. He went to the table that stood in front of them and ordered beef bouillon. He took the cup from Luis and said "You are the Purser, no?" This time it was a question and Luis answered in the affirmative.

"I am interested in the other people who are on the ship. It is important to know who you travel with, no? Who is in Cabin 8, A Deck, Port," he asked. Luis felt a tremor pass through him. The couple he hoped were unmarried lovers occupied that compartment. What was the reason for the German' interest in them. Was he going to cause trouble?

Luis temporized. "Do you know them?" he asked.

"No, I do not know them. I have seen them in ...ahh... the passageway. Are they German?"

Luis was relieved to know his maintenance of the Passenger List was not under attack. Nevertheless, he decided to give Herr Reichman as little information as possible.

"I do not know," Luis answered. "They both have American passports. One of them is named Druckrey and the other is named Nelson. I know nothing more about them."

"Thank you," said Reichman, with a sharp nod of his head. He then sat at one of the tables and drank the broth. So, he thought, they share the cabin but have different names on their passports. Decadent Americans. He finished the broth and left the Salon without further conversation, still wondering if they had been sent to watch him.

When he got to his Cabin, he was relieved to find the hair was still on the top of his cabin door where he placed it before leaving for the Salon. In his absence, no one had entered his compartment

* * * * *

It was after six when Ellie Sue and Paul left the deck chairs on the fantail of the Arbutus. "May I take you to dinner?" Paul asked. "I know a delightful restaurant, quite nearby. We needn't take a taxi. It is within walking distance, as a matter of fact."

"Only if it has a nautical atmosphere," was Ellie Sue's answer.

Paul walked her to her compartment. When she disappeared behind her cabin door, a cloud formed over Paul. The closer he got to his own port side compartment, the bigger and blacker it got. A grim reality faced him. He had to shower and change his clothes in that tiny room. That night he had to sleep there. Tomorrow morning he had to shower and shave and brush his teeth there - and that practically air tight compartment contained Clevis Dewlap.

Paul took a deep breath before entering his compartment. Clevis was still asleep on the lower bunk, farting and gurgling. The Mason jar was empty. Paul opened one of his suitcases, took out a change of clothing suitable for dinner with Ellie Sue and laid them on the bunk above a sleeping and mumbling Clevis Dewlap.

The water was tepid and the shower was quick. Paul shaved and combed his hair. He grimaced at the thought of eighty-four more hours of living from a suitcase and four nights in a bunk above Clevis Dewlap. With no movement of air inside the cabin, the place already smelled like a wet, long haired dog that had recently rolled in a number of things, all very smelly. What would it be like in another four days?

As he left the cabin and shut the door behind him, he considered the possibility of sleeping in the passageway or in a deck chair on the fantail.

When he approached Ellie Sue's cabin, his mood lightened. He knocked on the door. A voice from inside asked: "Is that you, Paul, honey?"

"Yes. El," he answered. "Are you ready yet?"

127

"Not quite, honey, but come on in."

He did. Ellie Sue was buttoning her blouse. She could have buttoned it ten minutes earlier, but she waited for Paul's arrival. She wore a delicate lacy brassiere. It did not escape Paul's attention.

When they entered the Salon, they saw Reinhold Reichman coming down the passageway on his way to dinner. Inside the Salon, the Magnussens were already seated. Ellie Sue and Paul went directly to their table and sat before an invitation was extended. They apologized for their presumption and explained their wish to avoid being seated with the German and listening to his expositions of the glories of the Third Reich.

With their table now filled, Professor Magnussen thanked the young couple for protecting them from the same peril.

Chapter 21

Revenge (and Romance)

Mary Louise was uncharacteristically silent as Ellie Sue and Paul sat at the Magnussen table. She looked grim and glared at her husband. Soon she recovered and, in way of explanation, said to Ellie Sue: "If my husband offers to buy you a martini in the Ship's Saloon, don't take it." The Professor smiled with deep satisfaction.

The soup course was finished when Clevis Dewlap appeared. He was crumpled and unsteady and hungry and obviously fully engaged in the experiment to test his theory that moonshine was an antidote for sea sickness. He went to Reinhold Reichman's table, sat down and announced: "Ahm clay vass doo lahp. Plee sta mee cha ahl," and he extended his hand.

The German didn't understand a word of it. The man didn't look like a Semite and the language might have been Finnish, but he wasn't sure. The extended hand suggested an introduction had been made, so he arose, shook the hand, clicked his heels, popped his head, and gave his name.

At the Magnussen table, the food was excellent and the conversation light and good humored. At the Reichman table, the food was excellent.

Reichman criticized the Treaty of Versailles and defended the German takeover of the Saar. Clevis didn't understand a word of it. He suspected his companion was talking about the Russian Czar. His southern courtesy, however, was displayed when he, nevertheless, occasionally nodded assent and made affirmative sounds.

Dinner completed, Clevis returned to his cabin and sampled the middle layer of the contents of another Mason jar. Then he retired and thought about the pitching and rolling that he knew would await the Arbutus as soon as it left the mouth of the Mississippi River and entered the Gulf of Mexico.

* * * * *

The other five passengers went to the ship's Saloon for an after dinner drink. Professor Magnussen, his afternoon experience in the Saloon, indelibly etched in his mind, asked for an Anchurian beer - a Cerveza Alemana. Mary Louise had not yet fully recovered from the shock of Luis Gogeasgoechea's venomous martini. She asked for a Drambuie. Paul and Ellie ordered gin and tonic. Then, remembering his conversation with the Professor, Paul ordered a martini "... for our very good friend from the German Republic."

Reinhold Reichman beamed. It was very nice to be accepted by the United Stateser, especially since he was of German background. The vague suspicion that Paul could be a secret agent evaporated. Luis reached for the Dutch Ginebre. This time he added a healthy portion of olive juice to the mixture and handed it to the German.

Reichman lifted his glass and turned to his companions. He clicked his heels, popped his head and toasted: "To the friendship between our two Nordic countries. Heil Hitler," and he drank. He froze for a second and his eyes widened. Rather than run the risk of insulting his new friends, he looked at Luis and said in strangled tones: "Sehr Gut."

Luis had mixed feelings. He finally found a man who liked his martinis, but he, unfortunately, was one of those stiff kind of Germans.

Reichman was obliged to finish the drink – but not all at one time. Immediately after the glass was empty, the German excused himself, thus destroying a sweetly smiling Mary Louise's plan to provide him with another of Luis' vile concoctions.

As Reichman left the Saloon, hurrying to his cabin for mouthwash and a Bromo Seltzer, he left four passengers with the broadest of grins on their faces. "Paul," said Mary Louise, "Now I'm positive you will go to heaven." The Professor chimed in with: "Well done, my boy. Did you watch his eyes when he took that first drink? I'll bet there was at least half an inch of white all around his irises. That'll teach him to bore me with his Nazi cant."

Watching it all from behind the bar, at first Luis was disappointed.

He had again failed to mix an acceptable martini. He found solace in the thought that he wasn't particularly fond of Señor Reichman and it looked like Professor Magnussen and his wife no longer hated him.

It was an enjoyable interlude. After "good nights" all around, Paul and Ellie Sue walked on the deck and the Magnussens retired to their cabin. During that first aboard-ship dinner and during the episode in the Saloon, Mary Louise watched Ellie Sue and Paul. Their exchanged smiles and sideways glances did not escape her. She was sure she was witnessing the beginnings of a shipboard romance.

Later in the evening, she suggested that thesis to the Professor who was ineffectually trying to read under the dim light that fought its way down from the weak bulb at the cabin ceiling to the compartment table. His response was: "Nonsense. If Herbert Hoover and Eleanor Roosevelt were aboard, you'd suspect them of a romantic liaison."

* * * * *

The sun was low in the western sky as the Arbutus sailed out of the muddy waters beyond the mouth of the Mississippi and into the deep blue of the Gulf of Mexico. Ellie Sue and Paul were alone, relaxing in the deck chairs on the fantail. They were there in time to see the sun set and the stars appear in the cloudless night. Paul held Ellie Sue's hand. He did not talk. Ellie Sue broke the silence.

"Is anything wrong, honey?"

"No. No. Everything is fine El, very, very (pause) fine." He looked at her and added: "It's been a marvelous day."

"It certainly has, honey, but something is bothering you. Now you just tell Ellie Sue what it is."

"All right," he said. "It's Clevis Dewlap. You've seen him. He's taken the lower bunk in our cabin and I can't sleep in an upper. He's put his clothing in the three upper drawers of the dresser. Now, that's not very important. I'm six feet three inches tall and I suppose its good exercise bending down to the floor, but I really don't like bottom drawers.

"More important, El, he's brought a goodly supply of home-made whiskey with him and I suspect there won't be any left by the time we get to Aguas Buenas. There are three empty pails set on the floor next to the pillow end of his bunk. I believe I know why. He will use them.

"Finally, El, Clevis is probably a good guy, but he emits some powerful odors. They don't come exclusively from his lungs and pores. That's as delicately as I can put it. The smell in our cabin is enough to make the angels weep and I have to spend four nights in there with him. El, I'd much rather spend them in this deck chair." Then he looked at her and said: "Especially if you were here." He squeezed her hand.

Ellie Sue looked at him. She speculated for a moment and made up her mind. "We can't have him ruining your cruise. I know just what to do about it." She arose, took his arm and said: "You come with me, Paul, honey." She led him to Cabin 9, A Deck, Port.

* * * * *

Inside Cabin 7, Mary Louise prepared to walk the deck for some night air. She opened the door to the Magnussen compartment in time to see Paul disappearing into Ellie Sue's cabin. Mary Louise grinned and quietly shut the door. She returned to the small table smiling an I-know-something-you-don't-know smile at her husband who sat across from her, still trying to read in the dim light.

When she didn't speak, he looked at her and said, "All right. What's up? You look like the cat that swallowed the canary. I expect you'll start purring in a moment."

"It's nothing, dear," she purred. "I was thinking about this afternoon and those two nice young people. Oh, I'm sure you're right." Professor Magnussen closed his book. This was an out of character comment from Mary Louise.

"I mean - the two of them," she continued. "The same chance as Herbert Hoover and Eleanor Roosevelt getting together. That's what you said. You're so astute, Charles. So much smarter than I am."

The Professor returned to his book. He couldn't concentrate on reading. Mary Louise's manner showed something was afoot. He thought: Could those two be shacking up? But how could Mary Louise know?

* * * * *

Inside Ellie Sue's cabin, she and Paul sat at the small table. "I believe I know you well enough, and I trust you," she said to him. "I'll shut my eyes while you undress and get into bed. Take the lower bunk. I like to sleep in an upper," she lied. "Then you shut your eyes and I'll put on my pajamas and get up there." And so it came to pass.

Ellie Sue peeked.

So did Paul.

Once in the bunks, they talked for a while and then the movements of the ship gently rocked them to sleep. It was peaceful. The only sounds came from the engines of the Arbutus, humming steadily on the darkened ship which, now well into a calm Gulf of Mexico, continued to gently roll from side to side.

It was well after midnight. The sounds of the Druckreys coming through the walls of the adjoining Cabin woke them. For a time they both lay still, silently imagining what was occurring on the other side of the bulkhead. Ellie Sue broke the silence.

"Are you awake, Paul, honey?"

"Yes, Ellie Sue. I suspect everybody aboard ship is awake. No one can sleep through that racket." They listened to the moans and ascending groans.

"I'll bet they're newlyweds, honey," Ellie Sue whispered.

"I'll bet you're right and I won't complain a bit, El. Those sounds are infinitely superior to the ones made by Mr. Dewlap."

"I kind of envy them, Paul, honey."

"I was just about to say the same, El."

They lapsed into silence and in a while the sounds from the next door cabin stopped, but neither Paul nor Ellie Sue slept. An hour later they were still awake and again Ellie Sue broke the silence.

"Can you help me down, honey?" she asked. The compartment was pitch black so Paul, naked, got to his feet.

Ellie Sue was sitting up with her legs over the side of the upper bunk. As Paul reached up to steady her, she edged forward and slid down Paul's body. Her arms were around his neck. She did not let go. His arms were around her body. He did not let go. He kissed her. They kissed again. Then they kissed again.

Early in the morning, Ellie Sue awoke to a kiss on the nape of her neck. On their sides, like two spoons, they shared the bottom bunk. She turned and answered the caress. An hour later, Paul dressed and went to the cabin he shared with a still soundly sleeping Clevis Dewlap.

When he returned with his luggage, Ellie Sue was dressed. Paul put his shaving gear, toothbrush and Ipana on the shelf above the sink in her bathroom. He opened his suitcase, took out his pajamas and opened the bottom drawer of the dresser. The bottom drawer now contained Ellie Sue's panties, brassieres and stockings. Ellie Sue was watching him. When he turned to look at her, she smiled. "I like the bottom drawers," she said, "but I like the bottom bunk only if you are there."

They walked to the Salon for breakfast.

Chapter 22

The Master Race and the Decadent Americans

Reinhold Reichman awoke at dawn. He shaved and dressed. After again placing a hair on the top of the door, he left his compartment and began an energetic walk around the deck. He met no one. The Dining Salon was empty. The deck chairs at the fantail swimming area were unoccupied. He returned to his cabin and donned a 1920's style two piece swimming suit.

Towel in hand, he walked to the fantail for an early morning dip. He stepped up the ladder and over the iron piping that supported the canvass lined pool and stood waist deep in water as warm as the Gulf air surrounding it. He lowered himself until his shoulders were covered and then stretched out his legs and floated on his back.

As he floated, he idly wondered if the water in the pool had been changed. It was still early. The sun had only recently risen over the horizon. The water was probably the same water that was there yesterday. His eyes widened as he wondered if any of the dark skinned deck hands might have bathed there during the night.

Reichman quickly left the pool and vigorously dried himself making sure none of the offensive water remained on his body. Then he sat in a deck chair, trying to relax. It was no use. The thought that he might have shared swimming pool water with a dark skinned man was too disturbing.

Reichman returned to his cabin and forget to check the hair to see if someone may have entered in his absence. He striped and again carefully toweled, making sure his body was completely dry before changing his clothing. He decided he would sun himself on the fantail, but never use the pool again.

* * * * *

In the meantime, a breakfast buffet had been prepared in the Dining Salon of the Arbutus. A tray of rolls was surrounded by containers of preserves, a platter heaped with small squares of butter and baskets of unpeeled bananas and other stranger looking fruits. A coffee urn stood over a burning container of canned heat. Cups and saucers, sugar and cream and a variety of juices were placed on the table beside it.

Osvaldo Carrera, sat behind the buffet. Ellie Sue and Paul were his first customers. When they entered the room, Carrera rose. "Please enjoy juice and coffee," he said, inviting them to the buffet. "The fruits are all very fresh. Will you have pancakes? Or eggs? Bacon or ham? Or sausage? Or, perhaps a cereal? Wheaties? Cream of Wheat?"

Ellie Sue was satisfied with coffee and juice. At the cook's suggestion, they both took a yellow/orange colored, roundish, husked fruit which, they were told, was a granadilla. Carrera disappeared into the galley to prepare Paul's ham and eggs and the couple sat at the same table they occupied the night before.

Paul didn't know what to say. He couldn't act as if the events of the last twelve hours hadn't happened, but he was afraid of making a comment that Ellie Sue might consider insensitive. Ellie Sue put him at ease. She touched his hand, smiled at him and said: "Thank you." Paul smiled and answered: "Thank you." He emphasized the second word.

They were on their second cup of coffee when Carrera brought the ham and eggs. Before Paul finished their meal, Reinhold Reichman came for breakfast. He wore a yachting cap, a v-necked sweater and knee length shorts. He looked very much like a European, trying to look very much like an American vacationer. When he saw Paul and Ellie Sue, he came directly to their table. "Good morning, Miss Bradshaw," he said to Ellie Sue and, as he sat, "Guten Morgen, Herr Eckert," to Paul.

When his motioned invitation to come to the buffet was disregarded, Osvaldo Carrera came to the table and took Reichman's breakfast order. "You will bring me orange juice, bread, pancakes, sausages and black coffee with sugar." Then he dismissed the cook with a wave of his hand. Carrera stiffened. A man's dignity was threatened when strangers gave him brusque and imperious orders. Courtesy, common among Latinos, should be extended to everyone, regardless of their apparent social position.

Carrera returned to the table with the buffet items ordered by Reichman. He brought no preserves or butter because they had not been ordered. He quickly returned to the galley before Reichman could correct his oversight.

Reichman directed his conversation to Paul. "You arise early, Herr Eckert," he said. "It is good. Everyone should arise early. As you Americans say: "Early to arise and early to bed.""

Paul finished his own version of the adage, saying to himself: makes a man healthy, wealthy - and dead.

"I arise early. I exercise every morning. I like to walk before taking breakfast. I walked around the ship this morning, but did not see you. Perhaps you arise before me, no?" Reichman continued. He sipped the coffee and, watching Paul's eyes, he asked, this time more slowly: "Perhaps you saw Mr. Druckrey or Miss Nelson this morning?" This time he waited for an answer. He saw no flicker of recognition when he mentioned the names and accepted Paul's answer denying any knowledge of them.

Carrera returned and served Reichman's pancakes and sausages. When the German asked him if Mr. Druckrey or Miss Nelson had come for breakfast, Carrera gave a short negative response and retired to his post behind the buffet table. Ellie Sue caught Paul's eye and gave an almost imperceptible nod toward the Salon doorway. Paul needed no other nudge. He pushed back from the table, leaving an unfinished meal behind, patted his lips with the napkin and said to the German: "It's been delightful sharing breakfast with you, but we must leave now. Auf wiedersehen," and he and Ellie Sue made their escape.

Auf wiedersehen, guten morgen, gesundheit and a few other phrases were the extent of Paul's German vocabulary. He learned the words from a Milwaukee roommate at the University of Wisconsin. They were enough to brighten Reinhold Reichman's morning. Here, he thought, was a 'landsman' - a Midwesterner of German heritage who, obviously, was favorably disposed towards him. The political scientist with the diabetic wife and the peculiar passenger who smelled so strongly of schnapps posed no danger to him. Druckrey and Nelson were a different matter. He suspected they were American secret agents.

In the companionway, Ellie Sue looked puzzled. "Paul, honey. Didn't that seem odd to you?" she questioned.

"What do you mean, El?"

"I mean that Mr. Reichman. He seemed terribly interested in Mr. Druckrey and Miss Nelson. I wonder why? And I wonder who they are."

* * * * *

Mary Louise and Professor Charles Magnussen were not early risers. They left their cabin for their first aboard-ship breakfast just as Ellie Sue and Paul, returned from their Reichman - abbreviated meal, and entered Ellie Sue's compartment at the far end of the passageway. Mary Louise nudged her husband, raised an eyebrow and purred: It looks like Herbert Hoover and Eleanor Roosevelt may have found (she paused for special emphasis) something in common."

"Nonsense," was his response. "You shouldn't leap to romantic conclusions on the basis of such fragmentary evidence. They probably had breakfast together and she's invited him to her cabin for some perfectly innocent reason."

"Perhaps to see her etchings?" answered Mary Louise, again looking like the cat that swallowed the canary. Magnussen turned to lock his compartment door when Luis Gogeasgoechea entered the passageway from the weather deck. He carried a tray of food, covered with a napkin.

"Good morning Señora. Good morning Sr. Professor." He stopped and backed up against the corridor's bulkhead. Mary Louise declined the implied invitation to pass before him. She was curious about the tray of food. Luis asked: "con permiso" and walked past them to the doorway of the Druckrey cabin.

The Magnussens watched as he knocked on the door. It opened far enough to allow a woman's hands to appear and disappear with the tray. Seconds later, the hand returned and gave Luis a dollar. A woman's voice said: "Thank you," and the door quickly closed. Luis, with a smile and another "con permiso," re-passed the Magnussens and walked out onto the weather deck.

"It might be sea sickness", Mary Louise declared. "Didn't you hear him last night? His distress kept me awake."

"No, Mary Louise, I didn't hear him last night," lied Professor Magnussen. "I enjoyed the deep and peaceful sleep that comes to those very few of us who have a clear conscience." He smiled and Mary Louise scowled. Then the doorway to Cabin 9 opened. Paul and Ellie Sue, dressed in their swimming suits, came into the passageway.

When two people of opposing sexes change their clothes in a very small room at the same time, it is exceedingly difficult to presume anything except an intimate relationship. As they walked down the corridor and on toward the fantail and their deck chairs at the ship's pool, the Magnussens greeted them.

Paul looked quizzically at El. "Did she say 'Good Morning, Eleanor' to you?" he asked. "Did she say 'Good morning, Herbert' to you?" Ellie Sue countered.

* * * * *

As they ate their breakfast, Mary Louise was mildly uncomfortable. Whenever her curiosity was unsatisfied, she became mildly uncomfortable. If her curiosity remained unsatisfied, she became fidgety. This morning she was particularly fidgety. Her curiosity about the couple in Cabin 8 had reached elephantine proportions.

"Charles," she said with a rising inflection, demanding his attention, "What do you know about the people in the compartment next to us?"

"Only that they pay attention to their own business, my dear," he answered, noticing and enjoying her fidgeting.

* * * * *

Charlotte Nelson and Harvey Druckrey were married in La Grange,

Illinois. That evening, the marriage was consummated a number of times in Chicago's Drake Hotel. The following morning, the Druckreys entered a compartment on the City of New Orleans and re-consummated their marriage in each of the states between Illinois and Louisiana.

On the day they boarded the Arbutus and found their way to Cabin 8, A Deck, Port, the door to the Magnussen Cabin was open. Mary Louise stood inside, considering which luggage would have to be available in the Cabin and which could be stored in the inaccessible hold. She saw the Druckreys go down the corridor and heard them enter the adjoining compartment.

She knew they were there, but, later, when she knocked at their door to welcome them and introduce herself, they did not answer. She heard what she thought were sounds of distress. This made her curious. Her curiosity did not surprise the Professor. He knew it took very little to make Mary Louise curious.

The first night at sea, through the thin walls separating their cabins, she heard faint moaning suggestive of pain and agony. At first, Mary Louise was convinced Mr. Druckrey suffered from acute sea sickness. Sea sickness was only a possibility and certainly not enough of an answer to satisfy a woman with an active imagination.

Mary Louise developed the theory that Mr. Druckrey's indisposition was not mere mal de mer, but evidence of a more seriously debilitating illness. After due consideration, she selected tuberculosis or cancer as appropriate diseases.

Professor Magnussen, on the other hand, developed the theory that it was none of her business and their two neighbors should be left to their own devices. He flatly refused to interfere and advised Mary Louise to adopt the same posture. Of course, this did not satisfy her. She wouldn't follow the Professor's advice in any event.

Mary Louise asked the Professor to knock on the adjacent cabin door and introduce himself as Doctor Magnussen. Perhaps they would think he was a medical doctor and invite him in. Then he'd find out just what troubled them. The Professor disregarded her request and refused to interfere.

Chapter 23

Curiosity
Stavros Stavropopolous
Intrigue

To Mary Louise's disappointment, their next door passengers did not appear for luncheon. With her curiosity unsatisfied, in desperation, Mary Louise decided to seek out the ship's Medical Officer. She meant to report the serious physical condition of their traveling companion. She meant to prod the Medical Officer into examining him, naturally, reporting all his finding to her.

Mary Louise's ability to speak Spanish (or Lebanese or Swahili, for that matter) was limited to the point of being non-existent. After unproductive attempts to discover the location of the medico via conversation with crew members, she decided to go straight to the top. She convinced herself a visit to the Captain was in order.

* * * * *

The Captain of the Arbutus was sometimes called Stavros Streptococcus. Actually, his name was Stavros Stavropopolous, but that name was too hard for the Central American Fruit Company's New Orleans accountants to handle. Everyone called him Captain Streptococcus and let it go at that. Sometimes his salary checks were drawn in that name. He didn't mind.

Captain Stavros Stavropopolous was firmly convinced all ills of humanity were caused by there being too damned many people in the world. He was acutely uncomfortable in the presence of others and enjoyed being Captain of a ship where his orders were law and no back talk was suffered.

If he was on the Gulf of Mexico, surrounded by water and far from the madding crowd - and if the ship's supply of Ouzo was sufficient - and if the crew was able to perform its functions with even marginal efficiency - and if there was no overt mutiny - and if the goddamned passengers would stay out of his way, then, as far as Captain Stavros Stavropopolous was concerned, the universe was in good order.

His bridge, therefore, was strictly out of bounds to all passengers. Signs in English, Spanish, Lebanese and Swahili made the ban very clear. Mary Louise, however, was never stopped by a sign she didn't like. She read the admonition, momentarily considered it, then disregarded it and proceeded up the ladder toward the bridge.

As she approached the Captain's territory, a Honduran crewman, half her size, tried to explain the prohibition. "You no go Capitán. You no go Capitán." Mary Louise simply glowered at him.

If the unfortunate man didn't stop her advance to the bridge, the crewman would incur the terrible ire of a terrible, Ouzo reeking Greek Captain. One glance at the determined set of Mary Louise's jaw convinced the man it was safer to scurry down the ladder. He would plead ignorance of her approach when later called to task.

Mary Louise met her match in Captain Stavropopolous. She entered the bridge and approached him intending to politely inquire of the whereabouts of the Medical Officer. Stavros saw her coming and adopted the same technique that served him so well on the few other occasions when passengers had the temerity to invade his sanctum sanctorum.

He screamed Greek imprecations at her, pointed to the door and yelled "OUT." This was repeated three times as, stern visaged, he advanced upon her. By the time of the third "OUT," to Stavros' comfort, she had retreated from the bridge and was halfway down the ladder to the weather deck. She didn't stop until she reached the Saloon where, to settle her nerves, she inadvertently ordered a martini from Luis.

When she calmed down a bit, she recognized the mistake. It was too late. Back turned towards her, Luis was already reaching for the bottle of Dutch ginebre. This time, he thought, I'll add sweet vermouth. Maybe that will help.

Mary Louise was too polite to simply spill the frightful mixture on the floor. Besides, Luis looked so hopeful as he watched for any sign of approval of his martini, she didn't have the heart to disappoint him. Knowing her tongue, throat and windpipe would all strenuously object to Luis' potion, she forced herself to take a tiny sip and then affected a thin smile and nodded toward him.

The tiny sip of the martini had the affect of recalling her original purpose - to find the Medical Officer. "Luis," she asked, "Where is the doctor?"

"Doctor? Doctor?" repeated Luis as his face fell. He had heard that question before - almost always directly after a passenger had tasted one of his martinis.

"Oh, I don't mean for me, Luis," Mary Louise hastily explained. "Your martini is really quite (pause) good," she said, knowing God would forgive her bald faced lying. "It's for one of the passengers, the one who is in the cabin next to us. I fear he needs medical attention. He moans and sounds so very ill."

"Oh, no Señora", said Luis. "He does not need the doctor. I have seen this thing many times before. He is not sick. He is, how you say, newlywed."

"Oh," said Mary Louise. "Newlyweds. Well - Yes - I see." In her confusion, without thinking, she took another sip of the martini.

* * * * *

After breakfast, Reinhold Reichman returned to his compartment. He looked for the hair he replaced on the top of his door when he left for breakfast. It was missing. Someone had entered his quarters. He unlocked the door and pulled his suitcases from beneath the bunk. The pistol was still inside the valise and the interior walls of the suitcase were untouched.

Everything appeared to be in order. They appeared to be in order, but only an amateur would break into a room and then leave evidence of the search. Reichman sat on the edge of the bed. He worried about Druckrey and Nelson. Could they have watched him leave for breakfast and picked the lock to the door when he was in the Salon?

Then he noticed the clean sheets. Someone had changed his

bedding. That would account for the missing hair on the top of the door. Still, he couldn't discount the possibility that his room had been searched. Reinhold Reichman had good reason for anxiety. A miscarriage of his mission would be a disaster - both for his country and for himself.

* * * * *

The German Ambassador to the Republic of Anchuria was in the twilight of his diplomatic career. In the 1920s, he served the Von Hindenburg government as its First Secretary in Sweden. In 1931, he was sent to Washington D. C. as First Secretary of one of his country's most important Embassies. With the German National Socialist party in ascendancy, the Reichstag fire and the subsequent "Enabling Act" which granted Adolf Hitler dictatorial powers, the nature of German diplomacy underwent drastic change.

The First Secretary was removed from the German Legation in Washington and sent into a form of exile. He was named the Third Reich's Ambassador to the small Central America Republic where he now served. However, in 1938, that insignificant diplomatic post assumed a front rank importance in German foreign affairs.

Anchuria's President Máximo Peña heard the rumblings of discontent in the church and among the army's junior officers. The threat of revolution was growing. Credible support from a strong foreign fascist government could help him destroy opposition and retain power. At his direction, his Minister of Foreign Affairs opened discussions with the German Ambassador and suggested a cultural interchange and a Friendship Treaty. What Peña wanted was a military alliance.

The Ambassador was not told that the Embassy clerk who encoded and decoded communications to and from Berlin was an Abwehr agent. That clerk's reports had already provided his Hamburg superiors with an accurate analysis of the problems of the Peña administration.

In Berlin, the growing dissatisfaction with Máximo Peña and his potential forcible removal from office were known. The Abwehr properly interpreted Peña's proposal for a Culture Treaty as an invitation to strengthen his regime with military assistance. It was the Third Reich's opportunity to get a foothold in the Americas.

But who would deal with Peña? The Ambassador was not a Nazi. The Reichswehr didn't trust him. Neither could the Abwehr's Embassy agent be used. His presence had to remain hidden from both the Ambassador and the Peña government.

In Hamburg, the Abwehr recommended their New York agent, Reinhold Reichman, be given the assignment. He had stolen the Americans' secret Norden Bombsight and his Nazi credentials were impeccable. He was selected to enter into preliminary secret negotiations directly with the President of Anchuria.

Hidden inside the lining of a suitcase he carried aboard the Arbutus, Reichman brought a sealed letter directed to President Peña and signed by Adolf Hitler himself. A second letter from Franz von Papen established Reichman's authority to represent the German Republic.

Reichman's instructions were clear. Germany would provide Peña with an air force, tanks and modern weapons. German advisers and technicians would be sent to train and, under Anchurian figureheads, direct the army. Germany would develop an Anchurian naval base at Villa Smit. Anchuria would become the strongest military force in Central America.

With a powerful army controlled by his fascist friends, there would be no danger of revolt against Peña and the Third Reich would have a secure base of operation in Latin America.

* * * * *

As he sat on his bunk, Reinhold Reichman wasn't thinking of world politics. He was thinking of Reinhold Reichman and his expectation of becoming the next German Ambassador to Anchuria. When Europe was unified and the slogan: "Today Germany, Tomorrow the World" became a reality, he might become the gaulieter of all of Central America. The treaty with Peña was the first step.

Reinhold Reichman was concerned. The knowledge of his presence and his purpose could result in intervention by the United

States. His expectations would de destroyed. Was his mission in danger of being discovered? Were American agents aboard the Arbutus? His fears and suspicions intensified.

Chapter 24

Morning Activities

Early in the morning, Luis and Osvaldo sat in the ship's galley, enjoying a cup of coffee. Osvaldo never disclosed his past to Luis. He trusted no one with information that could lead President Peña's police to him. Neither did he inquire into Luis' personal history. Perhaps it was this mutual lack of curiosity that made them such good friends.

They talked about the present and Luis was in no way reluctant to provide Osvaldo with all the gossip about the passengers and the crew of the Arbutus. As Purser, Social Director, Medical Officer and Bartender, he was an excellent source of information.

"He is from a place called Iowa and she comes from a place called Arkansas," he said to the cook, "They are sharing Number 9. the top bunk is never disturbed," he added with a grin.

"Is it their first trip to Anchuria?" Osvaldo asked.

"Yes, it is. There is only one visa in each of their passports. You should see the passports of Dr. Magnussen and his wife. They are filled with visas. They've been all over Central America. This is their third trip to Anchuria."

Carrera showed no interest in the Magnussens. "Tell me about the German," he asked.

"Ah, Señor Reichman," said Luis, throwing up both hands. "His visas are for Anchuria and the United States - no other places. Osvaldo, I do not like him. He is not simpatico." Luis slowly shook his head and added: "His cabin is very neat, Osvaldo. Very, very neat. His neatness is an obsession. His dresser is neatly filled with his clothing and when I go to change the sheets, the bunk is already made. Everything is orderly".

Luis paused for a moment, looking puzzled. "His suitcases seemed empty, but when I open them, I found a pistola, Osvaldo. It was loaded and had a funny thing on the end of the barrel."

Osvaldo showed no interest in the pistola. "Yes, Luis. These Aryan supermen are strange," he observed. They both laughed.

"The couple in Number 8 are not lovers," Luis volunteered. He seemed somewhat disappointed. "They are newlyweds and the señora has not yet changed her passport. It is still in her unmarried name." Then Luis smiled. "They spend most of their time in their cabin. Oh, Osvaldo, that reminds me. Do you have any canned oysters? They want oysters with every meal."

Osvaldo nodded and continued his questioning. "I must inquire about Señor Dewlap, Luis. Will he survive the trip to Villa Smit?"

"I believe so, Osvaldo. He remains ill, but not as ill as he was during his other cruises. He brought me a present. It is a jar of what he calls "moon shine." It is an alcohol, Osvaldo and it is clear - just like gin. I think I will use it if anyone asks for a martini."

* * * * *

Luis helped Osvaldo set the breakfast buffet with bananas, curuba, guama, tipaya and mango which, together with the juices, Americano coffee, breads, eggs (scrambled, fried or boiled), rice, red beans, ham, bacon and sausages that would be offered to the passengers as breakfast fare.

Paul Eckert and Ellie Sue Bradshaw were again the first to enter the Salon. Of all the fruits laid out on the buffet, they recognized only the bananas and the granadilla. "I loved the granadilla you suggested yesterday, Osvaldo," said Ellie Sue. "What should we have this morning?"

Neither had ever tasted guama, so they tried them. Carrera appreciated it. These two liked to experiment and that was good. Many turistas would eat nothing they didn't recognize. If they eat only what they can get in New York, he thought, then they should stay in New York.

Reinhold Reichman finished his morning calisthenics and his constitutional march - three times around the deck - before coming to the Salon for breakfast. As he made his selections from the buffet, he nodded to Osvaldo and said: "Good morning, my good friend." It was a perfunctory salutation. He did not smile at the cook and only glanced at him. From behind the table, Osvaldo answered "Good morning, sir." He emphasized the word 'sir'. It was his way to show his recognition of the German's false cordiality.

"What is this?" Reichman demanded as he pointed to one of the fruits, about the size of a flattish potato, but yellow and split in half. "It is called a tipaya, sir," Osvaldo answered. "It is a very fine fruit, sir, and it is very good for the digestion, but one should be careful not to eat too much tipaya, sir. Too much can cause a stomach pain."

Osvaldo had already explained to Ellie Sue and Paul that the tipaya, like the granadilla, was eaten seeds and all. He hoped the German would take the tipaya. He didn't intend to tell him about eating the tipaya seeds. He wasn't interested in being helpful to him. He would enjoy watching him trying to remove the seeds. Reichman, however, did not cooperate. He rejected the tipaya and took a banana instead.

* * * * *

As he served the passengers' meals during the previous two evenings, Osvaldo overheard Reichman's super nationalistic lectures to Clevis Dewlap. Only the Nazis, Reichman claimed, could save the world from the spreading cancer of Communism. Like many Latinos, Osvaldo Carrera's own Catholic Church inspired distaste of the atheism of Communism was not strong enough to overcome his more potent distaste for the totalitarianism represented by Anchuria President Máximo Peña or by the Third Reich. He had no affection for communists or for fascists.

Reinhold Reichman finished his order (pancakes and sausages, again). He picked up his nearly empty cup and went to the buffet. He poured a second cup of coffee, added two spoonfuls of sugar, turned and started toward the table occupied by Ellie Sue and Paul. They saw him coming. Both arose and headed for the weather deck.

They looked forward to a stroll in the fresh Gulf air and a relaxing time in the deck chairs on the fantail. Later they'd take beef broth in the Salon and then, as was now their custom, a pre-luncheon intimate interlude in the privacy of their compartment. A discussion of European geopolitics was at the very bottom of their list of priorities.

The Magnussens, already seated, watched their young friends make their escape from the Salon. They smiled at each other. The smiles disappeared when Reichman changed course and came to their table. "You are enjoying a marvelous morning," he announced as he sat down. The Magnussens weren't sure if it was a statement or a question. Mary Louise had to bite her lip to keep from saying: "Up until now."

The Druckreys did not come to the Salon for breakfast. Luis entered the Salon and whispered into Osvaldo's ear. He retired into the galley and soon returned with a tray. It held coffee, juice, toast, a dozen soft boiled eggs and the contents of a can of oysters. Luis delivered it to Cabin 8.

Clevis Dewlap also remained in his cabin. He scratched himself. He felt his face and wondered if he should shave. Not feeling very steady, he decided against it. Instead, he unscrewed the lid from another Mason jar and prepared to face his second day on the Gulf of Mexico.

* * * * *

It was nearly impossible to read by the light from the single bulb hanging from the ceilings of the Arbutus' cabins. The lighting in the Dining Salon was more than adequate. It was Professor Magnussen's practice to abandon his cabin in mid-morning in favor of the then empty Salon. He would chat with Osvaldo as he removed the buffet and took the breakfast dishes into the galley for washing. The Salon was then both comfortable and peaceful. Mary Louise was not aware of his sanctuary and he could read without interruption.

When Luis came to prepare the Salon for the passengers' morning refreshment, the Professor would retreat to his cabin. He'd return with Mary Louise to socialize with the other passengers who came to enjoy the mid-morning refreshment. At precisely eleven o'clock in the morning, Reinhold Reichman entered the Salon for beef broth. He did not find beef broth. He found Professor Magnussen reading at a table.

"Good morning, Herr Professor."

"Good Morning, Herr Reichman. Are you enjoying the cruise?"

"The literature clearly states beef broth will be served to the passengers in the Salon at eleven in the morning and at three in the afternoon. Is that not so?"

"Why, yes, Herr Reichman. I believe it does say that."

"It is eleven o/clock and there is no broth. On the German Lloyd's liners, at eleven o'clock there is broth. There is food too. The German liners offer hors d'ouevres, as well as broth at eleven o'clock."

"The German Lloyd's liners are luxury liners, Herr Reichman. This ship..." The Professor had no chance to finish his mild defense of Osvaldo and Luis.

Reichman interrupted him. "It is inexcusable, Herr Professor. I will speak to the Purser about this," and he left the Salon.

Reinhold Reichman did not find Luis. Instead, he found Mary Louise who was looking for her husband. Reichman believed a man, improving his mind by reading, should not be disturbed, particularly by his wife. However, for some reason he could not define, he was not well disposed toward Professor Magnussen. He told Mary Louise her husband was in the Salon.

Then Reichman began his bitter and abusive litany of complaints. The cabins, the lack of proper security and the shipboard services all received his attentions. The main focus of his diatribe was the lack of organization evident from the fact there was no beef broth in the Salon at eleven o'clock. He asked if Mary Louise had seen the Purser.

Mary Louise seized the opportunity. Carpe Diem, she thought to herself. "Mister Reichman, I am aghast by the apparent lack of organization and by the improper treatment you have received. I am only a woman," she said as she watched Reichman's head nodding in agreement, "and can do nothing about it. If I could make a suggestion, it would be to waste no time with the Purser. You should go directly to the Captain."

When he agreed, she directed him to the ladder leading to the bridge on the upper deck. She told him to pay no attention to the sign.

* * * * *

Mary Louise found Professor Magnussen in the Salon. He was with Osvaldo Carrera. They stopped their conversation as soon as they saw her. Carrera hurried into the galley and soon returned with two platters. One held pieces of dark rye bread. The other contained a scoop of raw chopped meat and slices of onion. Professor Magnussen nodded approval.

"There," he said to Osvaldo Carrera, "that ought to put you in good standing with Herr Reichman. In Ohio we call that a cannibal sandwich. It's very popular with our Germans."

Later, Reinhold Reichman returned to the Salon. After his visit to the Arbutus bridge, he looked shaken and somewhat subdued. Mary Louise smiled sweetly. The smile was not returned and Reichman made no reference to his encounter with Captain Stavros Stavropopolous. With rare silence, he enjoyed a cup of broth and a cannibal sandwich. He left the Salon without engaging anyone in political or any other kind of discussion.

* * * * *

After Clevis Dewlap began his day by administering a dose of anti-sea sickness remedy, he went back to sleep. In mid-morning he again awoke and, this time, got out of his bunk. He shook his head, looked around and didn't find his cabin mate. It must have been breakfast time, he thought, or, maybe, time for the noon meal.

His theory of using moonshine as a sea sickness preventative seemed to be working. For a day and a half, homemade alcohol produced a pleasant insensitivity to the pitch and roll of the Arbutus. True, it had been replaced with, at times, acute beverage poisoning, but Clevis was more than pleased with the trade off.

It was not an easy decision to leave the security afforded by the cabin with its bunk, supply of Mason jars and convenient buckets, but Clevis was ready to face the terrors of a walk on the weather deck. He dressed and, taking one more swallow from the Mason jar to prepare him for the ordeal, he left the cabin.

As he walked about the deck, Clevis was drawn to the sign that said: Salon. He thought it said: Saloon. Remembering he had given Luis a jar of his own product, it occurred to him the ship's store of liquor might include some Anchurian sugar cane based alcohol. He had developed a taste for it.

Once inside the room, Clevis recognized his error, but didn't retreat. It was easier to get something to eat than to explain the mistake. He took a cup of the soup that was thin and watery and salty and had no meat or vegetables in it. He would have sat at the same table with his cabin mate, but the young man was with a lady and Clevis was too polite to intrude.

He sat alone and merely gave them a friendly wave of the hand. Both Eckert and the lady smiled and returned his gesture. As he finished the broth, he looked out the Salon doorway and caught a glimpse of the ship's rail. It gently moved up and down as the Arbutus steamed over the waves of the Gulf of Mexico and toward its first port of call. That movement was enough for Clevis. He quickly returned to Cabin 10.

* * * * *

Later in the afternoon Paul and Ellie Sue left their quarters dressed in swimming suits and carrying towels and sun lotion. As they went through the passageway toward the weather deck, Ellie Sue grinned and then motioned Paul to her side. For a second they listened at the door to the Druckrey's compartment. Then they continued on their way to the fantail.

At the pool, they found Reinhold Reichman, stretched out in the afternoon sun. He wore his swimming costume, but had no towel. He did not intend to enter the water. As Paul and Ellie Sue approached him, the German arose from his deck chair. He was bare footed and did not click his heels. He popped his head and said: "Good afternoon, Fräulein Bradshaw. Good afternoon, Herr Eckert. Please join me?" Paul felt Ellie Sue's subtle reaction, but answered: "Of course," there being no other alternative he could think of.

At last Reichman would have an opportunity to speak privately with Paul Eckert. Now he could confirm Eckert's pro-German feelings and begin the process which, he believed, would lead to Paul's active support of the Third Reich. "May I call you Paul?" Reichman pronounced it 'Pawell'. "And may I call you Ellie Sue?" It came out 'Ailly Zoo'. "Please call me Reinhold." 'RRRINE holt'.

Reichman informed them he represented a Hamburg manufacturer and volunteered that the purpose of his visit to Anchuria was to find local commercial agents to sell German bicycles in that Republic. He mentioned they were very good machines and then abruptly questioned Paul: "The purges by the Russian Communists, they are terrible, no?"

When Paul answered: "They are disgraceful," Reichman moved directly into the discussion that would allow him to judge the extent and depth of Paul's support for Nazi principles. Or, at least, he tried to do so. Reichman would open a subject and Ellie Sue would close it. Her game was to see how long she could keep him away from whatever he wanted to talk about. Paul was a willing co-conspirator.

Question by Reichman: "The Czechoslovakian State is pieced together from many historically unassociated ethnic fragments and has no basis for its existence, don't you think so?"

Response by Ellie Sue: "Last night Paul found a flying fish flopping around on the deck. Isn't that interesting? Have you ever seen a flying fish, Reinhold?"

Answer by Reichman: "I have seen a picture."

Comment by Paul: "It probably was attracted by the lights on the ship. Don't you think so, Reinhold?"

Response by Reichman: "In Berlin we read of the New York Jewish agitators stirring your blacks into revolt. Do you think the Americans will wait until it is too late to control such 'untermenschen'?"

Response by Ellie Sue: "Were you in the German navy, Reinhold? How did you get that tattoo on the inside of your arm?"

Comment by Paul: "Here comes Luis. I think he's bringing us some broth. Do you like beef broth, Reinhold?"

* * * * *

When Paul and Ellie Sue didn't appear in the Salon for the afternoon refreshment, Luis knew they would be at the pool side. He would bring the broth to them. He came up the ladder to the fantail in time to hear Ellie Sue's question and see Reichman move his hand over his arm to cover the tattoo. Luis didn't expect to find the German on the fantail. He'd brought only two cups of broth. He served the two passengers he liked most and ignored the other. Then without comment, he turned and left the pool area.

When Luis had gone, Reinhold Reichman took pains to explain the tattoo. In 1933, he said, the Geheime Staats Polizei was organized under Hermann Goering to combat Communist street gangs. Those Communist criminals, he explained, were attempting to create chaos and destroy the will of the German people. He joined Goering's police and, as was the custom, he received the tattoo that identified him as one of its members.

Reichman admitted he did not have the proper temperament to be a good policeman. He quit the organization on the very day he was promised employment by the Hamburg bicycle company. He asked Paul and Ellie Sue to keep the tattoo a secret, saying he was not proud of once being a policeman.

* * * * *

Reichman left the fantail and walked back to his compartment. There is no point in trying to hold a serious discussion with Eckert when that young woman is around. Reichman considered women to be nearly non-persons. Hitler, he thought, is right about women. Kirche, Kuchen und Kindern - Church, Kitchen and Children.

Back inside his cabin, Reichman sat on his bunk. His paranoia came to the fore. He had not been careful. The tattoo had been seen. Did they believe his explanation? Would they keep his secret? He knew the tattoo could be removed. It would leave a scar. Would he need permission? If he asked for permission, would the Abwehr suspect him of disloyalty? Should he do it? No. It was best to leave matters as they were and never be seen in public unless wearing a long sleeved shirt.

155

When Luis returned to the then empty Salon, he told Osvaldo Carrera about the German's tattoo. Within the hour, everyone aboard ship knew of it - with the possible exception of the Druckreys. Carrera was one of the few people aboard the Arbutus who knew the tattoo was that of a member of the Geheime Staats Polizei, the organization everyone knew as the Ge-St -Po.

Chapter 25

The Captain
The German Embassy
The Druckreys
Planning Murder

Captain Stavropopolous was not displeased. In two more days the Arbutus would be safely moored at the Central American Fruit Company dock in Aguas Buenas. The unloading of the cargoes would be overseen by the First Mate. The unloading of the disembarking passengers would be managed by Luis Gogeasgoechea. He would also take care of the four passengers who would remain aboard ship. If any of them had a problem, it would become Luis' problem and not his.

As in the case of practically all of his landings at Aguas Buenas, Captain Stavropopolous had reason to believe nothing would happen to cause any anxiety or require him to deal with his crew, with any of the local personnel from the Central American Fruit Company or with any of the Anchurians. He disliked dealing with people, finding association with them to be only slightly preferable to being captured and tortured by the Apaches.

The Captain wiped his lips with the napkin from his breakfast tray, poured Ouzo into a water glass and took it with him to the bridge.

* * * * *

Ellie Sue and Paul were enjoying breakfast when the Magnussens came to their table, carrying the food they selected from the morning buffet. Mary Louise took juice, coffee and cereal. She would have preferred the ham and eggs her husband had ordered, but if she asked for them she would lose the opportunity to mention what she called Charles 'huge appetite' and to wonder (out loud) if he were gaining weight.

The ploy did not work. Before she could speak, the Professor explained to his table mates that his metabolism was such he easily maintained his weight at 195 pounds. He did not miss the chance to tell the young people that Mary Louise ate like a bird, but, nevertheless, was adding weight - "here and there" was the way he put it. The tables were neatly turned. Mary Louise was uncomfortable and did not enjoy her Wheaties.

Luis came into the Salon and whispered into Osvaldo's ear as he stood behind the buffet. The cook disappeared into the galley and, minutes later, re-appeared with a tray filled with dishes and glasses and covered with a large napkin. A note from Osvaldo lay under the napkin. It was addressed to the Druckreys and explained the ship's store of canned oysters was completely depleted. He promised an adequate supply would be re-stocked upon arrival in Aguas Buena.

* * * * *

In the German Embassy in Progreso, the Ambassador read his code clerk's request to be absent from his post for two days. When such requests came from his staff, it was his practice to approve them unless the work of the Legation required the man's presence. Since there was little work at the Legation requiring anyone's presence, approvals were only rarely withheld.

The Ambassador's world changed with the end of the disastrous 1914 war. He did not change with it. He remained true to his prewar principles. He was not in step with the philosophies of the 1938 rulers of Germany. He was not a Nazi and that fact was well known. That was the reason he had been reassigned to the diplomatic backwater of Anchuria, there to quietly awaited retirement.

The Ambassador felt uncomfortable with the clerk's request. There were few diplomatic surprises in Anchuria requiring immediate contact with Berlin. Diplomatic matters in Anchuria were so mundane that the Ambassador sometimes wrote his routine reports at least a week before they were due. They could be transmitted on Monday or Tuesday. Coding messages for transmittal to Berlin presented no problem. Decoding messages from Berlin was another matter.

Though it was impossible to predict when Berlin might send him a coded message, he had reason to believe he might receive one. There had been no answer to his communiqué reporting the overture made by Anchuria's Minister of Foreign Relations. His own suggestion for a cultural exchange had not been acknowledged. That communiqué was sent to Berlin over a month ago. An answer might come on Friday.

He again looked at the clerk's request. If he approved it, the man would be absent both Thursday and Friday. Then he would not know the contents of any message from Berlin until Monday. The Ambassador laid the request on his desk and looked out the window at the Central Highland landscape.

The code clerk had been in Anchuria for less than a year and was one of the new breed - an outspoken Nazi. The Ambassador harbored the suspicion that he was an Abwehr agent. To him, the use of his Embassy as a refuge for a spy was an anathema. He picked up the clerk's formal request. He had no reason to refuse to give the man a day off. With some reluctance, he approved and signed it.

* * * * *

As the Ambassador was signing the code clerk's request, aboard the Arbutus, Harvey and Charlotte Druckrey finished their afternoon meal. They agreed it was time they left the confines of their cabin and looked around the ship. Remembering the Arbutus had a swimming pool, they put on their suits and, hand in hand, walked to the fantail. They were disappointed to find two passengers already seated in deck chairs. They would not have the pool to themselves. Ellie Sue and Paul were equally disappointed to see their privacy invaded.

After brief introductions, the Druckreys entered the pool. They could not be seen by the occupants of the deck chairs, but Paul and Ellie Sue heard their murmured conversation and occasional exclamations of surprise, followed by quiet laughter. From inside the pool, Harvey and Charlotte could not see Paul or Ellie Sue, but they heard their murmured conversation and occasional exclamations of surprise, followed by quiet laughter.

The Druckerys emerged, set up their deck chairs and stretched out in the Gulf sun. Charlotte and Ellie Sue's sat next to each other. On either side of them, Paul and Harvey leaned back with eyes closed. The men were smiling, as if enjoying some private joke. Feeling more at ease, the women began to talk.

"Paul and I are in Cabin 9," said Ellie Sue. "I believe we're neighbors. You're in Cabin 8. Isn't that right?"

"Yes we are," Charlotte answered. Then she giggled. "We heard you," and after she saw Ellie Sue's knowing smile, she added: "too." The women exchanged the look the sisterhood uses to pass special information.

"Who's in Cabin 7?"

"That would be Professor Magnussen and his wife, Mary Louise. The Professor is a bit standoffish and his wife seems a little forward, but don't let them fool you. They're really very easy to get to know and they're both very nice. I'm sure you'd like them. Have you met Clevis Dewlap and Reinhold Reichman?" Ellie Sue rolled both rs in his name.

"Whoever are they?"

Ellie Sue began to describe them as Paul and Harvey entered the pool. "Clevis Dewlap...," she began.

* * * * *

Reinhold Reichman sat at the table in his cabin. He knew his compartment was being entered. Was it only by the one who changed his bedding? Was someone else watching him? He set traps. He placed a suitcase exactly seven inches from the leg of his bunk. Whenever he pulled it from beneath his bunk, he often forgot to measure to see if it had been moved. The second drawer of his dresser was left open by the width of a single dime. Whenever he opened the drawer, he'd forget to check the measurement. Occasionally, when he entered his cabin, he'd forget to see if the hair left atop the door had been disturbed.

What were Herr Druckrey and Fräulein Nelson doing in the corridor in front of his compartment? Their explanation of looking for a cabin on the other side of the ship was preposterous. The Purser must have explained the difference between port and starboard to them and, he was sure, accurately directed them to their quarters.

If they were counter intelligence agents, they could be English or Canadian, but probably American. They had no English accents and there was no reason Canadians should keep him under surveillance. Ever since he was questioned by the undercover agent who posed as a Customs official in New York, he felt he was being watched. Druckrey and Nelson, he concluded, were probably American agents masquerading as newlyweds.

Did they know his mission? Probably not. If they knew it, they would have killed him before he boarded the Arbutus. He pulled the suitcase from beneath his bunk. He carefully studied the lining. The letters hidden behind it could not be removed without leaving unmistakable evidence of tampering. There was none. Yes, he thought to himself, it is all very logical. They do not know my mission in Anchuria

He was sure they would follow him ashore at Aguas Buenas. They would follow him to the Embassy in Progreso. They would follow him to his meeting with President Peña. If they guessed his mission, the Americans would have time to react. They could overthrow the Peña government before German support could arrive to defend it.

He could kill them. He could kill them and throw their bodies overboard. If their bodies weren't found, there would be confusion and delay. By the time the Americans discovered what had happened, it would be too late to depose Peña.

The Arbutus would not dock for two more days. Druckrey and Nelson would be aboard the ship during the next two nights. There was time to kill them.

Perhaps a walk on deck would clear his head and help him make his plans. He put the suitcase back under his bunk, this time placing it eight inches from the leg. He left the cabin, placing a hair on top of the door before locking it. Then he walked down the passageway toward the fantail.

* * * * *

"It's almost time for morning broth, Charlotte," said Ellie Sue. "Do you and Harvey want to join us?"

Both answered "No" at the same time, and Harvey then added: "We'll stay here. You two go along."

"Want to be alone, eh," said Paul in as lewd and suggestive a manner as he could. Charlotte reached into the pool and splashed water at him. Ellie Sue took him by the arm and pulled him toward he ladder. They left for the Salon, leaving Harvey and Charlotte in the deck chairs behind the pool.

"They're OK," said Harvey and Charlotte agreed with him. "Just what did you learn about the other passengers? I heard you two ripping them apart. How many are there anyway?"

"Besides Ellie Sue and Paul there are only four - and we weren't ripping them apart, Harvey. Our neighbors are the Magnussens. The one who pounded on the wall last night was probably the wife, Mary Louise. The husband is a professor of something at some university somewhere. Ellie Sue says they're fun to be with."

"And the other others?" Harvey asked.

"Two men," Charlotte said. "One of them is from Mississippi and he has one of those peculiar southern names. Paul was supposed to share his cabin, but he moved in with Ellie Sue."

"A good move on his part, I would say," said Harvey.

"You don't know the half of it," said Charlotte. "This man - Clayborn or Clevon or some such name - brought a lot of moonshine with him. He spends most of his time in the cabin, drinking and throwing up."

"That leaves one more," said Harvey. I heard you two making a bunch of uncomplimentary sounds about somebody. It must have been him. 'Fess up now."

"All right," she said. "There's a German passenger. Ellie Sue doesn't like him. He clicks his heels and rolls his rs and bores everyone to death with his talk about Hitler and the new Germany and the Jews and the colored people. Ellie Sue says he sells bicycles for a German company. He is going to Anchuria to find agents and make contracts with them to represent the German concern."

"Well, Madame Private Eye," Harvey said, "You certainly have gotten a lot of information."

"You're an accomplished 'undercovers' agent, yourself, Harvey." They enjoyed the pun and laughed.

* * * * *

Reinhold Reichman didn't laugh. Half way up the ladder from midships to the fantail and unseen with the canvas pool between him and the Druckerys, he overheard the last part of their conversation. He silently backed down to the main deck and retreated to his cabin.

Now he had proof. His suspicions were confirmed. He heard the woman say: "He is going to Anchuria to find agents and make contracts with them to represent Germany's concerns." He heard the man call the woman a "Private Eye." That, he knew, was American slang for an Investigator. He heard her call him an "Undercover Agent." There no longer was room for doubt. Druckrey and Nelson were American Intelligence Agents.

He would have to kill them both. Now was a perfect time to do it. The other passengers would be in the Salon. He would shoot them and push their bodies over the side. Then he would join the others for afternoon broth. Reichman hurried to his compartment and retrieved his suitcase without bothering to measure its distance from the bunk leg. He opened it and took the Walther 9 mm pistol from the valise. The silencer was attached to its barrel. He slid the weapon under his belt and beneath his coat.

Reichman stepped out of his cabin and walked down the passageway to the weather deck. None of the crew and none of the passengers were in sight. He started to cross the weather deck to the ladder that led up to the fantail swimming pool and the Druckreys. Then he froze in his tracks.

An unsteady Clevis Dewlap came out of his cabin and yelled at him: "Haiy thar, Mistair Rockman. Mistair Rockman. Haiy Thar. Whar ya goin? They got that thin soup over thar in the sah lon." He paused between "sah" and "lon". "Lait's go get some."

Reichman glared at him. He turned toward Clevis and pulled his suit coat further over the Walther as Harvey and Charlotte, curious about Clevis' call, stuck their heads over the canvas pool and got their first glimpse of Clevis Dewlap.

Though Clevis had alerted them, Reichman was sure the American agents did not see him stalking them nor did they not see his pistol. It would be best if he left the impression he was simply taking a stroll. He walked to Clevis saying, loud enough for the American agents to hear and in his most amicable manner; "Yah, my good friend. We will go to the Salon."

Reichman's inner thoughts were not at all friendly. He was sorely tempted to add Clevis to the list of those he intended to execute. Once in the Salon, even the cook's specially prepared chopped raw steak and onion did nothing to improve his disposition.

Chapter 26

Frustration
Martinis

Reichman returned to the fantail later in the afternoon when the passengers were in their cabins, preparing for the evening meal. His quarry was no longer at the pool. Perhaps they would come to dinner. Reichman waited in the Salon until Luis left, carrying a tray of food for the Druckerys. How clever of them to stay out of sight, he thought.

After sun set, Reichman stood amid ships, partially hidden behind the cargo stored on the deck. He watched the passageway that led from Cabin 8 to the weather deck. The Druckreys didn't appear. It was after midnight when he crept into the port passageway and listened at the doorway of their cabin. He cautiously turned the door handle. It was locked. Finally, he returned to his own starboard compartment. Tomorrow, he thought. Tomorrow.

Reichman awoke early the next morning. It would be his last day at sea. In 24 hours, the S S Arbutus would dock at Aguas Buenas. After his morning calisthenics, he dressed and strolled around the weather deck until he saw Luis carrying the breakfast tray to Cabin Number 8. The American agents would remain hidden in their compartment, he thought, but I am patient. He went to the Salon for breakfast.

In mid-afternoon, Reichman stood in the shadows of the starboard passageway. He had waited there, watching, for more than an hour. Now he looked at his watch. It was after three-thirty. It was the time, he said to himself, when the Druckrey and Nelson might come to the fantail's canvas swimming tank. The other passengers would be in the Salon taking the broth. He hoped the drunken southerner would be asleep in his bunk.

Reichman's patience was rewarded. He saw the Druckreys walking down the port side of the ship toward the fantail. They carried towels and were dressed in swimming suits.

They would be alone and now he would kill them both. He would throw their bodies overboard. He would tell Luis they didn't want dinner or breakfast delivered to their quarters. Tomorrow morning he would disembark before their absence was discovered.

Reichman removed the Walther from beneath his coat. No one was watching as he pulled back the slide to move a shell into the firing chamber. He kept the weapon partially hidden next to his body as he cautiously moved across the mid-ships section of the Arbutus. When he got to the ladder leading to the raised fantail, he looked back and saw no one who could witness his acts of murder.

* * * * *

After he and Luis set the buffet table with the passengers' afternoon broth, Osvaldo Carrera returned to the galley and busied himself with the preparations for the evening meal. Osvaldo disliked peeling potatoes. It was his custom to do that job first. Then it was over and he needn't worry about it.

When the last pared potato joined the others in the kettle of cold water, Osvaldo picked up the pail containing the peelings and the other kitchen refuse that had accumulated since the noon meal. He headed for the 1938 version of a garbage disposal unit - the ship's rail on the leeward side of the vessel.

As Osvaldo prepared to dump the garbage over the side, he saw the Druckreys climb the ladder to the fantail swimming pool. Then he saw a movement on the weather deck. It was Reinhold Reichman. Osvaldo wondered why he behaved in such a furtive manner. He saw the German draw a pistol from his belt and approach the ladder. Carrera watched as Reichman aimed the pistol toward the backs of the heads that appeared and disappeared above the canvas top of the swimming pool.

Osvaldo didn't hesitate. He banged the garbage pail against the bulkhead, stepped out onto the open amid-ship deck and loudly sang the words to an Argentine tango: "Adios muchachos - compañeros - de mi vida..." Though apparently paying no attention , he moved to the windward side and watched Reichman from the corner of his eye.

When Reichman heard the pail hit the bulkhead and Osvaldo's singing, he stepped back down the ladder and ducked behind a crate of gasoline generators stored on the weather deck and destined for the Central American Fruit Company plantations. He replaced the pistol under his belt and hid on the outboard side of the crate as Carrera, singing noisily, crossed to the windward side of the ship and walked toward the German's hiding place, but gave no indication he was aware of his presence.

Carrera knew exactly where Reichman was concealed. Carefully estimating the direction and force of the wind, he dumped the garbage over the side. The wind picked it up and returned it to the ship - and to the place where Reinhold Reichman crouched. The ex-Storm Trooper was graphically reminded of the reason for the admonition: Never piss into the wind.

When the garbage hit him, Reinhold Reichman didn't hesitate. He jumped up, screaming in German at Carrera. The Druckrey heads appeared over the canvas swimming tank. They saw Carrera, apologizing in both English and Spanish to an apoplectic Reinhold Reichman who hurled German epithets at him. They saw Carrera begin to brush potato peelings from the irate Nazi. As he did so, Carrera pushed Reichman's coat to the side and exposed the butt end of the Walther sticking out from under his belt.

Reichman's screaming abruptly stopped. He jerked his coat over the pistol and, with as much dignity as he could assemble, walked back toward his cabin. Once more he had failed to eliminate the American agents. That stupid cook, he muttered to himself. He saw my pistol. If I shot the American agents, the cook would know I did it. No, I can't kill them now. I'll have to wait until they are ashore.

Alone in his cabin, Reichman worried. Twice the American agents had seen him amid ships. They must suspect he had identified them. They would be on their guard. It would be difficult to kill them before they followed him into Aguas Buenas. But, now aware of his own identity, once they were ashore it would be much easier for them to kill him. The possibilities of saving himself by becoming a double agent again occurred to him.

Osvaldo watched the German's retreating back. On his way back to the Galley, he smiled and waved at the Druckreys. They smiled, waved back and then their heads disappeared behind the canvas wall of the pool. Ever since the Gestapo tattoo was discovered, Osvaldo suspected Reichman was a Nazi agent. Why would he try to kill the newlyweds? Why was he going to Anchuria? To sell bicycles? Ridiculous. A vacation? Unlikely. No, Osvaldo guessed, Reichman had a more sinister purpose.

Carrera took eight steaks from the refrigerator. It would be the last time all eight passengers would share a shipboard meal. He hoped Clevis Dewlap would stay in his cabin. Then he would eat his steak for him. He rubbed salt and pepper into the steaks. He dropped them into a marinade and left them to absorb the flavors. Then he went to the Salon to clean up after the afternoon broth and prepare the room for the evening meal. The Salon was empty, save for Professor Magnussen. He was seated under one of the room's light fixtures, reading a book.

* * * * *

Later in the afternoon, Mary Louise came to the Salon. "Charles," she said, "I have a wonderful idea."

Without looking up from his book, Professor Magnussen answered: "In a minute dear. Just as soon as I finish this page."

"Oh, put that silly thing down, Charles. Listen to me."

"It's not a silly thing, dear. It's Ernest Hemingway's latest book, 'The Fifth Column'," he said. Without looking up, he re-read the same sentence for the third time.

Mary Louise was in one of her favorite elements. Her husband was trying to concentrate and she didn't mean to let him do it. "I was thinking about Herbert Hoover and Eleanor Roosevelt," she continued, paying no attention to the Professor's request for a few seconds of silence.

"All right. All right," he said, as he turned the corner of the page and set the book down. "What earth shattering matter involves Herbert Hoover and Eleanor Roosevelt?"

"They're such a nice couple and Ellie Sue is going all the way to Villa Smit and Paul is leaving the ship at Aguas Buenas and wouldn't it be nice if the four of us had a cocktail together tonight after dinner because tomorrow morning we'll all be busy, what with the hubbub of packing and Customs and all, and we could say a nice goodbye with time to tell them how much we enjoyed their company, because, certainly, that horrid Nazi and the drunken southerner are no fun and the Druckreys are so...," she paused a second before she said: "sick they seldom leave their cabin. Don't you think that's a nice idea, Charles?" she said without stopping to take a breath, nor even seeming to need to take one.

If Mary Louise expected cooperation from her husband, she should not have disturbed him and refused to allow him to finish the page he was reading. Vengeance is mine, thought the Professor. He picked up the book and straightened the corner on the page he had turned. He made believe he was reading and said: "I don't think so."

The Professor continued to pretend to be reading and not hearing Mary Louise as she continued to suggest a farewell party. For the rest of the afternoon, he had the satisfaction of frustrating her. Mary Louise would not give up. The Professor would listen while she pled her case and then he would refuse to agree, without giving any reason. It was a bad day for her.

Never underestimate the power of a woman.

* * * * *

The seating arrangements in the Arbutus Dining Salon were now well established. Clevis Dewlap and Reinhold Reichman, neither being able to understand the other, shared one table. The Magnussens, Ellie Sue and Paul were at another. The Druckreys took their meals in their quarters.

Clevis was unable to make any sense out of the foreigner's conversation. The accent was too much for him. He listened to Reichman. He nodded occasionally. A few times Clevis tried to explain the pleasure he found in turning hard wood logs into boards. His Nordic table mate couldn't fathom the Mississippi accent. He listened to Clevis. He nodded occasionally (and he wondered if Clevis had lynched any Negroes).

At the other table, conversation was more subdued. Mary Louise pouted. Ellie Sue was not her effervescent self and Paul, too, was quiet. Both knew they would part in the morning. "Mary Louise," said Ellie Sue to the still sulking wife of the Professor, "you seem quiet. Is there anything wrong? Do you feel ill?"

"No, dear, there's nothing wrong," she answered. Then a happy thought occurred to her and she said: "I feel wonderful. I'm going to miss you, Ellie Sue. I wish we could stay aboard with you," and she gave Paul a reproachful look. "Charles feels the same way. In fact, he wants to invite you and Paul for cocktails, just as soon as dinner is finished." She looked at her husband, smiled sweetly and added: "Isn't that right, Charles."

Knowing he had been trapped, Magnussen smiled and answered, as sweetly as he could: "Of course." Immediately thinking of revenge, he arose, went to the other table and invited Clevis Dewlap and Reinhold Reichman to the party. He planned to seat Mary Louise between the two of them. That would fix her.

Clevis pulled the napkin from where he had firmly tucked it beneath his chin. He stood up and (the Professor thought) said he'd be "rat pleased to jain yall fer a drank". Reichman got up, clicked, bobbed and said he would be honored, Herr Professor.

After dinner, Luis was in the ship's Saloon, preparing a bowl of heavily salted, thick, deep fried platano banana slices for his customers when the six passengers arrived. The Professor was successful in seating Mary Louise between Dewlap and Reichman.

The stiff German immediately asked for Scotch whisky and soda water, thus avoiding the risk of someone ordering a martini for him. Paul and Ellie Sue ordered gin and tonic. Luis smiled. He could mix gin and tonic. The Professor asked for a Cerveza Aleman. Luis was surprised to hear him ordered a martini for Mary Louise. Well, Luis thought, she knows what she's getting into. Clevis Dewlap admitted he had heard about martinis. Before anyone could warn him, he asked for one.

When the drinks arrived, Clevis took a martini, said: "Hare's too y'all," and downed it - all of it – all at once. Conversation stopped. Everyone looked at him. He waited a few seconds while the soft tissue of his mouth, throat and esophagus received the mixture. Clevis smiled and said it was a 'rat good drank'. They thought he was merely being polite but he ordered another.

After Paul and Ellie Sue had been served, Mary Louise quickly took the scotch and soda from Luis' tray and Reichman was left with the martini. He didn't want to offend his learned host by asking for a replacement. He felt he had to drink it - or, at least, sip at it. Maybe he could make it last all evening. Ellie Sue destroyed his plan.

She noticed Reichman's eyes involuntarily widen as he took his first sip of the Gogeasgoechea martini. Aha, she thought, I have him, and she proposed a toast to their hosts. Reichman had to drink. Mary Louise caught on and proposed a toast to the German Republic. Again, Reichman had to drink. The Professor ordered another round.

At every sip the German became increasingly pale. Whenever he showed any sign of wanting to leave the room, Ellie Sue or Mary Louise would propose a toast or engage him in political discussion. The Professor, after watching Clevis drink a third Gogeasgoechea martini with relish, toasted him. Then Clevis toasted the Confederacy.

Osvaldo Carrera entered the Saloon with a plate of hors d'oeuvres. He apologized to Reichman for the unfortunate incident of the early afternoon and, to make amends, brought him a separate plate that held a piece of rye bread heaped with raw, chopped meat and onion. Luis, pleased that Clevis actually liked his martinis, offered a round of drinks. Luis himself took rum and Coca Cola and mixed another for Osvaldo to take back to the galley.

Unbeknownst to Reichman, the ladies accepted only two drinks and Paul and the Professor each quietly disposed of three without drinking them. In the morning, the potted plant in the terra cotta vase next to their table was dead.

Clevis Dewlap stood up under the onslaught of four of Luis' martinis, but the ex-Storm Trooper did not. When Paul toasted the Rome-Berlin Axis, a wobbly Reinhold Reichman spilled his martini down his shirt front. He was so ashen he looked near death and they took pity on him. The party ended and Clevis helped Reichman to his cabin.

Chapter 27

Disembarkation

The Caribbean hurricane season begins in the late summer. Starting as tropical depressions off the coast of Africa, the storms gather power as they follow the Atlantic currents toward the New World. Some of them attain hurricane status. They tear through the Lesser Antilles and head straight for Anchuria's eastern port of Villa Smit.

Few hurricanes hit the Anchurian coast. Most of them turn north before landfall and, paying no attention to the orders of Llewellyn Black, follow the route of the Central American Fruit Company banana boats. They move up the Caribbean and the Gulf of Mexico and to the south coast of the United States.

Late summer is not the time for a banana boat cruise to Aguas Buenas. During early and midsummer, however, the voyage from New Orleans to Central America is a delight. The ship sails in a peaceful Gulf of Mexico, through a calm Yucatan Channel, past Isla Mujeres and into a serene western Caribbean.

Arriving at Aguas Buenas as the sun rises is an experience no one will forget. Watching from the deck of the Arbutus, the scene is impressive. The night darkness is complete except only for the stars and the ship's muted lights. Then, at the time described by Omar Khayyam as 'when dawn's left hand is in the sky', light begins to appears in the eastern sky and, on the western horizon, the rounded peaks of the Central Highlands can be recognized as slightly darker masses.

Then, at about sun rise, the dark colors of the coastal mountains begin to lighten and the indigos of the round topped hills change, first to very dark greens and then to lighter greens, as increasing light dissipates the blue hues. Finally, the yellow greens of the tropics are displayed by the growing sunlight.

At the shoreline the whitewashed Aduana Building and the Fruit Company warehouses are bright and showy. A thin golden line separates the various hues of green and the white buildings from the blue of the water of the Caribbean. It is the sand beach which graces the Aguas Buenas part of the Caribbean shore.

This is the shoreline that first attracted the 17th century Spanish explorers. After days of sailing past mangrove thickets, here they could land and look for provisions to refill depleted supplies. Not only was there an abundance of turtles and deer in the area, fresh water bubbled from many easily accessible artesian springs. The Spaniards marked the place on their charts as "Aguas Buenas" - Good Waters.

The navigator who drew the old chart was of an artistic nature. His outlines of the coast and the offshore islands were reasonably accurate. The unexplored interior of the country appeared as a large blank area on the map. He filled part of it with a directional design. One space remained open so, as an afterthought, he drew a line showing a river. It balanced the design and pleased his eye.

In those years, English pirates roamed the Caribbean in search of Spanish treasure galleons. They, too, visited the golden beach for rest and re-supply. This provoked the Spanish into establishing a garrison and the surrounding village became known as Aguas Buenas. The Comandante of the garrison reviewed the old charts with a local Chuchiba Indian cacique. He pointed to the old map maker's river and asked its name. The cacique answered: "Ramasajoti." Thereafter all maps showed the Rio Ramasajoti.

In the dialect spoken by the chief, the words "ra masa joti" meant: "No river there."

* * * * *

Approaching Aguas Buenas from the sea displays a pleasant scene of tranquility and indescribable beauty. A white ship sailing on a deep blue sea toward a golden beach lined with neat white buildings before a backdrop of multi-shaded greens, capped by the clear, lighter blue Caribbean sky and all seen through the orange booms of the Arbutus is, indeed, an unforgettable scene.

Charlotte and Harvey Druckrey were awake, but did not see it. They were engaged in the same activity which occupied most of their time aboard the ship.

Paul and Ellie Sue did not see it. They were not yet awake and shared the close quarters of the bottom bunk in Cabin 9 - she with her head on his chest and both comfortably asleep.

Professor Charles and Mary Louise Magnussen did not see it. The Professor was awake in the top bunk. Mary Louise was asleep in the lower. He would stay where he was until she was up and around. It was a peaceful time of day for him and he did not want to destroy it by waking her.

Clevis Dewlap didn't see it. He was enjoying his noisy inebriated sleep in Cabin 10. Reinhold Reichman did not see it. He lay in the lower bunk of Cabin 11, oblivious to what was going on around him.

The sun didn't seem to mind this lack of attention. It continued in its usual course. The ship's company of the Arbutus did the same. They docked the ship, lowered its gang plank and removed the weather deck covers from the holds. The orange booms began to lift machinery, imported goods and plantation supplies from the ship and lower them onto the dock from where they would go first to the Customs House and then on to their final destinations.

Osvaldo Carrera sat in his galley, preparing the fruit and food (and the bananas) to be served for the passengers' breakfasts. He paid no attention to the beauty of the scene. To him it was commonplace. He was accustomed to it. As George Bernard Shaw pointed out: In heaven, an angel is no one in particular.

Luis Gogeasgoechea did not see it. He had a lot on his mind. He lay in his hammock, thinking about carrying the luggage of the disembarking passengers to dockside and then to the Customs Building for review. He also thought about arranging a shopping trip for the ones who would remain aboard the Arbutus.

Four of the eight passengers would stay on the ship. One of them, Clevis Dewlap, would leave the ship when it reached Villa Smit. Sr. Dewlap wouldn't buy anything and that meant only the Druckreys and Ellie Sue Bradshaw would be available for a shopping tour. Well, it is better than nothing, thought Luis.

Later, after he had risen and taken breakfast, he visited the galley. Then he went to the door of Cabin 8, knocked and passed the tray of breakfast foods to Charlotte Druckrey. He advised her they were now securely tied to the dock in Aguas Buenas.

Through the door, he offered to personally take them to the markets where they could buy souvenirs. He promised to bargain for them to be sure they did not pay too much. He did not tell them they would visit only those merchants who previously agreed to give him a 25 percent commission on anything they spent.

Luis looked down the passageway to Cabin 9. He saw Paul's two suitcases in the passageway ready for the trip through Customs and was disappointed. He hoped Paul would decide to stay with Ellie Sue for the rest of the cruise.

In the same corridor, at the side of the door to Cabin 7, Professor Charles Magnussen's two suitcases were also ready to be carried to the dock and into the white Customs Building. Mary Louise was still engaged in packing, and repacking her luggage. Luis returned to his quarters. At ten o'clock he would begin to carry the luggage to the Customs cart on the pier.

On the starboard side of the Arbutus, Clevis Dewlap slowly regained consciousness, stretched and noticed the ship was not rocking. He looked out the porthole and saw land. The Arbutus was tied to a pier. He smiled. He decided he would forgo his accustomed morning glass of moonshine. He was in Aguas Buenas or, perhaps, Villa Smit. He wasn't entirely sure.

Clevis was in a pleasant mood. While he suffered from constant beverage poisoning during this first leg of his trip to Villa Smit, he congratulated himself because he had avoided the dreaded sea sickness which bedeviled him on his earlier voyages. Now he would be in port for a day. It was almost like being on dry land.

He got up, shaved a four day growth of beard and went to breakfast. The foreigner who talked so funny was not seated in his usual place at Clevis' table.

A girl and the man he now recognized as his cabin mate entered the Dining Salon. Dewlap arose and went to their table. (Author's Note: Here is a translations of Clevis Dewlap's compliment)

176

"This is the third time I've taken this trip, mister and I've never shared my room with a man as nice as you. Yes sir. Those other gentlemen all complained about me getting sick and everything, but I never heard a word out of you. I truly do appreciate it. If you ever get over to Villa Smit, you look me up, you hear. I'd admire giving you some real good drinking whiskey." It was clear that Clevis' anti-sea sickness remedy had kept him in such a condition that he didn't know Paul had abandoned their cabin.

After finishing his breakfast, Clevis Dewlap returned to his compartment. He counted the number of unopened Mason jars and, satisfied with the supply, decided to finish off the quarter inch of fluid remaining in the opened jar. Then he dropped onto his bunk, smiled, closed his eyes and went to sleep.

* * * * *

The Professor insisted Mary Louise finish her packing before visiting the Dining Salon. The Magnussens enjoyed a very late breakfast. As they left their cabin, they met Ellie Sue and Paul who were returning to the compartment they shared for the last four days. They squeezed through the luggage left in front of the door to the Magnussen compartment and heard faint moaning from the Druckreys as they passed their cabin.

Once inside their own compartment, they held each other. "I don't want you to leave, Paul. I want you to be here with me, honey. I'll miss you."

"And I want to stay with you, El. I mean it, El, I really mean it. I wish I didn't have to leave. It will only be a few days and we'll be together again. When we get back to New Orleans, I'd like to go to Salem with you. Would that be all right? Would you mind?" This was a commitment and they both recognized it.

"Oh, honey. Of course you can. I'd love it." They held each other in silence until Ellie Sue said: "I love you, Paul." He kissed her. Shipboard romance was supposed to stop when port was reached. Both parties were supposed to know that when they began their affair.

Neither was willing to believe it.

Ellie Sue smiled and relaxed. She didn't again ask Paul to stay aboard the Arbutus. She helped him say "good bye" and then he said: "I love you." Paul left their cabin and went to the fantail to be by himself until it came time to go through Customs. He wondered if he were doing the right thing.

Ellie Sue was a wonderful girl, he thought. She was smart. She had a great sense of humor. She had pretty eyes and a marvelous smile. She had a great sense of humor. She had such a nice laugh – not anything like Janie Hanstadt. Paul struggled with the thought of reversing his plan to visit Aguas Buenas.

He could stay with Ellie Sue on the Arbutus as it sailed on the Villa Smit, but the American Consul at Aguas Buenas, his parents' friend Mr. Wilder, would wonder where he was. The Consul would send a cable to Des Moines. Then things would get messed up. It was only four days. Then they'd be together again. And he would go to Salem with her.

* * * * *

Luis Gogeasgoechea again entered the Arbutus port side passageway leading to the cabins occupied by the Druckreys, the Magnussens and the two young gringos. He suspected the Druckreys would not leave the ship for a stroll in Aguas Buenas. He stopped at their compartment door and placed his ear against it. Smiling at the sounds which came from within, he moved on.

He viewed the Magnussen luggage, piled against their doorway, with mild disapproval. The ship's hold was emptied and some of the Magnussen's luggage was already on the pier. Why would anyone not intending to permanently migrate carry so many suitcases? It would take more than one trip to carry them all to the pier. He would have to get another cart from the Aduana for the suitcases of the other passengers. As he carried the Magnussen's baggage down the gangplank, he thought maybe the Professor would appreciate the extra work and leave a tip in the cabin. He guessed right.

When Luis returned for the luggage outside the starboard side of the ship, he hoped Paul Eckert's luggage would not be in the passageway. He hoped he would change his mind and stay aboard. Señor Paul and Señorita Ellie Sue were a nice couple. Luis was truly sorry they might now go their separate ways.

When he got to the end of the passageway, Ellie Sue was waiting for him. Her suitcases were packed and placed beside Paul's. She told Luis she would disembark at Aguas Buenas and asked him not to tell Paul because she wanted to surprise him. Luis happily joined in the plot. He carried both sets of suitcases to the dock.

Since the Druckreys and the drunken gringo would stay aboard ship, only the German's baggage was left to be carried to the customs cart. Luis walked down the starboard passageway to the Reichman cabin. No suitcases were outside the door. He knocked. There was no response. The martini, Luis had been told, was a very powerful drink, even more powerful than the aguardiente or the tequila. Well, he thought, he would give Señor Reichman another half hour to shake off the effects of the four martinis he drank during the previous evening. Then he would come back for the German's luggage.

Chapter 28

The Arrival at Aguas Buenas
Frederick Bergman

On the morning the Arbutus docked at Aguas Buenas, Osvaldo Carrera stood at the ship's rail and waited for the disembarking passengers to go ashore. He waved to Paul who followed Luis as he pushed the overflowing baggage cart to the Aduana building.

The Magnussen's were finishing breakfast and Sr. Reichman, Osvaldo knew, was otherwise disposed. He watched as Luis returned from the Customs building. He watched the Magnussens and Ellie Sue as they left the Arbutus and walked down the pier toward the Aduana.

Before he returned to the Arbutus, Luis told Paul the easiest way to get through the Aduana was to smile and point your finger at your luggage. Usually, he said, the Aduana Inspector would bring your suitcases and hand them to you without even opening them. Then he said the procedure was effective only if a one Peso note was wrapped around the finger when it was pointed at the baggage.

Paul didn't have a one Peso note. He used a five. True to Luis' report, his suitcases, with the Aduana approval stickers neatly affixed, were quickly passed to him, unopened.

The Magnussens came into the Aduana and Paul waited for them to have their baggage inspected. He expected a long delay, but there was none. All of their bags were identified and brought to the Inspector's table. He opened one of Mary Louise's large cases and carefully reviewed its contents. A dozen pairs of shoes, three evening dresses, two curling irons and a variety of cosmetics filled it.

The Inspector looked at the hat boxes, then at the steamer trunk, then at the other unopened suitcases and then at the Professor. The Professor gave him a resigned look. The Inspector nodded in sympathy and then passed the rest of the baggage without reviewing their contents.

When the Magnussen's luggage had been removed from the Inspector's table, two suitcases remained. Paul looked at Mary Louise, expecting her to claim them. The Magnussens grinned and looked at or, more accurately, slightly past him. Mary Louise was sporting her most Cheshirey cat smile. Paul turned and found Ellie Sue standing behind him.

Ellie Sue smiled sweetly and said: "Life on that boat was so boring after you all left. The Druckreys really aren't much for intellectual discussion. While Mister Dewlap is quite handsome and cosmopolitan, he falls just a wee bit short in comparison to you. I thought I'd join you. Do you mind, Paul, honey?"

Paul did not mind.

Ellie Sue's cases were quickly reviewed. As they left the building, they saw Luis Gogeasgoechea re-enter from the docks. He was carrying the luggage of Reinhold Reichman. Reichman was behind him, dressed in his white linen suit and wearing his Panama hat. The German walked slowly into the Aduana, coughing and with a handkerchief to his face.

"I hope he has a terrible hangover," said Ellie Sue. "Let's get out of here as fast as we can. I don't need a morning lecture on European politics."

* * * * *

The Magnussens were the first ones to leave the Aduana. Two cab drivers immediately descended upon them. Each drove a 1932 Model A Ford. One of the drivers saw the amount of baggage loaded on the cart that followed the Magnussens. He immediately recognized them. He had burdened his taxi with Mary Louise's luggage three years ago when the same two people emerged from the Aduana on an earlier visit to Aguas Buenas. That driver quickly disappeared to the far side of his taxi and busied himself with an unnecessary review of the condition of its left rear tire.

The Professor hired the other driver who didn't appreciate the magnitude of the job he had undertaken. He hoisted Mary Louise's

181

steamer trunk onto the luggage carrier welded to the back of his Model A. Then he filled the unused portion of the front seat with luggage. Then he struggled to tie the balance of the baggage to the top of his vehicle.

The loading operation was supervised by Mary Louise, the Professor being satisfied to watch her try to explain to a smiling and nodding cabbie that the hat box should go on top of the heavy suitcase. The shouted English phrase: "On top, damnit, on top" apparently has little meaning in the local dialect.

When Ellie Sue and Paul followed the Magnussens from the Aduana, the hidden taxi driver made his appearance. Paul, with Spanish/English dictionary in hand, attempted to hire him and Professor Magnussen decided to come to the rescue. He was sure no prior hotel reservation had been made for Ellie Sue and, he suspected, it was possible Paul Eckert was in the same boat.

"If," he volunteered, "you two are not too squeamish and have a natural inclination to investigate a wide selection of local wild life without leaving your room, I can recommend the El Palacio Hotel."

When she heard the words "El Palacio," Mary Louise squeezed her eyes tightly shut and her mouth affected a look suggesting she had just taken a big bite from a fresh lime. Years earlier, she had stayed in the hotel during the Magnussen's first visit to Anchuria.

"I make the suggestion," continued the Professor, "only because there is no other hotel in Aguas Buenas with its historic significance or, for that matter, running water. As a hotel, it wins no prizes, but it has a reasonably reliable electricity supply, a bar where you can find martinis only slightly less poisonous than the kind Luis concocts and, more importantly, good cold Anchurian beer. If you are a connoisseur of martinis, I recommend the beer."

"Thanks for the advice, Professor," said Paul, "but Ellie Sue and I will be staying at a guest house. It's called Casa Canada." Mary Louise gave her husband the "you-made-a-fool-of-yourself-again" smile. Magnussen ignored her. In unaccented Latin American Spanish, he informed their driver of the young couple's destination.

After their own driver unceremoniously pitched the last suitcase on top of Mary Louise's hat boxes, Magnussen joined her inside the taxi.

The other driver tied Ellie Sue and Paul's suitcases onto his luggage rack and they proceeded to Casa Canada. Looking somewhat like a mobile version of the leaning tower of Pisa, the Magnussen's Model A, followed Paul's taxi and embarked on a journey that would end on the top of one of the green foothills that began the ascent from the coastal plains of Aguas Buenas into the Central Highlands.

* * * * *

Less than a five minute ride from the docks, the first taxi stopped in front of a wooden house, set back on a grassy, treed lot. A sign attached to the gated stone wall surrounding the lot identified it as Casa Canada. Ellie Sue and Paul left the taxi and Paul, conferring with his bilingual dictionary, began the process of asking the driver to wait until they had taken their bags to their room. He intended to use the cab to get to the El Palacio for lunch and refreshment. For anyone who doesn't speak Spanish, communication can be a complicated procedure. A language barrier is a terrible thing.

Paul had gotten to "Esperar - aqui - maletas - in room. You understand? Room?" Sign language, at times, can break through the barrier. Paul pointed to the driver when he used the Spanish word for "to wait." Then he pointed to the ground beneath his feet when he gave the second word meaning "here." He paged through the dictionary, found another word and pointed to the suitcases. When he couldn't easily find the next one, he pointed to Casa Canada and used the English word "room."

Possibly because of Paul's thick gringo accent, the Anchurian didn't have the foggiest idea of what he was trying to say. He, too, used sign language. Silently he stood between Paul and the suitcases with the upturned palm of his right hand slowly moving up and down, indicating the unmistakable and universally understood sign for the demand of: "pay up."

Ellie Sue, in the meantime, walked down the tiled pathway past a flowering hibiscus tree and up the wooden steps leading to the entrance of the building. She noticed scrawny chickens scratching for insects in the broad leafed tropical grass lawn and caught a glimpse of a stable behind the building.

The Casa Canada was built on cement stilts, extending, perhaps, two feet above the ground. There was no attempt to discourage any air movement under the building and termites had only limited access to the wooden structure. She went up the steps to the front door. When no one answered her knock, she opened the screen door and entered the Casa Canada.

Ellie Sue found herself in what was once the entrance of a private home. A stairway on her left led to an upper floor and three small apartments. They were occasionally rented to others, but usually to the employees and visitors of the Central American Fruit Company.

Some ten feet inside the building and next to the staircase, a small reception desk served as a platform on which a Guest Registration Book was placed. A narrow passageway curved around the desk, through a doorway and into the owner's first floor living quarters.

From the top of the doorway, strings of beads hung close together. They allowed the passage of any vagrant breeze which might enter the room and, at the same time, discouraged the admission of flying insects. A fan, the size of an airplane propeller, hung from the ceiling and, turning slowly, kept some of the air moving.

There was no one behind the Reception Desk. "Hello? Hello?" Ellie Sue questioned. The beaded curtain at the end of the hallway moved. Someone watched her for a moment and, after deciding she posed no threat, he pushed his head through the hanging beads and, without ceremony asked in English: "What do you want?"

* * * * *

Ellie Sue introduced herself and inquired whether Mr. Paul Eckert had a reservation. The man then entered the room and stood behind the desk. "I am Frederick Bergman," he said. "I've been expecting Mr. Eckert." He seemed ill at ease.

Bergman looked beyond Ellie Sue, through the screened front door, and saw Paul, paging through his dictionary while the taxi driver stared at him suspiciously and still slowly moved his upturn palm up and down, up and down. Bergman and Ellie Sue walked to Paul and the empty street before the cab driver called the guardia and, possibly, created an international incident.

The Canadian's explanation, in Spanish, brought a smile of comprehension to the driver who said something which Paul interpreted as an apology for the misunderstanding. Actually, the driver's statement questioned why these silly foreigners couldn't learn to speak Spanish.

After he carried their suitcases to an apartment at the front of the upper floor, Frederick Bergman said: "I understood from Consul Wilder there would be only one of you. There will have to be an extra charge. I can't let you both stay for four Pesos a day. I believe six Pesos a day is fair."

He didn't wait for assent, argument or even comment. "Five nights will be thirty Pesos. You can pay me now." He held out his hand, took the Peso notes Paul handed him and shoved them into his pocket. Without a further word, Bergman turned, quickly walked to the hallway and disappeared down the stairs.

"He certainly isn't interested in winning the tact and congeniality contest", Ellie Sue Said. "He's the only man I've seen down here who appears to be in a hurry." And, as she surveyed the apartment, she added: "I declare, he seemed annoyed."

Chapter 29

Casa Canad
El Palacio

While Paul brought their suitcases from the hallway, Ellie Sue reviewed their Casa Canada apartment. She took Paul's arm and led him to the bedroom door. "Look, Paul, honey," she said, "a real bed. You won't hang over both ends - and it's wide. My, oh my, doesn't it look inviting."

"Now, don't you be in such a hurry, El," he said. "Let's go to the Palace Hotel for lunch. Then I really must visit with Mr. Wilder. I should thank him for his trouble and we can ask him what to do to keep out of mischief. Besides, sweet, the taxi is waiting." Ellie Sue pouted, then smiled, took Paul's arm and they marched out of the building.

The driver understood "Palacio Hotel" and the young couple got into the cab. As they drove away from Casa Canada, Paul looked through his dictionary to find the Spanish equivalent for 'ham sandwich and coffee, please' while Ellie Sue gently moved her hand over his upper thigh.

They were still within a few blocks of Casa Canada when the sharp crack of an explosion made them both jump. The taxi driver's head popped erect but, when no further sounds were heard, he re-adopted his unperturbed demeanor. The startled peon on the sidewalk, however, hesitated for only a moment. Then he ran.

"Whatever was that?" exclaimed Ellie Sue.

"Probably someone switched the ignition of a Model T on and off," said Paul. "That'll always make them backfire."

Their taxi passed an official looking building with a wide arched entrance. A number of uniformed men, all brandishing night sticks, were standing in street. Since there was no dead buzzard on the sidewalk, they returned inside, without bothering to chase the peon who had made a full speed turn down a side street.

The driver spoke something over his shoulder in way of explanation. Paul tried to decipher it. He understood the word "muerte" meant "dead", but the other word, "zopilote" baffled him. Soon they arrived at El Palacio and Paul paid the driver.

* * * * *

In the early 1930s, Paul's high school in Iowa demanded those planning to go on to college take three years of Latin. In deference to a large population of German farmers in the area - most of whom voted - the School Board included a few years of German in the curriculum.

When an Arts teacher had the temerity to propose the Board consider offering the young minds a course in the French language, he was determined (a) to be a partisan of the late, but still hated Easterner, Woodrow Wilson and (b) probably "effeminate". (That's the only word they could bring themselves to use to describe what they really meant.) His teaching contract was not renewed for the ensuing year.

Certainly no one in Des Moines would suggest the Spanish language be taught - not with the memory of Pancho Villa and his Mexican bandits' raid on Columbus, New Mexico (and the General "Blackjack" Pershing-led United States Army's long and unsuccessful attempt to catch him) still fresh after less than twenty years.

So Paul's ability to speak Spanish was limited. Prior to the summer of 1938, the only Spanish words he knew were "si," "no," and "mañana." More recently he expanded that vocabulary to include, "cerveza" and "cuanto." Those words were recently picked from a study of his English/Spanish dictionary and committed to memory as being essential to any program designed to prepare a person for a vacation in Central America.

Unfortunately, an English/Spanish dictionary does not teach one to understand what someone may say in answer to the questions "Beer?" or "How much?" As far as Paul was concerned, the taxi driver's response to the question: "Cuanto?" could have been made in Bantu, Hindi or Scottish - all equally unintelligible languages. Paul, however, was prepared for that particular eventuality. He pulled a fistful of various sized Anchurian coins from his pocket. He opened his palm and held them in front of the driver.

The man looked down and took a number of them from the outstretched hand. Then he looked up to determine if Paul really understood the amount of the quoted fare. As soon as he raised his eyes, Paul closed his fist and returned the balance of the coins to his pocket. That transaction successfully completed, Paul and Ellie Sue entered El Palacio.

* * * * *

El Palacio was built like a squared doughnut, two floors high. One could stand in the center of the ground floor, look up and see the sky. One of the interior walls of the ground floor housed its hotel Reception Desk and Administration Office. A stairway led to the rooms on the second floor. Another side of the ground floor was occupied by a souvenir shop and a place where white guayabera shirts and other tropical clothing could be purchased. The hotel bar filled half of the third inner walls.

Against the fourth wall, opposite the Reception Desk, a neglected fountain dribbled water into a basin containing growths of both green and brown algae. On either side of it, a few trees and some large leafed tropical plants managed to stay alive. A monkey on a light chain was tied to one of the trees. He spent his time snarling and regarding the guests with obvious contempt.

Big billed toucans had the run of the place. They would leave their orangish droppings (which look like corn curls) on the floors and furniture. They'd descended upon the guests at meal time, looking for handouts. With the tips of their long beaks, they'd catch bread or fruit tossed to them, work it back toward their tongues, swallow and stare at the guest with a look that unmistakably demanded:"more."

The swinging, double door entrance into the kitchen formed a part of one of the walls. The hotel's laundry and storage rooms were behind the kitchen. Inside the El Palacio's patio, on a pillar at the side of the swinging doors, a brass plaque commemorated something. A slightly elevated stage suggested the possibility of a place for a dance band.

The open center of the doughnut contained the chairs and tables of the hotel restaurant. When Paul and Ellie Sue entered that central patio, it was empty, except for three waiters seated at the table nearest the kitchen door. Their salaries were meager and tips were eagerly pursued.

All three arose and attempted to entice the customers to his part of the room. The winner was the one who pulled two chairs from one of the tables, ostentatiously dusted them with a napkin and welcomed the couple with a generous sweeping gesture of his hand and arm.

After they were seated, Paul briefly reviewed the proffered menu and understood nothing written thereon. Despite the distractions of Ellie Sue in the taxi, he retained the few words he picked out from the dictionary and he ordered lunch, slowly, pausing between words and making no attempt to modify his gringo accent.

"Yo - desear - una - sandwich - and - una - coffee," he said. "Wat kine of sahnweech, señor?" was the waiter's response. Ellie Sue giggled. "Well," Paul said, "Since you understand English, perhaps we'll have something else. What is this?" he said as he pointed to the menu item which cost fifty centavos.

* * * * *

From their table in the restaurant, the Reception Desk and the stairway leading to the hotel's second floor were clearly visible. Ellie Sue could see them. Reinhold Reichman brought his suitcases into the hotel and registered at the desk.

"Oh, dear," Ellie Sue said, "There's that awful German. He's staying here at the Hotel." Paul had kept the menu and was studying it to see if he recognized anything. He looked up in time to see Reichman walk up the stairway to the second floor and disappear into one of the rooms overlooking the patio.

While they waited for lunch, toucans hopped to their table. They stood on the floor, surrounding them and turning their heads and colorful beaks to the side, watching, with one eye, for any indication of a feeding. After a few minutes of inactivity, the birds retired. They came back as soon as the waiter brought food.

Ellie Sue saw the monkey. He seemed quite unhappy with his status as he grasped the trunk of his patio tree and glared at her. She decided not to try to pet it . Then, above the animal and on the second floor of the hotel, she saw Reinhold Reichman emerge from his room. He walked down the stairs leading to the main floor.

"Here he comes again. Don't turn around," she said to Paul, but before she could raise her hand to cover her face, Reichman saw them both. "He's seen us." Paul turned around in his chair in time to see Reichman lower his head and, without acknowledging their presence, purposely walk through the arch leading into the street.

Their avocado salad lunch came. After throwing pieces of bread to the toucans, again crowding around their table, Ellie Sue stretched and yawned and said: "I'm tired, Paul, honey. Let's go back to Casa Canada," and then she tilted her head and smiled at him.

Paul returned her smile. "I know, I know. I'm what you call 'tired', too." He smiled again and said: "Very tired, El. I really want to go back, hon, but I've simply got to at least say 'hello' and 'thanks' to the American Consul. He's a friend of the family, El. It won't take long."

Paul paid the bill and left a Peso tip. The waiter beamed. He wondered if all norteamericanos were as wealthy as this one. He watched the couple as they left and saw Paul bend down to pick up something orange and about two inches long. He didn't get there in time to warn him.

* * * * *

When Paul and Ellie Sue's taxi left the Aduana building earlier that same morning, the cab of Mary Louise and Professor Magnussen followed it. When they arrived at Casa Canada, the Magnussen taxi passed them and continued on its way toward the United States Consulate, located at the edge of the city and on one of the adjacent foothills.

The streets in the main part of Aguas Buenas were paved and kept in fairly good repair. As you moved away from the central part of the city, the deterioration of the roads proceeded in a geometric progression. Once beyond Casa Canada, the Avenida de la Revolución turned from cement to cobblestone. The surface of the road became more than somewhat uneven. The cobblestones were not uniform in size. They were, however, uniformly hard.

The Magnussens' taxi with its heavy load and tired springs bounced up the cobblestoned street toward the Consulate. Mary Louise and the Professor gripped the straps hanging from the inner sides of the Model A's back seat and tried to keep control of the packages and bags packed inside the vehicle as they, too, bounced up the street to the hilltop where their friend, Rud Wilder, would provide them with a room.

Twice the taxi's lurching dislodged a suitcase from the top of the vehicle. Twice the driver stopped and retrieved the suitcase. Twice he tossed it back atop the Model A. Twice the suitcase landed atop one of Mary Louise's now well crushed hat boxes.

The road turned and twisted until it arrived at a home surrounded by a whitewashed wall over two and a half meters high and topped by the sharp edges of broken bottles which had been set in concrete and meant to discourage unannounced midnight visitors.

A circular sign showed a stern, no-nonsense looking eagle sitting on a stars and bars shield. The eagle clutched an olive branch in one claw and lightning in the other. The sign was attached to one of two pillars which, separated by large iron gates, guarded the driveway entrance to the yard in front of the building. Lettering below the sign declared the place to be the office of the United States Consul General.

The iron gates were wide open. From the look of the growth of grasses beneath them, they were seldom closed. Without challenge, the taxi drove through the gate and into the court yard. There it was parked. The driver got out, surveyed the luggage with something other than unbridled enthusiasm and began to untie and unload it.

The Professor escaped from the baggage crowding the back seat and paid the driver. He added what he thought was an appropriate tip. The driver did not withdraw his hand. When his and the Professor's eyes met, he looked up at the luggage tied to his Model A and then back at his hand. The Professor nodded silently and added another Peso to the tip.

Magnussen went to the entrance of the Consulate. He pounded the heavy knocker against the carved mahogany door and watched the taxi driver struggle with the luggage. He was delighted with the condition of Mary Louise's hat boxes. He was even more delighted at the look on Mary Louise's face when she saw the condition of her hat boxes.

After the third knock, the Professor heard approaching footsteps and then, from inside the building, the words: "Oooh eees eeet?"

Chapter 30

The United States Consul General in Anchuria

The United States Consul General at Aguas Buenas had lived outside of the United States for nearly twenty years and retained few close friends in his native country. His visits to his homeland were limited to trips to Washington D.C., made for the purpose of reporting to his superiors and receiving briefings of current State Department attitudes and procedures.

During the course of his trips to Washington, he felt more and more like a stranger in his own country. When his business was completed, he would quickly return to his Consulate post. He was accustomed to the culture and pace of life in Latin America. He preferred them.

In 1938, Rutherford Birchard Wilder had been the American Consular Officer in Anchuria for five years. He enjoyed his work. He was not afflicted with the thinly disguised superior attitudes commonly found in Anglo Saxon and Nordic diplomatic and consular officials. He sincerely liked both Anchuria and the Anchurians. The Anchurians responded in kind. "Don Rud," as he was locally known, was a popular figure on Anchuria's northern coast.

Years earlier, Rud Wilder met the Magnussens in Colombia when he was a Consular official in Barranquilla. They met again when he was assigned to the Consulate in Aguas Buenas. This would be the Magnussen's third visit to Anchuria and Wilder looked forward to their arrival. On each of their visits, they brought him gossipy comments and observations of the follies and foibles of stateside life as it existed inside as well as outside the nation's capitol. They kept him in touch with the day to day life in his homeland.

It was Magnussen usual practice to question the Consul about life in the Republic of Anchuria and, later, travel to the country's university and to other cities, delving into local politics and keeping himself abreast of the matters of interest to an academic political scientist. On this visit, Mary Louise decided to remain at the Consulate in Aguas Buenas. This gave Wilder an excuse to re-introduce her to local society, sight see, shop with her and avoid the limited cares of his office.

As he waited for the Magnussens to pass through Customs and come to the Consulate, Wilder remembered the son of Helen Eckert. What was his name? Oh, yes. It was Paul. I certainly hope he doesn't take after his father, he thought. The unfortunate results of Rutherford Wilder's high school competition with Dave Eckert for the attentions of the pretty Helen, subconsciously at least, were still filed away in his memory.

* * * * *

The Consulate had only one car. It was a black Packard. Wilder would have preferred a Buick but the State Department thought otherwise. The President and Vice President of the Republic, as well as the Anchurian Ambassador to the United States all drove black Packards and the Anchurian government provided black Packards for the heads of their important government departments. In Anchuria, it became a matter of social standing to own a black Packard. Therefore, it was decreed that the Consulate should have a black Packard.

Wilder didn't know the young Eckert well enough to provide him with transportation although, in deference to Helen Eckert, he should send the Consulate automobile to meet him at the pier. On the other hand, he knew the Magnussens too well to send an auto for them. Mary Louise would be carrying enough baggage to keep a vigilant Customs Inspector occupied for a full day.

Wilder didn't want his man, Pedro, to be saddled with the job of loading and transporting Mary Louise Magnussen's luggage. If past history was a guide, it might take more than one trip to the Aduana building to bring her baggage to the Consulate. It was bad enough that Pedro would have to carry her gear from the taxi to the Consulate room reserved for visiting firemen.

The Consul General solved his transportation problem. He decided he wouldn't provide transportation for any of his guests. Both the Magnussens and young Eckert, he told himself, were capable of fending for themselves.

Wilder had timely advised Helen Eckert of the housing arrangements made for her boy at the local guest house. It was operated by Frederick Bergman, a Canadian who (showing little imagination) called the place Casa Canada. It offered facilities incalculably superior to those of El Palacio and was favored by anyone who had accurate information about the hotel.

As he sat in contemplation of the events of the day, Rud Wilder considered the owner of Casa Canada. His reputation for being what was known as "a snug man with a buck" was well established, but there was something else about him Wilder found to be peculiar. The man had no Canadian accent. When Bergman said "about," it was "ah bow t," and not "ah boo t." Wilder imagined Bergman might have been involved in smuggling whisky into the states from Ontario in the days when Prohibition was still the law of the land. It would account for his Americanized accent.

If the Canadian had been involved in smuggling booze, he could be hiding from gangster retribution for violation of some underworld commandment - or he might be avoiding the long arm of the law. With no extradition treaty with the United States, Anchuria would certainly be a good refuge for a man with the sort of income tax problems that put Al Capone in Alcatraz.

Either theory would explain the man's ready supply of money. It would also explain Bergman's reluctance to divulge any information of a personal nature. Wilder also thought Bergman may have been in the employ of a foreign government. But whose? If not Canada, it might be Great Britain.

The Consul's thoughts were disturbed when he heard the sounds of a Model A Ford racketing up the stony road to the hill where his home and office perched and received an occasional breeze from the Caribbean. He rightly guessed it was the taxi bringing Charles and Mary Louise Magnussen.

Pedro was Wilder's chauffeur, gardener, handy man and reporter of local goings on. He also heard the engines. He knew the Magnussens were scheduled to arrive and he headed for the back door to escape the baggage handling detail. He wasn't fast enough. Wilder called him back and pointed to the door. Its knocker had already announced the Professor's arrival. Pedro reluctantly went to it and inquired: "Oooh eees eeet?" hoping it was not the Magnussens arriving with their luggage.

* * * * *

Pedro and the taxi driver viewed the boxes, suitcases and steamer trunk. They exchanged knowing glances and proceeded to transfer the baggage. Wilder met the Professor and Mary Louise at the doorway. Abrazos and appropriate expressions of welcome and goodwill were exchanged. The three went into Wilder's den which doubled as his Consular office.

"Did you meet a passenger named Eckert? Paul Eckert?" the Consul asked. It was Mary Louise who answered.

"Oh, yes. He was in the Cabin two doors down from ours. Let me tell you about him." And that is exactly what she did. When she finished, she stopped, took a breath, and concluded with the questions: "Why do you ask? Do you know him?"

The Consul limited himself to acknowledging he knew the young man's family, had made a reservation at Casa Canada and had agreed to be helpful during the young man's stay in Aguas Buenas. "I'm glad he's arrived safely and in one piece," said the Consul. "I expect he may call upon us, but I wouldn't be terribly surprised if he didn't. Nothing this younger generation does - or doesn't do - would terribly surprise me."

"Well, he and his girl friend are at Casa Canada right now. Our taxi followed theirs," said the Professor, joining in on the conversation. "It's a small world. Eckert has a Political Science degree and I know some of his University of Wisconsin professors. Now it seems like we both know you. I'll like to see his face if he finds Mary Louise and me here in the Consulate."

Pedro brought small cups of strong Anchurian coffee for Wilder and the Professor. He brought green tea for Mary Louise. She quickly became bored by the conversation which dealt with the growing Nazi menace, the refusal of the U S government to sell the nonflammable helium to the Germans for use in their zeppelins, Japan's withdrawal from the League of Nations and Franco's Catalonia offensive in the Spanish revolution.

As she looked out the window into the Consulate garden, Magnussen's wife thought of the Anchurian artisan market where quality hand tooled leather goods, carved mahogany and interesting local pottery were available at reasonable prices. Her reverie was broken by the sound of a sharp report which echoed up from the center of the city.

"Is that the start of a revolution?" asked a wide-eyed Mary Louise.

"Oh, no", was Rud Wilder's response. "Don Carlos Mejia, probably found another rifle." Neither the Professor nor Mary Louise understood the significance of the explanation. The Consul General didn't enlighten them.

Later in the evening, the Professor and Mary Louise enjoyed dinner at the Consulate. The conversation centered on recent happenings in the United States - Fiorello La Guardia, the Republican Mayor of New York City - the Joe Louis/Max Schmeling fight - the continuing depression that showed few signs of alleviation.

Mary Louise had no interest in those matters. When an appropriate lull in the conversation occurred, she excused herself and went to the Magnussen's room to unpack. When she was out of earshot, the Professor looked at Wilder and said: "That should take care of her for the rest of the evening." Then he added: "And most of tomorrow, too." The two men retired to the Consul's den for brandy, cigars and more conversation.

Wilder answered the Professor's questions about the Peña government. They talked about the possibility of a treaty with the Third Reich. Magnussen said he planned to meet with Clemente Diaz, the dean of the University of Anchuria Law School in Progreso. Clemente Diaz' opposition to the Peña government was no secret. Wilder offered to let the Professor use the Consulate automobile.

It was nearly midnight when Magnussen retired. He could not

overcome the temptation to rouse a soundly sleeping Mary Louise. He put his hand on her shoulder and gave a gentle nudge. "Wha? What is it Charles?" she mumbled.

"Are you awake?" he asked

* * * * *

Rud Wilder had missed his usual mid-day siesta, but still, he enjoyed listening to the Magnussens tell of the daily happenings in state-side existence. His own private talks with the Professor were instructive. As he went to bed, he thought, there would be much to think about tomorrow.

Chapter 31

Will the real Frederick Bergman please stand up?
Panic Attack
Murder

During a heated debate in the Anchurian legislature, a Senator from the Province of Monte Verde said he thought his opponent, a Senator from the Province of La Playa, was a scoundrel, a thief and a liar. The Senator from the Province of LA Playa replied he thought the Senator from Monte Verde was a gentleman and a morally virtuous fellow. Then he added: "But, in this case we are both wrong."

With regard to the explosion heard that morning by all the Americans, everyone was wrong. Professor Mejia did not shoot a buzzard from the roof of the Comandancia building. No one played with the ignition of a Model T to make it backfire. It was not a shot signaling the start of a revolution.

* * * * *

In 1936, a guest registered at El Palacio Hotel under the name of Frederick Bergman. He listed his nationality as Canadian. In truth, he was an American accountant named Thomas Andersen. When he quietly left Villa Smit with the treasure he discovered in the beached fishing boat, it had been his intention to assume a new identity, travel to British Honduras and find a business in Belize to keep himself profitably occupied.

The condition of El Palacio and the complaints he heard from the employees of the Central American Fruit Company, who from time to time had to stay there, changed his plans. He bought a house in Aguas Buenas and remodeled it. When the work was done, it contained his living quarters and three apartments on the upper floor. He named it

"Casa Canada."

Tourists and other visitors plus a dependable number of people coming from or going to the Central American Fruit Company plantations provided a reasonable stream of customers. The business was profitable and easy to manage. Moreover, it gave Thomas Andersen time to engage in the activities he most enjoyed - fishing and beach combing. He had reason to be content. He had met his aims in life. He was not farming. He was not cold. He considered himself to be wealthy.

It was during a mid-July evening in 1938 when he returned to the Aguas Buenas after a day spent in the sun on a nearby golden beach. The following morning, the Arbutus would arrive in port. One of its passengers, a man named Paul Eckert, would take an apartment at his hostel. He would come to Casa Canada sometime late in the morning. There was no need for Andersen to rise early on the following morning. He could collect the rent and attend to his guest's needs at mid-day.

Andersen slept late and breakfasted late. As he was served the morning coffee, his servant proudly told him of an apartment reservation made during his absence. It had been made by the very important Senator Paco Mendez for the very important Senator Roberto Smit who was coming to Aguas Buenas.

The servant was proud of the reservation and unprepared for his master's reaction. Thomas Andersen was not at all pleased. His identity as the Canadian Frederick Bergman had been firmly established in Aguas Buenas. The coming visit of Senator Roberto Smit, his former employer, represented disaster. If Smit saw him, he would undoubtedly be recognized as the accountant who disappeared from Villa Smit almost two years earlier.

If Bergman's true identity as Thomas Anderson became known, it would only be a matter of time before he was also identified as the man who found the missing Sedalian money. Then, he feared, someone would take it from him. Confiscation of foreigners' assets often occurred in Latin Republics. Some Anchurian government official would surely take his Sedalian fortune. He could lose it and be poor again - but, thought Andersen, if Smit does not see me, perhaps I can avoid discovery. After all, Smit's reservation was for only two nights. Maybe I can leave Aguas Buenas before Smit arrives and return after he has gone.

Time was of the essence. The passenger from the Arbutus might be passing through the Aduana at that very moment. Bergman would like to stay until he collected the rent, but the risk was too great. Smit might come early. Bergman decided to take his cache and leave the city immediately. He would tell his servant to take the rent from the Arbutus passenger and he hoped the man wouldn't steal it.

With the decision made, he ordered his servant to bring his horse to the back door of Casa Canada. Alone in his first floor living quarters, Bergman removed two boards from the flooring under his desk. Beneath them lay the revolver he found in Chico Elizondo's boat. Beneath the revolver lay a thick leather saddle bag. The saddle bag was heavy with what was left of the gold and silver taken from the smuggler's boat.

Bergman lifted it from its sub-floor hiding place and opened it. He reached inside. Coins were in his hand when, to his consternation, he heard a knock on the front door of Casa Canada. A few coins fell as he jerked his hand from the saddlebag. Was in Roberto Smit? He hadn't time to replace the boards. He pushed the revolver and the saddle bag under the desk. He heard a woman's voice calling "Hello, hello?"

Bergman cautiously went to the doorway separating his apartment from Casa Canada's reception area. He peered through the beaded curtain and saw a young woman with pretty hazel eyes. When he asked what she wanted, her answer reminded him of the reservation made for Paul Eckert.

Bergman looked out the front door and after determining Roberto Smit was not present, he went to the street and translated Eckert's request that the taxi driver wait. He took the couple's suitcases to the hallway in front of the rented upstairs apartments and increased the room charges since there were now two guests, instead of one.

Bergman took thirty Pesos from Paul Eckert, and hurried back down the stairs. He stood, partially hidden, behind the doorway's beaded curtain. He knew the two guests would not keep the taxi waiting. As soon as he saw them leave, he returned to his apartment to finish his preparations.

The shot that disturbed the mid-day peace of Aguas Buenas was the shot that killed Frederick Bergman.

* * * * *

After lunch, Ellie Sue and Paul stepped out of El Palacio and into the bright sun of the tropical afternoon. There were no taxis in sight. Paul expected taxis would be stationed close to the city's best (only) hotel. The Aguas Buenas taxi cab drivers expected no one in his right mind would abandon a siesta in the cooler comforts of the hotel in favor of going anywhere in the noontime heat. Each driver was enjoying a nap inside his cab parked under a tree or in the shade of a building.

It was Ellie Sue who suggested a walk to their apartment. "It's only a few blocks, Paul, honey," she said. "It's straight up this street. I paid attention to where we were going while you had your nose in the dictionary. Come on." She steered him to the shaded side of the Avenida de la Revolución and they walked toward Casa Canada.

"You don't see much of a place from a taxi," she continued, "and a five block walk will help the digestion." Inwardly she smiled. Since Paul couldn't find a taxi, they couldn't go to the American Consulate. They were going to their apartment in Casa Canada. Outwardly, Paul smiled. Since he couldn't find a taxi, they couldn't go to the American Consulate. They were going to their apartment in Casa Canada and the walk would give them an opportunity for their first real look at Aguas Buenas.

As they went on down the Avenida de la Revolución toward Casa Canada, they walked past the broad arched doorway of the Comandancia Building and, softly, Paul chuckled and Ellie Sue giggled at the two policemen guarding the entrance. With chins on chests, both were seated in chairs, tilted back against the shaded interior walls of the open interior patio. Both were sleeping.

Few people were on the streets during the July afternoon heat. The shops were all closed. Ellie Sue and Paul stopped in front of one of them. The entire front of the store opened directly onto the street, with no intervening windows or doors or walls. An unrolled grid of iron bars hung down from the top of the store front. It was padlocked to an iron loop embedded in the sidewalk concrete. The air could enter the closed store, but a thief could not.

They looked through the bars at the goods displayed inside the building. Fruits and vegetables filled bins on the floor and the shelves contained canned goods. "Abaceria," said Ellie Sue, reading the sign that was hung on the outside of the building. "That must mean grocery store."

When they arrived at Casa Canada, it, too, showed no signs of life. They entered and went up the stairway to their apartment. Both were warm and perspiring after the walk. Paul commented: "Mad dogs and Englishmen go out in the noon day sun." Ellie responded: "Well, Paul, honey, I'm English, so you know what that makes you."

She went to the bathroom, turned on the shower and felt the water. It was warm. She took off her dress and half slip. Shoes, garter belt, stockings, brassiere and panties followed. She had just stepped behind the shower curtain and felt the water begin to run over her body when the curtain moved again. Paul joined her.

It was a very pleasant afternoon for Ellie Sue Bradshaw and Paul Eckert. Neither of them would ever read don Carlos Mejia's History of Anchuria.

* * * * *

John Keats claimed truth was beauty and beauty was truth. The logic of his claim cannot be defended, but who cares? Beauty is in the eye of the beholder and history is in the pen of the writer. Don Carlos Mejia's version of the Battle of the Ramasajoti River is just as truthful as the version set forth by the Sedalian historian - which is to say: both historians preferred poetry to fact. In 1938, only the few living survivors of the battle knew the truth and they weren't going to tell it. The true story may never be told.

Chapter 32

The Battle of the Rio Ramasajoti

In 1888, as a result of Lord Percy Grenville's machinations, intended to once and for all establish the national boundaries of Sedalia and Anchuria, war was declared simultaneously by the two countries. Both sent their armies into battle.

Lieutenant Luciano Espinosa, later President of the Republic of Anchuria, together with a complement of 120 intrepid followers, marched to the east from Aguas Buenas to meet, engage in desperate battle and defeat the hated invading Sedalians.

Lieutenant Mario Galvez, later President of the Republic of Sedalia, and 120 loyal Sedalians marched to the west from Ciudad Carillo to meet, engage in desperate battle and defeat the hated invading Anchurians.

Both armies soon became hopelessly lost in the swamps that separated the two Republics.

A few weeks later, the Galvez army consisted of 67 men. They were camped around a thatched hut, living on short rations and desperately searching for a way out of the pestilent miasma in which they found themselves. Luciano Espinosa's army had similar problems. His remaining 58 mutiny minded men remained together only because they were all in the same boat. Without being aware of it, he and his Anchurians were located a few miles to the west of the Sedalians.

During the previous day, each host, separated only by an alligator and poisonous snake infested swamp, had marched directly past the other. The two armies, each unburdened by the information that the enemy was now at its rear, seemed destined to march away from each other and miss the excitement of Armageddon. The Fates, however, had different plans.

Though history does not record it so exactly, the Battle of the Rio Ramasajoti began at 7:53 in the morning of July 23, 1888. At that moment, Flaco Cortines, a sergeant with the Luciano Espiñosa Anchurian contingent noticed camp fire smoke rising behind him from the west. At the same time, Gordo Lopez, a sergeant with the Mario Galvez Sedalian contingent saw smoke rising behind him from the east. The smoke came from the camp fires of the contesting armies.

Fear of unknown enemy forces did not paralyze either Sergeant Lopez or Sergeant Cortines. Training and experience, universally characteristic of sergeants in all armies, directed their thoughts and actions. The sight of morning smoke meant one thing to them - the presence of food.

Come hell or high water, the opportunity to find it would not be neglected. Each sergeant quietly informed his Lieutenant and the two pairs of men, each hoping to find something to eat, moved to the rear and, unwittingly, towards each other. The two enemies met at the sides of a dry creek bed.

Lt. Galvez quickly analyzed his position. His company's armaments consisted of machetes, his service revolver and the few rifles and ammunition which, during the march, hadn't been sporadically discarded by his soldiers as heavy and useless baggage. Unless firm action was immediately taken, his men would be slaughtered.

He and his sergeant tore off their shirts and waving them in the air, advanced into the dusty draw. There they met Lt. Espinosa and Sergeant Flaco Cortines, also carrying and waving white shirts. They had come to the same conclusion as had Lt. Galvez and Sergeant Gordo Lopez. In an attempt to avoid their slaughter, each tried to surrender to the other.

The four men sat on rocks in the middle of the dry creek bed and brought peace to their troubled lands. It was decided neither could surrender to the other. National honor would not permit it. A battle would have to be fought. Next, since both Lieutenants agreed it had to be around there somewhere, they carefully drew the location of the dry ditch on their respective maps and marked it: Rio Ramasajoti.

When battle plans were being considered, Sergeant Gordo and

Sergeant Flaco pointed out the armies were on the wrong sides of the ditch. The Anchurians were in Sedalia territory, and vice versa. Resolution of the problem was forthcoming. Time pieces were synchronized. The Anchurians would place themselves a soccer field's length upstream from the spot the Lieutenants then occupied. The Sedalians would position themselves at a place a soccer field distance below the spot.

At 2 o'clock, the Anchurians and the Sedalians would be ordered to fire every available weapon directly into the unoccupied position in front of them. Filing side-ways would be strictly forbidden. At 2:30, both Lieutenants would unsheathe their swords and lead their men in a spirited charge across the draw, routing the unseen enemy. Both armies would then be on its own side of the Rio Ramasajoti.

The armies would return to their capitol cities, properly claim they had driven the cowardly invader from their sacred soil and claim glorious victory. Those who deserted or died of disease would be counted as killed in action and generous pension paid to surviving widows.

Since that time, school teachers and professors in both Republics have glorified the military leaders who so brilliantly outflanked the invading army and courageously drove it from their beloved homeland. When those lieutenants assumed the Presidencies of their respective Republics, Gordo Lopez and Flaco Cortines were appointed Defense Ministers. This action not only gave official recognition for their assistance in the brilliant military maneuver, but also assured their silence.

Each Republic erected a pylon on its side of the spot where the dry river bed met the Caribbean. Brass plaques, affixed to the base of each monument, proclaimed the army of its particular Republic to have been the victor, praised its military leaders and vilified the enemy. Students from the University of Sedalia stole the plaque from the Anchurian pylon. Students from the University of Anchurian stole the plaque from the Sedalian pylon. The pylons, themselves, can still be seen by passing coastal steamers.

By the summer of 1938, there were 600 old liars in village squares in each of the Republics, mesmerizing youngsters with tales of their heroics during the Battle of the Rio Ramasajoti. July 23rd became a National Holiday in both Anchuria and Sedalia. In Aguas Buenas, a grand party commemorating the 50th anniversary was planned at the El Palacio Hotel. Senator Roberto Smit would address the celebrants.

* * * * *

Senator Roberto Smit was not happy. Except for trips to Progreso when the National Congress was in session, he seldom left Villa Smit. He was never happy when he had to leave his home. Smit would have preferred to stay in Villa Smit and quietly celebrate the anniversary of the Battle of Rio Ramasajoti, but Paco Mendez had asked him to be the main speaker at the Aguas Buenas party celebrating the 50th anniversary of the historic event. Senator Smit was a popular speaker, but he did not enjoy delivering addresses. He hated it. He made them as short as possible. That's why he was so popular.

Paco Mendez exercised good judgment when he reserved an apartment for Roberto Smit at Casa Canada. The owner, he told his fellow Senator, was a Canadian who operated a clean guest house with reliable modern plumbing. It had its own diesel electric plant for use on those occasions when the city's power generator broke down. Eight years earlier, during his last visit to Aguas Buenas, Smit stayed at El Palacio. That experience was one not calculated to instill a strong desire to return to Aguas Buenas.

Senator Smit's own personal wishes had to be disregarded. He told don Paco to inform the Mayor he would be honored to address the celebrants and he prepared for the trip to Aguas Buenas. The Senator didn't enjoy driving an automobile, but discretion also decreed he leave his chauffeur behind in Villa Smit. There was other special business in Aguas Buenas that required his attention. Few people knew the true purpose of his trip.

* * * * *

Ellie Sue and Paul were sleeping under the netting-covered bed in their apartment when Senator Roberto Smit arrived at Casa Canada.

There was no activity in the streets of Aguas Buenas. It was the hottest part of the day. As he got out of his Packard, the Senator wasn't thinking of the speech he had to make at the city's celebration. He was preoccupied with the political situation in his country.

Smit was well aware of the rumors of a pending pact between the Peña government and the Nazis. He knew how such a treaty would solidify Máximo Peña's control over Anchuria. Smit and Mendez had been loyal friends and confidants for many years and the two of them were considering a revolution. The rumors of the treaty were a catalyst for their conspiracy. After the Rio Ramasajoti celebration, Smit and Mendez would meet with others and determine the course of their action.

Smit carried his suitcase to the unattended Reception Desk in Casa Canada. After calling "allo" a few times, he stepped around the desk and passed through the beaded curtain that separated the reception area from the rest of the downstairs living quarters. Inside the room he found the body of a man, lying face down in a circle of blood. He caught his breath, but kept control.

After a few seconds, he kneeled beside the body. The man was unquestionably dead. The Senator took the corpse by the shoulder and turned it over. To his surprise, he recognized Thomas Andersen, the Madera Anchuria accountant who had been missing for over two years.

From his position next to the body, the Senator could look under the desk. He saw the floor boards that had been removed and the secret compartment they concealed. Whatever had been cached there was now gone, but a golden coin lay beside the leg of the desk. It was Sedalian. Smit's suspicions of the circumstances of Thomas Andersen's disappearance from Villa Smit were confirmed. The accountant had, indeed, found the money stolen from the Sedalian Agriculture Worker's union office.

Smit could not afford to be connected with the dead accountant in any way. Peña was a ruthless dictator and Smit's antagonism to his government was no secret. Peña would surely accuse, try and convict Smit of any crime on the flimsiest pretext. The Bergman/Anderson murder would certainly be used to destroy him and, perhaps Paco

Mendez, too. It would certainly destroy any plans for revolution.

The Senator's first impulse was to return to Villa Smit. That would mean abandoning the meeting with Paco Mendez and the anti-Peña forces. No, that alternative was unacceptable. Only one option made sense. He arose and went back to the Reception Desk. He picked up his suitcase and returned to his automobile. He drove the Packard up the Avenida de la Revolución, past the United States Consulate and on toward the country estate of Senator Paco Mendez.

Smit hoped no one would see him during the trip to the Mendez farm. As he drove to it, he passed a man on horseback. It made him very uncomfortable. He knew the Packard would identify him as an important government official. Evidence of his afternoon presence in Aguas Buenas might be discovered.

It was after two o'clock when he arrived at the Mendez finca. After don Paco welcomed him with an abrazo, Smit told him of finding the body of the owner of Casa Canada and identified him as Thomas Andersen, the Madera Anchuria accountant who disappeared from Villa Smit during the failed Sedalian revolt. He showed Mendez the Sedalian gold coin. It was all the poof needed to prove Andersen had found and the SINDETRAG treasury.

"Of course," said Paco Mendez, "you had to come here, Roberto. If there is risk, we both must share it. If anyone should ask, I will tell them I called you at Villa Smit and invited you to stay with me. We will go to the Aguas Buenas celebration together."

Mendez thought for a moment and then added: "It is very important that the Comandante find Bergman's killer. Tomorrow morning you must make an anonymous call to him. Tell him about the body. The sooner he finds the murderer, the safer we will be."

The Senators went to the veranda and Paco Mendez poured a scotch and water for his friend, Roberto Smit. They talked of revolution until 8. Then they ate. Then they talked more. Then they retired.

Chapter 33

The Comandante of the Guardia Civil
A lovely morning
Arrest

On the morning after the Arbutus docked at Aguas Buenas, the sun had risen when Sergeant Alberto Gonzalez brought a bowl of sugar and a cup of black Anchurian coffee to the Comandante of the Guardia. The Comandante put three teaspoons of sugar in the saucer alongside the cup. The Comandante did not like sugar in his coffee. He liked it strong and black, but he was also a nationalistic Anchurian. By putting three teaspoons of sugar in the saucer, he helped create the demand for the Anchurian sugar growers' product.

The Comandante had watched Anchurian governments come and go. He allied himself to no politician and represented no threat to whoever happened to be in power at the time. He outlasted them all because he had no political ambitions. He was happy being the Comandante of the Guardia Civil of the second largest city in the Republic.

Cup and saucer in hand, the Comandante slowly sipped the heavy black brew and walked to the window. From his office in the back of the Comandancia building, he could look south to the Central Highlands. In the morning, the sky was usually a cloudless blue and the many green hues of the mountains would be on display. Early morning was the Comandante's favorite time of day.

Men and women left the hills before sun rise and brought foods and fruits and woven goods and handmade articles to the markets. The muted sounds of their burros' hooves on cobblestones were not yet overpowered by the squawking of automobile horns and the urban bustle of this city of over twenty thousand inhabitants.

In the meantime, the warm air of the coastal plain was rising up the foothills, creating an agreeable movement of air. Later it would be hot, the breeze would disappear and the humidity would rise. Soon the city and its sounds and smells would come to life, but now one could stare out of the Comandancia building at the mountains behind the coastal plain and enjoy a cup of coffee in peace.

The Comandante broke from his reverie and considered the coming day's work. He expected some unpleasantness from Carlos Mejia. Yesterday, don Carlos tried to shoot a zopilote from the Comandancia building. It was the first time he missed. Today, the Comandante was sure, he would try again. Then it would be necessary to cross the street to the National Library, confiscate don Carlos' rifle and again lecture him on his obligation to uphold his position in society and be a peaceful citizen. The Comandante was favorably disposed to don Carlos. Like the Comandante, Carlos Mejia had no political ambitions.

As head of the Guardia of the City of Aguas Buenas, the Comandante did not look forward to the coming celebration of the anniversary of the Battle of the Rio Ramasajoti. There would be a lot of Cerveza Alemana and a lot of aguardiente flowing in and around the city. There would be fights, some with knives and some with machetes. It was to be expected during the celebration of such an important national holiday.

The Comandante instructed his men to use forbearance and bring to jail only those who were clearly dangerous. He, himself, planned to avoid the excitement. During the latter part of the evening when the jail would overflow, he would be enjoying the city's formal party at El Palacio. Today would be peaceful, but tomorrow evening would be hectic.

The phone rang. He turned from the window, set down the coffee and picked up the phone. "Bueno?" he asked. A voice answered: "There is a dead man in Casa Canada." The line was immediately disconnected.

* * * * *

When Ellie Sue awoke that same morning, with eyes still closed she rolled on her side. Instead of finding Paul, her hand touched only the sheet. She opened her eyes, simultaneously calling out "Paul, honey?"

Paul, in his pajama bottoms, was standing beside one of the open floor-to-ceiling jalousied windows separating the interior of their apartment from a tiny iron railed balcony that extended over the side of Casa Canada. He had been looking at the scenery of the Central Highlands, listening to roosters make various announcements from every corner of the city and watching Aguas Buenas come to life.

He turned from the window and walked to the bed. "Good morning, beautiful lady," he said and he kissed her. "You slept well?" She smiled, then answered "Mmmmmm" and pulled him down to her for another kiss. Paul offered no objection. Then he put his finger against her lips and said: "El, the first order of business this morning is to visit Mr. Wilder at the Consulate. Let's get that behind us." In order to avoid temptation, he rose and returned to the window.

"My, my. You Iowa boys are strange", she said, slowly moving under the sheet. When Paul didn't react, she got up and went to the bathroom for her shower. She returned, sat on the edge of the bed, dressed and surveyed the apartment's cooking facilities.

On legs twenty inches off the floor, a modern electric stove sat against the wall. It had three burners on its top left side and an oven on the right. She turned a burner on high. It worked. A small sink stood next to the oven. Ellie Sue saw it had only a cold water spigot. Heating water on the electric stove wouldn't be a serious inconvenience. A Westinghouse refrigerator (square, heavy and with a large drum on top) completed the kitchen equipment. They'll serve our needs, she thought.

"We really should have something to eat before we visit Mr. Wilder, honey," she said. "What would you like for breakfast?" In true Iowa fashion, Paul declared for ham and eggs. A search through the English/Spanish part of the dictionary provided the words: leche (for "milk"), jamon (for "ham") and huevos (for "eggs"). Ellie Sue memorized them and was ready to visit the Abaceria - the grocery store she and Paul passed when they walked from El Palacio to Casa Canada.

"Since you're paying for two people, we should have two pillows.

After you get dressed, honey, talk to Mr. Personality and see if we can get another one", she said. "I'll pick up the groceries," and she left.

* * * * *

Paul showered, dressed and went to the desk on the first floor of Casa Canada. No one was in the reception area. "Hello," he called out. There was no answer. "Is anyone here?" Still no answer. Paul walked through the beaded doorway and into the room behind it. It appeared to be empty although the door to the hostel's back yard was open.

Paul went toward the door and discovered the body of Frederick Bergman sprawled on the floor behind the desk. The hostel owner's shirt was soaked in blood. There was blood on the floor. Paul had no doubt the man was dead - and not from natural causes.

For a moment he stood without moving, looking at the body and wondering what to do. The man lay on his back. His mouth was open. His eyes stared blankly at the ceiling. His face was an ashen white, the blood having drained down to the parts of the body that were closest to the floor.

Paul noticed the boards lying on the floor beneath the desk and saw they had once concealed a hiding place. The compartment meant to be covered by the boards was empty except for a golden coin. He picked it up and turned again to the body.

From the coagulated condition of the blood, Paul felt certain the man had been dead for hours. Then he heard the noise of a group of people entering Casa Canada. They quickly came past the Reception Desk and through the beaded curtain.

Still holding the coin in his hand, Paul saw men wearing the uniforms of the Aguas Buenas Guardia enter the room. One of them drew his revolver and pointed it at his head. Another gave him a command in Spanish. Paul didn't understand the words, but he quickly put his hands up. There are times when translations aren't necessary.

Chapter 34

Interrogation

Paul was marched down the Avenida de la Revolución into the same building which, yesterday, had housed the two sleeping soldiers. Today he saw no humor in the way he was shoved through the arched entrance and into a room at the back of the building. He was roughly pushed into a straight backed wooden chair facing the Comandante's desk. He sat there for fifteen minutes. It seemed like a hour. Two men of the guardia stood beside him. Their rifles had ugly bayonets affixed to them. They scared him. He felt intimidated.

Of course, that was exactly how the Comandante wanted him to feel. After a few minutes alone in that room, seated in the uncomfortable straight backed chair, guarded by two men with rifles and bayonets, many of the Comandante's countrymen confessed before they were even questioned. Some admitted unrelated crimes perpetrated years before their arrest.

The Comandante entered the room. He said nothing. He sat behind his desk and looked at Paul through cold, hard eyes. He wondered if a more sophisticated gringo would react to the treatment in the same way as his own compatriots. There was another reason for the Comandante's silence. He didn't quite know how to begin.

The coagulated blood and rigor mortis as well as the absence of a weapon bothered him. It was clear Federico Bergman was killed yesterday. The Sedalian gold coin may have been a coincidence, but the Comandante smelled a motive. The unsolved disappearance of the SINDETRAG treasury from Ciudad Carillo in the neighboring Republic of Sedalia came to mind.

The young gringo traveled with a woman. Where was she? They were both Norteamericanos so he would have to be careful. The American Consul, don Rud, would stand for no nonsense when United

States citizens were concerned. He would have to be cautious until he had more evidence. Right now, all he had was a Sedalian coin and a weaponless man kneeling over a long dead body.

As he looked at Paul, he wondered, what kind of gringo is this? Is he overbearing like so many of the Fruit Company people? Or is he as naive as he appears to be? Perhaps it would be best to let him talk without questioning. What he says and how he says it will be instructive. "Will you have a cigarette, Señor Eckert?" asked the Comandante, extending his cigarette case toward Paul.

He seems pleasant enough, thought Paul. What was it Professor Magnussen said? In Latin America, offers should be made three times before you can accept. The first two offers are made merely to be polite. "No, I don't believe so. Thank you," he answered.

There was no second or third offer. This was not reassuring. The Comandante lit an Anchurian cigarette - dark uncured tobacco and sweet rice paper. He blew smoke into the air and continued to look straight into Paul's eyes.

Why doesn't he ask questions, Paul wondered. He speaks English well enough. Maybe I should demand to call Mr. Wilder. No. He'll think I'm uncooperative. Well, I've got nothing to hide. Let's get this over with.

"Sir," Paul said to the Comandante, "Do you want to know how I happened to find the body?"

"Yes, Señor Eckert. I'm very interested in learning everything you know about Señor Bergman."

The Comandante leaned forward in his chair. He stared into Paul's eyes and didn't move a muscle. This posture was usually enough to frighten the suspect or, at the very least, make him feel ill at ease.

Paul, feeling ill at ease, decided to keep Ellie Sue out of it. There was no reason to involve her in any unpleasantness. This whole affair was a matter of a mistaken impression. He could understand why the Comandante would think him guilty. A simple explanation would set things right in a hurry.

"Well, there's not much to tell," he said. "I was on board the Arbutus when it docked yesterday morning. This is my first visit to Anchuria." He looked up at the Comandante. There was no reaction he could read. "I'm on vacation," he added. Still no reaction.

"After I got through Customs, I went to Casa Canada and met - for the first time - this man Bergman." Paul emphasized the words 'for the first time'. For further emphasis, he added: "I never saw him before in my entire life." He paused. The Comandante continued to look directly into his eyes and said nothing.

Paul didn't like the way the conversation was going. It wasn't a conversation. The Comandante made him extremely nervous. Why didn't he say something? Paul felt his every statement may have been some kind of terrible admission. He began to think he had somehow been caught up in a surrealistic Franz Kafka novel. He became defensive.

"Look, I didn't spend much time with him. Maybe ten minutes, at most. I rented an apartment from him, that's all. I was only there long enough to leave my luggage. Then I went to the El Palacio hotel for lunch. When I finished, I walked back to the apartment. If Bergman was in Casa Canada when I returned, I didn't see him. I went immediately to my apartment and stayed there until this morning. I didn't see anything or hear anything out of the ordinary."

The Comandante recognized Paul's rising level of discomfort. He hoped his nervousness would continue and approach panic. He said nothing, didn't change his expression and continued to look directly at Paul.

When it became clear the Comandante wasn't going to break the silence, Paul continued: "This morning I went downstairs, ah, to get some extra bedding. No one was in the lobby, so I went behind that beady curtain into the office. At least, I thought it was the office. It looked more like a living room. That's when I saw the body.

"I went up to it and recognized it was Bergman. He was dead. He had been shot. I didn't touch anything. I was going to come here and tell the police. Then your men came into the room and you know the rest of the story."

Paul again looked at the Comandante, hoping to hear some comment or see some sign that would give him comfort or assurance. There was none. Paul felt a quiver of hysteria begin to disrupt his thinking. He fought for control. Well, he thought, two can play this game.

"And that's all I know." He said nothing more. He waited.

The Comandante continued to stare at him in silence. Finally, he put the cigarette to his mouth, again blew smoke in the air and asked: "Anything else, Señor Eckert?"

"No," Paul answered, "that's all. Except for the few minutes when I paid the rent, I didn't even talk to the man." Then he thought: Wait a moment. There's something funny here. Aloud he said: "Excuse me. How do you know my name is Eckert? I never introduced myself."

The Comandante arose. He picked up a copy of the Arbutus' Passenger List. He walked to the front of the desk. The chair occupied by Paul was placed far enough away from it to give the Comandante room to sit on its edge. He now looked down on Paul, further intimidating him. He drew on his cigarette and, after a few seconds, exhaled the smoke into the room. He slapped the ship Manifest into the palm of his hand.

"When a visitor comes to Aguas Buenas, the Comandante gets a report from the Inspector at the Aduana." He held the Manifest up and looked at it. "It tells me who has come to visit my city. When anyone disembarks - particularly one who is not an employee of the Fruit Company - everyone knows about it. We are a small city and we get few tourists. We wonder why a visitor comes to Aguas Buenas. We are inquisitive people and we ask questions."

Can it be this idiot thinks I have something to do with this? thought Paul. "Look," he said, "I'm a stranger here. I don't know the man who was killed. I don't why he was killed. I don't know who killed him. I don't know anything."

The Comandante made no comment. He looked down at Paul for a moment or two. Then he said: "I'm sorry, Señor Eckert, I was not listening. You see, I was preoccupied with another matter. My mind was wandering. I was 'sheep gathering', as you say up north in the United States. I was wondering what you smuggled into Aguas Buenas yesterday morning. Can you enlighten me?"

Oh my God, thought Paul, why didn't I just let the Customs Inspector open my suitcases? With some alarm showing in his voice, he said to the Comandante: "I didn't smuggle anything into Aguas

Buenas. I was in a hurry to get through Customs. I gave the Inspector five Pesos. He didn't look through my suitcases. It was an innocent affair - not too smart, I'll admit - but it was innocent. If I were smuggling anything, would I be dumb enough to put it in a suitcase where the Inspector could find it?"

The Comandante leaned a bit forward and looked down into Paul's face. Then he said: "In this country, Señor Eckert, when someone comes through the Aduana, it is our practice to wrap a one Peso note around the finger, point to the baggage and avoid the delays incurred by a review of its contents.

"If someone wishes to smuggle something into the country, it is customary to wrap a five Peso note around the finger. Though one Peso is enough to avoid unnecessary delay, five Pesos is a guarantee that there will be no need for unpleasant importation disclosures. If one Peso is sufficient, why would anyone spend more? Perhaps he is trying to be doubly sure the Inspector will not look into his luggage?

"Señor Eckert, you wrapped a five Peso note around your finger. Five Pesos is a lot of money. Is not the true reason for the large gift obvious?"

Paul regained his composure and answered: "I didn't know your local custom. I was told to wrap a Peso around my finger, but I didn't have one. I only had a five. I know it may sound implausible," he said as the initial shock of realizing he was a suspect wore off "but, what I've told you happens to be the truth, the whole truth and nothing but the truth."

There was still no response from the Comandante. So, Paul said to himself, he is going to remain silent. All right, I can stare off into space as long as he can. The Comandante returned to his chair behind the desk. He looked at Paul. It seemed like the young man had decided to speak no more, so it was time for the Comandante to begin. He snubbed out the butt of his cigarette in the ash tray and lit another. He stood up, looked out the window and said: "Señor Eckert. I'm going to tell you a story.

"One day a man, who says he is a tourist, comes to Aguas Buenas. His passport is issued at a place called Chicago. It is a place which, even here in a small town in a small country, we all know as a center of crime. The man says he comes here for a vacation. Few criminals from Chicago come to Aguas Buenas for a vacation." Then he returned to his chair and again stared straight into Paul's eyes.

"This (pause) tourist bribes a government official to pass his suitcases through the Aduana without review. This (pause) tourist does not tell me about this. This (pause) tourist goes not to our hotel, but to a guest house operated by a man named Bergman. He too is a foreigner. A Canadian. The Customs officials tell me they have never seen Bergman's passport. People think he is very wealthy, but no one really knows because Señor Bergman does not speak of it."

The Comandante puffed his cigarette and watched Paul. There was no reaction to the hint that Bergman had a substantial amount of money. He continued his narrative. "This (pause) tourist from Chicago goes directly to Señor Bergman with two suitcases whose contents have never been checked by our Customs Inspector. Is that not curious?"

Without waiting for a response, the Comandante continued: "A day after this (pause) tourist has brought uninspected luggage into my country, he is found kneeling over the body of the murdered Señor Bergman. The (pause) tourist has a Sedalian gold coin in his hand. Even now, when the (pause) tourist tells me about finding the body of a murdered man, he does not mention the gold coin. Is that not curious?"

The Comandante again picked up the Arbutus passenger Manifesto. He looked at it and continued. "A woman named Ellie Sue Bradshaw was a passenger scheduled to stay aboard the Arbutus and sail on to Villa Smit. She left the ship here in Aguas Buenas. Is that not curious?"

He picked up the Casa Canada Guest Registration book. "This Registration book tells me she shares your apartment at Casa Canada, but you do not mention her." He snapped the book shut, looked at Paul and said: "Is that not curious?"

The Comandante paused for only a few seconds before continuing. "I do not believe the (pause) tourist went to El Palacio for lunch. I believe he killed Bergman as soon as he arrived at Casa Canada. I believe he killed him for his money. I can find no other Sedalian gold coins in Casa Canada. Neither can I find the (pause) tourist's female accomplice. I believe she has the gold and the (pause) tourist was going to dispose of the body when he was arrested this morning."

The Comandante stood up. He was not sure Paul killed Bergman, but perhaps he knew more than he was telling. He hoped he had scared Paul to the point he would tell everything he knew. He put both hands on his desk, leaned across it and, continuing to stare into the young man's eyes, in a measured, firm voice, he asked: "That is what I believe, Señor Eckert. Perhaps we can drop this charade, Señor Eckert, and begin to tell the truth. Where is your accomplice?"

The word 'accomplice' gave Paul a terrible fright. He knew it meant Ellie Sue and he also knew it meant 'accomplice to murder.' As he tried to frame an answer, there was a knock on the door. The Comandante looked up. Before he could react, it opened and Sergeant Alberto Gonzalez entered the room. He gave the Comandante a business card. The Comandante read it, then held it in his right hand and tapped it a few times against his left thumb. Both he and Gonzalez left without saying a word.

Paul stayed in the chair. The guards, the rifles and the bayonets continued to intimidate him. Though he was innocent of any crime, the policeman thought he was a murderer. He was in serious trouble and in a foreign land. Prior to this time, Paul always felt an innocent man did not need an attorney. Now he fully understood it is the innocent man who truly needs the attorney and it is the guilty man who does not.

He would demand to see the American Consul. It was his constitutional rights - but he was in Anchuria where his constitutional rights meant nothing. Well, he decided, I will demand to see Rutherford Wilder and I'll answer no more questions.

Chapter 35

The Cavalry Arrives

On the morning the Comandante of the Aguas Buenas guardia looked out the windows of his office toward the Central Highlands, Ellie Sue left the Casa Canada and walked down the Avenida de la Revolución toward the Abaceria. The grid of iron rods protecting the open store from petty thieves was raised and the owner was behind the counter.

He arose from his chair when Ellie Sue entered. She asked for "leche" and got the unpasteurized milk that had been delivered that morning, fresh from the dairy. Without difficulty she found and pointed to the coffee and roll-like pieces of still warm bread on the shelves behind the grocer. Getting the ham and eggs was a bit more complicated.

Having used Spanish to ask for milk and having successfully received same, she confidently ordered ham. Instead of saying "jamon," she asked for "jabon." The store keeper handed her a bar of soap. Rather than admit a mistake, she took it, but lost the courage to ask for "huevos."

The pantomime of breaking an egg and dropping it into a pan produced the desired result. The abacero placed a dozen eggs on the counter and said "huevos." She repeated the word and he smiled and said "Si, señorita, si. Huevos."

The abacero grinned broadly. He nodded his head as a sign that he now understood her other order. He retreated into the back room and returned with a slab of ham. He put his finger on the soap and said: "Jabon." Then he put his finger on the meat and said: "Jamon." Ellie Sue repeated the words.

It is satisfying to be able to communicate in a foreign language, Ellie Sue thought, even if it requires the support of pantomime. The important thing is - I managed to buy the food for our breakfast. Now,

I'll pay for it.

Her question: "Cuanto?" elicited an answer from the abacero. The abacero's answer elicited a blank look from Ellie Sue. He recognized the expression of non-comprehension. From her clothing, her accent and her general demeanor, he knew she was a Norteamericana. Of course, he also knew she was not fluent in Spanish. She probably didn't understand the figure he gave her.

The abacero was pleased to have her as a customer. Like most of the middle and lower class Anchurians, he liked gringos. He wrote a figure on a piece of paper and showed it to her. The "1" looked like a triangular 'i' and the seven had a line through it. Ellie Sue paid the bill, picked up the groceries and was leaving the store when she heard a commotion coming from across the street.

She looked up and saw Paul surrounded by half a dozen men of the guardia. He was being led down the street from Casa Canada toward the building she had called 'the police station.' A young sergeant with a billed cap led the procession. He was followed by Paul and, a few steps behind, five guardia enlisted men brought up the rear. Their rifles were all aimed at Paul in a menacing manner.

Paul did not see Ellie Sue as he was shoved into the Comandancia Building. He was more than preoccupied by the shock of finding the body, being taken into custody and, particularly, by being followed by a group of men pointing rifles at him.

Ellie Sue's immediate thought was to drop the grocery bag and run to Paul. That would not have been smart and Ellie Sue was smart. She knew she couldn't help him. She also knew the United States Consul General could. That was their job, wasn't it - getting Americans out of trouble in foreign countries? What was the name of the man Paul knew? Wilder? Yes, Wilder was the American Consul.

She backed into the store and returned to the abacero. Then she said "taxi" with a rising inflection which changed the word into a question. The abacero was happy she returned and requested a taxi. In 1938, it was demeaning for a woman of substance to carry a package in Latin America. He took the bag from her and placed it on the counter while nodding his head in approval and saying "Si. Si, señorita."

He left his shop unattended and trotted toward a nearby plaza where taxis waited for fares. In a few minutes he was back, Ellie Sue was in the vehicle and it was on its way. The driver had no trouble understanding Ellie Sue's destination. "The American Consulate, please."

* * * * *

After answering the knock on the heavy front door of the Consulate, Pedro went to the dining room where Rud Wilder and the Magnussens were having breakfast. He announced to the Consul General: "Una señorita Americana le espera."

As soon as the words left his mouth, an agitated Ellie Sue entered the room behind him. She had no intention of being kept waiting. Mary Louise was the first to react. "Ellie Sue, what is the matter?" The Professor arose from the table and repeated: "Ellie Sue."

Ellie Sue barely acknowledged their presence and went directly to the third person. "Are you Mr. Wilder?" she asked of him. "Why, yes, I am," he said, somewhat surprised and then, looking at the Magnussens, he asked: "Do you know this young woman?"

For a moment confusion reigned. Like a Verdi operatic quartet without music, all four spoke at the same time. "Whatever is the matter?" "The police have Paul." "Yes, we know her. She was on the ship with us." "What did he do?" "Is he hurt?" "I don't know." "She's the friend of Paul Eckert, the one we told you about yesterday." "You must do something." "Are you all right?"

In a loud voice, Rud Wilder demanded: "QUIET. Sit down. Calm yourself. Be orderly." With a semblance of peace restored, Wilder continued. "Now let's see what this is all about."

The Professor identified Ellie Sue. Mary Louise winked at the Consul. She wanted to be sure he remembered Ellie Sue and Paul were more than mere friends and would ask no embarrassing questions. However, when Ellie Sue got her chance she did not equivocate. She began by saying she and Paul were vacationing together, then paused and corrected herself. "No, we are living together - and we love each other."

The admission was delivered with just a touch of defiance and an unwavering look into the faces of each of the other three. Mary Louise gave the nod and smile of understanding and support. The Professor and Wilder, more cynical, exchanged glances and, discreetly, said nothing.

"This morning I left Paul at our apartment in Casa Canada and went out to buy groceries for our breakfast. When I came out of the store, I saw the police - there were lots of them - taking Paul down the street toward the police station. I don't know why. I only know they took him away. I got a taxi and came here as quickly as I could. You must do something. You've got to get him out of jail."

Even before the Consul could ask Pedro to get the Packard ready for a ride into town, Mary Louise had risen from the table and put her arm around Ellie Sue. "Charles, Rud," she said, "Go down there and bring Paul back." Wilder nodded to Pedro who went to the garage and brought the Packard to the front of the Embassy.

Wilder slipped on his coat. This would be a more formal occasion so he also took his Panama hat. At the front door of the Consulate, he looked at Ellie Sue and said: "Stay here with Mary Louise." She started to remonstrate, but Wilder held up his hand and said, "No, Ellie Sue. You stay here. You can do no good at the Comandancia and you may get in the way. Charles and I will do what we can to bring Paul back."

* * * * *

Some of the gringo employees of the Central American Fruit Company's Anchurian operation affected a superior and imperious manner and showed no respect for the different culture of the country. Those employees left the unfortunate impression that all North Americans, at best, were boorish. Some of the other Fruit Company employees were quite different. They learned the language and acted as friendly guests in a friendly nation. They were the good will ambassadors.

In his capacity as the United States Consul General in Aguas Buenas, Rutherford Wilder cultivated friendships with as many people as possible. In particular, he developed close relations with those in positions of authority - military, political or social. To many Anchurians, he not only represented the United States, he was the United States. His reputation was excellent and he was respected.

Before he would use his friendship with Anchurian officials or bring his consular authority to bear to get a fellow American out of the hands of the Comandante, Rutherford Wilder had to be sure the American deserved his support. The Comandante's respect would be lost, if he pressed an unworthy cause. That loss of respect would soon extend beyond the Comandancia. In Anchuria as in the United States, rumor and gossip traveled faster than newspapers.

Rud Wilder trusted Charles Magnussen's opinion and held his analytic ability in high regard. As he knotted his tie inside the Consulate Packard, Wilder asked the Professor for his assessment of young Eckert. He was pleased when Magnussen's analysis was positive.

When Wilder and the Professor arrived at the Comandancia, Pedro, wearing the brimmed cap he proudly wore when performing his office of chauffeur, opened the automobile door for his passengers. They walked passed the guards standing in the wide arched entrance and the Consul gave his card to the Adjutant, seated behind the desk. Wilder called him by his first name, Alberto, and asked to speak to the Comandante - "inmediatamente, por favor."

Everyone in Aguas Buenas knew "don Rud." Those who disliked him did so because they were automatically antagonistic to the "Colossus of the North." Their animosity towards 'don Rud' was nothing personal. They simply disliked the United States and anything connected with it.

The Comandante was not pro U. S. but his adjutant, Alberto Gonzalez, was. He liked the United States and everything connected with it. He took "don Rud's" card and went to the Comandante's office. He knocked. Without waiting for an invitation, he opened the door and entered the room where Paul was being questioned.

Chapter 36

Release
A National Holiday
Exoneration

After seeing the Consul's card, the Comandante held it in his right hand and struck it against his left thumbnail a few times while he decided what to do. He could not keep the American Consul General waiting. He nodded his head toward the door and he and his Adjutant left the room. Paul Eckert remained in the chair in front of the Comandante's desk, wondering what had happened.

* * * * *

"Good morning, don Rud," said the Comandante, extending his hand. Wilder would have preferred an abrazo, but he shook the hand and introduced Professor Magnussen.

"I am honored by your visit, don Rud. What brings you to the Comandancia?"

"Señor Comandante, I hope you will excuse my interruption of your important business. I need your help. I seek a national of my country. His name is Paul Eckert and I am told he is here. Is that correct?"

"Yes, don Rud, that is correct. He is being questioned because of a very serious happening. It is the violent death of Señor Federico Bergman."

"Bergman," repeated Wilder, failing to disguise his surprise. "Frederick Bergman? He was killed?" The Comandante nodded.

"I am surprised," Wilder said evenly. Knowing nothing about the facts surrounding the death, he proceeded with caution.

"Of course," he said to the Comandante, "I know you would not question one of my countrymen without good and sufficient reason. Be assured, I have no desire to meddle into the internal affairs of the Comandante of the Aguas Buenas guardia and I do not question the laws of this friendly Republic. However, it is my responsibility to report incidents of this nature to my Department of State. Naturally I wish my reports to be entirely accurate, for only in that way can we avoid the possibilities of misunderstanding between our two great nations."

The implied threat of an incident which might bring down the power of the Department of State of the Colossus of the North did not escape the attention of the Comandante.

"I understand, don Rud," he answered. "I am pleased you have extended me the courtesy of your visit. I am not a politician and have no interest in international affairs. I am merely an officer in the Guardia Civil (pause) doing my duty." The last three words were emphasized. Then he continued: "When my investigation is completed, be assured a full report will be prepared and delivered to you for transmittal to our very good friends in Washington."

This was not what Wilder wanted to hear. The Comandante was refusing to turn young Eckert loose. Perhaps the young man had killed Bergman. The Consul needed more information. He would try a different approach.

"You are very kind, Comandante," he said. "I should tell you that this young man is the son of friends of long standing. While I do not know him, personally, I hope you will understand I feel obliged to advise my friends - his parents - of his situation and condition. Perhaps you could give me some information - in an unofficial manner, of course?"

The Comandante found himself in an uncomfortable position. One of the matters that disturbed him was the fact that Eckert had no gun when he was found kneeling over the body. If Eckert killed Bergman and was engaged in the dangerous business of doing away with the body, why would he not keep the gun with him? No weapon had been uncovered in either Eckert's apartment or the Bergman living quarters.

It was possible the woman accomplice now had both the gold and the gun. She may have decided to disappear, leaving Eckert to face the music. Still, it was a man and not a woman who called him to report the body at Casa Canada. The voice spoke Spanish. Eckert did not. Was it Bergman's servant? No. The accent was not that of an uneducated peon. Was there a third man involved in the matter? Perhaps the woman had another accomplice.

The Comandante was not inclined to consider Eckert to be a prime suspect in the murder, but it was possible he was somehow involved in the death or in the lesser crime of robbery. Certainly his actions were suspicious. The question was: What should he do now that the gringo Consul had entered the picture? Don Rud did not have a reputation of defending wrongdoers, even if they were gringos.

If he kept Eckert in custody and he was found to be entirely innocent and if the United States Department of State asked questions, the Peña government in Progreso would surely use the Comandante as a scapegoat. If anything went wrong, he would be blamed. Yes, his better interests were served by a more cooperative posture.

"Very well, don Rud," he said. "I received a telephone call this morning. The caller did not identify himself. He told me there was a dead man in Casa Canada. I went there and found your compatriot bending over the body of Federico Bergman. Bergman was shot and had been dead for some time. I am now questioning the young man. He has not been - how do you say it - completely candid with me.

"His baggage was not inspected at the Aduana when he arrived on the Fruit Company ship yesterday. He bribed the Inspector. When I found Señor Eckert, he had this Sedalia gold coin in his hand." The Comandante showed it to the Consul.

"The Casa Canada register shows he is living with a woman," he continued. "Sr. Eckert did not divulge any of these things to me." Then a thought occurred to the Comandante. He looked at Wilder and said: "I presume it is the woman who brought this matter to your attention?"

"You are very astute, Señor Comandante," said Wilder. "She is, indeed, the reason I am here. She is at the American Consulate right now and, of course, is at your disposition. The young man's failure to mention her is curious."

Professor Magnussen listened without comment. He went through Customs with Paul and knew the so-called bribery consisted of a 5

Peso note wrapped around a finger. He doubted Paul was capable of murder and he knew there was nothing either curious or sinister in his relationship with Ellie Sue. Then he smiled inwardly as he thought of a maneuver that would pay back Reinhold Reichman for his unwelcome lectures on German politics. He entered the conversation.

"Yes, Señor Commandant, it is, in fact, curious," the Professor agreed. "I am sure you have noticed another curiosity. The Fruit Company ship brought a visitor to Aguas Buenas named Reinhold Reichman. He is a German national. I must tell you, in confidence, Señor Comandante, while aboard ship, Herr Reichman acted in a very suspicious manner. The name, Bergman, is also German, is it not?"

"I can tell you, Señor Comandante," added Consul Wilder, lending support to the Professor's diversion: "Señor Bergman did not speak English with a Canadian accent. I know little about him and suspect he is also an enigma to you."

The Comandante speculated. Don Rud was a clever man. Clearly he and the Professor were trying to direct attention away from the young man and to the German. Was it a red herring? Or, was there substance to don Rud's suggestion? Was the German involved in a plan to rob Bergman? Was it he who called the Comandante, telling him of the death of Bergman?

It would not take long to find and question the man named Reichman. If he could account for his actions in a satisfactory manner, he could be eliminated from the equation. Otherwise, well, don Rud was a smart man and perhaps there was substance in his suggestion. In the meantime, he would be able to check Eckert's alibi and question the young woman.

It was apparent to the Comandante that the shot heard the previous day was not fired by don Carlos Mejia. It was the sound of the shot that killed Federico Bergman. If Eckert and the woman were at El Palacio when that shot was fired, then neither could have killed Bergman.

Yes, he thought, he could release the gringo into the custody of Consul Wilder. If the young man ran, it should be easy to find a tall, non-Spanish speaking gringo anywhere in Anchuria. If he ran, the United States Consulate would receive great criticism. The anti-gringo response in all of Central America would be enormous. There were few risks involved in putting the gringo into don Rud's custody.

* * * * *

Paul Eckert was still sitting in the straight backed chair when he heard the door open behind him. He turned to see the Comandante, Professor Magnussen and another man, dressed in a white suit, enter the room. They both approached him and the Comandante said: "Señor Eckert, I ask you no more questions at this time. This is Señor Wilder. He is your government's Consul General. I release you into his custody. You must not leave Aguas Buenas. You must tell Señor Wilder where you are at all times. He is responsible for you. You may go."

Paul didn't say a word as he followed Wilder and Magnussen from the Comandante's office, out of the building and into the Consulate automobile waiting at curb side. Only then did he speak.

"I'm certainly glad you two came along. I don't know how I can thank you. That guy thinks I had something to do with Bergman's . . ."

He didn't get a chance to finish the sentence. A shot rang out behind him. Paul ducked, thinking someone was shooting at him, but such was not the case. A dead buzzard fell from the top of the Comandancia to the sidewalk beside the car. A group of the guardia soldiers, with night sticks drawn, came running out into the street.

* * * * *

Mary Louise Magnussen did her best to keep Ellie Sue calm. She was not entirely successful. Ellie Sue would run to the Consulate's front door whenever she heard the racket of an automobile bouncing up the roadway. She was waiting there when the Consulate Packard finally arrived. Her greeting of Paul was not subdued.

During the ride back from the Comandancia building, Paul told about the five Peso bribe in the Aduana, his limited association with Bergman and his decision to keep Ellie Sue out of the questioning by the Comandante. Finding the body and being taken by the Guardia was a shock and Paul simply forgot about the coin.

Neither Paul nor the Professor saw the significance of the coin being Sedalian. To Rud Wilder, it was a sign that Bergman may have solved the by now widely known mystery of the Ciudad Carillo SINDETRAG treasury. By the time they arrived at the Consulate, Paul finished his story. As soon as he got out of the Packard, Ellie Sue was there to throw her arms around him.

"We had better get inside," said Rud Wilder. "It will rain soon." They did and it did.

In the Consulate den, Paul got the opportunity to repeat the report of his morning experiences for the benefit of Mary Louise and Ellie Sue. They listened carefully. Mary Louise made supportive sounds. Ellie Sue remained fearful and Paul couldn't understand how the Comandante could possibly suspect him of killing the Canadian.

Wilder reassured them both. The Comandante, he said, was no fool. If Paul were still a prime suspect, he would not have released him into the Consul's custody. As the Comandante's investigation progressed, doubtlessly he would discover both the motive and the real murderer.

The conversation became lighter when Magnussen told how he tried to insinuate Reinhold Reichman into the matter and bring him to the Comandante's attention. Mary Louise laughed and hoped the Comandante would subject him to an equally frightening interrogation.

It was Wilder who recommended Paul and Ellie Sue visit the Comandante and show him there was nothing mysterious surrounding their "joint vacation" (which was the way Wilder delicately described it). Without mentioning it, the Consul felt sure the Comandante, once he saw Ellie Sue, would no longer consider her to be an accomplice to any crime. Sound Latin instinct, he felt sure, would quickly identify the couple's true relationship.

The atmosphere surrounding the Consulate luncheon was pleasant as both Paul and Ellie Sue's fears subsided. Paul and Wilder talked about Iowa. Professor Magnussen talked about his coming visit with the Law School dean, Clemente Diaz, in Progreso and how he looked forward to the drive through the country side. Wilder suggested Paul thank the Comandante for the suggestion of using no more than one Peso to quickly pass Customs reviews.

Ellie Sue and Mary Louise talked about a shopping trip. They planned a visit to the Municipal Market the day after the fiesta commemorating the fiftieth anniversary of the Battle of the Rio Ramasajoti.

* * * * *

In two days the national holiday celebration would occur. A grand gathering at El Palacio was planned by the City of Aguas Buenas. Wilder, in his capacity as Consul General of the United States, would be one of the speakers at the party celebrating the great victory over the Sedalians.

Both Magnussen and Wilder expounded on the questionable validity of the various national histories of the 50 year old Battle, but they cautioned one and all to never, ever, by word, deed, or body language, indicate the version of the Battle adopted in any country in which they happened to find themselves was anything except the absolute gospel.

Though Wilder would be at the dais, he promised to secure a ringside table for his four friends. He knew Mary Louise wanted to go to the party. It would give her the chance to use one of her formals and the opportunity to see and be seen by the best of Aguas Buenas society. It might be fun for Eckert and Bradshaw to participate in a fiesta in the Latin tradition. Since they didn't understand Spanish, they would probably enjoy the speeches more than anyone else.

Though Mary Louise gave graphic warnings about the perils of a stay at El Palacio, both Paul and Ellie Sue decided it would be an adventure vastly preferable to remaining in Casa Canada above the room where Frederick Bergman had been murdered. They'd take their chances at the hotel.

At four o'clock, Pedro, in black coat and black billed cap, drove Paul and Ellie Sue down the cobblestoned Avenida de la Revolución to Casa Canada. They retrieved their luggage and were driven to the Comandancia building. The heat of the day having passed, the guards now stood at reasonable attention at the entrance to the building.

The Comandante had not been idle. In spite of the noonday heat, he questioned the waiters at the El Palacio. All remembered the gringo couple. One waiter, without hesitation, clearly described Paul, recalling how he tried to pick up an orange toucan dropping from the dance floor. El Palacio's Registration book gave Reinhold Reichman's name, nationality, passport number, where he came from, where he was going and where he would stay. The Comandante was told the German had not returned to the hotel during the previous evening, nor had he taken any meals at the hotel restaurant.

The Comandante found and questioned the cab driver who brought Paul and Ellie Sue to El Palacio. He told of Bergman's translation of the request to wait for the couple and take them to El Palacio for lunch. The driver was positive Bergman was alive when the two gringos re-entered Casa Canada.

The driver was also certain he heard a shot while both of his fares were inside his taxi in front of the Comandancia. His statement erased any question of their possible guilt. Paul and Ellie Sue were no longer suspected of any involvement in the death of Bergman before they entered the Comandante's office.

* * * * *

A smiling Comandante greeted Paul and Ellie Sue. "Good afternoon Señor Eckert - and you must be Señorita Bradshaw. I am enchanted," he said as he came from behind his desk and extended his hand to Ellie Sue. "It is a pleasure to see you again," he said, looking at Paul, "and, this time, in such a more pleasant atmosphere. Our first meeting," he explained to Ellie Sue, "was under highly suspicious circumstances. I hope you both will understand my reaction and forgive any inconvenience I may have caused."

The Comandante was capable of being both charming and disarming. He returned Paul's passport and, as a gesture of good will, offered to provide them with an automobile and a driver for a tour of the countryside surrounding Aguas Buenas. The offer was a reassured Paul. He was no longer suspected of killing Frederick Bergman. He and Ellie Sue both shared a welcomed feeling of relief and they accepted the Comandante's offer. A weight had been lifted from their shoulders.

The Comandante walked them to the Consulate Packard, awaiting them at the curb. He advised them to get inside the hotel because it was going to rain soon. As he watched the car carry the two young gringos toward El Palacio, three questions were foremost in his mind. Who killed Federico Bergman? Where was Bergman's servant? Where was Reinhold Reichman?

Chapter 37

Analysis
Another Murder

On Saturday morning, the Comandante gazed out the window of his office. The death of the owner of Casa Canada intruded in his thoughts and he was unable to enjoy the sights and sounds of early morning in Aguas Buenas. His mind insisted he think about the murder. He had no alternative except to do so. He turned from the window and sat in the chair behind his desk. He reviewed the results of his investigations.

When Federico Bergman first came to Aguas Buenas, he came on horse back - by land and not by sea. The Customs Inspector couldn't provide the usual kind of gossip and information picked up at the Aduana. Bergman stayed at El Palacio and the Guest Registration book still showed his entries. He claimed he had mislaid his passport and claimed he was Canadian. He came from Progreso and was on his way to British Honduras.

Bergman, however, stayed in Aguas Buenas. He bought a home and remodeled it into a guest house. The Casa Canada had a good reputation. More was known about it than about its owner. Federico Bergman kept to himself.

Yesterday morning, a phone call told him there was a body at Casa Canada. He went to the guest house and found a gringo kneeling over Bergman's body. When found, the young man held a golden coin in his hand. The coin was Sedalian. A few years earlier, gold Sedalian coins disappeared from the Ciudad Carillo Agricultural Workers' Union office. A secret compartment under Bergman's desk was empty. The motive for the murder seemed clear. Bergman had the Sedalian Sindicato's money and someone killed him for it.

Who placed the phone call? The two gringos couldn't speak Spanish. Certainly neither of them made the call. The one who placed the call spoke in the accent of an educated man. It could not have been Bergman's servant. Was it Reichman? Did Reichman speak fluent Spanish with an Anchurian accent? That would be a surprise.

Would anyone murder a man and then call the Comandante and tell him about it? No. Whoever called him was not a murderer. He may be a thief, but he was not a murderer. Still, why did he call him. What was his motive?

Who murdered Federico Bergman? Of the people who disembarked from the Arbutus, clearly Paul Eckert and the girl were guiltless. They were naive and innocent. At least, he thought, they were naive and innocent in matters of murder and robbery. In more private social relationships, he guessed, they might be quite artful.

The other disembarking passengers on the Arbutus included Professor Magnussen and his wife. It was not their first visit to Anchuria. Their cab driver, after complaining about the volume of their luggage, said he took them directly from the Aduana to the American Consulate. Don Rud confirmed the Professor and his wife stayed with him the entire afternoon and evening. The Comandante did not doubt the Consul General's word. The Magnussen's were not involved in Bergman's death.

The only other visitor was Reinhold Reichman. Was there any substance to the American Professor's hint of the German passenger being involved in the Bergman murder? Or was it merely a smoke screen to protect the young gringo? He suspected the latter, but he had been unable to find and question Reichman.

When there is a killing and a person disappears, along with a substantial amount of money, the finger of suspicion must point toward him. Reichman registered at El Palacio almost an hour after passing through the Aduana. This meant he could have entered Casa Canada when the gringos left, killed Bergman and then gone to El Palacio. When the Comandante searched Reichman's room, only two unopened suitcases were found.

El Palacio's Guest Registration book showed Reichman traveled under a German passport. His occupation appeared as 'Bicycle Manufacturer's Representative." He came from New Orleans and his destination was Progreso. His address in Progreso was given as the

Hotel Nuevo Mundo. The Nuevo Mundo Hotel in Progreso did not cater to foreign businessmen. Respectable people wouldn't go near it. Most of its clientele rented rooms by the hour.

The Comandante telephoned the Nuevo Mundo and was not surprised when no one had any information about a Señor Reichman. It was the answer they would give to all inquiries. The people at the Nuevo Mundo would deny knowledge of Jesus Christ himself. In that regard, the Comandante conceded, some of them would be telling the truth.

Why would Reichman stay at the Nuevo Mundo?

The Comandante looked at Reichman's suitcases, now on the floor near the table in his office. When he searched them, he found nothing out of the ordinary. They were neatly packed and all the available space was filled. Why would Reichman elect to disappear without taking any clothing with him? His disappearance could not have been premeditated.

Something happened that made Reichman decide to leave in a hurry. Where did he go? The German Consulate was in Progreso. None of the city's taxi drivers had been hired to take him there. Where was he?

Of those who disembarked from the Arbutus, only Reinhold Reichman could not be eliminated from suspicion of murdering Frederick Bergman. Reichman, however, was not the only man to disappear. The other was Bergman's servant and Bergman's horse was not in the stable.

Would a servant kill his Patrón? For money? For a large amount of money? Would an innocent servant, for fear of being blamed, steal a horse and run if he found his Patrón murdered?

There were more questions than answers. Anyone who knew Bergman had the Sedalian SINDETRAG treasury could have killed him. A Sedalian from Ciudad Carillo may have traced him to Aguas Buenas. An Anchurian in Aguas Buenas may have discovered his cache. The last entry in the Comandante's mental list of suspects had to be: "unknown third party."

The Comandante sighed. He knew, sooner or later, someone would begin to spend Sedalian gold pieces. Then he would find his murderer.

237

In the meantime, he could only continue to search for Reichman and Bergman's servant.

Well, thought the Comandante, mañana is another day and he began to think about the problems of keeping order during the celebration of the fiftieth anniversary of the Battle of the Rio Ramasajoti. It wasn't only the drinking and the quarreling that could be expected from the inhabitants of his city. People from the surrounding countryside would be drawn to Aguas Buenas for the fiesta. The Comandante also knew his own men would be of highly questionable sobriety as the evening wore on.

The Comandante's decision to put Sergeant Gonzalez in charge of the guardia while he attended the city's formal party at El Palacio was a good one. He owed it to his position to attend. It would be improper for him to refuse the Mayor's invitation. He and his office would be criticized for a failure to recognize civic responsibility if he wasn't there. Besides, if things went wrong, Alberto would have to face the criticism.

The Comandante hoped don Carlos Mejia had not yet found another rifle to replace the one he had so recently confiscated. Alberto Gonzalez interrupted his thoughts when he entered the Comandante's office. He did not bring the morning coffee. He brought disturbing news.

"Comandante," he said, "a man has been shot and killed behind the Fruit Company warehouse. The men have captured the murderer."

* * * * *

After the prisoner was taken to the Comandancia, placed in the uncomfortable chair between two members of the guardia, properly armed with rifles and bayonets, the Comandante questioned the policeman who made the arrest.

"Tell me what happened. From the beginning."

"Juan and I were in our kiosco at the docks. One of the estibadores came running to us saying there was a dead man at the warehouse. Juan and I went there. There were many estibadores standing there. We asked what happened. When they came to load the bananas from the railroad cars into the warehouse, one of them went behind the building to relieve himself. He found the body and yelled out. The others ran to see what happened and one of them came to the kiosco to tell us to come.

"We demanded to know who killed him and one of the estibadores started to run. We caught him and beat him. I brought him here while Juan went to get the doctor to come for the body."

The man was proud of his work and the Comandante said he would commend him in his report of the incident. He told him to ask the doctor to call him after he examined the body. The Comandante returned to his office where the running dock worker sat in the uncomfortable straight backed chair. The two guards stood silently beside him. The man had been there for nearly fifteen minutes, but to him, it seemed like a full day.

The Comandante intended to sit, light a cigarette and stare at him. He didn't get the chance. As soon as he came into sight, the dockworker cried out: "I didn't do it, Señor Comandante. I didn't shoot him. I saw a man shoot him, but I didn't shoot him, Señor Comandante."

The Comandante silenced him. He knew he should get the man's statement while he was still panicked. "Tell me what you saw. Tell me what you did and tell me the truth," he demanded in his most official and threatening tone.

"It was yesterday, Señor Comandante. We were taking the bananas from the railroad cars to the warehouse. At mid-day we stopped to eat. It was very hot in the warehouse and I was very tired, Señor Comandante. I went into one of the empty railroad cars behind the warehouse to rest. I saw two men. One took his gun and shot the other one. I was in a railroad car. I saw him do it, Señor Comandante. I didn't do it."

The Comandante held up his hand. "What are you called?" he asked.

"I am Mario. I am called Mario," was the answer.

"Tell me Mario, the man who shot the other one, what did he look like?"

"He was wearing a white suit, Señor Comandante. A white suit. He wore a white hat. Like the ones the patrones wear, Señor Comandante. Not like the ones we wear."

"And the other one, Mario, what did he look like?"

"He wore a guayabera, Señor Comandante. A guayabera and white pants but no hat, Señor Comandante."

"Tell me Mario, when the one man shot the other, did any of your friends hear it and come out of the warehouse?"

"No, Señor Comandante, no one came from the warehouse."

The Comandante stared into Mario's eyes and said in measured tones: "This morning, Mario, a man went behind the warehouse to relieve himself. He found a body and he yelled out. You and many other estibadores heard that yell and ran out of the warehouse to find what was the matter"

Then the Comandante stood up, put his hands on the desk and leaned forward and said: "Today, when men heard a shout, they came from the warehouse to see what happened. Tell me Mario, how is it on Friday a gun can shoot next to the warehouse and yet not one man comes to see what happened? That puzzles me, Mario. Tell me how that can happen?"

Tears came to Mario's eyes. "Oh, Señor Comandante. I do not know. There was no big noise. The man in the suit took the gun from under his coat and pointed it at the other one. I saw the other one fall backwards and blood come from his chest. It turned his guayabera red. I heard no big noise, only a sound like 'putt' - like 'putt', Señor Comandante. It was not a loud noise."

The Comandante was silent. He no longer stared into Mario's eyes in an attempt to intimidate him. He looked at his desk instead. Then, without looking up, he asked: "Then what happened, Mario?"

"Señor Comandante. The man put the gun back under his coat. He looked around. He did not see me. Then he walked away - toward the docks, Señor Comandante. He walked away. When he was gone I came from the railroad car.

"I was very frightened and I wanted to run, but I was afraid to run. If I did I was sure I would be accused of killing the man and I would be caught and the guardia would shoot me. If I went back to work and said nothing, maybe no one would find out about what I saw. Today, when the guardia came, I was so frightened I ran, Señor Comandante, I ran."

The Comandante again held up his hand and Mario was silent. "I have listened to what you say, Mario. If you have told me the truth, you have nothing to fear. You will stay here tonight. No one will beat you. Tomorrow morning you must tell me if you remember anything you have not yet told me."

Chapter 38

Identification
A Tour
The Abwehr Communicates
The Arbutus

The physician who served Aguas Buenas as its Coroner confirmed part of Mario's statement. The man had been shot in the chest. His wallet was missing and the body had no identification. The doctor had never seen the man before. He was a stranger to Aguas Buenas. The dock worker's descriptions of the murderer's clothing and the hotel clerk's description of Reinhold Reichman's clothes were identical.

It looked as if Reichman killed the stranger, but the Comandante was a cautious man. He wanted to be sure Reinhold Reichman was not the victim. Only four people could identify him. Two were women and the Comandante would not call upon them. He elected to ask the American Professor to identify the body.

The Comandante called the United States Consulate and explained his request to don Rud Wilder. He asked him to bring the Professor to the Comandancia Building. Within the hour, the Consulate Packard arrived and the three men drove to the doctor's consultorio. The body lay on a table. It was covered by a sheet. The sheet was blood stained. Flies rested on it. The doctor lifted the cover, exposing the dead man's head.

Professor Magnussen looked at the body for only an instant. He turned to the Comandante and aid: "This is not Reinhold Reichman. I have never seen this man before."

* * * * *

Paul and Ellie Sue finished luncheon at El Palacio. As they waited for

242

the car and driver promised by the Comandante, they watched the toucans beg for bread. Paul recognized the Adjutant as he came across the patio floor toward

"I am Sergeant Alberto Gonzalez", he said, smiling. "You will remember me, Sr. Eckert. I am the one who arrested you at the Casa Canada. You must be Señorita Bradshaw". Ellie Sue admitted it. "I am enchanted", he said, remembering a phrase often used by the Comandante.

"I am the Comandante's Adjutant", he said proudly, "The Comandante asked me to come and offer a visit to our countryside. The automobile is waiting. When you are ready, I will be honored to drive."

Alberto's father was a field worker for the Central American Fruit Company. The children of Fruit Company employees could attend the Company's school and it was there, as a child, that Alberto learned English. Now he was twenty years old and a sergeant in the Aguas Buenas Guardia. He was pleased to have been entrusted with the care of the two gringos.

Few tourists visited Aguas Buenas and few of them had an opportunity to see any of the coastal interior. Paul and Ellie Sue were among those few. With Alberto as their guide, they visited one of the Fruit Company's plantations and saw bananas growing on their large clustered stems. Alberto explained how the banana plants were cut back to the root every year and how, periodically, the land was flooded and left fallow in order to fight the Panama Disease.

As they drove toward the round topped foothills that led up to the Central Highlands, they passed an iron barred gate set inside a long whitewashed wall. "That is the finca of our Senator, don Francisco Mendez. He is called "don Paco" and is very wealthy. He has cattle and coffee and cotton." Then Alberto showed them trees with branches that grew together when they touched the branches of other nearby trees.

The three became friendly enough to joke together. Alberto stopped at every thatched roofed roadside stand and talked with the owner. There were many of them. Each one had a red metal chest marked Coca Cola. It was an advertisement that showed it was a place where refreshment could be obtained. The chests never contain ice. Only occasionally did they contain Coca Cola.

Once, when they stopped for refreshments, it began to rain. They ran under the thatched roof. "It will be a short rain, nothing more," said Alberto.

"What's that?" Paul asked, pointing to what appeared to be a pig skin hanging above and dripping into half of a 55 gallon drum. "That is a pig skin," Alberto answered. It's been boiled in the oil in that drum. It's called 'chicharron' and is very tasty." Ellie Sue made a face, but Paul bought a piece of it, together with half a dozen bottles of Cerveza Alemana, a few candy bars and some bananas.

In the afternoon they came to a beach on the Caribbean shore. They drank Cerveza Alemana and lunched on candy and bananas. Alberto showed them a kind of grass growing on small vines that crept along the sandy ground. The leaves were small and oblong.

"Here, Señorita. Touch the vine here."

She did and the small leaves attached to the vine folded in half and closed. "This is a very good grass," he explained. "It eats the tiny flies that bother you when you swim."

They stopped once more. Alberto cut the stalk of a plant growing at the side of the road. He shaved off the tough outer cover and gave it to Ellie Sue. "Here," he said, "try it. It is sugar cane."

Alberto knew it was the custom of the gringos to eat at six o'clock in the afternoon. He never understood that custom. The evening meal should be taken at 9 or 10 o'clock. It was nearly five and he felt he should take his charges back to their hotel.

"Is there anything you would like to see before we return?"

Paul wondered how Alberto, the Comandante Luis and Wilder were all such accurate rain forecasters. He said the Alberto: "There is something I'd like to know. How can you tell when it will rain and when it will stop?"

"That is an easy question, Señor Paul. Look to the mountains. The water comes from the sea. When the wind carries enough to the mountains, they become foggy and indistinct. The water won't pass over the mountains and it will fall very soon. Once the rain has fallen, you can again see the mountains. When you can see them, the rain will soon stop."

It's really quite easy when you can read the signals. It is quite a different matter when you can't read the signals. The German Ambassador in Progreso was about to become painfully aware of it.

* * * * *

In 1938, the Abwehr had not yet perfected the mikropunkt - the micro dot. Secret information was sometimes sent by geheimtinten - invisible ink. Transmitting confidential information by geheimtinten through surface mail took too much time. Coded messages were sent to the German Embassies by short wave radio. Different codes were used, depending upon the degree of secrecy assigned to the message. The Abwehr had its own codes, different from the ones used by the diplomatic services.

In Progreso, the radio operator and the code clerk were the only members of the German Embassy staff who were trained to receive and transmit short wave messages. All decoding, however, was done by the code clerk. The codes were secret and the radio operator was not privy to them. He would receive messages and give them to the clerk who would decode and deliver them to the Ambassador. On weekends the receipt of messages from Berlin was rare, but someone had to attend the radio every Saturday and Sunday.

On this Saturday at the German Legation, the short wave operator dozed in his chair, his head resting on the table in front of him. It was his turn to man the radio room. No one else was in the Embassy. It was safe to nod off. The earphones of the headset rested on the operator's temples. They were more comfortable there and he could still hear transmittals. It's hard to rest your head on a desk when bulky earphones cover your ears.

The sounds of the clicks of dots and dashes woke the operator. He moved the earphones to his ears and took down the letters. The coded message was gibberish to him. He took it to the code room, placed it on the clerk's desk and then returned to the radio room and resumed his rest.

* * * * *

Early Thursday morning, the Arbutus, sailing from Aguas Buenas, arrived at its Villa Smit destination. The orange booms began unloading cargo destined for Madera Anchuria and at nine o'clock Luis Gogeasgoechea entered the Arbutus galley. The tray with the bananas, soft boiled eggs and oysters was laid out and ready for him to deliver to the Druckreys.

Osvaldo Carrera was frying a steak. "It is for Clevis Dewlap?" he correctly guessed. "Yes," Osvaldo answered. "He has missed many meals and he must be very hungry. I told him steak was on this morning's menu and he is waiting in the Salon."

"That is good, Osvaldo," Luis said. "Señor Dewlap has not been much of a problem this trip." Luis set the Druckrey tray down and said: "Osvaldo, you are a good man ..."

Osvaldo stopped him before he could continue. "I do good deeds for those I like. If I ever needed steak or oysters, I'm sure you would get them for me."

"Yes, Osvaldo, you know you can count on me." Luis picked up the tray and went to Cabin 8. He knocked on the door.

"Is that you, Luis?"

"Yes Señora Druckrey." The door opened and Charlotte's hands came out to take the tray.

"We are in Villa Smit, Señora Druckrey. There is a store in town where you can buy Chuchiba Indian hammocks. They are very comfortable. They are very big. Two people can sleep in them." There was a pause before an answer came from the compartment.

"Can you take us there right after lunch?"

Chapter 39

Clevis Dewla
El Palacio
Identification
The Hawthornes

On Sunday morning, after loading a portion of its hold with Anchurian mahogany, the Arbutus weighed anchor and left Villa Smit, beginning its voyage to Aguas Buenas and, finally, back to New Orleans. Only two passengers, the Druckreys, remained aboard ship.

Clevis Dewlap had disembarked after saying his good-byes to Luis and Osvaldo. Once again on dry land, he moved his belongings into the company house assigned to him. He complimented himself on his planning. During the voyage he carried enough moonshine to protect himself from the dreaded sea sickness, to allow for a gift to 'Looie' and to provide two additional quarts for use in Villa Smit.

After a careful search, Clevis found the copper tubing and the washtub he used to construct his first Villa Smit still. Soon it would again be producing sugar cane alcohol. In the meantime, he had two full Mason jars for the following evening's celebration of the Anchurian national holiday.

* * * * *

In El Palacio, Paul Eckert awoke to the calls of roosters. They made sure everyone in Aguas Buenas knew the sun was about to start the day. He turned his head and looked at the girl beside him. "El," he said. "Umhmmn," she answered, rolled to her side and put her arm across Paul's chest.

Later, fully awake, Paul swung his legs over the side of the bed. "El, do you have a rifle?"

"Yes, I do, Paul, honey, but I ran out of ammunition last night. If you are attacked, you'll just have to engage them in hand to-hand-combat."

They were referring to the cockroaches inhabiting their bathroom. Yesterday, their first morning in El Palacio, Paul stumbled into the room for a shave and shower. He opened the mirrored cabinet above the sink. A dozen objects, the size and color of dead willow leaves, ran out at the speed of light. They were gone before he was able to comprehend what happened.

The cool and moist climate of the bathroom was preferred by the cockroaches. They didn't complain when the management of El Palacio insisted two human beings temporarily share their long established place of abode. Ellie Sue and Paul became accustomed to seeing them wave their long antennae at them and then, in a flash, disappear. A long lasting attachment with them, however, was impossible. The time Paul and Ellie Sue spent in the hotel room was too short to allow it to develop. They were never able to honestly claim they were friends of the cockroaches.

After breakfast, the young couple fed the toucans with the remains of their bread and fruit. Then they walked the streets of Aguas Buenas and watched the people prepare for the celebration of the anniversary of the Battle of the Rio Ramasajoti.

* * * * *

On Sunday morning, the Comandante remembered Mario. He was still in one of the cells in the basement of the Comandancia. A man should not be in jail on a national holiday unless he committed a serious crime. Mario's reputation and record had been carefully investigated. Nothing showed he was other than what he appeared to be - a simple dock worker. Clearly, Mario did not kill the stranger. Mario was brought to the Comandante's office and placed in the uncomfortable chair in the middle of the room.

"Mario," said the Comandante, "Today is the anniversary of the Battle of the Rio Ramasajoti." Mario sat before him, silent, but nearly trembling. "Only a criminal should be in prison," the Comandante said. Then he added: "I don't believe you are a criminal, Mario. I don't believe you killed the man behind the Fruit Company warehouse."

Mario almost violently nodding his head in agreement. He started to rise from the chair and intended to say "Gracias, Señor Comandante." The first syllable left his lips when he remembered the two soldiers who stood beside him with the rifles and bayonets. He quickly sat back in the chair, with difficulty suppressing his smiles, and saying nothing.

"You may go, Mario. You are free. Remember always, Mario, the truth will help you."

Mario looked at the soldiers beside him and, testing them, he slowly stood. They didn't try to stop him.

"Señor Comandante?" he said. It was a question. It was a request for permission to speak.

"What is it, Mario?"

"Last night, I remembered something."

"Tell me, Mario. What did you remember?"

"After the man in the white suit was killed, the man who shot him took the wallet from the dead man and hid it in the stones under the rails. I will show you where."

They went to the railroad tracks behind the Fruit Company's dockside warehouse. Mario dug in the stones and gravel supporting the ties. He retrieved a wallet and handed it to the Comandante.

The Comandante was not surprised when Mario led him directly to the spot where the wallet was buried. Poverty is a terrible companion and Mario was a poor man. He could be excused for burying the victim's wallet in the hope of digging it up again when things cooled off.

The Comandante removed the bills from the dead man's wallet and folded them against his palm. "I wish you good luck, Mario," he said as he extended that hand to the dock worker. Mario took it, shook it and, with the exception of a brief smile, gave no indication the bills had been passed to him. Now he had yet another reason to enjoy the coming national holiday.

When he returned to the Comandancia, the Comandante looked through the dead man's wallet. It contained a German Republic automobile driver's license but no other particularly useful information. The murdered man was Gerhard Strauss. Another German, the Comandante said to himself. Reichman, Bergman, Eckert. Now, Strauss.

The Comandante asked Alberto Gonzalez to bring the files listing the names of the people who disembarked from the ships that docked at Aguas Buenas. Soon the Sergeant returned with a file folder containing copies of ship passenger Manifests.

"I brought only the last five years", he said. "Will that be enough?"

"Thank you, Alberto. We'll see. Now, sit down and tell me about your day with the two gringos. What do you think of them?"

"I followed your instructions, Comandante," the Sergeant said. "They are very open and friendly. They show great affection for each other. I must tell you, it would be a surprise if either were of a felonious nature. Nothing they said or did was suspicious or made me think they were anything except two young gringo tourists."

"I'm happy to agree with your assessment, Alberto. Now tell me. Did you find any Sedalian coins?"

"No, Señor Comandante. I did what you said. I asked at every place we stopped. Nobody had seen one. I am sorry my inquiries have proven unhelpful."

"On the contrary, Alberto. Not finding coins can be as helpful as finding them." Gerhard Strauss. He traveled under a German Passport. He arrived in Aguas Buenas in 1937. His occupation was listed as: Embassy Employee.

The sergeant returned to his desk at the entrance of the building and the Comandante searched the passenger lists. One of them contained the name   Gerhard Strauss. He traveled under a German Passport. He arrived in Aguas Buenas in 1937. His occupation was listed as: Embassy Employee.

Tomorrow, when the German Embassy in Progreso was open, the Comandante would inquire of Gerhard Strauss. If Strauss was attached to the German Embassy and if he were missing, the Legation's First Secretary would be asked to come to Aguas Buenas to identify the body.

* * * * *

It was mid-day and it would be a long day. The celebration of the victory over the Sedalians in the Battle of the Rio Ramasajoti would begin that evening and go on at least until daybreak. The Comandante closed the shutters on the windows of his office. He pulled off his boots, rested his heels on his desk top and leaned back in his chair. He thought about the murders. If Reinhold Reichman murdered Strauss, he didn't attempt to hide his victim's identity. He wasn't interested in the contents of the man's wallet. Was he careless? What was the reason for killing the man?

Another matter bothered him. He had avoided thinking about it. One had to be very careful when dealing with persons of political or social importance. Casa Canada's Reservation Register showed Senator Roberto Smit reserved a room for the evening of the day of Bergman's murder. The Comandante wondered why Smit made no appearance at Casa Canada. As he dozed in his chair, he began to understand what might have happened.

* * * * *

Across the street from the Comandancia, don Carlos Mejia locked the front door to the National Library. It was closed for the day. In his capacity as National Historian, don Carlos would drive to Progreso where he would address the dignitaries attending the capitol city's Ramasajoti Day celebration. While in Progreso, he planned to buy a rifle to replace the one the Comandante had so recently confiscated.

* * * * *

In Central America, the measurement of time is an inexact science. Life is governed by considerations infinitely more important than the clock. Anchurians have their priorities properly arranged. This is particularly true with regard to social engagements. A definitive answer to the question: "When?" is never really expected. The only thing that begins on time in Anchuria is the bull fight (a terrible

251

translation of the term "fiesta brava").

"The party will begin at 7:30" doesn't mean the party will begin at 7:30. It means the party might begin at 8:30, or at 9:00, or, possibly 9:30. The only time "7:30" means "7:30" is when it is followed with the words "Hora Inglesa" ("English Hour").

The Aguas Buena party celebrating the Battle of the Rio Ramasajoti was advertised as beginning at 7:30 in the evening. At 7:30, Paul and Ellie Sue left their room and looked over the iron railing and down at the center of the squared doughnut's tiled first floor. They expected to see guests already in the hotel. Their expectations went unfulfilled.

The waiters were the only ones there. They had begun to clear the center of the open floor. Paul and Ellie Sue watched while tables and chairs were moved and an area was cleared for dancing. One of the waiters mopped up what appeared to be orange caterpillars lying on the floor. Ellie Sue nudged Paul, giggled and pointed to the waiter with the mop. Paul gave her a "let's change the subject" look.

When the waiters finished their work, there were two open spaces on the floor. One was in front of the dais. It would be used for dancing later in the evening. The other was around one of the trees that grew at the side of the patio. The tree was the home of the hotel's pet. The open space marked the territorial limits of the diabolic and aggressive chained monkey.

Paul and Ellie Sue watched as, twice, the animal charged at waiters who got too close. However, it was unable to nip them. From past experience, the waiters knew the exact length of the monkey's chain as well as the sharp pain of its bite. They stayed at least one foot beyond its range. This frustrated and angered the creature that had long nourished an enmity toward everything human.

About an hour later, the Consulate automobile arrived. Pedro, smiling in his brimmed cap and black coat (and smelling faintly of aguardiente), opened the Packard door and Consul General Wilder and the Magnussens entered El Palacio. It was 8:30 and they were early arrivals. Ellie Sue and Paul went down to welcome them.

Because they were the special guests of Consul Wilder, a table in front of the stage carried a reservation card marked: MAGNUSEN Y

ECART. It was set for only four because a space was reserved for the Consul General at the speakers' dais.

The Mayor of Aguas Buenas would never offend the Fruit Company by any action which might suggest an anti-U.S. frame of mind. As a result, Wilder's chair was one seat closer to the podium than that of the Consul General of Great Britain. It was the only other country to maintain a Consular office in Aguas Buenas.

In addition to the Mayor, Wilder and the British Consul, the dais would be occupied by Senator Paco Mendez, Senator Roberto Smit, and Henry Hawthorne. Henry Hawthorne was the newly appointed Operations Vice President of the Central American Fruit Company in Anchuria.

* * * * *

Henry Hawthorne was thirty years old. He had more than earned the right to be the Operations Vice President of the Central American Fruit Company in Anchuria. He had more than earned that right because he married Arbutus Black, the daughter of Llewellyn Black. Arbutus took after her mother, the iron willed Elizabeth Black. Henry, therefore, qualified to be rewarded with a Vice-Presidency. He also deserved to be pitied.

Llewellyn Black tried to give timely warning by advising him against the marriage, but Henry was too appreciative of Arbutus' large bust and too dumb to understand what was being told to him. Henry Hawthorne was not what might be called Ph.D. material.

When Henry married Arbutus, Llewellyn Black experienced mixed feelings. Whenever he looked at Henry, he shuddered. He made the best of it by thinking he had not gained a son-in-law, but had disposed of a daughter. Black did not believe losing this daughter was a tragedy. It was a circumstance he could best describe by repeating Hamlet's declaration: 'a consummation devoutly to be wished'.

When the knot was tied, the happy couple embarked on their honeymoon - a year long cruise around the world. With Arbutus out of his household, Llewellyn Black's domestic life was easier - not easy, but easier. Then the sullen and obstinate Arbutus Black and the obtuse

Henry Hawthorne returned to New Orleans.

Elizabeth Black insisted Henry be given a position in the Central American Fruit Company. To her amazement, Llewellyn agreed without hesitation. He expected Elizabeth would make such a demand and he was prepared for it. Black had already created a position in Aguas Buenas called Vice President in charge of Operations. It had no responsibility and no authority. Llewellyn Black got rid of both Henry and Arbutus by shipping them off to Anchuria.

No important north coast Anchurian social function would be complete without representation from the Fruit Company. Hawthorne was invited to speak at the Ramasajoti Commemoration dinner.

Chapter 40

Fiesta

Everyone on the dais was expected to make a few appropriate remarks. It was hoped and expected that the addresses would be brief. The final and main speaker was Senator Roberto Smit. He was selected as the main speaker because of his history. It was not because of his family history of developing a business that protected the Anchurian eastern border from Sedalian economic encroachment. He was selected because of his history of delivering short speeches.

By 9:30 the tables were filled and at 10:00, the program began. It began at 10:00 because Senators Mendez and Smit arrived at 9:50. The Mayor was the Master of Ceremonies. He started the celebration by introducing the other five men seated at the dais. Then he went on to recognize the important individuals in attendance.

They included the Comandante, the President of Cerveza Alemana, Professor Magnussen and Paul Eckert, who was introduced as an American industrialist from Chicago who came to Aguas Buenas to investigate eco0nomic development potentials. (The Customs official had spread the word that Paul's passport listed his occupation as "Capitalist.")

The Mayor also introduced others - many others. By the time he worked his way down to those who sat at the furthest table, the food was served and, in most cases, the soup course was finished.

Finally, the speeches began. Consul Wilder spoke in Spanish and received an ovation. Paul and Ellie Sue didn't understand a word of it. They feigned interest and applauded when everyone else did. The British Consul delivered his comments in English. He looked like the actor, Eric Blore, and his accent was so thick no one, including the Magnussens, Wilder, Ellie Sue or Paul, understood a word of it. Nevertheless, he was heartily applauded. Henry Hawthorne was the next to speak. He gave his speech in English. His speech was the cause of some excitement.

* * * * *

The Fruit Company provided materials designed to prepare its Central America executives for life in Central America. Included within the materials were a number of pre-printed speeches, both in English and in Spanish. They were to be used if an executive was called upon to deliver an address to some local Central American group. The file contained speeches appropriate for almost every one of the various celebrations annually held in each or any of the Republics.

Hawthorne searched the file and found speeches entitled: "For Delivery at Battle of Ramasajoti Celebrations." The speech for use in Anchuria was exactly the same as the one prepared for use in the Republic of Sedalia, except the names of the Republics were interchanged. One address praised the brave Anchurian patriots and the other praised the brave Sedalian patriots. One castigated Anchurian criminals and gringo imperialists. The other castigated Sedalian criminals and gringo imperialists.

Unfortunately, Henry Hawthorne carelessly picked up the one prepared for usage in the neighboring Republic of Sedalia. More unfortunately, he didn't recognize his error. Even more unfortunately, he delivered the speech at the El Palacio fiesta.

Hawthorne's remarks were not punctuated by applause. As the bi-lingual Anchurians translated his remarks to their non-English speaking table-mates, looks of consternation appeared on the faces of his audience. Angry murmurs arose at Hawthorne's accolade of the brave Sedalian soldiers who saved democracy by repelling the hated Anchurian invaders.

Henry Hawthorne sat down, satisfied he had performed well, but wondering why his words were greeted with shocked silence. When Ellie Sue overheard a statement made by the wife of the Mayor who was seated at the next table, she leaned over toward the Professor and asked: "What do the words 'estupido' and 'hijo de puta' mean?" "Never mind," was the Professor's response.

Senator Paco Mendez limited his comments to the historic significance of Aguas Buenas as the birthplace of the Republic of Anchuria and the home of the patriots who defended the Republic and defeated the Sedalians. He ended with the assurance that the brave men of Aguas Buenas would always defend the Republic against all dangers, foreign and domestic. He emphasized "domestic."

Senator Roberto Smit was the last to speak. Paul, now on his third Cerveza Alemana, rubbed his leg against Ellie Sue. Mary Louise noticed it. Professor Magnussen tried not to look bored and almost succeeded. The Senator spent five minutes describing the bravery of the Anchuria militia on the Ramasajoti battle fields and the bravery of his progenitor who secured the nation's boundary from further Sedalian encroachment by building Villa Smit so close to the Sedalian border.

The second half of his speech dealt with the bravery of the men of Aguas Buenas when they were threatened with bombardment by English warships during the previous century. (The British Consul General looked uncomfortable.) Senator Smit mentioned the recent loss of liberty by European nations. He ended his speech with a statement of the necessity of defending the Republic against all dangers, foreign and domestic. He emphasized "domestic."

Roberto Smit's speech received a standing ovation from the celebrants. They knew his was the last speech they would have to endure. The Senator had bested his usual performance, speaking for only eleven minutes. It was truly appreciated. The party could now begin in earnest.

Those at the dais removed their coats and ties. The few men in the audience who were not wearing guayabera did the same, excepting only the waiters and the British Consul who felt the situation required formality. The Comandante walked towards Senator Smit while others congratulated him on the excellence of his speech. Senator Paco Mendez intercepted him.

"Ah, Señor Comandante," he said "a pleasure to see you. I hear there has been some unpleasantness here in Aguas Buenas."

"Yes, Señor Senator. An unfortunate affair. The owner of the Casa Canada and, yesterday, another man - both murdered."

"So I am told," said Mendez. "I am sure you will find the wrongdoer."

"Did I see you enter with Senator Smit?" the Comandante asked. "We are honored when two illustrious Senators grace our celebration."

When the Comandante changed the subject, Mendez' reaction was immediate. Was the Comandante going to Roberto Smit to question him? Had Smit been seen at Casa Canada? Or perhaps his reservation had been discovered? Offense is better than defense, thought Mendez.

"You are very kind, Señor Comandante," he said. "This matter at Casa Canada - it was only by good fortune that Senator Smit was not there. I made reservations for him, but, on reflection, I thought it would be most ungracious of me not to invite him to my finca. Luckily, he accepted my invitation before he left Villa Smit. Otherwise he would have gone to Casa Canada and his life may have been endangered."

"Yes, yes," answered the Comandante. "A man like Senator Smit deserves good luck." When he left without further question, Paco Mendez was relieved. Bergman/Anderson's death posed no immediate problem to him,.

The Comandante, too, was satisfied. Now he correctly guessed the identity of the man who called to tell him of the body in Casa Canada. It was clear. Senator Smit arrived at Casa Canada, found the body and then hurried to don Paco's finca. He was the one who called the Comandante.

No murderer would direct the guardia to the body of his victim. Smit was no murderer and Smit was too honorable to be a thief. There was no need to embarrass him. His secret was safe with the Comandante.

The waiters were busy. They scurried among the tables, picking up and carrying empty glasses to the bar. Then they scurried from the bar back among the tables, delivering replacements. The chairs on the dais were removed and replaced by an orchestra consisting of seven marimbas. One of the musicians doubled on the saxophone.

Their favorite song was: "Jamaican Rumba." Before the sun rose on the following day, they played it many, many times. As soon as the marimbas began, the floor was crowded with dancers. The music was loud. It was lively. There was a background rumble of happy conversation and laughter.

Professor Magnussen saw Mary Louise begin to keep time with her foot and he nearly panicked. She was perfectly capable of committing the outrage of asking him to dance. Rather than run the risk, he arose and went to the cluster of people surrounding Rud Wilder. He returned to the table with the Consul, gave him his seat and asked him to keep Mary Louise out of jail. He excused himself, saying he would leave the party since he must rise early and drive to Progreso. He, thus, successfully avoided dancing and Mary Louise could do nothing except call him a coward.

Wilder and Mary Louise danced. Paul and Ellie Sue waited for a fox trot and watched the Mayor dance a merengue. They tried to learn the footwork of the dance by observation. Mary Louise and Wilder came off the floor in time to see the Comandante approach the table. "May I join you?" he asked.

"Certainly," said the Consul General, "the Señor Comandante, is always welcome at our table."

The relief Paul experienced when the Comandante told him he was not a suspect in the death of Frederick Bergman had worn off and was replaced by memories of the intimidating interrogation. The Comandante read Paul's mind. "I hope my questioning did not upset you," he said to Paul as he moved a chair to their table.

"No, no, of course, not," said Paul and then he added: "Well, as a matter of fact, yes. Yes, it did upset me and it still upsets me."

The Comandante raised his hand, palm forward to stop further comment and quickly said: "Then I apologize to you. It is my job to ask questions. I tell you in all honesty, it is clear you are not involved in this unfortunate happening. I hope we can forget the matter. It is in the past. Let us enjoy the evening."

The rum, the Cerveza Alemana and the aguardiente all flowed freely. The Comandante spelled the Consul and danced with Mary Louise. Paul danced with Mary Louise. The Comandante taught Ellie Sue to dance the merengue and she taught Paul. Mary Louise taught everyone to dance the latest craze from the States - the Lambeth Walk.

Ellie Sue divined the meaning of the Spanish word "estupido." No one would explain the meaning of the Mayor's wife's phrase "hijo de puta." She kept pressing the Comandante for a translation. After the Anchurian rum had its effect, the Comandante finally capitulated. He gave the literal word for word translation: "son of a female dog."

Ellie Sue got the point. She had heard Henry Hawthorne's speech and his idiotic reversal of hero and enemy. After telling the Comandante she entirely agreed with the lady's characterization, a thought occurred to her. She and the Comandante put their heads together in conspiracy.

The marimba band played a fox trot and the conspirators went to the table occupied by Henry Hawthorne and the large busted, but plain faced Arbutus Black Hawthorne. The Comandante danced with Arbutus and Ellie Sue danced with Henry. It was heavy weather for the Comandante. Arbutus insisted on leading. Though her rhythmic abilities were more than merely limited, he stood up under the pressure and survived the dance.

As Ellie Sue danced with poor Henry Hawthorne, she maneuvered him to a place on the floor where his backside moved nearer and nearer and finally too near to the monkey's tree. Once she brought him into range, the animal wreaked terrible Anchurian vengeance for Henry's clumsy faux pas. The animal attached itself to and bit a piece from Hawthorne's gluteus maximus.

As she returned to her table, Ellie Sue winked at the Mayor's wife. The Mayor personally delivered a gin and tonic to her. Ellie Sue became popular with the Anchurians and she enjoyed the party. The monkey also enjoyed the party. It had a good time. The Comandante began to think, perhaps, gringos weren't that bad after all.

Chapter 41

The Morning After
The Market

On the day after the celebration of Anchuria's glorious victory at the Battle of the Rio Ramasajoti, Professor Magnussen was in the Consulate dining room at seven. By the time he finished breakfast, Pedro had filled the Packard's gas tank and parked it at the front door of the Consulate.

When Pedro saw the Professor drive the auto out of the courtyard and through the pillared entrance, he went to his room above the Consulate garage. He was glad he didn't have to take the Professor to Progreso for the meeting with Clemente Diaz.

Pedro was not feeling well. He had a headache. His stomach was queasy. He needed bed rest. At noon a driver would deliver a Rolls Royce to the Consulate. Don Rud had made the arrangements to borrow it when he shared some scotch and soda with his British counterpart during the previous evening at El Palacio. At noon, Pedro had to be dressed and ready to drive to the Municipal Market, but he now had a few hours to rest and allow his body to repair the damage it had suffered during the previous evening's celebration.

It was very late when Paul and Ellie Sue left the dance floor to return to their room in the hotel. Paul awoke at ten. Ellie Sue, wearing his pajama tops, had already chased the cockroaches from the bathroom cabinet. They showered, he shaved, she put on her face and they spent the rest of the morning walking, admiring the colonial architecture of the older part of Aguas Buenas and enjoying the sights and smells of a city born in a different culture. At noon, they again shared their lunch with the toucans and then retired for an early afternoon siesta.

During their first visit to the Consulate, Mary Louise and Ellie Sue had planned a shopping tour. Mary Louise said she'd pick them up at three. They both suspected it was "three o'clock - Hora Inglesa."

Because the Professor bailed out early, Rud Wilder spent the greater part of the time between yesterday's midnight and today's sunrise dancing with Mary Louise to the music of seven marimbas and an occasional saxophone. He was sincerely sorry that the Professor never learned to dance. He was equally sorry that both he and Mary Louise had learned to dance.

The two of them got back to the Consulate at six thirty in the morning. It was now two in the afternoon and he awoke to a knocking on the door of his bedroom. It was Mary Louise. "Wake up, Rud. It's afternoon. The sun is shining. It's a beautiful day for shopping." He put a pillow over his head and said: "I'm going to strangle her. I'm going to strangle her."

* * * * *

Senators Smit and Mendez left the celebration soon after the speeches and returned to the Mendez finca. As was his custom, don Paco arose early. As was not his custom, don Roberto also arose early. They had morning coffee on the hacienda's patio and discussed the event that would shape Anchurian history.

Gossip about the death of Bergman, the disappearance of his servant and the mystery of the SINDETRAG treasury had circulated at the celebration party. The Comandante appeared to accept don Paco's explanation of Senator Smit's presence at his finca and there was no hint or indication of any knowledge that would draw them into the investigation or affect their plans for removing President Peña from office.

The Senators knew they must strike soon. Days earlier, Osvaldo Carrera had telephoned Senator Mendez from the Central America Fruit Company dock, giving him the disquieting news of the presence of a suspected Nazi agent. It was essential to develop support from the students, neutralize the military and secure armament as quickly as possible. Investigation of the Aguas Buenas murders could prematurely expose their plot. Moreover, the threat of an alliance between Peña and the European fascists was real.

If a so-called Friendship Treaty were signed, no one would attempt to overthrow Peña. With the military support of the Nazis, his power would be absolute. All of his opposition would face exile or death. Time was of the essence. Later in the morning, other major players whose support was essential to the planned coup d'etat would meet at the Mendez finca. The threat of the Treaty and the presence of a Nazi agent, they both hoped, would galvanize their co-conspirators into action.

The time for decision had come. Delay would destroy their plans. If all went well, within three weeks the coup could take place. Mendez and Smit sipped their morning coffee and prepared for the meeting of the conspirators. At ten o'clock, the first black Packard turned through the entrance to the Mendez finca.

* * * * *

The Comandante slept late on Monday. He entered the Comandancia at three in the afternoon. He was in a good mood. Alberto Gonzalez reported no major disasters. His men, though somewhat subdued and hung over, were mostly present and/or accounted for.

A phone call to the First Secretary of the German Embassy in Progreso confirmed Gerhard Strauss was the Legation's Code Clerk. The First Secretary admitted Strauss was not at his post. The Comandante reported the murder and his evidence that the victim was the missing clerk. Descriptions matched. The First Secretary said he would come to the Comandancia on Tuesday.

The death of Gerhard Strauss created problems for the German Ambassador. No one in the Legation could de-cipher the message that had arrived from Berlin on Saturday. The murdered clerk must have had a special cipher which had not been disclosed to the Ambassador. The Ambassador's suspicion that the code clerk was an Abwehr agent was proven to the old diplomat's satisfaction.

* * * * *

Since colonial times, in certain streets and squares of Aguas Buenas, vendors displayed their goods in the shade of sheets of cloth stretched over poles. There they sold vegetables and fruits and the wooden carvings and pottery and woven products made in their homes. The sites of these markets did not change throughout the years.

As the population of the city grew and the demand for their products increased, more vendors appeared. They set up shop at the same places that housed the old markets. In the mid-1930s, automobiles were imported and the narrow streets of the central part of Aguas Buenas became congested. The Mayor of the city had a serious traffic problem. He solved it by constructing a Municipal Market building at what was then the outskirts of the city.

The building was spacious and had running water and electricity. It contained stalls where vendors could hawk their goods. Fruits and vegetables were in one section, meats in another and dry goods in a third.

The floor of the building was made of cement and long troughs were cut into it. The troughs ran past the backs of the stalls and out into the open where they carried the building's effluvia somewhere. No one was interested in knowing exactly where, but it was somewhere downhill from the Market. The water inside the Municipal Market evaporated as it slowly ran through the troughs. It had the effect of cooling the building during the heat of the day.

Each morning housewives and the maids of the more well-to-do households came to the market to buy fresh foods. Halves and quarters of beef and pork and goat hung from S shaped hooks in the butcher's cubicles. A city ordinance required the meat to be encased in cheesecloth, but, consistent with the Latin's insistence on personal liberty, no one, butcher or customer, paid any attention to it.

If pork were ordered, the customer would point to the chunk of hanging meat that looked most appealing. The butcher would strike it with the flat side of his cleaver. The flies would scatter. He would take the meat down, place it on his heavy table and whack off the number of kilos ordered. Then he'd re-hang the meat and wait for another customer.

The best time to get the meat was early in the morning, before the sun had the opportunity to warm the building and activate all of the flies that swarmed there. The city of Aguas Buenas was justly proud of its Municipal Market. When compared to the previous markets, it was a vastly more pleasant and sanitary place to shop.

The dry goods portion of the market displayed the work of the artisans. Before dawn, mestizos could be seen trudging down mountain paths and narrow roads toward Aguas Buenas with a dozen handmade chairs or huge woven net bags filled with pottery tied to their backs. The best time to buy those items was in the early evening when vendors would be ready to return to their villages. They wouldn't want to carry their goods back with them. The prices would drop.

It was three o'clock in the afternoon when Pedro tooted the horn outside El Palacio. Only Mary Louise was waiting in the Rolls Royce. Rud Wilder had begged off, claiming he had to prepare, encode and send an overdue report to Washington.

As Pedro drove his three passengers to the Municipal Market, he explained the intricacies of the negotiation of purchase/sale agreements at the Municipal Market.

* * * * *

1. Whatever the seller says in response to your question: "How much?" you must clutch at your heart, look outraged and make a statement like: "That must be your telephone number." or, "I asked how much for the — was worth, not how much my accent was worth."
2. Never answer the Seller's question: "How much will you pay?" until very late in the negotiation. Then make it close enough to his last quote to elicit further bargaining because you will probably have to increase the figure.
3. Practice by bargaining for something you don't want and have no intention of buying. It will give you a feel for the extent of the final discount the seller is willing to give on his goods.
4. If the Seller will let you walk away without continuing to try to sell the item, he has probably given you his lowest price.

* * * * *

With his advice given, Pedro delivered Mary Louise, Ellie Sue and Paul to the entrance of the Municipal Market, wished them good luck and silently hoped Mary Louise's purchases would fit inside the automobile. Then he parked the car under the trees of the nearby plaza, tilted the brimmed cap over his face, slid back in the seat and snoozed.

Within minutes of entering the market, Mary Louise had wandered down one of the aisles separating the stalls. Paul and Ellie Sue walked down another. They remained separated in the maze and met only when they returned to the Rolls Royce.

Pedro's advice was valuable to Paul and Ellie Sue even though it presumed the bargainers all spoke the same language. It was slow going but, with his Spanish/English dictionary in hand, Paul finally successfully concluded the bargaining for the purchase of a hand woven wool blanket. At first, he had no intention of buying it.

The blanket was offered for six and a half pesos, but quickly came down to five pesos, eighty-five centavos, the seller giving ten percent off the top. Paul asked, in Spanish: "...Eso.. (pause).. es.. (pause).. la deuda.. (pause).. hipotecaria?" (Is that the mortgage debt?)

The seller smiled and said: "Very good. How about five pesos?"

"It is too much."

"How much will you give me?" (Question disregarded.)

"Too much."

"It cost me four pesos. I will sell for four and a quarter pesos."

"Still too much. I don't need a blanket."

"It is cooler in the hills."

"I'm not going to the hills."

"All right, four pesos, but that's my lowest price."

"Still too much." Paul turned to go.

"It is beautiful work, Señor. Feel how thick it is."

"It is excellent work. I admire it very much. But it is too expensive."

"I like you and your wife. I have not made a sale all day. I will sell it to you below cost - three and a half pesos. Perhaps it will change my luck."

Paul bought the blanket for three pesos.

Ellie Sue bought a mahogany bowl with the face of a Mayan goddess carved on its inner base. Her system was more direct and didn't take much time. The bowl was offered at two pesos. Ellie Sue offered one. The seller offered one and three quarters. She said: "No," and started to walk from the stall. The seller followed her and kept talking. Ellie Sue kept walking until she was nearly in the outer aisle. Then she turned, took out one peso and held it up in her hand. The seller knew she meant business, so he gave her the bowl and took the peso.

The next purchase represented the classic struggle between a willing buyer and a willing seller. Paul found a colorful hammock, loosely woven from strands of coconut fibers. Paul wanted it. The seller wanted to sell it. Paul knew the seller should give a fifty percent discount. The seller thought he could get away with a smaller price adjustment.

The battle raged for nearly twenty minutes. They were fifty centavos apart. Paul broke the deadlock. He put the hammock in the seller's left hand. He put four pesos in the seller's right hand. He told him he would count to five and if the seller didn't hand him the hammock, he would take back the four pesos. At the count of five, the seller handed him the hammock. Then the seller invited them to the back of his stall for a "cafecito." As he poured out the small cups of black coffee, he told them how much he enjoyed dealing with them.

The final purchase was made from a flower vendor. The cost of two dozen gladioluses was so small they didn't have the heart to bargain with her. Then Paul and Ellie Sue carried their treasures back to the automobile.

They arrived in time to see Pedro struggling to put a reddish colored clay pot, nearly three feet in diameter, on top of the Rolls. As Paul helped him tie it down, he noticed it was placed on top of a carved mahogany door that lay flat on the roof of the vehicle.

On the way back to the Consulate, Mary Louise explained she followed Pedro's advice and practiced by bargaining for things she didn't really want. "...but the prices were reduced to such a small amount I just couldn't resist buying the door and the pot."

That evening, Rud Wilder took the threesome to dinner at a restaurant in the hills overlooking the city. With a background of Caribbean music, played by seven marimbas and, occasionally, a saxophone, they ate long, Anchurian river shrimp, fried in butter and garlic. They watched the sun set behind them in the Central Highlands as the Caribbean changed its colors and the lights of Aguas Buenas slowly lit up below them. It was very romantic, a fact that did not escape the attention of Paul and Ellie Sue - or of Mary Louise and Rud Wilder for that matter.

Much later in the evening, Professor Charles Magnussen returned to the Consulate. As he walked down the hallway to the guest room, he saw a carved mahogany door and a large reddish colored pot. He knew who owned them. He knew Mary Louise had left them in the hallway to make sure he noticed them.

He decided to make no mention of them. Mary Louise seemed to be sleeping when he entered the room. He turned on the lights, but she showed no signs of life. Then he said, softly: "Is that a banana spider on the pillow?" Mary Louise's immediate reaction gave unmistakable proof that she had not been sleeping.

Chapter 42

The Arbutus
The First Secretary
Resolution
Union

Late in the evening, before the last day of Paul and Ellie Sue's visit to Anchuria, the Arbutus returned from Villa Smit and was again docked at the Central American Fruit Company pier in Aguas Buenas. Before the sun had risen the next morning, lines of "estivadores" carried stalks of banana from the Fruit Company warehouse to the holds of the Arbutus. The ship would be fully loaded in the early afternoon and, later, it would leave port and sail back to New Orleans.

In the morning, Ellie Sue and Paul packed their bags and went to the Consulate for brunch with the Magnussens and the Consul General. After the meal, Mary Louise pulled Paul to the side and whispered in his ear: "Don't let her get away." Then she did the same to Ellie Sue.

When the good-byes were all spoken, Paul and Ellie Sue got into the Packard and, for the last time, bounced down the cobblestone road from the Consulate to the center of Aguas Buenas. Soon they were at the Central American Fruit Company pier. Pedro, in black coat and black billed cap, carried their luggage up the Arbutus gangplank and into Cabin 9, A Deck, Port. He refused the tip until its third offer and then returned to the Consulate automobile.

As they unpacked in their cabin, Luis Gogeasgoechea knocked on the door. He welcomed them back aboard the Arbutus and, after looking down the passageway to make sure Captain Stavropopolous was not about, he reached under his jacket and gave them a complimentary bottle of Ouzo.

Luis told them the only other passengers were the Druckreys and since they were always "otherwise occupied," he would be able to spend all his time attending to their wishes. He was happy to see they were still happy.

After Ellie Sue and Paul left for the Arbutus, the Professor told Rud Wilder about his conversations with Clemente Diaz. They were particularly productive and his work in Anchuria had taken less time than he thought. He planned to use the extra time in Sedalia to undertake additional studies. He decided to leave the following afternoon.

Then he made the announcement that chilled Mary Louise. Transporte Anchuria, C. A. had a Ford Tri-motor airplane flying between Aguas Buenas and Santa Elena. He had already reserved two seats. He and Mary Louise would fly from Anchuria to Sedalia.

Though Professor Magnussen was never overly enthusiastic about the prospect of flying, he had weighed the pros and cons of air transportation. The list of advantages included: (a) Mary Louise was afraid of flying; (b) Mary Louise had only one day to re-pack; (c) Mary Louise could carry only that amount of baggage allowed by the airline; and, (d) in future Latin American study trips, she would not be able pack as if she were planning to accompany Admiral Byrd on a year long visit to the South Pole.

The major disadvantage was: he was afraid of flying and would probably throw up. It was a good trade-off, he thought. Professor Charles Magnussen was now willing and eager to use air transportation. Noting Mary Louise's reaction to his decision, he thought to himself: That ought to pay her for throwing my typewriter ribbon overboard.

Rud Wilder agreed to arrange to send the door, the huge pot and the balance of her luggage to the Magnussen's Bowling Green address by surface transportation. The Magnussens would be in Ohio long before the shipment was delivered.

* * * * *

As Ellie Sue and Paul boarded the Arbutus, the First Secretary of the German Embassy, in his chauffeur driven Mercedes Benz, arrived at the Aguas Buenas Comandancia Building. The First Secretary was ostensibly there to investigate the death of the embassy code clerk and arrange to send his body to Germany. He had a hidden agenda. Like Gerhard Strauss, he too, was an Abwehr agent. He was the one who sent Strauss to Aguas Buenas to meet Reinhold Reichman and bring him to Progreso to begin negotiations with President Máximo Peña.

The First Secretary was more interested in learning the whereabouts of Reinhold Reichman than in dealing with the corpse of the code clerk who, he thought, was probably killed for the money in his wallet. He presented himself to Alberto Gonzalez at the Comandancia.

The Adjutant delivered the diplomat's card to the Comandante. After a short wait, he ushered him into the Comandante's office where he was invited to sit on the uncomfortable straight backed chair that faced the Comandante's desk.

"Will you have a cigarette, Señor Secretary?" he asked. "The unfortunate death of Gerhard Strauss is, I presume, the reason for the honor of your visit," he continued.

"Thank you," answered the diplomat, taking a cigarette from the pack offered by the Comandante. "The Ambassador must report this incident to Berlin. I will need a full report of the facts surrounding the death and of the status of your investigation."

The Comandante was not insensitive to the slight undertone of arrogance. This man didn't politely ask. His statement was more of a demand. The Comandante resolved to give him the least information possible.

"There is little I can tell you, Señor Secretary," he answered. "You already know how the body was found. Of course, we will continue to aggressively seek out the murderer and I will immediately inform you of all relevant discoveries. In the meantime, Señor Strauss' ring, watch, wallet and handkerchief will be deposited with you." The Comandante paused and then added: "You will sign a receipt."

What insolence, thought the First Secretary. I will remember this man. "Of course," he said as he signed the document: "you must have a record of the delivery of personal effects. Tell me, Señor Comandante, do you have any idea who might have committed this terribly barbaric act - or why it was done?"

"Be assured our investigation continues, Señor Secretary and when we have facts, we will report them to you." The Comandante rose giving the indication that the interview was over. The First Secretary remained seated. He drew on the cigarette, blew the smoke and then looked up at the Comandante. "There is another matter which requires discussion," he said.

"How may I serve you?" replied the Comandante as he returned to his chair.

"We have received an inquiry concerning a German citizen named Reinhold Reichman," he lied. "We are told he was a passenger on the S S Arbutus which docked here, last week, I believe. A relative in Germany has received no communication from him and is worried...."

The Comandante interrupted the Secretary with: "Ah, Señor Reichman. Yes, I can help you, Señor Secretary. Señor Reichman came through our Aduana last Thursday morning. He registered at El Palacio, left the building and has never returned. His hotel bill remains unpaid.

"The owner of the hotel is quite interested in finding him. He has asked me to look for him, but Sr. Reichman is nowhere to be found. If Señor Reichman contacts your Embassy, you will tell me?" and the Comandante again arose from his chair. This time the First Secretary also got up.

When the First Secretary returned from his visit with the Comandante, the Ambassador advised Berlin of the death of Gerhard Strauss and of the disappearance of Reinhold Reichman. The Ambassador also asked Berlin to re-send the undecipherable Saturday message. It was his way of telling them he knew his Embassy housed an Abwehr agent. He didn't expect a response. He didn't get one.

The Ambassador's next message from Berlin was easily decoded from a lower grade diplomatic cipher. It told him a new code clerk would arrive in two weeks. The Ambassador presumed he, too, would be an Abwehr agent.

* * * * *

In Hamburg, news of the murder of Gerhard Strauss and the disappearance of Reinhold Reichman sent a shock wave through the Abwehr. Strauss had been ordered to meet Reichman when he disembarked at Aguas Buenas. Was Strauss murdered by some waterfront thug? If so, where was Reichman?

The Abwehr was sure there was more to Strauss' death than a simple random killing. Strauss may have been killed by American agents and Reichman may have been captured. Was he now divulging Abwehr secrets to the Americans?

That possibility was too dangerous to overlook. The New York agent who replaced Reichman was advised. His contacts were warned to keep a low profile and be ready to travel to Canada on short notice. The Treaty with Peña would be delayed until it could be determined what happened to Reichman.

* * * * *

It was nearly noon when the German First Secretary left the Comandancia building. The Comandante closed the shutters on the windows of his office and removed his boots. He leaned back in his chair and again analyzed the two murders. He had already developed a scenario that had the ring of truth.

The motive for the deaths was obvious. The coin Paul Eckert found when he discovered the body as well as the false floor hiding place under Bergman's desk suggested the Canadian had found the missing SINDETRAG treasury. Perhaps Bergman wanted to move his Sedalian gold to Germany, or change it into German Reichsmarks. Perhaps he confided in and sought the assistance of a German Embassy code clerk. Diplomat pouches and luggage were never reviewed by Customs Agents.

Perhaps Strauss hired an expatriate German to come to Aguas Buenas, ostensibly for the purpose of smuggling the gold to Germany, but, in reality, for the purpose of killing Bergman and taking his hoard. Instead of getting a fee for the service of laundering Bergman's gold, Strauss could pay a fee to his German associate and keep everything else for himself. Perhaps, that associate decided to kill Strauss as well as Bergman and disappear with the entire cache.

This is more than an interesting scenario, thought the Comandante. Yes, he said to himself, it could have happened. In his mind, he reconstructed the scene.

When the Arbutus arrived at Aguas Buenas, Gerhard Strauss, was waiting for Reinhold Reichman. Strauss intended to perfect the robbery scheme with Reichman and return to Progreso. There he would put himself in the company of witnesses who could remove him from any suspicion of a theft in Aguas Buenas.

Reichman, however, had different plans. He would not share Bergman's hoard. Robbery would be replaced by murder. When the Arbutus docked, instead of meeting with Strauss, Reichman went directly to Casa Canada.

He found the young gringos were there and waited until they left for lunch at El Palacio. Then he met with Bergman and told him how he would change his gold and silver coins into a currency that could be freely invested or spent. When Bergman showed his hoard, Reichman killed him. Then he went to El Palacio and registered for a room in order to establish his own alibi. He would appear to be a visitor who just arrived on the Arbutus and had no connection with Frederick Bergman.

After leaving his luggage in El Palacio, Reichman went to the docks to meet with his embassy clerk accomplice. Reinhold Reichman killed Gerhard Strauss. He must have decided to immediately disappear with what was left of the SINDETRAG treasury.

Bergman's servant discovered the body of his patrón at Casa Canada. What fear he must have felt. The Comandante couldn't blame him for running. He took his patrón's horse and is in one of the neighboring Republics by now. The Comandante concluded Reichman and the Sedalian gold were far from Anchuria. Too bad, thought the Comandante. It is doubtful the German will be brought to justice.

Only one thing bothered him. The gun that killed Bergman had no silencer. The sound of that shot was heard at the Comandancia building, two blocks from Casa Canada. The shot that killed Strauss made no sound. Did Reichman kill Bergman before he had time to put the silencer on his gun barrel? Later, in El Palacio, did he put it on and then kill Strauss?

In the Comandante's experience, it was only Charlie Chan of the movies who was able to answer all questions that arise during the investigation of a crime. Real life was different.

* * * * *

Late that same afternoon, Captain Stavros Stavropopolous stood on the bridge of the Arbutus as it left the Anchurian coast and moved into the Caribbean Sea. So far it had been an uneventful trip. He sailed from New Orleans to Villa Smit and got the Arbutus unloaded, reloaded with tropical wood and bananas, and now was sailing back to New Orleans.

Except for short confrontations with a strange American woman and a strange German man, it had been a pleasant voyage. With any luck, he might complete the trip without speaking to anyone else. It could be close to a perfect trip. As he stood there, he heard the door to his bridge open. Oh no, he thought. Another terrible confrontation.

He turned to see Paul Eckert and Ellie Sue Bradshaw enter his sanctum sanctorum. "Out, out," he screamed as he advanced upon them with an extended arm and forefinger pointing to the door. They did not retreat. The two stood their ground. "Out! Out!" he repeated, but this time a bit slower and not so loudly. Still they did not move. "Out? Out?" he questioned in a more conversational tone.

"Captain," said Paul, "We want to get married." Ellie Sue nodded her approval. Captain Stavropopolous heard the statement, but it didn't seem to register. "You have the authority to marry us," said Paul. "Oh, you will marry us, won't you, Captain?" said Ellie Sue in her soft Arkansas voice. If Captain Stavropopolous had any doubt about what he was going to do, Ellie Sue removed it.

That evening, before dinner, Captain Stavros Stavropopolous performed the first marriage of his career. The bride, the groom and four people attended the ceremony. Harvey Druckrey was the best man and Charlotte was the bridesmaid. Luis Gogeasgoechea and Osvaldo Carrera both gave the bride away.

Weddings often have strange effects on the observers. Women cry.

Men reminisce. After the Bradshaw/Eckert wedding, Stavros Stavropopolous behaved in an uncharacteristic manner. Instead of hurrying away from the (to him) large assemblage of annoying people, he toasted the couple and presented them with a bottle of Ouzo. An hour later, when safely back in his quarters, he thought the ordeal really wasn't so bad.

And the S S Arbutus sailed to New Orleans.

CODA: 1753. (It.:-L. cauda tail.) Mus. A passage added after the natural completion of a movement, so as to form a more definite and satisfactory conclusion.

CODA
FIRST

WHATEVER HAPPENED TO FREDERICK BERGMAN AND THE TREASURY OF THE CIUDAD CARILLO SINDETRAG

The Comandante's conclusions concerning the murder of Frederick Bergman were not entirely accurate. He had no way of knowing what had happened during the twenty four hour periods immediately before and after the Arbutus arrived in Aguas Buenas. Reinhold Reichman did not kill Frederick Bergman.

When the S S Arbutus docked and Paul and Ellie Sue passed through the Aguas Buenas Customs House and found their way to the Casa Canada, Frederick Bergman (erstwhile Thomas Andersen) had a problem. His servant told him of Senator Roberto Smit's apartment reservation.

If his Villa Smit employer saw him, Bergman's true identity would become know and his cache of Sedalian gold would become imperiled. He decided to take his hoard and disappear until the Senator left Aguas Buenas and returned to Villa Smit.

Bergman sent his servant to saddle his horse. He went to his apartment and, from its hiding place beneath his desk, removed the saddlebag containing the coins he'd taken from the fishing boat, abandoned on the shoreline near Villa Smit.

Paul and Ellie Sue's arrival at Casa Canada delayed his departure. Surprised by Ellie Sue's "hellos", he shoved the saddlebag under his desk. He was pleased to see the guests kept their taxi waiting. It meant they planned to leave soon. He registered them and put them in their apartment as quickly as possible

Bergman watched as Paul and Ellie Sue left for the El Palacio. He re-entered his living quarters, intending to upon retrieve his treasure and leave his servant to deal with Senator Smit. The saddlebag was

278

open and now lay on top of his desk, its contents exposed. His servant stood inside the patio doorway, facing him.

The servant looked at the saddlebag and then at Bergman. "You have much money, Señor Bergman", he said, "and I am a poor man."

Bergman did not answer.

"It is not right for you to have so much and for me to have so little."

Bergman did not answer.

"I think you should give me some of your money."

The North Dakota accountant quickly considered his alternatives. The expected arrival of Senator Roberto Smit was no longer his only a threat of exposure. His wealth was now known by his servant. He could not trust the man to keep silent. Unless permanently silenced, he would be paying him for the rest of his life.

Recollections of his years of poverty coupled with fearful thoughts of the threat of loss of his wealth crowded into his mind. He had to protect his money. He had to take it to a safer place - to British Honduras or one of the Caribbean islands - but first he had to eliminate the danger posed by his servant. He had to kill him.

As Bergman lunged toward him, he saw the servant lift his hand from behind his back and point a revolver at him. It was the last thing Bergman saw. He fell dead, a bullet in his heart.

The servant was panic stricken. He stood in the room, petrified, while fear, guilt and terror assailed him. He had committed an unpardonable sin. He had killed his patrón. He could hide, but the Comandante would surely find him. No one would help a servant who murdered his patrón. He could expect no mercy. He must run away.

He would go quickly, before the death of Señor Bergman was discovered. Should he leave the money behind? No, that would be foolish. Señor Bergman was dead and could not use it. He would take it with him. If he did escape, perhaps the money would help him forget his terrible crime.

He stuffed the revolver inside the saddle bag. When it was securely closed, he carried it to the horse taken from the Villa Smit stable when Thomas Anderson disappeared and Frederick Bergman was created to replace him. It was mid-day and few people would be on the street.

Perhaps he could get to the road leading away from Aguas Buenas without being discovered.

The servant led the horse from the courtyard and away from Casa Canada. He walked down the quiet side streets until he came to the trail that went up the foothills and joined the road between Aguas Buenas and the neighboring Republic of Nuevo Leon.. There he mounted his patrón's horse and was soon out of sight.

The road he traveled passed the finca of Senator Mendez. To avoid being seen, he would ride past the finca after the sun was down and continue on the road until the following morning. He'd spend tomorrow's daylight hours hiding in the jungle and, at night, continue his journey until he safely inside Nuevo Leon.

An hour later, the servant urged the horse down the road and away from the scene of his crime. The further he was from Aguas Buenas, the safer he felt, but distance did not remove the feeling of guilt which continued to plague him. He had killed his patrón. Everyone would look for him. The thought made him ill. He was sure the black Packard that came up behind him was the guardia. Was it fear that caused his stomach to knot in pain? To his relief, the automobile passed without stopping.

As he rode on toward the finca of Senator Paco Mendez, his thoughts kept returning to what had happened that afternoon. When he brought the patrón's horse to the door at the back of the Casa Canada, he looked through the doorway and saw a coin on the floor. He went inside and picked it up. Then the saw the false floor beneath the desk and the saddlebag. He saw the coins in the saddlebag.

The saddlebag was very heavy when he raised it to the top of the desk. As he lifted it up, he saw the revolver which still rested in the floor beneath it. He picked up the gun and saw his patrón back through the beaded curtain, watching the Casa Canada entrance and waiting for his two guests to leave. The servant silently stood up and held the weapon behind his leg to hide it from his patrón's sight.

He hadn't meant to kill Bergman. "I was defending myself," he said out loud in a vain attempt to excuse his own guilt. "He attacked me." Then, after a pause, he said: "The Patrón could not use that much gold. No one could use that much gold. He should have given me some. It wasn't much to ask. I didn't mean to shoot him," he again said aloud to no one in particular. Still, his conscience kept repeating: "Your patrón is dead and the Comandante will look for you. He will find you and the guardia will shoot you".

The servant nudged the flanks of the horse with his heels. The pain returned to his stomach. It is silly to have one's stomach in knots. What is done is done, he thought. It must be accepted. Pain in the stomach will not change it. As he rode down the road, his pain continued. He tried to quiet his conscience by forcing himself to think of different matters.

No one knows me in Nuevo Leon. I will change my name. With my money I will buy a small finca. I will find a beautiful young woman with broad hips. I will be happy. He turned and looked back to once again make sure the coin filled saddlebag was securely fastened to the back of the saddle and, again, he felt the sharp pains in his stomach.

During the next hours, his agony increased. He planned to ride all night, but by the time the sun set, the pain was too great. It no longer subsided. It was now constant. He could not ride. He needed rest. Ahead and to the side of road he saw the glimmer of a kerosene lamp shining through the open window of a thatched hut. He found and followed the path that led to it.

* * * * *

Senator Paco Mendez liked to begin the day contemplating the scenes of the Central Highlands. It was his well-established practice to sit at a table beneath a tree on the carefully attended lawn behind his hacienda. There he would have his morning coffee and enjoy the sounds and sights of the awakening day. His visiting friend, Senator Roberto Smit preferred to sleep late. That was convenient. Don Paco liked to be alone in his early contemplations.

On the morning following the arrival of Senator Smit, don Paco arose at 6:30. He dressed and went to the kitchen where Maria already prepared the strong, black coffee he took at the start of every day. She heard him descending the stairway and poured the heavy liquid into a small cup. As was her well-established custom, she was ready to hand it to him when he entered the kitchen.

This morning, in addition to her regular morning greeting of "Buenos días, Patrón," she told him one of his field workers wanted to speak with him. It was not customary to disturb El Patrón until after he finished his coffee. "Who is it?" he questioned.

"El Indio," was the answer. Mendez knew El Indio. He was the son of one of his father's kitchen helpers who was sixteen years old when El Indio was born. The boy, now a grown man, had lived on the Mendez property for his entire life. He had been a field hand since his childhood.

It is the obligation of a good patrón to care and provide for those who serve him. Mendez was a good patrón and El Indio was a loyal worker, always showing don Paco proper respect and deference. That he would come to the main house and ask to speak to the Patrón in the morning was, indeed, unusual.

Senator Mendez thought the matter must have been one of great importance to El Indio. Still, it was a bad precedent to speak to one of the men before taking his morning coffee. He asked Maria to tell El Indio he would meet with him after he finished his cafecito.

This morning Mendez could not enjoy his cafecito. In another day he and Roberto Smit, would meet with political allies to plan revolution. Smit's discovery of the murder in Casa Canada was disturbing. If anyone saw the Senator leaving the hostel, both of them could be drawn into the Comandante's investigation.

President Peña would use that investigation to destroy the two Senators and Mendez knew his fellow conspirators would immediately abandon the coup if it was learned he or Smit had been questioned in a matter of murder. Don Paco had not slept well and now one of his men had the temerity to disturb his morning ritual. He impatiently drank the coffee and, with a wave of his hand, signaled El Indio to approach.

Partially hidden, the Indian stood in the shadows of a portico at the side of a stone storage building. When don Paco signaled to him, he slowly came forward. His hands, side by side, clutched the brim of his sombrero. His steps were small. His head bent forward and he kept his eyes toward the ground. When he was fifteen feet from his patron, he stopped, not daring to come closer. He stood there waiting for permission to speak.

After a moment, Mendez said to him: "Indio, why do you come to me so early in the morning?"

"It is matter of grave concern. I hope the patrón will forgive me for bothering him."

"I know you would not disturb my morning unless it was a matter of importance. You know I will protect you as I protect all who live and work on my land. Speak."

"Last night, Patrón, it is late and a man comes to my hut. He rides a horse. He cries out in pain. I bring him inside. I give him water. He clutches his stomach. I see no wound. He is sick. Very sick, Patrón." El Indio paused. Still holding tightly to the brim of his sombrero, he raised his eyes and, for the first time, looked directly at Mendez.

Mendez did not like this news. Would the fates be so unkind as to visit him with a second death - with another complication to disrupt his plans? The presence of the guardia investigating a death on his ranch would be most inconvenient.

"Tell me, Indio," he said, "is the man better now?"

El Indio quickly looked back to the ground. "No, Patrón," he said. "The man is not better. He is dead Patrón. I do not know what to do, Patrón. Please, Patrón, tell me what to do."

Senator Paco Mendez studied the bottom of his demitasse cup. He thought: I must avoid any problem. That means I must hide the body and deny any knowledge of the death. He looked at El Indio and asked: "Who have you told of this unfortunate occurrence?"

"No one, no one, Patrón," said El Indio. "When the man is dead, I walk here to the hacienda to ask you what to do. I stand here for two hours and tell no one what has happened."

"Not even Maria?" Mendez asked.

"No Patrón," answered El Indio. "I told her only that I must speak with you. I did not tell her why."

Mendez was relieved. "You did well, Indio," he said. "Now we must see what can be done to protect you from harm."

* * * * *

283

The Senator saddled a horse and El Indio walked behind him as he rode to the thatched hut. The body of the man who killed Thomas Andersen lay in the corner. Though Mendez did not recognize him, the man's clothing marked him as a laborer and not a member of the middle or upper class. That was good. A missing laborer should require no serious investigation by the Comandante.

The horse the dead man rode was still tied to a post outside El Indio's hut. Mendez left the Indian with the corpse and returned to the horse. He looked in the saddlebag and found a revolver and a cache of golden coins. Mendez immediately recognized them as Sedalian. Bergman must have had the SINDETRAG treasury, he guessed. The dead man on the earthen floor of El Indio's hut must have killed him for it.

"Indio," he called. "Come here. Tell me truthfully, Indio, do you know what is in this saddlebag?"

"No, Patrón, I do not. When this man dies, I am too much afraid to do anything but to sit and to think what to do. I am fearful someone will think I killed him. I am afraid to stay here with him. At first I think I will run away, but then I think I will speak with you. I walk to your hacienda and wait until the sun rises. Then I ask Maria to say I want to talk with you. It is the truth, Patrón."

"I will help you, Indio," said Mendez. "I will tell you what you must do. First, bring the body out. Put it on his horse and carry it into the forest. There you must bury it. At least one meter deep, Indio. Return on the horse to my stable. Wait there. It is very important that you say nothing about this, Indio. You must never say anything. If you say anything to anyone, I will not be able to help you and the Comandante will find you and you will be executed..

When El Indio re-entered his hut, Mendez transferred the heavy saddlebag to his own horse. He helped the Indian tie the body over the saddle of the dead man's horse. El Indio brought a shovel from his hut. With the bridle in his hands, he led the horse into the jungle.

As he rode back to his finca, Mendez decided he must tell only Roberto Smit of finding the body of the murderer. The others need not know what had happened. The Sedalian gold, he thought, cannot be used for some time. If it were circulated, it might be recognized as taken from the Sedalia SINDETRAG. Too many questions would be asked. It would be best to hide the coins in a secure place and wait until memories softened. They would be useful at another time. El Indio presented another problem. He might talk. If he did, the information he possessed could destroy the planned revolution. El Indio, too, should be put in a secure place.

* * * * *

When he returned from El Indio's hut, Paco Mendez rode directly to the stable. Roberto Smit was now on the veranda and Mendez called to him. Inside the stable, Mendez asked: "Have you spoken with the Comandante, Roberto?"

"Yes Paco. I called him after coffee - fifteen minutes ago. Let us hope he finds the killer quickly."

"Let us hope the Comandante does not find the killer too soon," Mendez said to a confused Roberto Smit.

Mendez showed Smit the coin filled saddlebag. He told him El Indio's story and said the body of the murderer was being buried in the jungle. It was imperative that the death of the murderer and the presence of the Sedalian money be concealed, at least until after the coup. Together the Senators buried the Sedalian gold under the stable's dirt floor.

The murder of Frederick Bergman was no longer a mystery to them. The motive was the SINDETRAG treasury and the murderer was now dead, a victim of a ruptured appendix. The death of the murderer and the presence of the Sedalian gold had to be concealed. Only the two Senators knew when the gold was hidden. Only Mendez and El Indio knew where the body was buried.

Bergman's horse was also a problem. If found at the Mendez finca and identified by its brand, he would become involved in the investigation of Bergman's murder. Mendez and Smit agreed the risk of disclosure by El Indio as well as the danger represented by Bergman's horse had to be eliminated. They planned to do so.

CODA
SECOND

WHATEVER HAPPENED TO REINHOLD REICHMAN

As the Comandante of the Aguas Buenas Guardia Civil suspected, the Sedalian gold was never circulated. No trace was found of Reinhold Reichman. The Comandante often wondered where he was. A few people knew. Luis Gogeasgoechea was one of them.

On the morning of July 20, when some of the New Orleans passengers on the Arbutus were preparing to disembark at the port of Aguas Buenas, Luis Gogeasgoechea was performing his duty of carrying the passengers' luggage from the ship the Customs House.

Reinhold Reichman's suitcases were not in the companionway when Luis first went to carry them to the pier. Later he again walked down the starboard passageway to the German's cabin. Again there was no luggage outside his door. Luis knocked. There was no response. He called out: "Señor Reichman," and there was no answer.

After trying the door and finding it open, Luis entered the compartment. He found Reichman lying on his back. His left arm hung limply over the side of the bunk. He wore the same clothing he'd worn at the previous evening's party. His mouth was open. His eyes stared up at nothing. From the grotesque position of the body, Luis suspected he was dead.

Luis entered the compartment and closed the door behind him. He approached the body and touched it. It was lifeless. In a state of shock, he sat at the small desk. Guilt and terror held him in their grip. He knew what had happened. His martinis had killed the German. Many times he had been warned by passengers that his martinis were venomous. Once a missionary had made him promise, with one hand on the Book of Mormon, to never, never, never mix another martini.

But the martini was a challenge and Luis was committed to learn to make a good one or die trying. Now a man had died and he, Luis Gogeasgoechea, had killed him. What to do? What to do? He could not simply leave the compartment and let events take their course. When the body was discovered, he couldn't merely say he knew nothing about it. It was his job to get the luggage to the Aduana. If the German's luggage was not carried to the Aduana building, it would look suspiciously like Luis already knew the Nazi was no longer among the living. No, he could not ignore the body. He had to do something.

Too many people knew Reinhold Reichman drank four of his martinis during the previous evening's party. Certainly the death of the German would be traced directly to him. Then he thought of Clevis Dewlap. He too had consumed Luis' martinis, but he appeared to be healthy when he ate breakfast this morning.   Luis   heard   of snake handlers who became immune to serpent's venom. Clevis Dewlap's system was well accustomed to the effects of alcohol in a variety of different and highly concentrated forms. Perhaps he had built up an immunity.

If only the Arbutus were at sea, Luis thought. Then he could throw the body overboard. When the German was missed, people might think he got drunk, fell off the ship and drowned. There would be no body and no autopsy to show the telltale signs of the Gogeasgoechea martinis.

Perhaps I could throw him overboard now, thought Luis. But Clevis Dewlap carried Reichman to his quarters last night. He knew Reichman couldn't walk without assistance. Dewlap would know the German hadn't fallen overboard. Grasping at straws, Luis thought: Maybe the gringo was so drunk he would not remember what had happened last night.

After all, he, too, drank martinis and was quite intoxicated when he helped Reichman from the ship's Saloon. This morning at breakfast, Señor Dewlap didn't remember Señor Eckert had left his cabin when the Arbutus was still in New Orleans. He didn't even know Señor Eckert hadn't spent a single night with him.

If Clevis remembered, he reasoned, it could be said the German must have revived and gotten up during the night, taken a walk on the weather deck for fresh air and fell into the sea. Yes, if the body were never found, everyone would say he must have decided to take a late night walk and fell off the ship. Luis would be safe from criticism. No one would know his martinis had really killed the German.

Could he stuff Reichman's body through the porthole? No, the portholes were painted shut and no one could open them. Besides, Reichman's cabin was on the side of the ship that was tied up to the dock. Oh, thought Luis, if only they were at sea. Everything would be so simple.

If he were to consign the body of Reinhold Reichman to the waters at the port of Aguas Buenas, he would have to carry it from Cabin 11 on the starboard side of the ship to the railing on the port side of the weather deck. He could not do it alone. He would need help. He could ask Osvaldo Carrera to help him dispose of the body. If he did so, Osvaldo would know the reason for Reichman's death. That, too, would be risky.

Perhaps, when it was over, he could kill Osvaldo. No, Osvaldo was a friend and friends do not kill friends. He would have to run the risk. Yes, he would explain his problem and ask Osvaldo for help. Luis left Reichman's cabin, and hurried to the galley behind the Dining Salon. There he found Osvaldo Carrera.

* * * * *

Nervously, Luis began the conversation. "Osvaldo, my friend, I have a very troubling problem," he said.

"Tell me, Luis, what is it? If I can help, surely I will do so," Osvaldo answered.

"Thank you, my good friend, Osvaldo. I will tell you. You know the German, Reichman, no?"

Luis saw Osvaldo stiffen, and then say softly: "I do, Luis, but, please remember, he is a Nazi."

"Well, my very good friend, Osvaldo," Luis continued, "he is now a dead Nazi and I do not know what to do. I find him dead in his cabin this morning."

Osvaldo watched Luis, but said nothing for a moment. Then he put his hand on Luis' shoulder and, looking into his eyes asked: "Why is he dead, Luis?"

"That is a part of my troubling problem, my very, very good friend Osvaldo. Last night he drinks four of my martinis. No one ever does that before. He looks very ill when Señor Dewlap carries him from the Saloon to his cabin. But, Osvaldo," Luis said, almost pleading for understanding and agreement, "the German should have known better than to drink four of my martinis."

"This morning he lies dead in his bunk and he is still wearing the suit he wore last night. Osvaldo, I am sure I kill him with my martinis. I am sure the guardia will say I murder him. I do not know what to do, but I think I should throw the body over the side when no one is looking. I will need your help, Osvaldo."

Osvaldo Carrera watched his friend closely for a few moments while he made up his mind. Then he said: "All right, Luis, I will help you. We must do something soon, before the Aduana Inspector comes on board to find why one of the passengers on his list does not go through the Customs."

They returned to Reichman's cabin and Osvaldo took control. "Sit down, Luis," he said. "Calm yourself. We must think. We cannot merely drop the body over the side while the ship is in port. Soon or late it will float to the surface, even if we weigh it down. Then many questions will be asked.

"No, we cannot throw it overboard here in port. That means we must hide it until we are again at sea. We will put it in the galley food locker where it will be cool. I alone have the key. It will be safe there."

"But what if we are seen, Osvaldo?"

"We will wait until the passengers leave for the Aduana and then carry it quickly to the galley."

"But the crew and some of the passengers will still be on board, Osvaldo."

"The crew will be amidships busy loading bananas into the hold, Luis. The Druckreys, I am very sure, will be in their cabin."

"But what of the drunken gringo, Osvaldo?"

"We must hope he will do as he has done since we left New Orleans and remain drunken until we arrive in Villa Smit."

"You are my very good friend, Osvaldo. I will not forget your help."

"Friends help friends, Luis," said Osvaldo, and then he continued, "But, we have yet another problem. When the Customs Inspector does not find Señor Reichman or his baggage in the Aduana, he will wonder where he is. He will come to the ship to search for him, but calm yourself. I have a plan. Go. Carry all the baggage - including Reichman's - to the Aduana. Then come here. I will watch them leave the ship and meet you here.

* * * * *

Osvaldo stood at the starboard rail and waited for the disembarking passengers to go ashore. He waved at Paul when he followed Luis and the baggage cart disappeared into the white Aduana building at the foot of the pier. He watched Luis return to the ship and, shortly thereafter, first the Magnussens and then Ellie Sue walked down the gangplank and on toward the Customs building.

Then Osvaldo returned to Reichman's cabin. Luis was waiting for him. Together they carried the body to the ship's cold storage compartment. There the corpse was propped up against the bulkhead where it could contemplate the bananas, tropical fruits, eggs and the balance of the meats stored for the passengers' meals.

The two men went back to Reichman's cabin. While Luis packed Reichman clothing, Osvaldo dressed in the dead man's tropical white linen suit. Intending to throw it overboard with the body, Osvaldo took Reichman's Walther pistol with its attached silencer and slid it under his belt.

When Ellie Sue's baggage had been reviewed and the four disembarking passengers left the Aduana, Luis, carrying the German's suitcases, entered the building from the dock. Osvaldo followed him with Reichman's Panama hat shading his eyes and a handkerchief pressed against his face. Luis wasted no time getting back to the safety of the Arbutus.

After Reichman's bags were inspected, Osvaldo emerged from the Aduana. Both taxis were gone and he was alone. The handkerchief now served a double purpose. No one looking at a photograph of Reichman could say the man in the white linen suit was not he. And, more important to Osvaldo, no one would recognize him as the sought after Osvaldo Vargas.

Osvaldo went directly to the public telephone next to the Central American Fruit Company warehouse.

"Osvaldo, why do you call me?" asked Senator Paco Mendez when he answered the phone in the den of his hacienda. "This is dangerous."

"It is an extraordinary affair, don Paco," was Osvaldo's response. He told him of the German passenger who said he represented a German bicycle manufacturer. "On the first day of the voyage, I enter his cabin and find nothing about bicycles. During the voyage from New Orleans, he does not talk about bicycles. Strange for a salesman, no? His talk is all of the Nazi government.

"When Luis tells me of the tattoo which identifies him as a member of the Gestapo, I conclude Reinhold Reichman comes to Anchuria not to sell bicycles but to give Nazi support to the Peña government. For two days I wonder what to do. Then I see him try to kill two passengers.

"On the last night aboard ship I can wait no longer. He alone eats raw meat and onions. During the farewell party aboard the Arbutus, I put poison in his hors d'ouevre and I kill him."

"It is a very serious matter, taking a man's life, my friend," said Paco Mendez, "but, Osvaldo," he continued, "we live in a very serious time. We have all been aware an agent of the Nazi government might soon arrive in Anchuria. This Reichman, in all probability, is that man. I believe you took the proper action."

Osvaldo, relieved to receive such support, nodded in agreement. Then don Paco asked; "Osvaldo, what will happen when the body is found? What will you say?"

"Don Paco, the body will not be found." He explained how Luis Gogeasgoechea was convinced his martinis had killed the Nazi and would, therefore, remain very silent about all aspects of the death and the disposal of the body. He told Mendez of his plan to leave a trail of the German's passage through the Anchurian Customs office and to his arrival and registration at the El Palacio.

Osvaldo paused and then added: "Tomorrow the Arbutus will leave port and sail for Villa Smit. The body of our German friend is in the ship's food locker. I assure you it will not be aboard ship when we dock at Villa Smit."

Paco Mendez finished the conversation by saying: "You are a brave man, Osvaldo. You will be rewarded. Be careful."

* * * * *

Osvaldo replaced the receiver and left the dockside phone booth. The estibadores were inside the warehouses, waiting for the noon time heat to pass. No one was working on the docks. The Panama hat and white linen suit are a fine disguise, he thought as he picked up Reichman's suitcases and began to walk to El Palacio. Whoever sees me will think I am Reinhold Reichman.

And someone did.

Osvaldo had taken no more than a dozen steps when a voice behind him called out: "Herr Reichman, Herr Reichman. Willkommen nach Anchuria. Ich bin Strauss. Gerhard Strauss. Es tut mir leid. Ich bin späte."

Osvaldo turned to see a blond man wearing a guayabera hurrying toward him. He had no idea what the man was saying, but it was obvious he had been mistaken for Reinhold Reichman. It was equally obvious that the blonde man had to be silenced.

"Der Abwehr sie haben mir gespracht."

Osvaldo put his finger to his lips and said "Shh, shh." He left the suitcases on the ground and motioned the stranger to follow him. He led him to the railroad tracks behind the Fruit Company warehouse.

* * * * *

Later, at the El Palacio Registration Desk, Osvaldo, still disguised as Reichman, gave the German passport to the desk clerk who duly noted name, number and place of issuance in the register. In answer to the clerk's question, he said he was going to Progreso and he would stay in the Nuevo Mundo Hotel. It was fitting, he thought, to leave a record showing the Nazi Reichman was going to stay in a Progreso hotel commonly used by prostitutes and criminals.

Osvaldo took the key and carried Reichman's luggage to the second floor of the hotel. He entered his room, put the unopened suitcases on the bed and, as he descended the stairway leading to the main floor of the Hotel, he saw Ellie Sue Bradshaw and Paul Eckert at a table in the Hotel restaurant. He turned his head, quickly left the building and returned to the safety of the galley of the Arbutus.

Later during the evening of the following day, when the moon was down and the Arbutus sailed toward Villa Smit, Luis and Osvaldo carried the body of Reinhold Reichman from the galley food locker and consigned it to its final resting place in the Caribbean Sea.

CODA
THIRD

WHERE WAS PROFESSOR MAGNUSSEN WHEN ELLIE SUE AND MARY LOUISE WENT SHOPPING

On the morning after the celebration of the Anchurian victory at the Rio Ramasajoti, three black Packards came through the iron gates guarding the entrance to the Mendez finca. The occupant of each was welcomed by both conspiring senators and ushered into don Paco's den.

The first to arrive was Colonel Ricardo Pedregal. Though he was the son-in-law of don Paco, his rank in the Anchurian army was not achieved as a result of family connection. Had such been the case, he would have been a General.

During the previous Rivadavia presidency, Pedregal was invited by the United States Army to study infantry tactics at a post in Georgia. He was an apt pupil and, had Rivadavia not been assassinated, he would, at least, be a member of his country's general Staff.

Because of his father-in-law's known antagonism to the Peña government, Pedregal was frozen into the rank of Colonel. As long as Peña was President, Ricardo Pedregal would be a Colonel. He had good personal reasons to support a change in government.

There were other good reasons for including the Colonel within the revolutionary Junta. The Pedregal family was well respected and the Colonel was popular with the junior officers. They all held the old generals responsible for their various complaints - lack of advancement - low salary - poor organization. Colonel Pedregal listened to their grumbles and commiserated with them. His popularity grew as the popularity of the senior officers fell.

Military force or its threat is an important element in revolutions. If the Generals themselves do not actively support the revolt, success can be achieved only if the army rebels against them or sits on the sidelines. If active army support for a rebellion cannot be achieved, ate the very least, army neutrality is essential. The hunter, treed by the grizzly, said it well: "Oh, Lord, if you can't help me, for heaven's sake, don't help that bear."

Colonel Pedregal was an enthusiastic participant in the planning of the coup. It was his assignment to neutralize the army. The job was in good hands.

The second Packard to enter the Mendez courtyard carried Clemente Diaz, the lawyer and dean of the University of Anchuria Law School. Diaz would never die of extreme conservatism. In his classes and in his writings, he constantly railed against the Central American Fruit Company and he viewed the United States with more than passing suspicion. His students left the University imbued with liberal thought. As is the similar case with students from United States universities, as they matured, most of them got over it.

In a culture of inordinate respect for the educated, few governments were strong enough to attack students or professors. Popular support was immediately on the students' side and it must be remembered, most of the students came from families wealthy enough to send their children to the University. When there was a student uprising, presidential change often resulted. Professor Clemente Diaz carried weight with the students.

Diaz recognized Senator Mendez' Fruit Company connection and had little respect for him, but Diaz was also adamant in his opposition to President Peña. Alarmed by Peña's admiration of Hitler, Mussolini and Franco, Diaz knew a Friendship Treaty with the Third Reich would be a national disaster.

Mendez and Smit considered student/intellectual support to be important to their plans. They correctly guessed Diaz, albeit reluctantly, could be convinced to support the proposed coup. He hated Peña more than he hated the Fruit Company.

It was Senator Smit who, a month earlier, approached him with talk of sedition. It took over two weeks to get Diaz to agree to meet and consider forming a revolutionary Junta and he made it clear he would support a coup only if three conditions were met. First: Paco

Mendez would not be a member of the Junta; Second: he, himself, would head the Junta; and, Third: elections would be held within a year.

Mendez agreed to the conditions. He could be patient. His own personal ambitions could wait. A successful coup was of primary importance and Diaz could provide considerable support. Politics does, indeed, make strange bedfellows.

When Clemente Diaz arrived at the Mendez finca, he, Colonel Pedregal and the two Senators went to don Paco's den. Mendez began the meeting with a statement.

"There has been a development of which you should all be aware," he said. He told them of his dock-side telephone conversation with Osvaldo Carrera. He reported how a Nazi agent had been sent to Anchuria and how, before arrival in port, he had unexpectedly died. Without offering any further explanation, he reported the man's death would temporarily defer the negotiation of the Treaty between Nazi Germany and the Peña government.

Mendez emphasized the temporary nature of the delay and said the time for planning was finished. A commitment for action was necessary if Anchuria were to remain free and outside the Nazi sphere of influence.

Then the third Packard arrived at the Mendez finca. The guard opened the gate and Professor Charles Magnussen drove to the hacienda and entered the house. Senator Mendez introduced him.

"Friends, our enterprise is at a critical stage. I have, therefore, taken the liberty of inviting a man who will be important to our cause. He is a man in whom we can place complete confidence. Professor Charles Magnussen is a respected Norteamericano professor of Political Science. He is here as a representative of Señor Llewellyn Black."

When the name of the President of the Fruit Company was mentioned, Clemente Diaz stiffened.

Magnussen spoke briefly. He said he directed his efforts as a political scientist to Latin America because of his admiration for its culture and history. He told the conspirators how Llewellyn Black had become interested in his writings on Latin American politics and, from time to time, consulted with him. Magnussen emphasized how Black disliked the Peña dictatorship and detested the European fascists.

Magnussen described Black as a major contributor to the Democrat party in the United States and a man whose opinions carried weight with important politicians in Washington D.C. When Black became aware of a possible attempt to overthrow Peña, he asked the Professor to assess the viability of a successful coup.

If that coup were supported by men of substance, Magnussen told them, Mr. Black would supply the revolutionary Junta with rifles and ammunition. Black would also communicate directly with President Franklin Roosevelt. He would alert him to the dangers posed by the German/Anchurian Friendship Treaty and ask him to keep the State Department from taking any action that might impede the success of the coup.

Black would also ask Roosevelt to order an Anchurian foreign aid package to serve whatever purposes the Junta might reasonably request once they had assumed power. If this Junta were committed to act, Magnussen would advise Black to ship weapons and contact his political friends in the White House.

When Magnussen finished his comments, it was Clemente Diaz who asked: "And?"

Magnussen looked at Diaz, paused, and then asked: "And what?"

"Precisely," was Diaz' response. "And what does the President of the Central American Fruit Company want in return for his support? Land? Am I right? Is it more land he wants?"

"I understand your question, Professor Diaz. I asked Llewellyn Black the same one. Let me assure you, there are no strings attached to the offer. There is no quid pro quo. Llewellyn Black wants nothing more than a stable democratic government in Anchuria."

Clemente Diaz was impressed, but he didn't quite believe it. However, with Senator Mendez out of the Junta and the Fruit Company making no immediate demands, Diaz gave his formal support to the enterprise and the Junta was formed. The die was cast.

* * * * *

In Washington, D.C., during the Arbutus' return voyage to New Orleans, the clerk in the United States Department of State Code Room finished deciphering a transmission from Anchuria. The report was assigned a high priority. The clerk sealed it in an envelope and called for a messenger for delivery into the hands of the Chief of the Central America desk.

The report repeated the rumors of a potential liaison between the President of Anchuria and the Third Reich. It identified Reinhold Reichman as the German agent who was sent to meet with Peña and begin Treaty discussions. With no additional comment, the death of that agent was noted.

"The sending of an agent to Anchuria tells us the Peña government is much nearer to alliance with the Nazis than was suspected. Time is of the essence."

The report went on to raise the specter of a German submarine refueling station at Villa Smit and U-boat attacks on oil tankers proceeding to the United States from Aruba, Maracaibo and Vera Cruz as well as the disruption of the critical shipments of bauxite from Jamaica.

"When war comes, such a development would mean part of our war effort would be diverted from the Atlantic to the Caribbean to protect our raw material supply lines. Moreover, Anchurian support of the Axis would have a dampening effect on the willingness of its neighboring Republics to cooperate with us."

Then came the good news.

"A revolutionary Junta has been formed. It is composed of three men. Professor Clemente Diaz, the Dean of the University of Anchuria Law School, will serve as its titular head. Colonel Ricardo Pedregal and Senator Roberto Smit will be the other members.

"The man who organized the revolt and who will be the behind-the-scenes power is Senator Paco Mendez. He and Senator Smit both have a close association with Llewellyn Black and the Central American Fruit Company.

"A successful coup should mean elections will be held sometime next year. Though Clemente Diaz is the head of the Revolutionary Junta, I'm sure Senator Paco Mendez will be the next elected President of the Republic. He will probably be friendly to us.

"The Comandante of the Aguas Buenas guardia is apolitical and will probably keep out of any conflict. That has been his pattern in the past and we know of nothing which might encourage him to change. Though the coup is well organized, if success is to be insured, additional muscle in Aguas Buenas is needed.

"The accuracy of our information is unquestionable. With Llewellyn Black's help, M was accepted as the representative of the Fruit Company at the meeting when the Junta members committed themselves to execute the coup. The Junta knows M only as an academic and a friend of Black, not as our agent."

After again emphasizing the need for arms in Aguas Buenas, United States Consul General, Rutherford Birchard Wilder finished his report with a quotation from Macbeth: "If it 'twere done when 'tis done, then 'twere well it were done quickly."

* * * * *

At a United States Army ordnance depot, a sergeant ordered a work crew to clean out a section of the warehouse. Until recently, it served as a storage area for obsolete Spanish American War .30.40 Krag rifles and shells. He was happy to see the last of them.

Soon, U. S. Army trucks arrived at the Central American Fruit Company docks in New Orleans. They unloaded oblong wooden boxes. After the trucks departed, the boxes were stenciled "farm machinery" and then loaded into the hold of the S S Arbutus.

CODA
FOURTH

WHATEVER HAPPENED TO CLEVIS DEWLAP, EL INDIO THE MAGNUSSENS, OSVALDO CARRERA, LUIS GOGEASGOECHA, THE DRUCKREYS, THE ECKERTS, LORD PERCY GRENVILLE III AND THE REVOLUTION

El Indio was in Villa Smit. He never told anyone about the burial of the dead traveler. He never told anyone how his patrón gave him a horse and asked him to deliver it to the lumber company at Villa Smit. He never told anyone how he was ordered to take only the little used back trails or that his patrón promised him a reward.

El Indio received a great reward. He now lived in a house - not a hut, but a house. He shared it with a very important man. That man operated the very noisy machinery that ran the very big saws that cut the logs into boards. Though he was very important, that man was El Indio's friend and treated him well.

El Indio was further rewarded. He was given a job. He would pile the boards inside the sheds next to the very noisy machinery that ran the very big saws. He was given gloves to wear on his hands and shoes that had iron over the toes. He wanted to save the shoes and use them only on special occasions, but he was told he must use them every day.

They said he would receive pesos for his work at the end of each month. El Indio was sure he was the luckiest man in the world. Now that he was wealthy, he could afford a more or less permanent liaison with a woman. He hoped the very important man, who he called "don Klay Bees," would let a woman live with him in their house. Perhaps if don Klay Bees also had a woman he would understand.

* * * * *

A few days later, two young Chuchiba Indian women, all of their belongs wrapped in shawls and placed on the ground beside them, sat in the middle of the unpaved street in front of the company house Madera Anchuria provided for Clevis Dewlap and El Indio. They looked for a signal from El Indio telling them either to enter the building or wait at the edge of town.

Inside the house, Clevis Dewlap and El Indio sat at the kitchen table. Two water glasses and a Mason jar, now half filled with cane alcohol, sat on the table. The Indian wanted something that much was clear to Clevis. Exactly what he wanted was still a mystery.

El Indio spoke only Spanish and the Chuchiba dialect of the Miskito Indian language. Clevis Dewlap spoke no Chuchiba, but he picked up a rudimentary "pidgin Spanish" speaking ability during his previous Villa Smit employment. He and El Indio were able to communicate, but only at a very basic level. Both of them went through life with few people able to fully understand them. They were used to it.

The negotiation was slow. El Indio would take a sip. He would say nothing for a minute. Then he would make a statement like: "It is lonely here." He would wait for a response. Clevis would take a sip. He would delay for a minute to see if El Indio had anything else to say. Then he would respond with something like: "Perhaps you are right." Then it was El Indio's turn.

It was nearly midnight. Over the past four hours, the conversation had progressed favorably for El Indio. He sipped, waited and then said: "There are two fine young women outside who might stay here and cook and clean for us." Clevis took the kerosene lamp and walked to the front door of the house.

* * * * *

Aboard the Arbutus, Osvaldo Carrera was elated. Since 1935, when President Juanito Rivadavia was assassinated, he had lived incognito and hoped for a revolution to overthrow the government.

Osvaldo recognized Senator Paco Mendez as the man best able to launch a successful revolt against Peña. Mendez was a wealthy man.

He had the support of the Central American Fruit Company. He hated Máximo Peña and his heavy handed dictatorship. He had strong ties with politicians and with landed families. His son-in-law was a popular army colonel, and, Osvaldo suspected, the Senator coveted the Presidency.

Osvaldo acted as the liaison between Paco Mendez and Llewellyn Black. When the Arbutus docked at Aguas Buenas, Osvaldo would contact the Senator to give and receive information. On his return to New Orleans, he would telephone Black.

It was Black who advised Osvaldo that Professor Charles Magnussen would be his eyes and ears when Mendez asked for help in arming the Central American Fruit Company workers in Aguas Buenas. On board the Arbutus, Osvaldo and Magnussen had many opportunities to meet in the Salon and talk. Magnussen was well prepared to attend the meeting at the Mendez finca on the day after the anniversary of the Battle of the Ramasajoti.

Now Osvaldo Carrera knew the revolution would soon occur. He was elated. Soon he would return to his homeland and resume his real identity as Osvaldo Vargas.

* * * * *

While Osvaldo sat smiling in the Arbutus' galley, Luis Gogeasgoechea stood behind the bar in the ship's empty Saloon. In spite of the unpleasantness with Herr Reichman during the previous voyage to Aguas Buenas, Luis was not a quitter. He opened the Mason jar of Clevis Dewlap's moonshine and carefully measured out a portion. Then he opened the dusty bottle of Dry Vermouth.

Fearlessly he poured first the moonshine and then the Vermouth into a water glass. He added a cherry and swizzled the mixture around with his finger. He shut his eyes tightly, lifted the glass to his lips and swallowed. After a few moments he opened his eyes. He violently shook his head from side to side. The martini was terrible. What was left in the glass was poured down the drain.

* * * * *

In Santa Elena in the Republic of Sedalia, the Magnussens were comfortable in their hotel room. They had found another matter in which they were in total agreement. Each of them wanted to travel by airplane. The Professor was very uneasy in flight, but he enjoyed it because it severely limited the amount of baggage Mary Louise could carry. Mary Louise was also uneasy in flight, but she enjoyed it because it made her husband nauseous.

* * * * *

In Des Moines, Paul Eckert handed a Sedalian gold coin to the owner of Cowdery's Jewelry. It was the one he held in his hand when he was arrested in Aguas Buenas. The Comandante gave it to him as a souvenir. "Now, Charlie," he said, "don't drill a hole in it. Make a gold ring to fit tightly around it and hang the ring on a gold chain. And keep it quiet. El's birthday is on the 29th and I want to surprise her."

* * * * *

In LaGrange, Illinois, Angie Lundler finished transcribing the dictation. She was worried. Ever since young Harvey returned from his honeymoon in the Caribbean, he seemed so pale and weak. Perhaps he has malaria, she thought. It was ten o'clock in the morning and the young man was not yet at his desk in the Druckrey Insurance Agency. Even his father began to notice his son's tardy appearances at the office and began to grumble about it.

* * * * *

In London, Lord Percy Grenville III quietly listened as his stock broker extolled the virtues of investment in an Anchurian mining company.

"Percy," he said, "the Spaniards didn't get all the gold in the New World. Those 18th century mining methods were very crude. What they threw away can, by modern methods, produce profitable gold deposits. In addition to reworking those old Spanish mines, the Central

Highlands are rich in gold and silver which has never been exploited

"Central America Mining Company shares are a real bargain. The financial statement is solid. The best families of Anchuria are behind it. You know what's happening to the price of gold in the world today. Think about it, Percy. Think about it. There's money to be made in Central Am Mining."

Lord Percy studied his broker. Then he said: "John, when I was a small boy, my grandfather put me on his knee and he told me there were three things I should always remember. He said: 'Don't go out with chorus girls. Don't draw to inside straights. And never, never, never, ever invest in Anchuria.' He told me the family always had bad luck there. I think I'll follow grandfather's advice."

* * * * *

Days later, early on a pleasant tropical morning in Aguas Buenas, Wilder wiped his straight edged razor on a cloth to remove the shaving soap. He looked into the mirror and contemplated the events of the last four weeks. Then he heard a rifle report. It was too early in the morning for don Carlos Mejia to assassinate a zopilote.

When he heard additional firing and the shooting continued, he smiled, closed his straight edge razor and put it away. He called to Pedro and asked him to get a supply of cots and blankets and extra food. Local supporters of the Peña government would soon be asking for asylum. In spite of their anti-gringo rhetoric, they usually came to the United States Consulate whenever a successful revolution occurred.

- End -

Other Books by Galen Winter

THE AEGIS CONSPIRACY
A Conspiracy Within a Conspiracy - Supporting Lord Acton's Epigram: Power Tends to Corrupt. Absolute Power Corrupts Absolutely

THE CHRONICLES OF MAJOR PEABODY
The Questionable Adventures of a Wily Spendthrift, a Politically Incorrect Curmudgeon, an Unprincipled Wagered and an Obsessive Bird Hunter

THE JOURNALS OF MAJOR PEABODY
A Portfolio of Deceptions, Improbable Stories and Commentaries about Game Birds, Waterfowl, Dogs and Popular Delusions

THE BEST OF THE MAJOR
Stories For Men Who Smoke Cigars, Drink Single Malt Scotch, Own Shotguns, and Like Hunting Dogs

BACKLASH
A Compendium of Lore and Lies (Mostly Lies) Concerning Hunting, Fishing and the Out of Doors

BACKLASH II
More Tales Told by Hunters, Fishermen and Other Damned Liars